The Anthology of Colonial Australian Gothic Fiction

The Anthology of Colonial Australian Gothic Fiction

Edited by Ken Gelder and
Rachael Weaver

MELBOURNE
UNIVERSITY
PRESS

MELBOURNE UNIVERSITY PRESS
An imprint of Melbourne University Publishing Ltd
187 Grattan Street, Carlton, Victoria 3053, Australia
mup-info@unimelb.edu.au
www.mup.com.au

First published 2007

Cover design by Nada Backovic
Typeset by J&M Typesetting
Printed in Australia by Griffin Press, SA

National Library of Australia Cataloguing-in-Publication entry
The anthology of colonial Australian gothic stories.

Bibliography.
ISBN 9780522854220 (pbk.).

1. Short stories, Australian - 19th century. 2. Gothic
Literature - Australia - 19th century. I. Gelder, Kenneth.
II. Weaver, Rachael.

A823.087290801

Contents

Ken Gelder and Rachael Weaver
The Colonial Australian Gothic   1

John Lang
The Ghost Upon the Rail (1859)   11

Mary Fortune
Mystery and Murder (1866)   31

Marcus Clarke
The Mystery of Major Molineux (1881)   45

'Tasma' (Jessie Couvreur)
Monsieur Caloche (1890)   87

Ernest Favenc
A Haunt of the Jinkarras (1890)   105

Ernest Favenc
Doomed (1899)   113

Rosa Campbell Praed
The Bunyip (1891)   117

Francis Adams
The Hut by the Tanks (1892)   127

Contents

Henry Lawson
The Bush Undertaker (1892)   *139*

'Price Warung' (William Astley)
The Pegging-Out of Overseer Franke (1892)   *147*

Hume Nisbet
The Haunted Station (1894)   *173*

Guy Boothby
With Three Phantoms (1897)   *193*

'Coo-ee' (William Sylvester Walker)
The Evil of Yelcomorn Creek (1899)   *203*

Barbara Baynton
A Dreamer (1902)   *215*

Mary Gaunt
The Lost White Woman (1916)   *223*

William Hay
An Australian Rip Van Winkle (1921)   *231*

Katharine Susannah Prichard
The Curse (1932)   *261*

Notes on the Authors   *265*
Publication Sources   *272*
Acknowledgements   *274*

The Colonial Australian Gothic

IT might surprise some contemporary readers to know that in colonial Australia there was a remarkable level of activity in popular literary writing and publishing. Alongside the prolific *Bulletin*, magazines and newspapers like the *Australian Journal, The Lone Hand, The Queenslander, The Boomerang, The Australian Town and Country Journal* and the *Australasian* played host to a wide variety of colonial popular writers, some of whom we have collected in this anthology. Australian colonial popular novels were also often issued by prestigious British publishers, and a number of these—like Methuen, Macmillan and Heinemann—in fact ran their own 'Colonial Libraries'. Several authors in this anthology were published under these imprints; Hume Nisbet's *The Land of the Hibiscus Blossom: a Yarn of the Papuan Gulf* (1888), for example, was reprinted ten years later as part of Heinemann's Colonial Library of Popular Fiction, a lively although rather short-lived publisher's series. Colonial Australian writers worked across a diverse range of popular fiction genres. Travel and explorer adventure stories were especially in demand; so were gold rush and bushranger adventures. Colonial romance was popular, too, and so was comic melodrama. The relatively new genre of crime fiction rapidly rose to prominence in colonial Australia: Fergus Hume's *The Mystery of a Hansom Cab* (1886) is reputed to have sold 20,000 copies in Melbourne alone in the first year of its publication, quickly becoming an international bestseller. Another key popular genre in colonial Australia—the subject of this anthology—was the Gothic.

The Gothic had developed as a popular narrative form in Britain towards the end of the eighteenth century, specialising in an intense blend of the supernatural, family romance and gloomy atmospherics. The first identifiably Gothic novel was Horace Walpole's *The Castle of Otranto* (1764) but it was Ann Radcliffe who popularised the form with a series of Gothic romances beginning with *The Mysteries of Udolpho* (1794). The genre flourished in the nineteenth century, spreading beyond its European sources to America—most notably, in the writings of Edgar Allan Poe and Nathaniel Hawthorne during the 1830s and 1840s. It came to Australia, then, as an imported genre; but as we want to show with this anthology, it also quickly developed a set of distinctive local characteristics. European and American influences were indeed sometimes strongly visible in colonial Australian Gothic fiction. For example, the burning and collapse of the outback homestead in Nisbet's 'The Haunted Station' (1894) would obviously have recalled the apocalyptic climax to Poe's 'The Fall of the House of Usher' (1839). The title of Marcus Clarke's 'The Mystery of Major Molineux' (1881) is a direct echo of Hawthorne's macabre tale 'My Kinsman, Major Molineux' (1831); and William Hay's 'An Australian Rip Van Winkle' (1921) self-consciously references Washington Irving's 'Rip Van Winkle', a Gothic fantasy published more than a hundred years earlier in 1819. Colonial Australian Gothic stories were in a kind of dialogue with features or tropes of the genre already popularised elsewhere—which is why Clarke's story gives us an already-ruined Castle Stuart in early colonial Tasmania, or why Nisbet's haunted station recalls an English park and its nearby lake seems 'more like the moat of some ancient ruin than an ordinary Australian water-hole'.

In 1856 the German-born immigrant Frederick Sinnett—a journalist who founded the *Melbourne Punch* the previous year—wrote an essay about Australian literature in the *Journal of Australasia* in which he soundly dismissed the possibility of the Gothic genre ever taking root in colonial Australia:

> There may be plenty of dilapidated buildings, but not one, the dilapidation of which is sufficiently venerable by age, to tempt the wandering footsteps of the most arrant *parvenu* of a ghost that ever walked by night. It must be admitted that Mrs. Radcliffe's genius would be quite thrown away here; and we must reconcile ourselves to

the conviction that the foundations of a second 'Castle of Otranto' can hardly be laid in Australia during our time.

But the Gothic *did* take root in colonial Australia, and quite soon afterwards, too. This anthology begins with John Lang's 'The Ghost Upon the Rail' (1859), a story that in fact gives us a nocturnal ghost and which is also conscious of evoking the singularity of its Australianness in an otherwise imported genre. 'It was a winter's night', the story conventionally begins—and then it adds, 'an Australian winter's night—in the middle of July'.

It might be helpful to regard the colonial Australian Gothic as a restaging of European and American Gothic tropes, even as it departs from them in order to assert its identity as a unique and popular local genre. The singularity of the colonial Australian Gothic was most strikingly expressed in an often quoted phrase from Clarke's 1876 Preface to the posthumously published collected poems of Adam Lindsay Gordon—a champion horseman with 'a manly admiration for healthy living' who had shot himself a few years earlier. Clarke had been speculating about the defining national characteristics of colonial Australian poetry, which seemed mostly to be about scenery and Nature: all in the context of Gordon's suicide. He turns, perhaps unexpectedly, to the *American* Gothic for his inspiration by recalling the poetry of Poe. The Australian landscape evokes a 'weird melancholy': this is the 'dominant note' of Poe's poetry for Clarke, but it is restaged here in order then to define something specific about the Australian bush landscape in a passage that gets increasingly, and wildly, Gothic as it goes along:

> The Australian mountain forests are funereal, secret, stern. Their solitude is desolation. They seem to stifle, in their black gorges, a story of sullen despair … In the Australian forests no leaves fall. The savage winds shout among the rock clefts. From the melancholy gums strips of white bark hang and rustle. The very animal life of these frowning hills is either grotesque or ghostly. Great grey kangaroos hop noiselessly over the coarse grass. Flights of white cockatoos stream out, shrieking like evil souls. The sun suddenly sinks, and the mopokes burst out into horrible peals of semi-human laughter. The natives aver that, when night comes, from out the bottomless depth of some

lagoon the Bunyip rises, and, in form like monstrous sea-calf, drags his loathsome length from out the ooze. From a corner of the silent forest rises a dismal chant, and around a fire dance natives painted like skeletons. All is fear-inspiring and gloomy. No bright fancies are linked with the memories of the mountains. Hopeless explorers have named them out of their sufferings—Mount Misery, Mount Dreadful, Mount Despair.

The Gothic seems to have taken over Clarke's Preface at this point, hyperbolically transforming the Australian bush into a monstrous, occulted place. There is something more than 'weird melancholy' here, something that animates and spectralises the bush as the definitive setting for nightmare and terror. The presence of this peculiar passage in a Preface to a posthumous book of colonial poetry may seem extraordinary enough; but in fact this Gothic rendering was not uncommon in colonial narratives about the Australian bush, as almost all of the stories in this anthology strikingly show. In Rosa Praed's 'The Bunyip' (1891), a party of colonials are camping near a lagoon in the bush on their way to a settlement that is yet to be established. They pass the time by telling stories about the bunyip, a creature no one has actually seen but which—as they talk about it—infects the bush around them with a 'luxurious terror' and sense of foreboding. Talking and storytelling, strange noises, coo-ees and distant cries: these all work to render the bush Gothic and disorient the settlers-to-be who literally lose their way when they set out to discover the source of their horrors. In 'The Bunyip', storytelling itself—the campfire yarn, for example—summons the Gothic, as if the settlers themselves have called it forth and willingly surrendered to its power. We see something similar in Francis Adams' story, 'The Hut by the Tanks' (1892), with the experienced bushman Jonnie Holmes reluctantly telling his story, only to become possessed by it as the night goes on. Holmes is also lost in the bush, an event which leads him to regard even *himself* at one point as 'a sort of ghost'. Although he dismisses the bunyip as 'bunkum', the bush is nevertheless increasingly occulted with the shadowy black ball of the 'bush ghost', the curlew 'bansheeing up around me', and so on.

The colonial Australian Gothic especially relishes the aural effects of the bush, which are always imaginatively rendered: like the owl in Mary Gaunt's 'The Lost White Woman' (1915) which cries mournfully and looks like 'a lost soul'; or, more strikingly, when the narrator in Nisbet's 'The Haunted Station' conflates the cry of a kookaburra with the laugh of an 'exultant devil' and 'the wail of a woman, intermixed with the cry of a child'. The coo-ee is an archetypal bush cry, usually of greeting and recognition. In a story like William Sylvester Walker's 'The Evil of Yelcomorn Creek' (1899), however—and Walker's pseudonym was *Coo-ee* – the cry instead conveys 'a sort of quivering despair … It was a death-cry if ever there was one'. For the colonial Australian Gothic, the bush is invariably a place of settler disorientation and death, as if the promise of settlement can never be fully realised. In Barbara Baynton's story 'A Dreamer' (1902), a woman travels through the bush on her way to her childhood home. But nobody recognises her, and the familiar countryside takes on an alien and sinister, even sadistic, quality, with the tree branches lashing against her face. In 'Tasma's' 'Monsieur Caloche' (1890), a young French immigrant is cruelly whipped by the wealthy colonial capitalist Sir Matthew Bogg, and flees into the bush. The 'oppressive calm of the atmosphere' in this story highlights the sadistic violence of the event and structures the bush as a Gothic site which closes down the promise of a fulfilling colonial future. Henry Lawson's 'The Bush Undertaker' (1892) is perhaps the bleakest of these stories—even though it is set on Christmas Day—sealing the bush off from the outside world as if its grisly events unfold in a kind of Gothic vacuum. The old shepherd buries and exhumes bodies in the bush as a way of passing the time, giving recognition to a settler's final destitution and tying the colonial Gothic to a kind of deadpan realism that serves to make what occurs all the more disturbing: with the bush undertaker only too familiar with 'all that is weird and dismal'.

Guy Boothby's 'With Three Phantoms' (1897) is another Christmas story, ending in a northern Queensland settlement at the edge of the frontier on Christmas Eve, 'a sweltering mockery of the day'. This is an intensely Gothic version of the colonial explorer narrative, usually characterised by masculine heroics and expanding horizons. Here, however, events unfold in a tropical 'Inferno', and the mood is one of claustrophobia and suffocation, its explorer stumbling out of the desert as though returning from the dead. The colonial Australian Gothic can often locate itself at the outskirts of civilisation, its protagonists lost or disoriented or abandoned. The genre isolates its settlers from the colony, giving us solitary characters confronted with singular events. In Ernest Favenc's 'A Haunt of the Jinkarras' (1890) and Walker's 'The Evil of Yelcomorn Creek' (1899), prospectors searching for precious stones journey into forbidden zones and animate some kind of indigenous or pre-indigenous phantasmagorical vision, with dire consequences. Praed's 'The Bunyip' has the narrator and his brother travelling up country to meet a 'dray, loaded with stores and furniture for the new home to which we were bound'. These are settlers who are yet to settle; their disorientation in the bush occurs before they can properly establish their home, as a moment of weirdness that sees the colonials united again at the end but only in tragedy and reflection. In Nisbet's 'The Haunted Station', the narrator is another solitary figure, a condemned murderer and escaped convict who flees the civilised world. Delirious and starving, he comes across an isolated homestead that the story describes in a very particular way: 'an intermediate kind of station' built by squatters, but made of wood, preceding what the story calls 'stateliness and stonework'. It is as if this homestead materialises just before the point at which colonial wealth establishes itself with certainty. The story's Gothic events seem somehow connected to the homestead's 'intermediate' status, with the place simultaneously empty and possessed, vacant and yet full of ghastly spectral presences.

In other stories in this anthology, the Gothic effects arise *after* the accumulation of colonial wealth when properties are already well established. Indeed, colonial wealth is literally implicated in the Gothic here, already marked by the seeds of its own decline and dissipation. Lang's 'The Ghost Upon the Rail' sees a relatively unproductive pastoralist usurping the property of a 'very productive' farmer. Later on, that property and its contents are systematically auctioned off, as if the story feels obliged to offer some sort of detailed inventory of the after-effects of a Gothic experience. In Clarke's 'The Mystery of Major Molineux', we again see two neighbours defined through their property and wealth. The successful magistrate Captain Rochford's property is acquired 'under the operation of the colonial land laws', but his 'cheerful residence ... was in marked contrast to the gloomy mansion and overgrown garden of the owner of Castle Stuart'. Although Major Molineux's neighbouring property is just as much the result of colonial success—'a huge, colonial-built, red brick house'—it is nevertheless cast in this story as a 'desolated and death-haunted ruin': a place which puts an end to colonial optimism, with Molineux's wealth bringing nothing but misfortune, despair and death. Like any archetypal haunted house, Castle Stuart is also a burial ground, disturbed by the violence of the past to which it is so intimately connected. By the time we get to Hay's late colonial story, 'An Australian

Rip Van Winkle', however, the haunted house takes on a more whimsical set of characteristics. Jake is an experienced stockman, although romantic and given to melancholy: 'slightly more melancholy', the story tells us, than Robert Louis Stevenson, who he also resembles. He finds himself drawn to a homestead hidden away in the bush and previously inhabited by a beautiful woman, now dead, who he had once known and seemingly admired. This homestead is haunted not by colonial violence, but by its own past as a fully domesticated home, a place of particular civility and cultivation—with its various ornaments, its 'intimate, pretty things', its apple orchard, and so on. What makes this a *late* colonial Australian Gothic story is that it looks back at this moment of fully embodied settlement, and then empties it out: turning the homestead into a place which now seems 'inconceivably desolate, ruined, and alone'. We see something similar in the last story in this anthology, Katharine Susannah Prichard's 'The Curse' (1932), where an abandoned settler's hut is reclaimed and strangled by a wild, animated bush landscape. This is the end point of the colonial Australian Gothic, where settlement is disembodied and becomes phantasmagorical, the hut appearing becalmed and ethereal, 'dim, ghostly, in calm seas'.

Mary Fortune's story, 'Mystery and Murder' (1866), gives us another haunted colonial property in Tasmania. Its owner, Mr Longmore, is a highly respected and well-known resident, but he is also concerned to protect his property from any undue outside influences, 'my early residence in the colony having made me very cautious in guarding against surprise of any kind'. The Gothic, of course, tends to infiltrate even the most tightly secured mansion, like a kind of virus producing unearthly symptoms among its inhabitants. But there is also a fear of things getting *out*, and a need to keep the phantasmagorical visions of the Gothic – as well as the reasons for them—a secret. At the end of Fortune's story, Longmore leaves Hobart Town, 'glad to escape anywhere from a place so fraught with horrible memories'. In Clarke's Tasmanian-based story, the narrator, Julius Fayre, also leaves Hobart Town in horror, 'and I have never revisited it'. Some characters are lucky enough to escape the Gothic and start all over again: in Nisbet's story, the escaped convict recovers after his ordeal to become, more mundanely, a 'Queensland back-country doctor'.

For Clarke, however—as well as for other writers in this anthology—the Gothic and the mundane seem to co-exist. Major Molineux's 'melancholic craze', Fayre tells us, 'was one which blended itself so inextricably with the affairs of his daily life'. We might sometimes think of the Gothic as a marginal edge-of-the-frontier genre, which it can certainly often be. But the Gothic can also unfold closer to home, and closer to the colonial homestead. Castle Stuart is the scene of various partially hidden stories of past disappearances and violent deaths, some of which are teased out of Molineux's taciturn convict servant for a little bit of money. There is in fact a convict grave on the property, belonging to a character who barely makes it into the story: the 'forger' Arthur Savary, whose wife had eloped with a relative of Major Molineux. It is worth noting that this character's real-life near-namesake Henry Savery, credited with writing Australia's first novel, *Quintus Servinton* (1831), was himself a forger and a convict, dying at Port Arthur in Tasmania in 1842: around the time at which Clarke's story is set. Clarke, of course, was the author of an iconic colonial Australian Gothic novel, *His Natural Life* (1874), about a condemned convict, Rufus Dawes, who is transported to Port Arthur. By the 1870s, Port Arthur was no longer a penal colony and was falling into disrepair; but its ruination seemed to lend the place all the more readily to the Gothic imagination. In one of his journalistic pieces on Port Arthur, published in the *Argus* in July 1873, Clarke concluded with a description of how convicts here were 'subjected to a lingering torment, to a hideous debasement, to a monstrous system of punishment futile for good and horribly powerful for evil; and it is with feelings of the most profound delight that we record the abolition of the last memorial of an error fraught with so much misery'. Twenty years later, William Astley ('Price Warung') published a long series of stories which graphically itemised the debasement of transported felons in what Astley called the *System*. His convicts were labourers enslaved to the colonial project of nation-building, clearing forests or—like the narrator in Nisbet's 'The Haunted Station'—building roads. Astley's 'The Pegging-Out of Overseer Franke' (1892) takes its convicts even beyond the isolation of the penal colony into a sequestered Gothic realm where good men are corrupted by the tyranny and violence they encounter. In Astley's bleak vision of colonial life, the System—which sees colonial nation-building literally depend upon the utter debasement of convicted criminals—is turned into a kind of Gothic machine, driven and unstoppable.

Port Arthur has been a kind of primal site in Tasmania, or Van Diemen's Land as it was then called: a place where people disappear or are violently killed or become hopelessly deranged. The colonial Australian Gothic is drawn to primal or primordial landscapes, no doubt reflecting the early sense that even relatively proximate places were—in spite of the rapid development of the colony—still wild and unknown. Gaunt's 'The Lost White Woman' tells us that 'in 1839 they knew less about Gippsland'—the story's setting—'than we do about Central Africa'. In this story, a group of shipwrecked settlers are massacred by 'black figures, with skeletons marked on them in white' a description that recalls those 'natives painted like skeletons' in Clarke's Gothic fantasy about the 'weird melancholy' of the Australian landscape that we quoted above. Gaunt's story unleashes its tropes of wild savagery in a way that is not untypical of the colonial Australian Gothic, turning its Aboriginal figures into deathly apparitions. Something similar happens in Walker's 'The Evil of Yelcomorn Creek' and Favenc's 'A Haunt of the Jinkarras', as well as Favenc's 'Doomed' (1899) which reverses Gaunt's narrative about Aboriginal violence against colonials by showing five young settlers killing an Aboriginal woman and the baby she is nursing, and then reanimating the woman as the final spectral vision each settler sees before his own early violent death. The colonial Australian Gothic is intimately tied to the violence of settler life in Australia: colonials killing other colonials, Aboriginal people killing colonials, and colonials killing Aboriginal people—like the brutal sub-inspector of Police in Boothby's story, who would massacre local Aborigines 'until there remained not a man among them to tell the story'. The genre turns towards precisely those stories of death and brutality that might not otherwise be told in colonial Australia, playing out one of the Gothic's most fascinating structural logics, the return of the repressed: quite literally, as graves are dug up, sacred burial grounds uncovered, murder victims are returned from the dead, secrets are revealed and past horrors are experienced all over again. In this way, the colonial Australian Gothic gives us a range of vivid, unsettling counter-narratives to the more familiar tales of colonial promise and optimism we are often asked to take for granted. In many cases these strange renditions of colonial anxieties and failure are indeed weird and melancholic; compelling as they are, they can also seem downright desolate and destructive.

John Lang

The Ghost Upon the Rail

1859

CHAPTER I

IT was a winter's night—an Australian winter's night—in the middle of July, when two wealthy farmers in the district of Penrith, New South Wales, sat over the fire of a public-house, which was about a mile distant from their homes. The name of the one was John Fisher, and of the other Edward Smith. Both of these farmers had been transported to the colony: had served their time; bought land; cultivated it; and prospered. Fisher had the reputation of being possessed of a considerable sum in ready money; and it was well known that he was the mortgagee of several houses in the town of Sydney, besides being the owner of a farm of three hundred acres, which was very productive, and on which he lived. Smith also was in good circumstances; arising out of his own exertions on his farm; but, unlike his neighbour, he had not put by much money.

'Why don't you go home, John, and see your friends and relations?' asked Smith; 'you be now very warm in the pocket; and, mark my words, they would be very glad to see you.'

'I don't know about that, friend,' replied Fisher. 'When I got into trouble it was the breaking of the heart of my old father and mother; and none of my brothers and sisters—in all seven of 'em—have ever answered one of my letters.'

'You did not tell 'em you were a rich man, did you?'

'No; but I don't think they would heed that much, lad; for though they are far from wealthy, as small farmers, they are well to do in the world, and in a very respectable position in the country. I have often thought that if I was to go back, they would be sorry to see me, even if I carried with me 100,000*l.*, earned by one who had been a convict.'

'Bless your innocent heart! you don't know human natur' as I do. Money does a deal—depend on't. Besides, who is to know anything about you, except your own family? and they would never go and hint that you had been unfortunate. Why, how many years ago is it?'

'Let me see. I was then eighteen, and I am now forty-six—twenty-eight years ago. When I threw that stone at that man, I little thought it would hit him, much less kill him; and that I should be sent here for manslaughter. But so it was.'

'Why I recommend you, John, to go home is, because you are always talking of home and your relations. As for the farm, I'd manage that for you while you are away.'

'Thank you, Ned. I'll think about it.'

Presently the landlord entered the room, and Smith, addressing him, said, 'What think you, Mr. Dean, here is Mr. Fisher going home to England, to have a look at his friends and relations.'

'Is that true, Mr. Fisher?' said the landlord.

'Oh, yes,' was Fisher's reply, after finishing his glass of punch, and knocking the ashes out of his pipe.

'And *when* do you think of going?' said the landlord.

'That'll depend—' replied Fisher, smiling. 'When I'm gone you will hear of it, not before; and neighbour Smith here, who is to manage the farm during my absence, will come and pay you any little score I may leave behind.'

'But I hope you will come and say good-bye,' said the landlord.

'Oh, of course,' said Fisher, laughing. 'If I don't, depend upon it you will know the reason why.'

After a brief while the two farmers took their departure. Their farms adjoined each other, and they were always on the very best of terms.

About six weeks after the conversation above given, Smith called one morning at the public-house, informed the landlord that Fisher had gone, and offered to pay any little sum that he owed. There was a small score against him; and while taking the money the landlord remarked that he was sorry Mr. Fisher had not kept his word, and come to bid him 'good-bye.' Mr. Smith explained that Fisher had very good reasons for having his departure kept a secret until after he had left the colony; not that he wanted to defraud anybody, far from it,' he added; and then darkly hinted that one of Mr. Fisher's principal reasons for going off so stealthily was to prevent being annoyed by a woman who wanted him to marry her.

'Ah! I see,' said the landlord; 'and that's what he must have meant that night when he said, "*if* I don't, you'll hear the reason why." '

'I feel the loss of his society very much,' said Smith, 'for when we did not come here together to spend our evening, he would come to my house, or I would go to his, to play cards, smoke a pipe, and drink a glass of grog. Having taken charge of all his affairs, under a power of attorney, I have gone to live at his place, and left my overseer in charge of my own place. When he comes back, in the course of a couple of years, *I* am going home to England, and he will do for me what I am now doing for him. Between ourselves, Mr. Dean, he has gone home to get a wife.'

'Indeed!' said the landlord. Here the conversation ended, and Mr. Smith went home.

Fisher's sudden departure occasioned some surprise throughout the district; but when the explanation afforded by Mr. Smith was spread abroad by Mr. Dean, the landlord, people ceased to think any more about the matter.

A year elapsed, and Mr. Smith gave out that he had received a letter from Fisher; in which he stated that it was not his intention to return to Sydney; and that he wished the whole of his property to be sold, and the proceeds remitted to him. This letter Mr. Smith showed to several of Fisher's most intimate acquaintances, who regretted extremely that they would see no more of so good a neighbour and so worthy a man.

Acting on the power of attorney which he held, Mr. Smith advertised the property for sale: the farm, the live stock, the farming implements, the furniture, &c., in the farmhouse; also some cottages and pieces of land in and near Sydney and Paramatta: with Fisher's mortgagors, also, he came to an agreement for the repayment, within a few months, of the sums due by them.

Chapter II

About a month previous to the day of sale, an old man, one David Weir, who farmed a small piece of land in the Penrith road, and who took every week to the Sydney market, butter, eggs, fowls, and a few bushels of Indian maize, was returning to his home, when he saw, seated on a rail, the well-known form of Mr. Fisher. It was very dark, but the figure and the face were as plainly visible as possible. The old man, who was not drunk, though he had been drinking at Dean's public-house, pulled up, and called out, 'Halloa, Mr. Fisher! I thought you were at home in England?' There was no reply, and the old man, who was impatient to get home, as was his horse, loosed the reins and proceeded on his journey.

'Mother,' said old Weir to his wife, while she was helping him off with his old top-coat, 'I've seen either Mr. Fisher or his ghost.'

'Nonsense!' cried the old woman; 'you could not have seen Mr. Fisher, for he is in old England; and as for spirits, you never see any without drinking them; and you are full of 'em now.'

'Do you mean to say I'm drunk, mother?'

'No; but you have your liquor on board.'

'Yes; but I can see, and hear, and understand, and know what I am about.'

'Well, then, have your supper and go to bed; and take my advice, and say nothing to anybody about this ghost, or you will only get laughed at for your pains. Ghostesses, indeed! at your age, to take on about such things; after swearing all your life you never believed in them.'

'But I tell you I saw him as plain as plain could be; just as we used to see him sitting sometimes when the day was warm, and he had been round looking at his fences to see that they were all right.'

'Yes, very well; tell me all about it to-morrow,' said the old woman. 'As I was up before daylight, and it is now nearly midnight, I feel too tired to listen to a story about a ghost. Have you sold everything well?'

'Yes, and brought back all the money safe. Here it is.'

The old man handed the bag over to his partner, and retired to his bed; not to rest, however, for the vision had made so great an impression upon his mind he could not help thinking of it, and lay awake till daylight, when he arose, as did his wife, to go through the ordinary avocations of the day. After he had milked the cows, and brought the filled pails into the dairy, where the old woman was churning, she said to him—

'Well, David, what about the ghost?'

'I tell you I seed it,' said the old man. 'And there's no call for you to laugh at me. If Mr. Fisher be not gone away, and I don't think he would have done so without coming to say good-bye to us, I'll make a talk of this. I'll go and tell Sir John, and Doctor Mackenzie, and Mr. Cox, and old parson Fulton, and everybody else in the commission of the peace. I will as I'm a living man. What should take Fisher to England? England would be no home for him after being so many years in this country. And, what's more, he has told me as much many a time.'

'Well, and so he has told me, David. But then, you know, people will alter their minds, and you heard what Mr. Smith said about that woman?'

'Yes. But I don't believe Smith. I never had a good opinion of that man, for he could never look me straight in the face, and he is too oily a character to please me. If, as I tell you, Mr. Fisher is not alive in this country, then that was his ghost that I saw, and he has been murdered!'

'Be careful, David, what you say; and whatever you do, don't offend Mr. Smith. Remember, he is a rich man, and you are a poor one; and if you say a word to his discredit, he may take the law of you, and make you pay for it; and that would be a pretty business for people who are striving to lay by just enough to keep them when they are no longer able to work.'

'There's been foul play, I tell you, old woman. I am certain of it.'

'But that can't be proved by your saying that you saw a ghost sitting on a rail, when you were coming home from market none the better for what you drank upon the road. And if Mr. Fisher should be still alive in England—and you know that letters have been lately received from him, what a precious fool you would look!'

'Well, perhaps you are right. But when I tell you that I saw either Mr. Fisher or his ghost sitting on that rail, don't laugh at me, because you will make me angry.'

'Well, I won't laugh at you, though it must have been your fancy, old man. Whereabouts was it you saw, or thought you saw him?'

'You know the cross fence that divides Fisher's land from Smith's? near the old bridge, at the bottom of Iron Gang Hill?'

'Yes.'

'Well, it was there; I'll tell you what he was dressed in. You know that old fustian coat, with the brass buttons, and the corderoy waistcoat and trousers, and that red silk bandannah handkerchief that he used to tie round his neck?'

'Yes.'

'Well, that's how he was dressed. His straw hat he held in his left hand, and his right arm was resting on one of the posts. I was about ten or eleven yards from him, for the road is broad just there, and the fence stands well back.'

'And you called to him, you say?'

'Yes; but he did not answer. If the horse had not been so fidgety, I'd have got down and gone up to him.'

'And then you would have found out that it was all smoke.'

'Say that again, and you will put me into a passion.'

The old woman held her tongue, and suffered old David to talk all that day and the next about the ghost, without making any remark whatever.

CHAPTER III

On the following Wednesday—Thursday being the market-day in Sydney—old David Weir loaded his cart, and made his way to the Australian metropolis. True to his word with his wife, he did not mention to a soul a syllable touching the ghost. Having disposed of his butter, eggs, poultry, and maize, the old man left Sydney at 4 P.M., and, at half-past ten, arrived at Dean's public-house.

He had travelled in that space of time thirty miles, and was now about eight or nine from home. As was his wont, he here baited the horse; but declined taking any refreshment himself, though pressed to do so by several travellers who wanted to 'treat' him. During the whole day he had been remarkably abstemious.

At a quarter to twelve the old man reharnessed his jaded horse, and was about to resume his journey, when two men, who were going to Penrith, asked him for 'a lift'.

'Jump up, my lads,' said old David; and off they were driven at a brisk walk. One of the men in the cart was a ticket-of-leave man, in the employ of Mr. Cox, and had been to Sydney to attend 'muster.' The other was a newly-appointed constable of the district. Both of these men had lived for several years in the vicinity of Penrith, and knew by sight all the inhabitants, male and female, free and bond.

When they neared the spot where the old man had seen the apparition, he walked the horse as slowly as possible, and again beheld the figure of Mr. Fisher, seated on the upper rail of the fence, and in precisely the same attitude and the same dress.

'Look there!' said old David to the two men, 'what is that?'

'It is a man!' they both replied; 'but how odd! It seems as if a light were shining through him!'

'Yes,' said old David; 'but look at him, what man is it?'

'It is Mr. Fisher,' they said, simultaneously.

'Hold the reins, one of you,' said old David; 'I'll go and speak to him. They say he is at home in England; but I don't believe it.'

Descending from the cart, the old man, who was as brave as a lion, approached the spectre, and stood within a few feet of it. 'Speak!' he cried, 'don't you know me, sir? I am David Weir. How came you by that gash in your forehead? Are you alive or dead, Mr. Fisher?' To these questions no answer was returned. The old man then stretched forth his hand, and placed it on what appeared to be Mr. Fisher's shoulder; but it was only empty air, vacant space, that the intended touch rested upon!

'There has been foul play!' said the old man, addressing the spectre, but speaking sufficiently loud to be heard by both men in the cart. 'And, by heaven, it shall be brought to light! Let me mark the spot;' and with these words he broke off several boughs from a tree near the rail, and placed them opposite to where the spectre remained sitting. Nay, further, he took out his clasp knife and notched the very part on which the right hand of the spectre rested.

Even after the old man returned to the cart, the apparition of Mr. Fisher, exactly as he was in the flesh, was 'palpable to the sight' of all three men. They sat gazing at it for full ten minutes, and then drove on in awe and wonderment.

Chapter IV

When old David Weir arrived at home, his wife, who was delighted to see him so calm and collected, inquired, laughingly, if he had seen the ghost again. 'Never mind about that,' said the old man. 'Here take the money, and lock it up, while I take the horse out of the cart. He is very tired, and no wonder, for the roads are nearly a foot deep in dust. This is the fifteenth month that has passed since we had the last shower of rain; but never mind! If it holds off for a fortnight or three weeks longer, our maize will be worth thirty shillings a bushel. It is wrong to grumble at the ways of Providence. In my belief it is very wicked.'

'Well, I think so too,' said the old woman. 'Thirty shillings a bushel! Why, Lord a bless us, that ull set us up in the world, surely! What a mercy we did not sell when it rose to nine and sixpence!'

'Get me some supper ready, for as soon as I have taken it, I have some business to transact.'

'Not out of the house?'

'Never you mind. Do as I tell you.'

Having eaten his supper, the old man rose from his chair, put on his hat, and left his abode. In reply to his wife's question, 'Where are you going?' he said, 'To Mr. Cox's; I'll be home in an hour or so. I have business, as I told you, to transact.'

The old woman suggested that he could surely wait till the morning; but he took no head of her, and walked away.

Mr. Cox was a gentleman of very large property in the district, and was one of the most zealous and active magistrates in the colony. At all times of the day or the night he was accessible to any person who considered they had business with him.

It was past two o'clock in the morning when David Weir arrived at Mr. Cox's house, and informed the watchman that he desired to see the master. It was not the first time that the old man had visited Mr. Cox at such an hour. Two years previously he had been plundered by bushrangers, and as soon as they had gone, he went to give the information.

Mr. Cox came out, received the old man very graciously, and invited him to enter the house. Old David followed the magistrate, and detailed all that the reader is in possession of touching the ghost of Mr. Fisher.

'And *who* were with you,' said Mr. Cox, 'on the second occasion of your seeing this ghost?'

'One is a ticket-of-leave man, named Williams, a man in your own employ; and the other was a man named Hamilton, who lived for several years with Sir John Jamieson. They both rode with me in my cart,' was the old man's answer.

'Has Williams returned?'

'Yes, sir.'

'It is very late, and the man may be tired and have gone to bed; but, nevertheless, I will send for him.' And Mr. Cox gave the order for Williams to be summoned.

Williams in a few minutes came, and corroborated David Weir's statement in every particular.

'It is the most extraordinary thing I ever heard in my life,' said Mr. Cox. 'But go home, Weir, and you, Williams, go to your rest. To-morrow morning I will go with you to the spot and examine it. You say that you have marked it, Weir?'

'Yes, sir.'

The old man then left Mr. Cox, and Williams returned to his hut. Mr. Cox did not sleep again till a few minutes before the day dawned, and then when he dropt off for a quarter of an hour he dreamt of nothing but the ghost sitting on the rail.

CHAPTER V

The next morning, or rather on *that* morning, Mr. Cox, at eight o'clock, rode over to the township of Penrith, and saw Hamilton, Weir's second witness. Hamilton, as did Williams, corroborated all that Weir had stated, so far as related to the second time the spectre had been seen; and

Hamilton further volunteered the assertion that no one of the party was in the slightest degree affected by drink.

There was a tribe of blacks in the vicinity, and Mr. Cox sent for the chief and several others. The European name of this chief was 'Johnny Crook,' and, like all his race, he was an adept in tracking. Accompanied by Weir, Hamilton, Williams, and the blacks, Mr. Cox proceeded to the spot. Weir has no difficulty in pointing out the exact rail. The broken boughs and the notches on the post were his unerring guides.

Johnny Crook, after examining the rail very minutely, pointed to some stains, and exclaimed 'white man's blood!' Then leaping over the fence, he examined the brushwood and the ground adjacent. Ere long he started off, beckoning Mr. Cox and his attendants to follow. For more than three-quarters of a mile, over forest land, the savage tracked the footsteps of a man, and something trailed along the earth (fortunately, so far as the ends of justice were concerned, no rain had fallen during the period alluded to by old David, namely, fifteen months. One heavy shower would have obliterated all these tracks, most probably; and, curious enough, that very night there was a frightful downfall, such a downfall as had not been known in the colony for many a long year), until they came to a pond, or water-hole, upon the surface of which was a bluish skum. This skum the blacks, after an examination of it, declared to be 'white man's fat.' The pond in question was not on Fisher's land, or Smith's. It was on Crown land, in the rear of their properties. When full to the brink, the depth of the water was about ten feet in the centre; but at the time referred to there was not more than three feet and a half, and badly as the cattle wanted water, it was very evident, from the absence of recent hock prints, that they would not drink at this pond. The blacks walked into the water at the request of Mr. Cox, and felt about the muddy bottom with their feet. They were not long employed thus when they came upon a bag of bones, or, rather, the remains of a human body, kept together by clothing which had become so rotten it would scarcely bear the touch. The skull was still attached to the body, which the blacks raised to the surface and brought on shore, together with a big stone, and the remains of a large silk handkerchief. The features were not recognizable, but the buttons on the clothes, and the boots were those which Mr. Fisher used to wear! And in the pocket of the trousers was found a buckhorn handled knife, which bore the initials, 'J.F.,' engraved on a small silver plate. This was also identified by Weir, who had seen Mr. Fisher use the knife scores of times. It was one of those knives which contained a large blade, two small ones, a corkscrew, gimlet, horse-shoe picker, tweezers, screw-driver, &c. &c. The murderer, whoever it might be, had either forgotten to take away this knife, or had purposely left it with the body, for all the other pockets were turned inside out.

'Well, sir, what do you think of that?' said old Weir to Mr. Cox, who looked on in a state of amazement which almost amounted to bewilderment.

'I scarcely know what to think of it,' was Mr. Cox's reply. 'But it is lucky for you, David, that you are a man of such good character that you are beyond the pale of being suspected of so foul a deed.'

'I, sir?'

'Yes, you. If it were not that this dead man's property is advertised for sale, it might have gone very hard with you, old man. It would have been suggested that your conscience had something to do with the information you gave me of the ghost. But stay here, all of you, with the body until I return, I shall not be absent for more than an hour. Have you a pair of handcuffs about you, Hamilton?'

'Several pair, sir,' replied the constable.

CHAPTER VI

After leaving the dead body, Mr. Cox rode to Fisher's house, in which Mr. Smith was living. Mr. Smith, on being informed of the approach of so exalted a person as Mr. Cox, one of the proudest men in the colony, came out to receive him with all respect and honour. Mr. Cox—who would not have given his hand to an 'ex-piree' (under any circumstances), no matter how wealthy he might be—answered Mr. Smith's greeting with a bow, and then asked if he could speak with him for a few minutes. Mr. Smith replied, 'Most certainly, sir;' and ordering a servant to take the magistrate's horse to the stables, he conducted his visitor into the best room of the weatherboarded and comfortable tenement. The furniture was plain and homely, but serviceable, nevertheless, and remarkably clean. The pictures on the walls formed rather a motley collection, having been picked up at various times by Mr. Fisher at sales by public auction of the effects of deceased officials.

Amongst others were two valuable oil-paintings, which had originally belonged to Major Ovens, an eccentric officer, who was buried on Garden Island, in the harbour of Port Jackson. These had been bought for less money than the frames were worth. There were also some Dutch paintings, of which neither Mr. Fisher nor those who had not bid against him little knew the real value when they were knocked down for forty-two shillings the set—six in number!

'I have come to speak to you on a matter of business,' said the magistrate. 'Is the sale of this farm and the stock to be a peremptory sale?—that is to say, will it be knocked down, *bonâ fide*, to the highest bidder?'

'Yes, sir.'

'And the terms are cash?'

'Yes, sir.'

'Sales for cash are not very common in this country. The terms are usually ten per cent. deposit, and the residue at three, six, nine, and twelve months, in equal payments.'

'Very true, sir; but these are Mr. Fisher's instructions, by which I must be guided.'

'What do you imagine the farm will realize, including the stock and all that is upon it?'

'Well, sir, it ought to fetch 1500*l*., ready money.'

'I hear that *the whole* of Mr. Fisher's property is to be sold, either by auction or private contract?'

'Yes, sir.'

'What will it realize, think you, in cash?'

'Not under 12,000*l*., I should say, sir.'

'One of my brothers has an idea of bidding for this farm: what about the title?'

'As good as can be, sir. It was originally granted to Colonel Foucaux, who sold it and conveyed it to Mr. Thomas Blaxsell, who sold it and conveyed it to Fisher. But as you know, sir, twenty years' undisputed. possession of itself makes a good title, and Fisher has been on this farm far longer than that. All the deeds are here: you may see them if you please, sir.'

'There is no occasion for that; as Mr. Fisher's constituted attorney, you will sign the deed of conveyance on his behalf?'

'Yes, sir.'

'What is the date of the power of attorney?'

'I will tell you, sir, in one moment;' and opening a bureau which stood in one corner of the room, Mr. Smith produced the deed, and placed it in Mr. Cox's hands.

With the signature of Fisher, Mr. Cox was not acquainted; or, at all events, he could not swear to it. He had seen it—seen Fisher write his name, it is true: but then it was that sort of hand which all uneducated and out-door working-men employ when they write their names, a sprawling round-hand. But as to the signatures of the attesting witnesses, there could be no question whatever. They were those of two of the most eminent solicitors (partners) in Sydney—Mr. Cox's own solicitors, in fact.

'And the letter of instructions, authorizing you to sell by auction, *for cash;* for it says in this power, "and to sell the same, or any part thereof in accordance with such instructions as he may receive from me by letter after my arrival in England." '

'Here is the letter, sir,' said Mr. Smith, producing it.

Mr. Cox read the letter attentively. It ran thus:—

Dear Sir,—I got home all right, and found my friends and relations quite well and hearty, and very glad to see me again. I am so happy among 'em, I sha'n't go out no more to the colony. So sell all off, by public auction, or by private contract, but let it be for cash, as I want the money sharp; I am going to buy a share in a brewery with it. I reckon it ought, all together, to fetch about 17,000*l.* But do your best, and let me have it quick whatever it is.

> Your faithful friend,
> John Fisher.

There was no post-mark on this letter. In those days the postage on letters was very high, and nothing was more common for persons in all conditions of life to forward communications by private hand. As to the signature of the letter, it was identical with that of the power of attorney.

'All this is very satisfactory,' said Mr. Cox. 'Is this letter, dated five months ago, the last you have received?'

'Yes, sir. It came by the last ship, and there has not been another in since.'

'Good-morning, Mr. Smith.'

'Good-morning, sir.'

CHAPTER VII

Riding away from Fisher's late abode, Mr. Cox was some-what perplexed. That power of attorney, drawn up so formally, and signed by Fisher in the presence of such credible witnesses, and then the letter written, signed, in the same way by the same hand, were all in favour of the presumption that Fisher had gone to England, leaving his friend and neighbour Smith in charge of his property, real and personal. But then, there were the remains! And that they were the remains of Fisher, Mr. Cox firmly believed.

When he had returned to the pond, by a circuitous route, Mr. Cox ordered the blacks to strip from a blue gum tree, with their tomahawks, a large sheet of bark. Upon this the remains were placed, carried straightway to Fisher's house (Mr. Cox, upon horseback, heading the party), and placed in the verandah. While this proceeding was in progress, Mr. Smith came out, and wore upon his countenance an expression of surprise, astonishment, wonder. But there was nothing in that. The most innocent man in the world would be surprised, astonished, and in wonderment on beholding such a spectacle.

'What is this, Mr. Cox?' he said.

'The last that I have heard and seen of Mr. Fisher,' was the reply.

'Of Mr. Fisher, sir?'

'Yes.'

'These were his old clothes,' said Mr. Smith, examining them carefully: 'most certainly this was the old suit he used to wear. But as for the body, it can't be his; for he is alive, as you have seen by his letter. These old clothes he must have given away, as he did many old other things, the day before he left this; and the man to whom he gave 'em must have been murdered.'

'Do you think he could have given away this knife?' said David Weir. 'To *my* knowledge, he had it for better than twelve years, and often have I heard him say he would not part with it for 50*l*.'

'Give it away? Yes!' said Smith. 'Didn't he give away his old saddle and bridle? Didn't he give away his old spurs? Didn't he give away a cow and a calf?'

'He was a good man, and an honest man, and a very fair-dealing man, and in his later days a very righteous and godly man, but he was not a giving-away man by any manner of means,' returned old David.

'And if he gave away these boots,' said Hamilton, 'they were a very good fit for the man who received them.'

'This man, whoever he is, was murdered, no doubt,' said Mr. Smith, with the most imperturbable countenance and the coolest manner. 'Just look at this crack in his skull, Mr. Cox.'

'Yes I have seen that,' said the magistrate.

'And that's where poor Fisher's ghost had it,' said old David.

'Fisher's ghost!' said Mr. Smith. 'What do you mean, Weir?'

'Why, the ghost that I have twice seen sitting on the rail, not far from the old bridge at the bottom of the hill yonder.'

'Ghost! you have seen a ghost, have you?' returned Mr. Smith, giving

Mr. Cox a very cunning and expressive look. 'Well, I have heard that ghosts *do* visit those who have sent them out of this world, and I dare say Mr. Cox has heard the same. Now, if I had been you, I'd have held my tongue about a ghost (for ghosts are only the creatures of our consciences) for fear of being taken in charge.'

'*I* taken in charge!' said old Weir. 'No! no! *my* conscience is clear, and what I have seen and said I'll swear to. Wherever I go, I'll talk about it up to my dying hour. That was the ghost of Mr. Fisher that I saw, and these are remains of his body.'

'If I were Mr. Cox, a magistrate,' said Mr. Smith, 'I would give you in charge.'

'I will not do that, Mr. Smith,' replied Mr. Cox. 'I feel that my duty compels me to give *you* in custody of this police-officer.'

'For what, sir?'

'On a charge of wilful murder. Hamilton!'

'Yes, sir.'

'Manacle Mr. Smith, and take him to Penrith.'

Mr. Smith held up his wrists with the air of an injured and pure-minded man, who was so satisfied of his innocence that he was prepared for the strictest investigation into his conduct, and had no dread as to the result.

CHAPTER VIII

A coroner's inquest was held on the remains found in the pond, and a verdict of 'wilful murder' was returned against Edward Smith. The jury also found that the remains were those of John Fisher, albeit they were so frightfully decomposed that personal identification was out of all question.

The vessel in which Fisher was reported to have left Sydney happened to be in the harbour. The captain and officers were interrogated, and in reply to the question, — 'Did a man named John Fisher go home in your vessel?' the reply was 'yes,' — and on the custom-house officers coming on board, as usual, to took at the passengers and search the ship, to see that no convicts were attempting to make their escape, he produced his parchment certificate of freedom, in which there was a description of his person.

'And did the man answer exactly to that description?'

'Yes, making allowance for his years, on looking at the date of the certificate. If he had not, he would have been detained, as many convicts have been.'

'And during the voyage did he talk of himself?'

'Frequently; he said that he was a farmer near Penrith, that after he had served his time he went to work, earned some money, rented a farm, then bought it, and by industry and perseverance had made a fortune.'

'Did he ever mention a Mr. Smith — a friend of his?'

'Often. He said he had left everything in Mr. Smith's hands, and that he did not like to sell his property till he saw how he should like England after so long an absence. He further said that if he did not come back to the colony, he would have all his property sold off, and join some trading firm in his own country.'

The solicitor who had prepared the power of attorney, and witnessed it, said that a person representing himself as John Fisher, of Ruskdale in the district of Penrith, came to them and gave instructions for the deed; and after it was duly executed, took it away with him, and requested that a copy might be made and kept in their office, which was done accordingly. In payment of the bill, twenty dollars (5*l.* currency), he gave a cheque on the bank of New South Wales, which was cashed on presentation; that the man who so represented himself as John Fisher was a man of about forty-six or forty-eight years of age, about five feet eight inches in height, and rather stout; had light-blue eyes, sandy hair, and whiskers partially gray, a low but intelligent forehead, and a rather reddish nose.

This description answered exactly that of Mr. Fisher at the time of his departure from the colony.

The cashier of the bank showed the cheque for twenty dollars. Mr. Fisher had an account there, and drew out his balance, 200*l.*—not in person, but by a cheque—two days previous to his alleged departure. He had written several letters to the bank, and on comparing those letters with the letter Mr. Smith said he had received from England, they corresponded exactly.

Opinion was very much divided in the colony with respect to Mr. Smith's guilt. Numbers of persons who knew the man, and had dealings with him, thought him incapable of committing such a crime, or any heinous offence, in fact. The records were looked into, to ascertain of what offence he had been convicted originally. It was for embezzling the sum of twenty-two shillings and four-pence, which had been intrusted to him when he was an apprentice for his master, who was a market-gardener, seedsman, and florist. As for the story about the ghost, very, very few put any trust in it. Bulwer was then a very young gentleman, and had never dreamt of writing about Eugene Aram; nor had Thomas Hood contemplated his exquisite little poem on the same subject. Nor had the murder of the Red Barn been brought to light through the agency of a dream. The only instance of ghosts coming to give evidence of murder were those of Banquo and Hamlet's father; and Shakspeare was not considered an authority to be relied upon in such a case as that of Fisher.

Smith's house and premises, as well as those of Fisher, were searched in the hope of finding apparel, or some garment stained with blood, but in vain. Nor did the inspection of Smith's letters and papers disclose aught that strengthened the case against him. On the contrary, his accounts touching Fisher's property were kept entirely distinct from his own, and in memorandum-books were found entries of the following description: —

Sept. 9. Wrote to Fisher to say P. has paid the interest on his mortgage.

Sept. 27. Received 27*l*. 10*s*. from Wilson for year's rent of Fisher's house in Castlereagh Street.

Nov. 12. Paid Baxter 3*l*. 12*s*. due to him by Fisher for Bullock Chains.

No case had ever before created, and probably never will again create, so great a sensation. Very many were firmly impressed with the belief that Weir was the murderer of the man who wore Fisher's clothes, crediting Smith's assertion or suggestion that he had given them away. Many others were of opinion that the remains were those of Fisher, and the man who murdered him had robbed him of his certificate of freedom, as well as of the cash and papers he had about him, and then representing Fisher had got out of the colony, and made Smith a dupe.

CHAPTER IX

The anxiously looked-for day of trial came. The court was crowded with persons in every grade of society, from the highest to the very lowest. Mr. Smith stood in the dock as firmly and as composedly as though he had been arraigned for a mere libel, or a common assault—the penalty of conviction not exceeding a fine and a few months' imprisonment.

The case was opened by the attorney-general with the greatest fairness imaginable, and when the witnesses gave their evidence (Weir, Hamilton, Williams, and Mr. Cox), every one appeared to hold his breath. Smith, who defended himself, cross-examined them all with wonderful tact and ability; and at the conclusion of the case for the prosecution, addressed the jury at considerable length, and with no mean amount of eloquence.

The judge then summed up. His honour was the last man in the world to believe in supernatural appearances; but with the ability and fairness that characterized his career in the colony, he weighed the probabilities and improbabilities with the greatest nicety. To detail all the points taken by the judge would be tedious; but if his charge had any leaning one way or other, it was in favour of the prisoner.

The jury in those days was not composed of the people; but of military officers belonging to the regiment quartered in the colony. These gentlemen, in ordinary cases, did not give much of their minds to the point at issue. Some of them usually threw themselves back, and shut their eyes—not to think, but 'nod.' Others whispered to each other, not about the guilt or innocence of the prisoner at the bar, but about their own affairs, whilst those who had any talent for drawing, exercised it by sketching the scene, or taking the likeness of the prisoner, the witnesses, the counsel, the sheriff, and the judge. But in this case they seemingly devoted all their energies, in order to enable them to arrive at the truth. To every word that fell from the judge during his charge, which lasted over two hours, they listened with breathless attention, and when it was concluded, they requested permission to retire to consider their verdict. This was at half-past five in the afternoon of Friday, and not until a quarter to eleven did the jury return into court, and retake their places in the box.

The excitement that prevailed was intense, and when the murmurs in the crowd, so common upon such occasions, had subsided, amidst awful stillness the prothonotary put that all-momentous question, 'Gentlemen of the jury! what say you? Is the prisoner at the bar guilty, or not guilty?'

With a firm, clear voice, the foreman, a captain in the army, uttered the word—

'GUILTY!'

Murmurs of applause from some, and of disapprobation from others, instantly resounded through the hall of justice. From the reluctant manner in which the judge put the black cap upon his head, it was evident that he was not altogether satisfied with the finding of the jury. He had, however, no alternative, and in the usual formal manner, he sentenced the prisoner to be hanged on the following Monday morning, at eight o'clock.

Smith heard the sentence without moving a single muscle, or betraying any species of emotion, and left the dock with as firm a step as that which he employed when entering it. His demeanour throughout the trail, and after he was sentenced, brought over many who previously thought him guilty to a belief in his innocence, and a petition to the governor to spare his life was speedily drafted and numerously signed. It was rumoured that the chief-justice who tried the case had also made a similar recommendation, and that the governor, in deference thereto, had ordered a reprieve to be made out; but not to be delivered to the sheriff until seven o'clock on Monday morning. It was further stated that the governor was of opinion that the finding of the jury was a correct one. The press of the colony did not lead, but fell into, the most popular opinion, that it would be tantamount to murder to take away the life of any human being upon such evidence as that given on the trial.

CHAPTER X

On the Monday morning, so early as half-past six, the rocks which overlooked the jail-yard in Sydney, and commanded a good view of the gallows, were crowded with persons of the lower orders; and, when at a little before seven, the hangman came out to suspend the rope to the beam, and make other preparations, he was hailed with loud hisses and execrations, so emphatic was the demonstration of the multitude in favour of the condemned man. By seven o'clock the mob was doubled; and when the under-sheriff or any other functionary was seen in the court-yard, the yells with which he was greeted were something terrific.

At five minutes to eight, the culprit was led forth, and at the foot of the gallows, and near his coffin (according to the custom prevailing in the colony), was pinioned, preparatory to ascending the ladder. Whilst this ceremony was being performed, the shouts of the populace were deafening. 'Shame! Shame! Shame! Hang Weir! He is the guilty man! This is a murder! a horrid murder!' Such were the ejaculations that resounded from every quarter of that dense mob assembled to witness the execution; while the calm and submissive manner in which Smith listened to the reverend gentleman who attended him in his last moments, heightened rather than suppressed the popular clamour.

At one minute past eight the fatal bolt was drawn, and Smith, after struggling for about half a minute, was dead! Whereupon the mob renewed their yells, execrations, hisses, and cries of 'Shame! Shame! Shame! Murder! Murder! Murder!' These noises could not recall to life Mr. Smith. He had gone to his account, and after hanging an hour, his body was cut down; the coffin containing it conveyed, in an uncovered cart, to Slaughter-House Point (the last resting-place of all great criminals), and the grave filled in with quick-lime.

There was a gloom over Sydney until the evening at half-past six o'clock. Almost every one was now disposed to think that the blood of an innocent man had been shed. 'The witnesses were all perjured, not excepting Mr. Cox;' 'the jury were a parcel of fools;' and 'the governor, who would not listen to the judge, a hard-hearted and cruel man.' Such were the opinions that were current from one end of Sydney to the other. But at the hour above mentioned—half-past six in the evening—the public mind was disabused of its erroneous idea. At that hour it became generally known that on the previous night Mr. Smith had sent for the Rev. Mr. Cooper, and to that gentleman had confessed that he deserved the fate that awaited him; that for more than two years he had contemplated the murder of John Fisher, for the sake of his wealth, which was equal to 20.000*l.*: that the man who had personated Fisher, and executed the power of attorney, had gone to England, and written thence the letter upon which he so much relied in his defence; was a convict who resembled the deceased in person, and to whom he (Smith) gave Fisher's certificate of freedom: that it was his (Smith's) intention to have left the colony as soon as the proceeds of the sale came into his possession; partly because he longed to lead the last portion of his life in England; but chiefly because, from the day on which he committed the murder, he had been haunted by that ghost which old Weir had truly sworn he saw sitting on the rail: that the deed was done by a single blow from a tomahawk, and that the deceased never spoke after it was inflicted. He protested that the man who had personated Fisher, in respect to the execution of the power of attorney, and who had escaped from the colony, was ignorant of his (Smith's) intention to murder Fisher; and that the letter which had been forwarded from England was only a copy of which he (Smith) had told him to despatch a few months after he had arrived at home. He concluded by saying, that since he struck Fisher that fatal blow his life had been a burden to him, much as he had struggled to disguise his feelings and put a bold front on the matter; and that he would much rather, since he had been convicted, suffer death than be reprieved—although he hoped that until after the breath had left his body, his confession would be kept a secret.

Mary Fortune

Mystery and Murder
(from Memoirs of an Australian Police Officer, No. VI)

1866

IN Tasmania ten years ago I met with an adventure of so singular a character that it has been the subject of much thought during my leisure hours in the intervening space of time, the more so as the mysterious portion of it remains unexplained to this day.

One evening during one of the winter months I was seated in my quarters in Hobart Town, engaged in making memoranda of my day's occupation, when a gentleman who had requested to see me was shown into the apartment. Although he had not the slightest knowledge of me, I recognised him at once. It was Mr. Longmore, a merchant of Hobart Town, and one who had the character of being a steady, worthy, and withal wealthy gentleman. He was a widower, the father of one only daughter, and resided on the outskirts of the town, in a handsome residence situated very near to that part of the Derwent which bears the name of Sullivan's Cove; in fact, its waters rippled at the bottom of Mr. Longmore's own grounds.

'I have the pleasure of speaking to Mr. ——, the detective officer, I believe,' said he after having at my invitation seated himself.

'Yes,' I replied, 'and you may spare yourself the trouble of introducing yourself, Mr. Longmore. I have the honour of knowing you well by sight as well as by reputation.'

'Well, I suppose I need not be surprised at your recognising me,' replied he with a staid smile, 'although I do not recollect having ever met you before, but it is quite in your way to be observant.'

'It is, Sir, and now in what way can my present services avail you?' I could not help noticing that the gentleman looked uneasy and hesitant, and not at all so easy in his manner as I should have expected to find a man so conversant with the world as Mr. Longmore.

'I scarcely know what to say to you, Mr. ——,' he said, shifting uneasily upon his chair. "I came with the purpose of disclosing to you something so extraordinary and singular as to be scarcely credible, and now I am doubly inclined to fear that its very singularity may occasion doubts in your mind as to my judgment or want of common sense."

'You need not be at all afraid, Mr. Longmore,' I responded encouragingly, 'that I shall draw any false inference from any communication that you may do me the honour of making to me in confidence. Your well known character as a gentleman of clear judgment and sound common sense is a sufficient guarantee that any information you may give me, or communication you may make, will be well worthy of attention.'

'Thank you!' replied he, 'but in this matter I am positively afraid that my ordinary judgment is at fault, but if you can afford me time, I will relate the circumstances, and allow you to form your own opinion upon the matter.' Of course I signified my readiness, nay anxiety, to listen, and Mr. Longmore commenced thus:—

'My house is, as I dare say you know, at this side of the suburbs, and quite near to the river. I reside in it with my only daughter and three servants, one male and two females. The house has no upper story, and the front windows are French ones, and all open into the grounds; the back part of the establishment, stables, yard, &c., being separated from the front gardens by a high stone wall. Into the back yard the kitchen and ordinary apartments open, so that unless through the house itself no communication can be held by any of the servants with the pleasure grounds in front, unless, indeed, they were to go down and approach by the river. I tell you all this, so that you may be in the same position as I have found myself, as to the possibility of finding a natural solution of the singular difficulty which I am about to relate to you. The door of communication between the front and back portions of my house I am particularly careful to secure every night myself, my early residence in the colony having made me very cautious in guarding against surprise of any kind, and my daughter's safety is, of course, of more moment than my own, so that I am even more careful in these matters than I might have been.'

'This night week I had retired at my usual hour, or perhaps a little later. Everything was quiet, my daughter as well as the servants having some time before sought their sleeping apartments. It was a wild, dark night, but as I have always been in the habit of burning a lamp all night my room is of course lighted, although dimly. I had been for some time asleep when I awoke, but what awoke me I cannot say. The first thing however, upon which my eyes rested was a form—a figure, or the semblance of one. It was standing at the foot of my bed, and was that of a female. At first I was not alarmed, the idea that it was my daughter having immediately suggested itself; so I raised myself upon my elbow for the purpose of inquiring if anything was the matter. As soon as I did so I at once perceived that the face was a stranger to me.'

'The figure was a slight and not tall one, attired in a white robe, and there was a horrible expression of terror in the white features, whose deathlike pallor was increased by the contrast presented by the longest and heaviest black hair I ever saw, and which hung in a mass over her left breast, and reached down to her knees. Her dress was of some silken material, for I heard it rustling, and down over the whole of the front, and also upon the large, loose sleeves, it was absolutely clotted with blood.'

Here the narrator stopped, apparently quite overcome with the bare recollection of the scene that he had been describing, and I must confess that I could scarcely repress a smile at such emotion being felt by a person of Mr. Longmore's sense and experience, about such a piece of absurdity, and I dare say he read the expression of my feelings in my face, for he remarked, 'I can scarcely feel surprised that you should be inclined to treat the matter as a joke, Mr. ——; it is a very singular story to relate, and I do not expect you to give it credence without proving its truth yourself.'

'Oh, I hope, Sir,' I hastened to observe, 'that you do not suppose for a moment that I doubt your veracity, only to my professional mind the apparition looks very like a hoax which some one is playing off upon you; but if you will continue your narrative of the facts we can talk of these things afterwards.'

'I have very little to add. The appearance which I have described has visited me every night since, in spite of fastened doors and windows, each night waving its hand impatiently as if desiring me to follow.'

'And you never followed?'

'No! I must confess that I felt too horrified to attempt moving while the figure stood so immediately in my vicinity. I felt frozen to the bed as it were; indeed, I assure you it is a fearful sight!'

'Will you permit me to inquire seriously, Mr. Longmore, are you at all superstitious?'

'In the sense in which *you* mean, I am not superstitious. If I met with anything so singular in appearance as to be quite beyond the ordinary run of natural events, before setting it down to be supernatural or apparitional I should certainly do my utmost to find a natural cause or causes for it, as I have done in this instance; failing in that, however, I am ready to acknowledge that there *are* "stranger things in heaven and earth than are dreamt of in our philosophy." Still, had I been as really superstitious as you appear to think me, I should not have been here to ask your more practised assistance in trying to unravel this mystery.'

'Well,' I replied laughingly, 'I am certainly inclined to feel certain that we shall easily prove this visitation not to be one from a spiritual kingdom; for, indeed, Mr. Longmore, I do not believe in ghosts!'

'Of course, because you have never seen one.'

I did not reply to this observation of my visitor, as I could easily perceive his nerves had been much affected, and without wonder certainly; the appearance of such a figure in one's bedroom night after night, in spite of locks and bolts, was enough to shake any person's judgment; nevertheless I had not the slightest doubt that the professional cunning upon which I prided myself would expose the trick of some conspiracy, formed, I had a confidence, for no good purpose.

'Have you mentioned this to any one, Mr. Longmore?'

'No, I have not; I was afraid of alarming my daughter; and I do truly hope that you will be able to get to the bottom of it. The very knowledge of such an unaccountable visitation, such a horrible appearance, being night after night in the immediate neighbourhood of my unsuspecting girl, is almost overwhelming me. What steps will you take?'

I considered for a moment before I replied, and then I mentioned my intention of spending that very night in Mr. Longmore's bedroom.

'Could you get me in without any one suspecting that you had a visitor?' I inquired; 'and could you manage to let me occupy your room in secresy also?'

'Oh! easily! Mention an hour when you will be at the side entrance into the garden, and I will admit you myself. It is quite usual for me to smoke a cigar near the river after dusk.'

And so we made suitable arrangements, and Mr. Longmore left me. I sat down then and considered the matter on all sides. What object could any one have in thus acting the ghost in the bedroom of a man of Mr. Longmore's well known strength of mind? Indeed, from what I knew of that gentleman's character, I was much surprised at the weakness he had shown in connection with this matter, the earthly, and I had no doubt criminal, nature of which only wanted a little keen sighted perseverance to be proved.

As to ghosts, and entrances effected without any existing means of ingress or egress, bah! it was all fudge. My intention, in the first place, was to see, if possible, this singular apparition, and while doing nothing more than simply affecting to be the ordinary occupier of Mr. Longmore's bed for the first night, to make all the use of my eyes that I possibly could, and be guided in any further attempts at unravelment by my observations.

Well, at the appointed time I was conducted by Mr. Longmore into his bedroom, and the servants having retired as well as Miss Longmore, I was at liberty to examine the room at leisure. The apartment was a good sized one, perhaps sixteen feet by twenty-two, and had two large French windows that opened on a verandah which ran along the front of the house. These windows consisted each of a single sheet of plate glass in handsome mahogany framework, and faced directly the Derwent, called, as I have before mentioned, at that spot Sullivan's Cove. With its head against the wall, opposite to the windows, stood a large elegant bedstead, with a canopy at the head, from which depended rich damask curtains, which curtains, however, only formed a shelter to the head of the bedstead, leaving the foot entirely unprotected. On the right hand of the bed was the door opening into a dressing-room that communicated with the other portion of the establishment, and at the wall at the left hand was the toilet and its appliances, upon which stood a deeply shaded night lamp. There was also a chimney in the room, but as the grate was one of the stove description I did not trouble about it. It was evidently too small to admit of any personification of a ghost whatever. As I did not care to be seen at the windows that night, and, besides, as I had no wish to prevent the spirit from gaining entrance, I left the windows and doors entirely to Mr. Longmore's inspection, taking his word for it that they were fastened as usual.

After this was all right we seated ourselves beside a table, where my entertainer had taken care to have refreshments, and after having each partaken of a glass of wine I lit my cigar, begging my host to excuse my invariable practice before retiring. It had not escaped my keen observation that the gentleman on whose behalf I had volunteered to encounter a ghost had shown indubitable signs of a mind ill at ease ever since he had ushered me into his house, and taking advantage of the wreaths of smoke that soon curled up between my lips, I watched him as he sat opposite to me more closely than I should otherwise have had an opportunity of doing.

He was gazing down at the floor, and occasionally sipping his wine in an abstracted manner, with a thoughtful and troubled expression upon his face, but looking up once, and encountering my eyes steadfastly, and I suspect searchingly, fixed upon his countenance, he became red and pale by turns, and at length addressed me hurriedly,

'I am afraid, Mr. ——, that I have done wrong in this business, as I have given you trouble in the matter I think. I believe I should have told you everything.'

'Certainly, Mr. Longmore,' was my reply; 'if you seek my professional services in this business, I think I have a right to know everything which you know yourself in connection with it.'

'It is true—it is quite true, and yet I think you will make allowance for my disinclination to speak of this circumstance. There are some things of the past so painful that I may be excused if I feel a disinclination to allude to them.'

'Well, I can only say, Sir, that if you regret having at all mentioned the subject to me, forget that you have done so, and nobody shall be the wiser for me at any rate.'

'No, no! you quite mistake me. I am anxious to tell you at once what I should have informed you of before, and that is simply that—this—this apparition bears the semblance of one with whom I was too well acquainted.'

'May I ask of whom?'

'My wife!'

'Your wife?' I exclaimed, and then checked myself at once, as the cause of Mr. Longmore's awkwardness and evident trouble of mind flashed before me at once. I now remembered having heard a great deal of gossip about this said wife. She had eloped years before from this very house in a most disgraceful manner, and with a most disgraceful and low rascal.

Of course, I respected my host's feelings now, and felt sorry that anything should have occurred with which I had any connection to bring the memory of the transaction again before him.

'And you think that the figure resembles that person?' I inquired.

'It is herself!' was the determined reply.

'Well, I must say that I think it very likely that it is. What more probable than that she should be acquainted with some outlet from this room which you do not know?'

Mr. Longmore shook his head.

'It is not her *alive*,' he said.

'Do you then really and positively believe that this visitation is a supernatural one?' I inquired in much surprise.

'I do! I am willing that every means of discovery should be tried, but when you have seen *it* I think you will acknowledge that I *must* believe it is supernatural!'

This was very positive and very singular to me. That any man in these days of enlightenment, and possessed of his full allowance of brains, should insist upon the *existence* of a *ghost*—if I am not making a 'bull' in so saying—was a matter beyond my comprehension, and as I turned into Mr. Longmore's stately bed after that gentleman had taken up his quarters on a couch in the dressing-room, I am afraid I allowed myself to consider for a moment how long in all probability it was likely to be before this far-seeing merchant should become the inmate of some asylum, where the beds would not be half as soft or the rooms as luxurious as were the one which I occupied as the tenant temporary of this 'haunted house.' I had not removed my clothes, and my revolver lay handy; indeed, since the last communication of my host I had fully made up my mind to bring the matter to a determination that very night. This ghost, be it as active as it liked, would have to use all its supernatural power to enable it to escape from my clutches, for I had no doubt that I should succeed in 'grabbing' the *late* Mrs. Longmore before she had time to invoke the powers of darkness, or find her usual mode of egress. An officer of ten years experience in the detective force was not born yesterday! And so I lay thinking over things quietly, hour after hour striking upon the ornamental clock that stood upon the mantlepiece until it was half-past one.

It was a cloudy night, and a chill wind blew up from the cove, which made a sighing and a sad whispering among the trees that shaded the house, and the lately risen moon, now streaming in through the verandah, and casting shadows of vine leaves and creepers upon the carpet—shadows that waved and shook, as the agitated air outside waved and shook the foliage outside—was occasionally obscured, and left the room almost in complete darkness, as I had before lying down screwed down the lamp as low as possible. I had entirely made up my mind by this time that, by some means or other, the conspirator or conspirators had found out my presence in the apartment, and had thought it safer not to attempt any of their pranks upon me. At this moment the moon was cloud-enveloped, and the room nearly, but not quite, in darkness, when suddenly, and without any apparent reason—I had seen nothing—I had heard nothing—I felt myself getting cold, cold as the dead; and then, and not until then, I heard a rustling as it were of silk, and involuntarily my eyes settled upon the space at the foot of the bed. There was a distinct shadow there, but only a shadow, out of which my eyes could form no distinct figure or semblance; in a second or two, however, it grew white—whiter, and at length stood out visibly and clearly against the dark background, the white dressed woman, with the long black hair hanging unfastened over her left breast, and with the red blood staring horribly from the rich white silk of her robe! But her face—oh! I could not help feeling at that moment that it was not possible for a living face to look so by any contrivance whatever. I was horror-stricken—I could not breathe. I felt as if all my faculties were frozen into my eyes, and they could not move from the dreadful figure, which now lifted an arm and waved me as if to follow. The face of this woman, as Mr. Longmore had said, was full of agony and terror itself, and although this continued for only a few seconds, I was for the time paralysed. I made an effort, however. 'Am I going to allow myself to be made a laughing-stock of?' I asked myself, and perhaps the touch of the pistol which I felt at this moment against my fingers, helped to recall me to myself; at any rate, I bounded out of the bed, rushed toward the figure, determined to grapple with it to the death. It was gone! Not a moment, not a second did I lose. I pushed back the bolt of the window near which the figure had disappeared, opened it, and rushed on the verandah. There stood the phantom on the lawn, rendered now visible by the moonlight, which had struggled through the clouds, and it was still beckoning to me to come! I was in a perfect frenzy of rage, and of horror, also, I must confess; and, taking a steady aim at the vision with my revolver, I fired, and then rushed toward it again. There it was still, but a little farther off, still beckoning! and so I followed and still followed without appearing to gain on it in the slightest; and as I was now joined by Mr. Longmore, whom the report of the pistol had aroused, he accompanied me.

The figure in white moved directly in the direction of the river, which, as I have said before, was in the front of the house, and down to which the grounds belonging to Mr. Longmore extended.

As we followed hastily, having now given up all idea of a capture, I could see the cove rippling in moonlight, and the masts of the shipping at the quays, until they were hidden by the intervening shrubbery that fringed the bottom of the lawn, and formed a slight barrier between it and the shore of the river. This shrubbery extended around a grassy hollow not far from the edge of the water, in a spot so low, that it was occasionally a receptacle for the surplus rain-water that lodged in it, and formed a pond. It was quite dry, however, at the time I write of, and I only became aware afterwards from Mr. Longmore himself that such had frequently been the case. On reaching the centre of this grassy hollow, the figure stopped until we came within a distance of about twenty yards, and then, wildly tossing its clasped hands above its head, it appeared to fall prone upon the earth. But not a vestige of anything did the most rigid search discover; not only was there nothing on the ground when we reached it, but there was nothing to see or hear on the shore, or in all the shrubbery; and so, as the moon had again become invisible, Mr. Longmore and I went back again to the 'haunted room.' He was as pale as a corpse, and I tell you, I was not sorry to be helped to a glass of good wine.

'What do you think of it?' he whisperingly inquired, as the stimulant revived and strengthened him.

'Let us speak of it by daylight, Sir,' I replied, flinging myself upon a sofa, and, truth to say, I was positively ashamed to say what I *did* think of it, I did not close an eye before the day broke; and as soon as it was at all light enough I commenced a regular and thorough examination of the room. I could make nothing of it. I positively could *not* account for the entrance of the bullet-proof visitant of the night. And then I walked down to the foot of the lawn, and sat down close to the spot where the figure had vanished, and took a cigar to clear my intellect and soothe my agitation, for I am an inveterate smoker.

As I smoked I observed that, at the bottom of this little hollow, the ground, which was elsewhere covered with green fresh looking grass, was covered for a small space with a layer composed of what appeared to be a mixture of dead leaves and chips and rushes, mixed with soil of some kind; in short, just such a sediment as might have been left as the deposit of a dried-up pool. And on a closer examination I fancied I could detect signs of a late disturbance of the soil in that particular place. What could possibly have suggested to me the idea of making a search *in* the ground there I am totally unable to explain: it was one of those singularly instinctive thoughts for which there is no accounting; certain, however, it is that I decided upon going at once, before I took another step in the matter, to get the assistance of one of the force to examine this hollow, before any one would be likely to be on the river, or about to make observations on our movements.

Returning, then, to the house, I found Mr. Longmore just dressing, and looking miserable, pale and wretched. I felt sorry for the man; but, as my silence would be, I had no doubt, more grateful to him than any sympathy I could bestow upon so tender a matter, I simply informed him of my intention, and, taking with me the key of the side gate, I went toward the police camp.

Going along Macquarie-street, however, I fortunately met the very man I should have chosen as an assistant, where I wished for a close mouth. I despatched him for tools, and when he again joined me, we proceeded on our return to Mr. Longmore's.

Again, before commencing what seemed such a silly task as rooting in that spot of ground, I asked myself what object I had in view, or what suspicion led me to do so; but I could not reply to the question, even to my own satisfaction.

'What do you expect to find?' inquired Mr. Longmore, who stood beside us when we commenced shovelling the loose soil from the place.

I could only shake my head, and in a few moments the spade of my companion scraped against some wooden substance, at the empty hollow sound of which Mr. Longmore's face grew deathlike.

'Perhaps you had better go up to the house, Sir,' I said.

'No,' replied he, with an effort, 'Go on!'

Quickly then we uncovered a deal case with a loosely fastened, ill fitting lid: it was about four feet long by three wide, and perhaps two feet deep, and looked like a soft goods case, which, I dare say, it had been. Well, we lifted it from the hole, Mr. Longmore still standing silently and inactively beside us, and I am certain that I myself was more surprised than either of my companions at the result of our labours, as I was the only one who really knew how entirely without reasonable cause I had set to work with spade or shovel in that unlikely place. As soon as the box was set upon the undisturbed ground, I prized off the rough lid with my spade, and it fell over to the side, exposing a lining of zinc, which was bent down without any attempt at evenness, and which entirely concealed what remained below it. We unfolded it bit by bit, gradually exposing a horror so terrible, that I wish to heaven I had never seen it!

Many a night since, when some midnight duty has found me on a lonely patrol, have I fancied in the darkness the figure in that deal box. It was a dead woman, and the *fac simile* of the phantom that visited me in the darkness of the night before! The figure lay upon its right side, the knees slightly drawn up so as to enable it to fit in the case; and it was dressed in the identical rich white silk, every fold of which seemed familiar to me. The long heavy black hair was loose, and, gathered at one side, lay scattered over the left shoulder; and upon the skirt of the blood-stained dress, and under the hair, where it lay clogged and clotted, remained still the handle of a Spanish knife, the blade of which had passed directly through the unfortunate woman's heart! Although the body lay upon its side, as the space was confined, the head was turned so that the face looked upward, with the glaring wide open eyes fastened in a look so full of fear and horror, that I can never forget it, and with one glance at the well known face, Mr. Longmore sank to the ground in a swoon. He had recognised his wife!

It had all passed over in the usual way, an inquest resulting in an open verdict, and a large offered reward posted on the walls, and printed in the *Gazette*; and Mr. Longmore had long left Hobart Town, glad to escape anywhere from a place so fraught with horrible memories.

One night I was seated in the very same room where, twelve months before, Mr. Longmore had sought and found me about this business of mysterious termination, when a tall young man of about seventeen inquired for me, and gained admittance. He looked like a sailor, and proved to be something of the sort. In his hand he held a paper, which he opened out, and handed to me. It was one of the posters to which I have alluded, commencing under the offered reward with the usual 'whereas,' &c. The paper was torn and partly destroyed, but not sufficiently to hinder one from perusing the principal parts of it.

'I suppose you remember that, Sir?' said the young sailor; and, when I replied in the affirmative, he entered into the following narrative, which I shall give as nearly as possible in his own words.

'I only came to this port last night, and to-day I went into a shop to buy some toggery, and the woman wrapped some of the things in that paper. When I came to look over it, I thought that I could give some information about it, and when I asked a policeman about it, he referred me to you.'

'Well, my man,' I replied, 'sit down and tell me what you can.'

'About twelve months ago I belonged to a brig called the "Water Snake," owned and commanded by a man of the name of Walter Cuvier.'

I rather started at this, for this Walter Cuvier was the name of the man with whom the murdered Mrs. Longmore had eloped.

'I was cabin boy in the "Water Snake," and had been in that brig a couple of years.'

'Can you tell me,' I here inquired, 'what Captain Cuvier did with his vessel? In what trade was he?'

'Well, you know, Sir, that was none of my business. He traded on his own account, and I think principally in contraband goods. Well, as I said before, I was cabin boy in the "Water Snake," and all the time I was in her, the captain had his wife with him; at least, a woman who passed for his wife, and I believe that the body found in this bill was the woman we used to call Mrs. Cuvier.'

'What makes you think so?'

'I think I am sure of it, and I'll tell you why, Sir. The captain and the missis did not live very comfortably at times, and when he was drunk, he was a brute, and I think the missis herself took a drop too much, so they had terrible shines at times. Well, we came from Calcutta here, and, tired of being kicked and cuffed, I determined to bolt the very first chance, and give Cuvier leg-bail for it. We cast anchor in the Cove in May last I think, and that very night, as I was in the pantry washing up the glasses, I heard a terrible row between the captain and the missis in their state room, she insisting on 'going back' somewhere, crying her eyes out all the time, and he swearing he'd kill her first, until at last he told her to "go back and be―― to her." Shortly after the captain ordered the boat to be lowered, and took me into the cabin to help him with a box like the one described in this; and as I went back afterwards to get something he had forgotten, I saw Mrs. Cuvier getting ready to go ashore. She was dressed in a very handsome white silk gown, and she filled me out a glass of wine, and shook hands with me, saying she was going to leave the ship, and going to her friends; and I thought nothing of it, having, as I said before, heard the talk between her and the captain. Well, I and one of the sailors rowed them ashore, and landed them on the beach near some trees, and it was a wild dark night. So Mrs. Cuvier shook hands with the other man, and bid him goodbye, and the captain told us to shove off again, and wait for him up at a tavern he pointed out along shore, saying he had a few words to say to the missis before he went, and then he gave us the price of a drink or two, and we went off, leaving him and herself sitting on the box that he said had the woman's clothes in. Well, that was the last I saw of them, for as soon as my mate had a glass or two, I took the chance and made tracks, and stowed myself aboard the ship "Chester" that sailed for Calcutta the very next morning, and that's all I know about it.'

'And you never saw nor heard of Cuvier or his vessel since?'

'No, Sir; and if I had done I'd have given both her and him a wide berth.'

And I never heard of him since either. God only knows if he still lives to drag a miserable consciousness of his crime through a wretched existence, or if he has gone to meet with its punishment before a higher tribunal than that of man. Many a time have I pictured to myself the miserable and guilty woman returning once more to the neighbourhood of a child and of a husband whom she had disgraced; but perhaps whom she still loved. How often, during the abuse and the ill usage of him for whom she had sacrificed everything, had her breaking heart yearned for the peace and rest of the home she had left! and then determined to brave everything—to throw herself at the feet, perhaps, of her injured husband— to beg the intercession of her child—did the demon murder her upon the threshold of her hopes, and within sight of the very window lights of the home she longed to enter once more. And who can tell who and what was the midnight visitor to Mr. Longmore's bedroom? Was it a bodily presence of some one acquainted with the murder, and who wished to make it known without being known in the affair? To solve the problem in that manner seemed to me impossible, considering all the opposing circumstances, so it has remained a mystery to this day—a mystery into which I carried the closest investigation, without being any wiser by the inquiry.

Marcus Clarke

The Mystery of Major Molineux

1881

Extracted from the Diary of an Army-Surgeon.

HOBART TOWN, 6TH AUGUST, 1839.

'I HAVE come to the conclusion to-day that the strange behavior of Major Molineux has something in it which is quite beyond ordinary eccentricity. I think that I have found in him a case worth studying.

When I arrived here, ten weeks ago, from Calcutta, I was insufferably bored with the place, and cursed Grosscot for inducing me to visit it. An officer of Irregular Horse may find some enjoyment in playing billiards at the Ship, or in drinking brandy and water at the barracks, but for a man of forty, compelled to take compulsory leave of a profession in which he delights, Hobart Town possesses few charms. When I prescribed a dose of quietness and pure air for myself, I did not intend to live utterly without intellectual society; but the old Major has given me something to think about.

Let me first describe him. He is a tall, thin, muscular man, of commanding presence and military bearing. He has white hair, a white moustache, and a very red face. He is always tightly buttoned and braced. He carries a thick stick, and wears buff gloves—a common sort of fashion enough for retired officers. But with all this there is something more. His blue eyes are always withdrawing themselves from you to furtively glance behind you. I have turned round a dozen times, when playing whist with him, to see if anybody was overlooking my hand. His large, long, white fingers are perpetually twitching and working, and he has a habit of drawing one hand through the other, as though to disencumber himself of a glove. His voice is singularly low and soft for so large a man. You expect, from his manner of walking and sitting, that he will presently roar out at you, but he speaks in a singularly apologetic sort of way, in an undertone, and without any assertion of authority.

The most curious idiosyncracy of Major Molineux, however, is this: He ceases to be on each Thursday in the week.

A constant visitor to the Union Club, I have observed that the Major never makes his appearance on that day. Suggesting to McBride (manager of the Derwent Bank) that perhaps the old gentleman was unwell, I was told that he never appears on Thursdays. Debating with Johnstone (of the—1st) if it would be well to ride over and visit the invalid, I was told that the Major never receives visitors on Thursdays, and being anxious to send a small cheque for a night's losings at whist, on Wednesday, I was told by the postmaster that I might as well wait until Friday, as no letters were taken in at Castle Stuart on Thursday morning.

Castle Stuart is a huge, colonial built, red brick house on the road to New Norfolk. It is sunk in a spacious bush-park, not unadorned with shrubs and trees planted at some expense. The stables are unusually large, and the out-houses almost like barracks. In former days the Major kept a large household, but since the sudden death of an orphan niece, to whom he was much attached, he has persistently refused to entertain company, and contented himself with the humblest retinue. An old man, and a woman still older who acts as cook, are, with their master, the sole inmates of Castle Stuart.

It can readily be understood that this condition of affair has given rise to some comment. Hobart Town is not a large place, and, as the society consists almost entirely of military officers and the civil service, the strange conduct of the Major has been food for scandal during many a day. He, however, appears to busy himself but little with the conjectures concerning him. He rides into town twice a week for his rubber of whist, and, apart from his day of seclusion, comports himself like every other half-pay officer in similar circumstances. Bagally, the man, and Mary Pennithorne, the maid, are deaf to all hints and persuasions. Indeed, the old woman is almost imbecile, and the man, a queer, wizened old rascal—a manumitted convict—who walks lame and has a trick of talking to himself—professes to know nothing whatever concerning his master's eccentricity.

Now, there is nothing very remarkable in an old bachelor, who has lost the only person for whom he may be presumed to care, keeping a sparse table and living an inexpensive life. But this weekly seclusion is a puzzle to the whole community. No one seems to think that the Major has had any event of importance happen to him on a Thursday, nor that it is necessary or proper for him to shut out, at that particular time, the world and its surroundings. The death of Miss Tremayne occurred on a Monday, and, moreover, it was noticed—so they tell me—that the Major had begun to avoid society on Thursdays before that sad event took place.

The first time that this remarkable dislike to be seen abroad on the fifth day of the week openly manifested itself was—I am informed at the club—at a *levée* given by Governor Arthur on the occasion of his arrival. Everybody in the city who had any pretensions to social rank attended as a matter of course, and no military or naval officer could have absented himself without causing the gravest scandal. Major Molineux attended, but his behaviour was said to be most extraordinary.

His carriage drove up to Government House with the blinds closely drawn. After some seconds, the door was opened and the Major, dressed in full uniform, and leaning on the arm of Miss Tremayne, appeared. His face was, in strong contrast to its customary hue, of a death-like paleness, and a clammy perspiration beaded his brow. On stepping out into the light he placed his hand before his eyes, as though to shade them from the sun, and then drew himself up with an effort, as though nerving himself for some dreadful task. He pressed his niece's hand with the air of one who might take an eternal farewell, and then tottered, rather than walked, through the corridor. He passed through the special door set apart for those having official cards of entry, and, making his way straight for the dais, attempted to tender his respects to the representative of his Sovereign. His Excellency, who had heard of Major Molineux's services, would have detained him with some words of kindly recognition, but, at the moment he stretched out his hand, the Major paused, and fixing his eyes on the group behind the Governor, seemed as though about to utter some startling announcement. His mouth remained open, but no sound issued from it, while the convulsive working of his features betrayed some powerful emotion. One of Colonel Arthur's staff stepped forward and took the unfortunate gentleman by the arm. The contact seemed to recall him to himself, and, stammering some incoherent excuse, he allowed himself to be led to his carriage, where his niece waited for him in an evident condition of anxiety.

The next morning he called on the Governor and explained that a sudden indisposition, for which he could not account, had prostrated for the moment his physical powers. His excuses were, of course, accepted, with many expressions of regret for his illness, but since that day he has never quitted his house on a Thursday. Some months afterwards Miss Tremayne died, and the Major then dismissed his servants and commenced to lead the solitary and strange existence in which I found him.'

CHAPTER I

I have just read the above, which was written nearly forty years ago, when I was on a visit to Hobart Town to recruit my health, which a long residence in India with the regiment to which I had been attached as surgeon had considerably impaired. For reasons which will, in the course of this narrative, be apparent to the reader, I found it inconvenient to continue any daily record of one of the most remarkable cases which ever came under my experience. Indeed, it became—as will be seen—advisable that there should be no written statement extant of Major Molineux's misfortune, and for half a lifetime I have put away my knowledge of the facts as one puts away some family secret. But the sight of the faded ink of my diary, and the certainty that, ere long, I shall be incapable of narrating the occurrences which influenced the whole of my subsequent career in life, have induced me to briefly state as much as I may of one of the saddest and most terrible histories ever confided to a professional ear.

JULIUS FAYRE, M.D.,
Late Surgeon-Major.

Apart from the peculiarity which I have recorded in my diary, no man could be more courteous than Major Molineux, and few more entertaining. He did not ask me to Castle Stuart, it is true, but he was good enough to devote many mornings to making me acquainted with the beauties of the country more immediately surrounding Hobart Town, and entertained me by many amusing anecdotes of early colonial days. He, too, had been in India in early manhood, and we passed many a pleasant hour in comparing notes as to our travels and experiences in that wonderful country. Entering the army at an age when most men are fagging in the cricket field, or spelling out their daily modicum of Horace, Major Molineux had seen much service in many countries. His genial manner, soft voice, and dignified bearing added much to the charm of his narratives.

Though for the most part self-educated, as must necessarily be the case when a man enters early on the business of life, he had accumulated more than considerable information on many topics not generally touched upon save by very active minds. In addition to his fund of anecdote, and his acquaintance with what may not inaptly be called the personal history of our more celebrated military campaigns, he was a naturalist of no mean attainments, an accomplished taxidermist, well read in the literature of natural science, and possessed of by no means a contemptible knowledge of physiology. I was agreeably surprised one day, shortly after our first acquaintance, to find that his response to some casual remark of mine, upon an experiment recorded in a medical journal which I had received from England, betrayed an acquaintance with the subject which would have been notable even in a professional man, but which, coming from a layman, was quite remarkable.

'Yes,' said he, in reply to my query, 'I take a great interest in matters of that nature—a very great interest.'

He seemed about to say more, but turned the conversation abruptly, nor could he be afterwards brought to resume the discussion.

One other subject was, as a matter of course, *taboo* between us—the existence of such a day of the week as Thursday. I once purposely mentioned the day, affecting not to be aware of his antipathy to it, but the result forbade me to repeat the experiment. Major Molineux became visibly disturbed. The colour left his face, and he trembled violently. His appearance, in fact, was that of a man who had just received some nervous shock, or who had unexpectedly swallowed some nauseous and poisonous substance. He recovered himself with difficulty, and took occasion to make a hasty departure. He did not wholly resume his friendly relations with me for some days, being apparently fearful lest, by inadvertence, I should again offend, and though my curiosity was piqued almost beyond endurance, I took care not to risk the loss of so polished an acquaintance by impertinent intrusion into that which, after all, was no business of mine.

The time passed pleasantly. Our bi-weekly 'rubbers' and our almost daily conversations continued to our common content. My leave had nearly expired, and I had already begun to make preparations for carrying my reinvigorated liver back to the land of hepatalgia, when one of those accidents which are the providences of romance occurred.

The next neighbour of Major Molineux was a gentleman named Rochford. He, too, had been in the King's service, and, like my friend, had sold out, in order to settle down upon the fine estate which he had acquired under the operation of the colonial land laws. Captain Rochford—for he assumed brevet rank on the sale of his lieutenant's commission—owned a somewhat similar house to that of Major Molineux, for all the houses in that colonial day were built on the same plan, and after the same pattern. But the cheerful residence of Captain Rochford was in marked contrast to the gloomy mansion and overgrown garden of the owner of Castle Stuart. Not only were the grounds of Ashmead Park kept in the completest horticultural condition, but the house was enlivened by a constant gaiety, in which the good magistrate's charming daughter took a conspicuous part.

Miss Beatrice Rochford was, when I first knew her, a beautiful young girl of sixteen, having at once that exquisite complexion and that nobly rounded figure the possession of which makes the native-born of the most delightful of the Australasian colonies a sort of commingling of Devonshire loveliness of face with Spanish splendour of form. She was the only child, and both her father and her mother spoiled her. Allowed to have her own way in everything, she would have grown up without culture, and almost without education, had it not been for the more than sisterly friendship displayed by Miss Tremayne. While Miss Tremayne lived she exercised over the excitable and impetuous nature of Beatrice an influence greater than that of any other person.

From all that I could gather, Agnes Tremayne had been a girl of rare promise. Miss Rochford told me that all she knew of music—and she played brilliantly—had been taught her by her dead friend, and her mother confidentially informed me that, had it not been for the Major's niece insisting that Beatrice should share her studies, the water-colour drawings which decorated the breakfast-room at Ashmead would never have been executed.

One day Miss Rochford showed me a portrait of Agnes Tremayne. It was a miniature, very beautifully painted on ivory by the celebrated Wainwright, and represented a fair girl with lofty forehead and large grey eyes.

'A refined and delicate face,' was my comment as I handed back the picture.

'And a good face,' said the impetuous Beatrice, kissing the miniature. 'No one knows what she endured in that dreadful house.'

'You rouse my curiosity,' I said. 'What is this mystery concerning Major Molineux?'

'I don't know,' said Miss Rochford. 'I think poor Agnes knew, and the knowledge killed her. You are aware that they say the house is haunted.'

'They say that of all houses which are shut up. Pray, what shape does the familiar spirit take?'

'You laugh, of course, Dr. Fayre, but, nevertheless, there is something horrible to me about Castle Stuart. The closed windows, the desolate garden, that horrible old cripple, and Mary Pennithorne, with her toothless mouth—ugh! the thought of it makes me shudder.'

'But, my dear young lady, there is nothing horrible in lameness, and though the absence of teeth may render Mrs. Pennithorne unsightly, the poor woman is to be pitied rather than shuddered at.'

'Of course. But I cannot help shuddering at ugly things. Even the Major, for all his soft voice and smooth ways, is sometimes repulsive to me. I think of him shut up in that lonely place every Thursday in the week, and wonder what horrible act of wickedness he is committing, or what dreadful penance he is inflicting on himself for some past crime.'

'You have never been to the house, then?'

'Never since poor Agnes's death. Nor would I go even if I was asked. I rode up once to escape a thunderstorm, and went round to the back of the stables. They were empty; the windows of the rooms were boarded up, and not a creature was about the place, not even a dog. When I turned the corner, I could see the room which had once been Agnes's bedroom. The curtains had been taken down, and the window was wide open, like a great blankly-staring Eye. It was horrible, and I turned Sultan round, and never drew rein until I was at our own park gates.'

'But this is mere fancy, Miss Rochford. There is no reason to suppose that Major Molineux is anything but the best and kindest of men. I have felt nearly as much interest as you do in the matter, and all my inquiries but serve to show me that your father's old friend is most honourably esteemed.'

'Then why does he shut himself up for twenty-four hours every week?' persisted the laughing beauty, with that carelessness as to the motives of others, and that inability to understand the unconventional, which is peculiar to the young and happy. 'I should dearly like to discover his secret. Would not you, Dr. Fayre?'

'I confess that I should be glad if he would reveal it to me,' I replied, 'for, as you say, it is a most puzzling business.'

'Then we will penetrate the mystery together,' said she, flashing a dazzling smile on me from between her red lips. 'Here is my hand upon it!' but, ere I could imprison the tiny fingers, she was gone.

I did not dream how sadly and how soon her jest would be realised.

CHAPTER II

I have said that Miss Rochford was allowed to have her own way by her parents. She did, in fact, as she pleased; stayed at home to paint and read for the best part of one week, and during the next would close the piano, put away her unfinished watercolours, fling her books into a corner, and go scampering over the country upon her Arab horse, Sultan.

I have heard my Indian friends say that, if an Arab horse is not docile, he is more difficult to manage than any other. Sultan was certainly a proof, in some sort, of the truth of this statement. He was awkward in the stable, and even his own groom was not without some little dread of him. When mounted by a stranger, he seemed to lose all control over himself, and though Beatrice Rochford was absolutely without fear, and rejoiced in sitting her plunging and rearing steed, her father was always threatening to exchange the beautiful but unruly creature for a more placid, if less showy, animal.

But the wilful girl pouted and coaxed by turns, until the good Captain pressed his grizzled moustache upon her smooth, young brow and withdrew his determination for that time. He had, indeed, a well-merited admiration for his daughter's skill as a horsewoman, and, during some of our many pleasant riding parties, I have often reined my steed alongside his more mettlesome hunter to watch Beatrice, as, sitting well back in the saddle, with her hands low on her horse's wither, her veil blown like a streamer from her hat, and her dainty figure swaying like a willow to every bound of the snorting horse, she allowed the delighted beast to take his own course through bush and brake, until, with heightened colour and ringing laugh, she flung him on his haunches not five lengths from where we stood.

She was a feather-weight, and her hand was as light as gossamer, but Sultan had been perfectly bitted, and dropped his head to the curb like a colt. So long as his temper was not crossed he was perfection.

'You shall never sell him, papa!' the lovely girl would cry after one of these daring flights, and the noble horse arched his muscular neck to the caress of the stroking whip-handle, as though to ask pardon for his occasional outbreaks of ill-humour.

One day we were returning from a long ride to New Norfolk, a charming village situated on the banks of the Derwent, which in some places assumes the aspect of an English trout-stream. The day had been chilly, for we were approaching winter, and fires had already made their appearance in the hospitable rooms of Ashmead. The road lay by the side of the stream, which brawled and foamed, some distance below us, over its rocky boulders, and the unwonted coldness of the air, together with the peculiar aspect of the swiftly-flowing brook, brought distant England vividly to my thoughts.

'How like this is to a scene in one of the mountain counties of England, Rochford!' I said.

'It is,' he returned. 'I wonder if either of us will see them again?'

The question was a pertinent one, and I fell into a reverie of recollection in which all but the existence of home and friends was for the moment forgotten. I was aroused by an exclamation from Captain Rochford, and, raising my head, became conscious that Beatrice was no longer with us. My companion's horse fretted under the restraint of the bridle, and I guessed that, finding us both wrapped in thought, she had, with her customary impulsiveness, galloped off down the rocky road alone.

'Let us push on,' I said. 'It is getting dark. We shall overtake her soon.'

'It is not that,' said Rochford. 'Look there!' and he pointed to a turn of the road which, visible to us on account of our elevated position, could not be seen by anyone in the gap through which Beatrice was evidently riding.

A bullock team attached to a waggon loaded with timber, apparently cut from the land of Major Molineux, had 'camped' in the track. The driver was asleep by the side of the road, and the animals had taken advantage of the absence of his formidable whip to snatch a few moments' respite from their toil. There were eight in all, and they were disposed right across the road, one of the polers and the two leading bullocks lying down.

Rochford shouted at the full strength of his voice, but the man did not stir. He was evidently drunk. I could distinguish, or thought I could distinguish, the rapid ring of Sultan's hoofs in the pass, as he was being urged at the top of his speed to the collision which awaited him. I, too, called out, but the word that rose to my lips was 'Beatrice!' I knew in that moment that the liking I—the middle-aged army surgeon—had for this beautiful and wayward girl, who was almost young enough to be my daughter, was a feeling warmer than mere friendship.

Breathless we awaited that which we knew must come. It was useless, worse than useless, to follow down the gap. We should only encourage the horse to greater speed, and should see nothing of the catastrophe. It came at last. Round the rock at full speed wheeled the flying horse, and simultaneously his rider saw the danger. There was but one chance, and that was balked. Just as she reined Sultan for the desperate leap, the drunkard tried to rise.

A less uncertain-tempered horse might even then have escaped. But the Arab saw the uncouth figure with the hated whip, swerved, fell on the great horns, recovered himself, with a scream of pain, and rolled backwards over his rider twenty feet sheer into the river.

How we reached the spot I never knew. There are some actions which, under great excitement, one performs automatically. I was told afterwards that I had fastened my bridle swiftly to a branch, and, leaping down from crag to crag, had gained a jutting point below the spot where the unhappy girl had fallen, had plunged into the stream, and, dragging her from the dead horse, had drawn her to the bank. I only remember standing, in my wet clothes, beside her, watching some faint colour of life gradually creep back to her white lips, while her father, like a man beside himself, galloped off to Castle Stuart for assistance.

When he returned with old Bagally, I had regained my composure. Nothing steadies the nerves of a surgeon—if he loves his profession—like an immediate necessity for the display of his utmost skill. Beatrice was cold and almost pulseless, her left arm was broken, and, when I raised the eyelids from the once lovely eyes, nothing remained of those large and liquid pupils but two scarcely perceptible specks.

'I have bad news for you,' I said; 'I cannot, of course, speak definitely yet as to the full extent of her injuries, but Miss Rochford has broken her arm, and has received severe concussion of the brain.'

'I will borrow Molineux's carriage,' said Rochford.

'No,' said I; 'I am not prepared to risk the journey. Miss Rochford must be taken to the house at once.'

The lame servitor looked askance, but Captain Rochford made light of all objections. 'Molineux would never be so absurdly fanatical as to refuse us his hospitality in such an emergency,' he said; 'I will answer for him.' So, making a litter with saplings and blankets brought from the house, we carried the still unconscious girl through the open door and placed her in a room to which Mrs. Pennithorne directed us.

I set the broken arm at once, and apprehended no danger on that score; but, on examination, I found a comminuted fracture of the skull, with displacement of the external table, and dreaded the result upon so highly sensitive and delicate an organisation as that possessed by my patient. It was clear that she must remain where she was for some days, perhaps for weeks, and I recommended my friend to continue his journey home with all speed and send out Mrs. Rochford to act as nurse.

'I will remain here until you return; and, indeed, if Major Molineux will permit it,' I added, 'I will stop for the next twenty-four hours, at all events.'

Rochford departed, and, in obedience to my summons, Mrs. Pennithorne appeared. She was a pale woman, with a strangely frightened air, and furtive, light-blue eyes. The misfortune of which poor Beatrice Rochford had spoken was very apparent, and certainly very repulsive.

'Let me have candles and a fire,' I said to her. 'I must stop here to-night. When do you expect Major Molineux home?'

'He is at home now, sir,' replied the old woman, in a low voice, which her imperfect articulation rendered almost unintelligible; 'but he cannot see anyone.'

For the first time I remembered that it was Thursday evening.

CHAPTER III

A bright fire, and homely but plentiful preparations for supper, exercised on me their cheering influence, and I succeeded in shaking off a certain depression of spirits which had seized me so soon as the imperative necessity for attending to my patient left me leisure for reflection.

The old housekeeper had, according to my directions, contrived accommodation for Mrs. Rochford in the same room with her daughter, while I was given a bedroom in the next corridor. Supper was served in a spacious apartment downstairs, which seemed to be used by the master of the house as dining-room and library combined. A portrait of the deceased Miss Tremayne, painted by the same hand which had executed the miniature in the possession of Beatrice Rochford, hung on the wall over the chimney, and beneath it was placed the Major's dress-sword and some withered branches of cypress. A heavy writing-table of solid fashioning occupied the embrasure of one of the windows, and lying upon it were some three or four volumes, evidently freshly imported from London.

A new book has always an irresistible attraction for me, and, moreover, on this occasion I was anxious to see what sort of literature my eccentric friend affected. Judge of my surprise to find that three of the works treated of the higher Mathematics, and the fourth was the last speculation of a physician, whose name had a European fame, upon Insanity!

Taking up the lamp, I examined the shelves. I expected to find there works which a military man of culture would naturally purchase, and I was not mistaken. The Life of Sir David Baird, Orme's Hindostan, and Southey's Peninsular War, elbowed Dubosc's History of the Prince Eugene and Mackenzie's Tippoo Sultan, while Churchhill and Harris' Voyages sat pleasantly alongside Barclay's Universal Traveller, and the early volumes of the Despatches of the Duke of Wellington. Oliver's Entomology, and Labillardiere's Plants of New Holland, together with some fragments of Bewick, filled in the spaces between Shaw's Lectures on Zoology, while Audubon's Birds of America, with some few volumes of fiction, enlivened the higher shelves. The best of the collection, however, was almost entirely composed of treatises on Mathematics and the latest works on Mental Disease. Not only were Bayle, Boyle, and La Place in their due place of honour, but the Norwegian Abel sat up beside them, and the latest volume of the Philosophical Transactions had between its leaves a paper covered with calculations made in dispute of Hopkins' statements anent luni-solar precession and nutation.

A row of folios, in sheepskin, bore the honoured names of Galen, Hippocrates, and Avicenna. The best editions of Harvey, Bichat, and Fothergill lay, with the last number of the Medical and Surgical Transactions, near them, while I could see that the Swiss edition of Tissot bristled with page-markers. But on the table were piled books which seemed strangely out of place in the house of a military officer, however cultured. Boehave de Goster, Didier, Cabanis, and Schenck are not authors which one would expect to meet out of the library of a physician, nor are the *Opuscula* of Van Helmont, *le science de l'homme* of Bartletz, or *Lehesätze* of Prochascha, works with which a retired major of the line would be likely to soothe his leisure hours.

I was interrupted at once in my researches and in my reflections by the arrival of the carriage containing Captain Rochford and his wife.

As may be readily imagined, the poor mother was in a condition of great anxiety. Nor was her trouble much alleviated by a visit to the sick-room. Miss Rochford was still unconscious, and though, by the application of wet cloths to the head, I was enabled to keep the inflammation in check, I could as yet offer no decided opinion as to the result of the case.

It might, indeed, be even yet necessary to use the trephine, but I did not desire to alarm either of the parents, and I made the best assurances I could of their daughter's ultimate recovery.

'One thing,' I said, 'is absolutely necessary—perfect quiet. If you move Miss Rochford from this house until I am fully satisfied that she can bear the journey, I will not be responsible for the consequences. To-morrow we will, if you choose, call in the family doctor. To-night the case is under my care.'

Captain Rochford was good enough to express his perfect confidence in my skill, and took leave of us in terms which seemed to indicate that his mind was at ease. I pressed him to stop, but he declined.

'I learn from the old man, Bagally,' he said, 'that Major Molineux has been informed of our presence in the house, and that nothing but the extreme urgency of the case induces him to allow us to remain. I will come back again in the morning.'

Although I defended our involuntary host from the grave charge of discourtesy, I felt that, perhaps, it was well to intrude upon his strangely enforced privacy as little as possible. Having paid a last visit to my patient, and given directions for my immediate recall in case of need, I returned to the dining-room, determined to enjoy myself for a few hours by browsing among the scientific pasturage so curiously and so liberally provided.

I found it impossible to fix my attention on the page. Speculations which, at another time, would have enchained me, vaguely glimmered into my consciousness and disappeared again before I could grasp them. Insignificant and forgotten events of my past life suddenly sprang into my memory with startling distinctness, and an apparent importance wholly disproportioned to their true value as factors in the sum of my existence. I recalled faces of my boyhood, and seemed to hear voices, long ago silent, whispering about me. The wind had risen with the moon, and the night foreboded tempest. The rushing of the swollen stream mingled with the lashing of the rain, as it beat faster and faster upon the panes, while the distant flapping of some unhinged shutter gave querulous and doleful token of the desolation which reigned around the mysterious and ill-omened house.

I more than half-repented that I had insisted upon the establishment of Miss Rochford in a place so dismal and so fraught with gloomy recollections. But her removal would have been attended with graver danger, and my better sense informed me that my fears were merely fancies engendered by shaken nerves and mental strain. Resolving to get the poor girl into the more cheerful society of her own domestic circle without delay, I adjusted another log on the fire, and endeavoured to rally my faculties into some more pleasant mood.

Alas! I but succeeded in making myself more uneasy than before. The chink of the falling embers sounded like low, warning cries, the roar of the river became a threatening voice, the scream of the blast was like the last appeal of some wildly parting soul, the indistinctly-heard rustling of the trees seemed to urge flight.

Through this medly of sounds and sensations the intermittent flap of the loose shutter recurred at irregular intervals, like the sound made by one who, with failing strength, and yet passionate persistence, would gain shelter from some pursuing terror. I felt horribly alone. From above me looked down the sad, wild eyes of the dead girl, and about me were only the tokens of the strange, perhaps hideous, speculations of the mysterious recluse.

At that moment I heard a stealthy football in the passage.

Without pausing to think, I flung wide the door, and confronted the intruder.

At first I felt inclined to burst into laughter. Old Bagally was creeping towards the staircase with a tray, upon which was spread meat and wine.

'Bringing me something to eat?' I said, ashamed of my abrupt outbursting from the door, and yet glad of this momentary companionship with humanity.

'It is for the Major, sir,' said he, endeavouring to pass, and seeming unaccountably agitated.

'But the Major doesn't want two forks and two knives, and all that meat,' said I. 'Perhaps someone sups with him?'

'What is that to you?' said the old man, with a sudden, savage snarl, making as though, having both hands engaged, he would have bit me sideways in his wolf-like fury. 'You have had all you want; if not, I'll bring you more. Leave us alone. We have our own ways,' and, vouchsafing no further parley, he climbed the stairs which led to his master's apartments.

More puzzled than ever, I returned to the gloomy dining-room. Had I stumbled into a house of madmen? Was the unreasoning terror of the toothless beldame but a form of idiocy? Was the old convict, with his ape-like skull and his canine rabidity, a maniac?

And the master of this desolated and death-haunted ruin, who shut himself up for one day in the week, and enshrouded that day with such precautions against being taken unawares, that his very food must be conveyed to him at night, and by stealth—what was he? Was he, too, insane? Had he brooded upon madness until he had become mad himself? Was he doing penance, as Beatrice had suggested, for some frightful crime? Did those doors, behind which he lived his forlorn life, conceal some poor relative whose sad calamity was held a misfortune to be bolted in and barred away from men?

Or—most horrible thought of all—did he keep concealed above, and watched by the crazy pair, some poor wretch upon whose dazed brain and diseased body he might practice devilish experimental arts, if haply he might work out one or other of the wild theories propounded in some of the more speculative of his philosophers? Even as the thought shaped itself, there rang through the house a series of piercing shrieks.

CHAPTER IV

In another instant I was at the head of the stairs, but paused in my onward flight, for the sounds issued from the room occupied by Beatrice and her mother.

Mrs. Rochford was lying on the floor senseless. Ringing the bell furiously, I raised her to her bed, and, with the assistance of the old woman, whom the cries of the unhappy lady, not less than my importunate summons, had brought to the spot, I succeeded in restoring her to consciousness. Her first words were:

'Is it gone?'

'What?' I asked.

'The white face at the window!' said Mrs. Rochford. 'That imploring, maddened face!'

'What can she mean?' I asked Mary Pennithorne, but the old woman, moping and mowing, made no reply.

'See, madam,' I said, flinging wide the lattice, 'the storm has passed, and with it the cause of your alarm. Some leafy branchlet carried by the wind, perhaps even some more wrathful gust than usual, has, while rousing you from sleep, given form to a passing dream. Look, the sky is almost cloudless.'

And in truth, the tempest had, during the time we had been occupying ourselves with the frightened woman, quite passed away. The scene was one of exquisite peacefulness. The clouds had almost withdrawn, and the wet trees sparkled in the beams of a glorious moon, which rode high in a serene heaven. All felt the influence of the scene. Beatrice, sunk in her stupor, alone was ignorant alike of sounds and sights; but her mother composed herself with a smile at her former fears, and as I sought my comfortable couch, I felt that science and sentiment alike bid me laugh at the ungrateful fancies which an atmosphere surcharged with electricity could breed in a brain usually so cool as mine.

The excitement of the day caused me to sleep longer than my wont, and it was nearly eight o'clock when I awoke. I discovered by the hot water jug, with its carefully placed towel, that the rude valetage of Bagally had already been exercised in my chamber, and, before I had completed my *toilette,* the old servant introduced himself with the compliments of his master, and information that breakfast would be ready for us in half-an-hour.

Captain Rochford had already arrived, and with him I visited the sick-room. Beatrice was still insensible, but Mrs. Rochford was up and dressed. Rochford laughed at her story of the ghost, and, gathering courage from my assurance that the patient was progressing favourably, we went down to breakfast in something like good spirits.

Major Molineux received us with more than courtesy. He lamented the accident, but trusted that the skill of a surgeon so well known as myself, and the careful attention of a mother so devoted as Mrs. Rochford, would soon restore his fair guest to her wonted health.

'I'm afraid,' he said, as he assisted us to the dish before him, 'that my poor house is but a gloomy place for a convalescent, and I trust that Miss Rochford's convalescence may be early. Such as are the resources of the place, however—command them. I regret that I was unable to render you any personal assistance yesterday, but I must compensate for my enforced neglect by devoting myself to all your services during the next few days.'

The language was of the politest, but there was no mistaking its meaning. Rochford and I looked at each other. It was quite evident that Major Molineux did not desire that we should pass another Thursday under his roof.

'I trust that Miss Rochford may be able to travel to her own home before this day week,' said I, somewhat pointedly. 'In the meantime, let me thank you for the courtesy with which we were received, and especially for the hospitality of last night.'

The hand with which the Major was lifting the teacup to his lips trembled slightly, but he said, merely, 'It was a wild night—a night of storms. I trust you were not disturbed.'

'I was most terribly disturbed,' said Mrs. Rochford—I think I have said that she was not a woman of much force of character, or quickness of apprehension—'I had the most shocking dreams. A white face at the window—'

'Nonsense, Mary,' interrupted Rochford; 'you were nervous.'

'There is no one in the house but myself and the two servants,' said the Major, who had completely regained his composure, 'and I am sure neither of them would have the temerity to disturb your slumbers. Pray,' he added, turning in stiff condescension to old Bagally, 'have *you* been amusing yourself by terrifying my guests?'

The old man seemed dumb-stricken. He tried to speak, but words failed him. Lifting up his hands with a gesture of terror, he made for the door, and, turning as he went, displayed again that wolf-like savagery of aspect, the which I had observed on the previous night.

'A curious fellow,' said Major Molineux, cracking the shell of his egg, 'but faithful. An old convict, of course. I have touched some tender chord, perhaps.'

Perhaps he had, for Dame Pennithorne waited upon us during the rest of the meal, and even brought the Major his cigar-case, when we found ourselves in the dilapidated but spacious verandah, prepared to seek the solace which, in those days, was supposed to lie in Manilla tobacco.

The conversation, of course, was of the accident and its results. The prospects of the patient's recovery, the punishment to be meted out to the self-indulgent bullock-driver, the quality of Sultan's temper, and the equestrian skill of Miss Rochford, were all debated in turn. A learned discussion was held upon fracture of the skull, and I was compelled to illustrate as best I might the operation of the trephine. At last exhausted with surgery, and convinced that he was thoroughly competent to treat a similar case, should he ever meet with one, Rochford betook himself to visit the scene of the accident, and left me alone with our host.

Major Molineux seemed uneasy. He got up and paced the broken tiles of the piazza floor, talked of twenty things in a breath, and flung away his half-consumed cigar, only to light another an instant after.

'You are restless this morning,' I said, willing to gain, if I could, some information concerning the mysterious seclusion of yesterday. 'Did you not sleep well?'

'Oh, yes,' returned the Major, indifferently, 'I slept well enough,' and then he fixed his eyes on the wall behind me with that strange stare of which I have already spoken, and wiped from his brow some large beads of sweat which had suddenly appeared there. 'I seldom sleep very soundly.'

'Indigestion, I suspect,' I continued, in a careless tone. 'A man who eats enough for two people at about midnight can scarcely wonder if he suffers from nightmare.'

With a visible effort my interlocutor withdrew his gaze from space, and looked me in the eyes.

'Then you saw Bagally with the tray,' said he. 'I am ashamed of my voracious appetite,' he added, with an attempt at a smile, 'and try to laugh myself out of my gluttony by demonstrating to my actual vision that I do, in fact, partake of a double portion of food.'

'Your notion is ingenious, but I fear that you will never effect a cure by its means. Let me feel your pulse.' He gave me his wrist. The hand was hot and dry, the pulse full and bounding. 'I will write you a little prescription which may do you good. Give me a sheet of paper,' and I led the way to the library. 'There,' said I, folding the sheet; 'though I saw Woodville and Sowerby on your shelves, I doubt if you are fully acquainted with the virtues of the lily tribe.'

'You have been among my books, then,' said the Major, looking round.

'I have, and am surprised to find so excellent a collection of works in—pardon me for saying it—so unexpected a place.'

'Books are my only companions,' said Major Molineux, and, as he spoke, he scanned the table a little nervously, as though to see which of the volumes had attracted my attention.

Determined to penetrate the secret which I was now convinced existed, I pressed my advantage. 'I see that you study the higher Mathematics. This calculation on the variation of parameters is not made by a school-boy, while here'—and I lifted from the table a sheet of paper—'is something headed, "*Probability that an event observed several times in succession depends upon a cause which facilitates its reproduction*," in which the calculation is made by finding the equation of the logarithmic curve.'

Major Molineux changed colour, and took the paper from my hands. 'I did not know that I had left the records of my folly thus carelessly exposed,' said he. 'The fact is that I have always been a lover of anything which approaches an exact science, and the calculation of probabilities is a fascinating subject. I am foolishly fond of it,' and, as he spoke, he tore the paper into pieces and flung them into the basket at his feet.

'Some men say that mathematicians are mad,' I said. 'If this be so, you have the antidote as well as the bane, for seldom have I seen, even in the libraries of my professional brethren, so fine a collection of works on Mental Disease as that which I examined last night.'

I had gone too far for his patience.

'Doctor Fayre,' said he, 'you are my guest, and my house is at your disposal so long as the illness of my old friend's daughter compels you to remain in it; but let me remind you that an old man who lives by choice a recluse, may have sought such seclusion in order that he might be spared these very comments upon his private tastes which you have just been pleased to make,' and, bowing stiffly, he left the room.

CHAPTER V

He did not appear that day, nor at breakfast the next morning. I felt that I deserved the reproach which his absence conveyed, and was angry with myself for having so far permitted my curiosity to outrun my discretion. But the more I reflected upon the circumstances of the case, the more convinced did I become that Castle Stuart held within its walls some mystery of mind or body, upon the like of which it was not given to man to frequently look; and, despite the Major's rebuff and my own self-consciousness, I resolved not to abandon my quest. In pursuance of this resolution I sauntered out into the garden the next afternoon, thinking to fall in with the old servant. I was not disappointed. I found him standing in a little glade, or opening in the brushwood, staring with all his might at the upper windows of the house.

'What interests you?' I cried, taking a guinea from my pocket. 'Can you not spare time for a little friendly chat?'

He looked nervously about him, pocketed the gold piece, and, pointing to a coarse patch of verdure at his feet, whispered:

'It was here he did it.'

'Did what?' I asked.

'Cut his throat,' said the old man, 'and they buried him here, with a stake through his heart. But that can't hold him.'

'What do you mean, man?' I asked, experiencing a fresh access of horror at this hideous and unexpected story. 'Who is buried here?'

'Savary, the forger; him as found his wife gone as well as his liberty. This was where he saw them walking. The Captain was a handsome man, and Mrs. Savary had been a beauty, they say. She died mad for all that,' and he laughed the discordant laugh of one whose experience of life has been of the sort to make him rejoice in others' woe.

'What was the Captain's name?'

'Tremayne. He was the Major's brother-in-law. *He's* dead too, and Savary will soon see them all out.'

'Does his ghost walk, then?' I asked, attempting a laugh; but the day was cloudy, and a cold wind seemed on a sudden to chill me.

'Ask Mrs. Rochford. She saw him last night. Listen. Two years ago I was sitting up with the old hag in the kitchen, when I heard the door-bell. It was blowing a storm like it was last night, and the wind went shrieking round the house as if it wanted to get in and tear us. It was the Major's Thursday, and I daren't go near him for my soul. I crept to the door, thinking some traveller had got out of his track, for no one who knew us would come to Castle Stuart; but before I could open it there was an awful screech, and something went whirling round the house like a pack of dogs. I heard them bellowing and grunting at the back, and ran upstairs to look. I looked out of that window'—he pointed to the room where Mrs. Rochford had slept the night before—'and I saw something like a herd of huge swine on Savary's grave, rooting, and snarling, and slavering in it, and then I slammed to the window, for some awful thing with a white face was there trying to save itself from those hellish beasts. The noise continued for five or six minutes, and then the sky cleared like it did last night, and I saw no more.'

'You have a cheerful imagination, my friend,' said I; 'but, pray, do you couple this delectable story with your master's day of seclusion?'

Once more the ugly look came into his face. 'Nay, I know nothing of that; and it's no business of yours either, though you are a doctor. Doctors cannot cure Major Molineux's complaint.'

'Then you think that he is ill?'

'Not I; he's well enough.'

'Look ye, Bagally,' I said, determined to try a last chance, 'you are too sensible a man to believe this nonsense about ghosts, and suicides, and hunted souls. I am a doctor; I shall be here some days. I may be able to do your master good. Tell me'— and I exhibited another guinea— 'what is the mystery in connection with Major Molineux?'

'He is possessed by a devil,' said Bagally; and then, as if he had said too much, made for the house with grotesque, uneven strides, and left me standing on the coarse grass that sprung from the dishonoured grave where the suicide lay with a stake through his heart.

A voice roused me from my reverie. Major Molineux himself was at my side.

'Fayre,' said he, 'I have overheard the last words of your conversation. I do not expect you to pay attention to the vulgar fancies of an ignorant hind. The story of the wretched being who lies buried at your feet is neither part of my history nor does it concern my family. The romance which was sought to be woven around his name and that of my dear sister's husband has been long ago proved false, and it was perhaps the gratification of a desire to preserve from derision the last resting-place of a man more sinned against than sinning which caused the report to first obtain circulation. When my niece came to live with me I caused the fence, which formerly surrounded Arthur Savary's grave, to be removed, and, unless some chattering imbecile like old Bagally had informed her of the story, this portion of the park possessed for her no more interest than any other. The fantasies of women are innumerable.' He spoke rapidly, and with some heat. It was quite evident that he expected a reply, and a direct one.

'No one, Major Molineux,' said I, 'is less superstitious than myself, but I have seen so much of what is termed superstition resolve itself into fact, that I am not prepared to pronounce any fantasy of the imagination as wholly baseless. But before we proceed further, let me feel sure of my ground. I came here only in my character as a physician in attendance upon a patient who has been made unavoidably your guest. I find myself face to face with an extraordinary enigma, yourself. Your peculiar studies, your secluded life, above all, your strange disappearance from all society on one day in the week, have combined to raise in me a curiosity which I cannot stifle. What is the mystery which darkens your life?'

Major Molineux planted himself firmly on his feet, and took both my hands in his own. His face was deadly pale, and he seemed to be nerving himself for a great effort. 'Do not turn from me. Do not shun me,' he said. 'Had it not been for your persistence, I had never spoken. Bagally is right. One day in each week I am possessed by a devil.'

'Come, come,' said I, a little shaken, despite my self-control, as the powerful old man searched my eyes with his, 'there are many sorts of devils—devils of wrath, and devils of discontent, and we all are now and then at the mercy of such.'

'Ay,' said Major Molineux, 'but to be possessed, as I am, by—no, I cannot speak it, I could not repeat, nor could you listen to the tale. Forget what I have said, and'—he pressed my arm with painful violence—'swear to mention to no living soul that which I have unguardedly betrayed.'

'A physician's lips are sealed without an oath,' said I. 'You may rely on me. And now I must see Miss Rochford. Let us go in.'

He regained his self-possession before we reached the house, and not during the day was the subject again mentioned between us. I thought it better for the development of the case to permit my patient—for so I now considered him—to begin a confidence which I feared might be withdrawn if I pressed him too closely. Seeing that I touched only on indifferent matters, he presided at dinner with his customary composure, and entertained us all with the stores of a mind acquisitive of information and fastidious in the imparting of it.

'The old gentleman was never more amusing,' said Rochford, as I parted from him in the hall. 'When we move Beatrice, I'll ask him to come to Ashmead; the change would do him good.'

'Ask him, by all means,' said I, 'and I will second your entreaties. If we can once break the chain of recurring events in his life we may give him another lease of it. Our intrusion, unwelcome though it was at first, has already roused him into something like gaiety. Miss Rochford should be well enough in a fortnight to be moved, for her case looks in every way favourable.'

'How can I ever repay you for your kindness?' said Rochford.

I knew a method by which he could repay me a thousandfold, but I did not think it wise to mention it at that moment. Alas! events soon occurred which rendered it impossible for me to ever ask that favour which I prized so highly.

On Wednesday afternoon, Major Molineux begged to see me alone. He led the way to his library, carefully closed the door, and, after much prelude, began to talk about his malady.

'I wish to ask you,' said he, 'if it is possible for a man to be mad and know that he is mad?'

'There are different kinds of madness,' said I, feeling that I must speak with caution. 'An insane man may have lucid intervals during which he reviews acts done during the period of his insanity, and condemns them. A man may have an uncontrollable impulse to commit a certain act—as to jump out of a window, for instance—and yet be quite conscious of the folly, and even wickedness, of his morbid promptings. I knew a case in India of a soldier who was seized with just such a morbid desire. He felt compelled to murder some one very near and dear to him, and at last deserted in order to do it. Arrived in the town where the intended victim lived, he absolutely had himself tied up by the people of the inn, until the proper authorities could be sent for to secure him. Some months afterwards the object of his morbid lust for blood died, and the man at once recovered. He described his sufferings while resisting his impulse as terrible. Surely no devil worse than this could possess a man. And yet he could hardly be called mad.'

'You give me a few grains of comfort,' said Major Molineux, 'though I have no such fearful impulse as that which you describe. Every week, from ten o'clock on Wednesday night until ten o'clock on Friday morning, I am the prey to the most bestial and awful delusion which it has entered into the mind of man to conceive. I know that the fault is in my own brain, and that I am but the dupe of imagination. But where that fault lies I have sought in vain to find. Science brings me no solace, and, though my sense laughs at my imagination, I dare not confront the hideous thing which my imagination has created to mock my sense.'

'You are not alone in your misfortune, dear sir,' said I. 'There have been many men, haunted by phantoms, who have lived to make them but a source of amusement. The operation of ghost seeing is simple enough. We recall a landscape, which we have seen. We will it to return, and it is instantly present. That is to say that we project from us that which we wish to recall, and look at it, and listen to it, as if it were again external to us. An artist draws a dead face from memory, while a musician plays an air forgotten by his hearers—the same effort too, of will, which recalled the lineaments of a corpse, and the notes of the opera, could people a house with ghosts, and fill the darkness with the voices of the dead.

'Ah,' said the Major, with a sigh, 'mine is no such illusion as those which you have mentioned. No voices of angel or of demon speak to me. No faces, grotesque or enchanting, present themselves to my gaze. My delusion, and delusion it is, though sometimes I am half persuaded of its truth, is so horrible, so damning, so fearful in its naked insistence of the beast in our fallen natures that I have been tempted not once, but a hundred times, to set my spirit free from the soul-destroying bands which enwrap it.'

He spoke with sober vehemence, and appalling earnestness.

'That this feeling is part of the delusion I know, but that does not make it more bearable. For nine years I have endured a weekly agony, compared with which, the keenest torments of man's devising are as naught. In body and in soul I have suffered more than tongue can tell. Save that my reason did not desert me, I should have speedily qualified myself for a place beside the poor wretch over whose grave I confessed my secret; and yet I ask you, can I lay claim to the possession of reason, when I am the sport of an imagining so foul as that which torments me?'

'But,' said I, gently, 'you have not yet told me the nature of this delusion.'

'I dare not,' said Major Molineux. 'You would quit the house. To no human ear can I speak the history of my unspeakable degradation.' He rose suddenly.

'To-morrow is Thursday,' he said, 'come into my room to-night, and *see* what I dare not speak,' and he left me.

Miss Rochford had regained consciousness, and I hoped that the next few days would see her in a fair way of recovery. Mrs. Rochford had laughed off her fears, and attributed, as I did, the visitant's face to a more mortal source than that of the wandering soul of a suicide. Rochford was in high spirits at the approaching departure, and even Mrs. Pennithorne seemed less terrified than usual. I could not have had a more propitious hour for the investigation of the mystery which had baffled me, and I waited with much anxiety for midnight, which—being about the time I had seen Bagally on the previous week—was, I thought, a customary hour with the Major for taking his oddly-timed meal.

I was not amiss in my calculations. As the timepiece in the hall rang out the hour, the old convict appeared with the tray.

'Your master has desired me to see him,' I said, 'and I will go up with you.'

'As you please,' said Bagally, roughly; 'but take care.'

He led the way along the great corridor until he came to a double door.

'If he is not waiting on the other side,' said he, 'you'll be lucky,' and, opening a slide in the panel, he pushed in the tray with its burthen, bolting the panel quickly.

I stood uncertain how to act. Bagally turned to descend the stairs.

'Will you not go in?' I asked.

'Not for all the money in Hobart,' said the man, his very hair bristling. 'Listen.' I bent my ear to the door, and could distinguish the confused sounds of voices.

'Who is with him?' I asked. But the old servitor had left me. I was alone, and from the other side of the oak panel came a sound which caused my blood to curdle in my veins. In another instant I should have fled.

'Molineux! Major Molineux!' I cried, and rapped at the panel. The door shot back, and I entered. The passage was pitch dark; but in the distance I could see a lighted candle in what appeared to be a bedroom.

I advanced towards it. The door shut behind me, and I felt someone place what seemed to be a hand on my shoulder.

Major Molineux was right. Words refuse to lend themselves to the depiction of that which the horror fixed eye saw in that lonely chamber.

Chapter VI

Mrs. Rochford was the only person whom I met at the breakfast-table the morning after my visit to Major Molineux's room. The Major himself, for reasons which I could readily appreciate, desired to postpone, as long as possible, an interview with one who had become possessed of his unhappy secret, and Rochford had intimated his intention of arriving later in the day. Now that his daughter was out of danger, there was really no real reason for his presence, which, indeed, was a daily element of disturbance in the sick room.

'When do you think that Beatrice can be moved?' asked Mrs. Rochford. 'I long to have her at home again under my own roof; for, though Major Molineux is most kind and attentive, I experience a sense of depression in this house which I cannot shake off.'

'I quite agree with you that the sooner Miss Rochford is got home the better,' I replied, 'though the feeling of which you speak is attributable only to your own anxiety, and perhaps in some measure to the unwonted quietude of Castle Stuart after the bustle of Ashmead. Nevertheless, we must be cautious. I never like to disturb a case of fracture, however slight, for at least twenty days, and we have been here but barely seven.'

'True,' she said; 'this is Friday. I had forgotten,' and her glance at the vacant place at the foot of the table noted to me the circumstance which had escaped her memory.

Some slight confusion in my manner must have betrayed me, for, with a woman's quickness, she said suddenly, 'Doctor Fayre, you look worn and ill this morning. Tell me, do you know anything about this mystery of Major Molineux?'

'My dear madam,' I said, 'I am a doctor, and I cannot speak even indirectly of matters which have come to my knowledge in the exercise of my profession. Major Molineux has been complimentary enough to ask my advice upon certain points connected with his health, but I am as yet but very partially informed as to his case.'

'Nay,' said she, 'I did not mean to put an impertinent query; but it has occurred to me that, in return for the Major's kindness to my daughter,

Beatrice might, by-and-bye, rouse him from his melancholy, and even win his confidence as to the secret cause of his malady.'

If you have ever chanced, when in conversation, to hear a phrase innocently uttered which conveys to your private ear a world of esoteric meaning, you will comprehend the quick pang I felt at this sudden approximation of two ideas. Beatrice and my patient of last night! That pure girl and that most unhappy being, whose hideous hallucination made him doubtful of his humanity! When a student in Paris, I had seen the body of a beautiful girl exposed on a dissecting-table for some needful demonstrations in anatomy. The sight shocked me then, and as, obedient to the law of association, the picture of that nerveless figure, so passive under the searching knife and exploring eye, rose again before me, I almost saw the pallid features shape themselves into a likeness of those of Beatrice.

'Do not think of such a thing, madam,' I cried. 'It is quite impossible. Miss Beatrice must never know aught of the—' and I stopped abruptly. Was I not already committing myself?

Poor Mrs. Rochford quite failed to appreciate my fervour, but I was glad to see that she attributed it more to zeal for her daughter's welfare than to any serious illness affecting Major Molineux.

'I had no intention, of course,' she said, 'of urging the project now, but by-and-bye, when change of air and scene might be tried on both—'

'Let us defer the consideration until then,' I said; and with some difficulty succeeded in retaining my composure sufficiently to sit out the untasted meal.

Left to myself, I began to reflect. Upon what a hideous thing had I stumbled! Far from being, as I had suspected, the melancholic craze of a hypochondriac—who might believe himself a teapot or a wash-hand basin, Tiberius Cæsar, or Alexander the Great—the hallucination of Major Molineux was one which blended itself so inextricably with the affairs of his daily life that he could no more escape from it than he could stay his pulse at will. Bound as I was by the most solemn pledges of personal and professional honour, I had taken upon myself the burden of a frightful secret which I must lock for ever in my own heart, or share, and sicken in the sharing, with the unhappy man whose choking breast was its only other repository. And, having acquired the knowledge of this polluting horror, I must bear it with me for ever; for, did my skill haply succeed in removing from my companion's mind his belief in the absolute entity of it, still the image of it was there stamped upon the brain, and ready to start into grisly life again at any instant.

Nor was it possible to fix the idea in words. Even now, after thirty years, I can recall the agony of mind with which, pacing in the deserted park by the lonely grave of the suicide, I strove to bring the abstract horror of the thing into some shape, that I might grapple with it and defy it. In vain. It eluded my mental grasp as a jelly-fish slips through the fingers. Formless and void, it yet was there—a foul and filthy thought, profaning the shrine of sense.

And he—the wretched man, in whose brain-cells this more than chimæric growth of shame and horror had been fed and fostered—what was my suffering to his? I saw clearly the line which separated the delusion of the one day from the comparative sanity of the other six. I could trace, far down in the beginnings of mental being, the first growth of the appalling thought which now mounted reason's throne and shook the sceptre of judgment. *I* was no believer in the damning mystery. Mine was, after all, but the experience of one who, meeting a leper uncovered in the by-way, has to wash in many waters ere he can return to forget that loathsome sight, among men of sound flesh and healthy limb. But the leper—poor ruin—knowing his own bitter fate—cut off for ever from the intimacy of the honest, put away from the sight of the noble, the very manhood which, supporting him in his trial, urges him to retain what semblance to his fellow-men the cankering corruption may have left him, and make an exit from life while he is yet a step removed from rabid putrescence—what far-reaching depths of anguish and of shame has not his soul plumbed in the swift descent of its despair?

One thing was certain. Having thus possessed myself of the knowledge of Major Molineux's terrible story, I was bound, by every tie of honour and humanity, to alleviate his sufferings. Such of my brethren who are read in the literature of insanity will understand me when I say that I shuddered at the task. I am not what the world terms a religious man, and in those days I was perhaps less so than the experience of a long life has taught me since to be; but, in reviewing the case of this unfortunate gentleman, I found myself involuntarily offering up a petition to a Higher Power on his behalf. I had—during the long vigil of the dread night—mastered all physical symptoms, and arrived at the conclusion that, though science might palliate the tortures of the sufferer, she could not restore him 'whole and in his right mind.' 'I am possessed by a devil,' the poor man had said to me; and I did not profess to have the power of exorcism. Still, much might be done. The relief to his burdened mind must be already great, and if I could but prevail on him to discuss the theme—and my flesh crept with disgust as the thought thrilled my nerves—in calmness, haply some break in the continuity of the hallucination would be discovered whereby I could prevent the recurrence of the phenomena, or at least destroy the regularity of their appearance. The trial, distasteful as it was, should be made, and I sought the house, to give directions to Bagally to send to Hobart for some drugs with which I had resolved to begin the treatment.

I found the old servant in something of an anxious mood. He was evidently desirous of knowing how I had sped with his master, and I thought it a good opportunity to ascertain how much or how little he himself had learned.

'I had a long conversation with Major Molineux last night, Bagally,' said I; 'and I have every hope that I may do him some good. Pray, when did you first observe the symptoms of his illness?'

'I have lived with him for seventeen years,' said the convict, with something approaching to tenderness in his voice, 'and for the first eight years he was the same as the rest of us. Then he began to keep to the house and avoid company, then to his room, and so by degrees to what you know him.'

'Have you ever seen him during one of his attacks?' I asked.

'Never, thank God! but I have seen them as have—God help 'em!'

'Whom do you mean?'

'Miss Agnes. She saw him; and she never held up her head after. 'Twas one of them windy nights, like the one I was telling you about. When the screeching began, it seems that Miss Agnes got frightened, and ran out, calling for her Uncle. The old woman there slept next Miss Agnes, and she says she heard the Major's door open, and him come out to her. Then Miss Agnes cried out upon God to save her; and when Pennithorne got to her she was lying, fainted, in the passage. She was took with shivering that night, crying out on names we didn't know for someone to help her. The doctor—'twas old Murchison—said 'twas a cold she took in running out from her warm bed to the passage. We knew better, Pennithorne and I. 'Twas fright she died of.'

'I am afraid that Mrs. Pennithorne is as much a romancer as you are,' said I, with a most unsuccessful attempt at a smile. 'Dr. Murchison was, no doubt, quite correct in his diagnosis. However, I want you to go into the town for these few matters,' and I handed him the paper. 'The Major has consented to submit to my treatment; but you know how sensitive he is, and I trust to your discretion to make no remarks either to him personally or to others.'

'You needn't fear,' returned he, unhitching the bridle from its peg. 'I've lived too long here not to know how to hold my tongue.' He hobbled to the door, and then came quickly back with awkward gesture, meant to indicate self-possession. 'Cure him,' he said, and thrust something into my hand. It was one of the guineas I had given him over the suicide's grave.

Pondering over the confirmation of my worst fears, which the manner of the death of poor Miss Tremayne gave me, I resolved to see if I could obtain any information from Dame Pennithorne. The kitchen was a large one, and amply furnished with necessary utensils of all sorts. Our visit had compelled an almost entire change in the domestic policy of the household, and evidences of plenty, and even luxury, abounded. A fat-faced wench, employed in assisting a boy scullion to scour a huge fish-kettle, destined to contain our Friday fare, directed me to a door which led into a sort of stillroom or housekeeper's closet—the private apartments of the woman to whom Miss Rochford had taken so strong a dislike.

Mrs. Pennithorne was seated before the empty grate, staring, with all her dazed might, into the fuelless fireplace. She did not hear me approach, and, coming close behind her, I tapped her lightly on the shoulder. The effect was curious. She did not start nor scream; she simply trembled violently, turning, as she did so, her head slowly round, until her glassy eyes—round and unspeculative as those of a fish—met mine. Her toothless mouth, open, in the curve of expectation, seemed not unlike that of a cod. Had I taken her hand I should have almost expected to find it cold.

Slowly her senses undazzled, and she recognised me. 'I was thinking of you, sir,' she mumbled, her wrinkled cheeks flapping together like bellows. 'But I daren't speak to you.'

'Why not? What mystery can you have to conceal?'

She looked round her again with that frightened air of which I have before spoken, and then suddenly clutching my arm, with all her choppy fingers distended like the claws of a bird, she whispered to me:

'Take her away, doctor. For God's sake, take her away.'

'You mean Miss Rochford,' said I. 'Now, listen, Mrs. Pennithorne; I want you to tell me what you know of Miss Tremayne's death. It took place in that very room, did it not? Answer me.'

She stared wildly, gaping and goggling after her unpleasant manner. From the adjacent kitchen came the laughter of the scullion and the cook-maid.

'Come, Mrs. Pennithorne,' I repeated, 'recollect yourself. What took place before Miss Tremayne's death?'

'She met *him*,' said the old woman, nodding at the wall nearest the house. 'I know nothing more. But there is a curse upon this house, which brings agony and woe to all who live in it.'

I looked at the crone with aroused curiosity. Was my conjecture right, and was she, too, a victim to some form of mental aberration? It was likely enough. There is contagion in insanity, and it might be that the lonely life led by a woman of her age, whose constant employment was speculation upon a mystery in another's life, had rendered her also a monomaniac. I felt a sudden repulsion to the house and its belongings. The old woman had no coherent tale to tell; and if she had? The atmosphere seemed hot with the breath of madmen. I paid a hurried visit to Beatrice, saddled my horse myself, and galloped into the town. I felt that I must have a few hours of commonplace life, or I, too, might become the sport of those unseen agencies which take up their abodes in pampered bodies and neglected minds.

Chapter VII

Soothed and sustained by a night's rest in the unromantic precincts of the Club, I returned to Castle Stuart with all the cobwebs swept out of my brain, and with a positive professional delight at the prospect of the cure of Major Molineux.

I found my poor friend anxiously awaiting my arrival, and, so soon as lunch was disposed of, he drew me aside.

'I have felt an inexpressible relief,' he said, 'since I revealed to you my fearful trouble, and something like hope begins to light up the darkness within.'

'That is a good symptom,' said I; 'and now we will have a little physical history to follow upon the mental one.'

I asked him a series of questions upon his general health, and found, as I expected, that he had been for years a stranger to anything like regularity of life. He ate when he pleased and what he fancied, walked but little, and would often sit for a day together without moving from the table where he pursued his physiological studies. He was emaciated in body, but of late, and as his malady had progressed, he had become more and more addicted to the use of large quantities of animal food, with which he drank weak brandy and water.

'I find,' said he, 'that I grow less and less able to eat vegetables or bread without experiencing serious inconvenience, not merely as regards indigestion, but as concerns the extent and pressure of that which I know to be a delusion of the brain.'

'Of course,' I replied, with that wisdom which doctors affect when they are at fault for a diagnosis; 'the normal condition of things in the body is changed when certain substances are taken into it; and, in certain other conditions of it, moreover, there are produced within it organic products which affect the organs of the senses and interfere with their functions. Indian hemp, opium, and a thousand other substances, have the power to set to sleep some senses and open others, while—and this I suspect is at the bottom of your sorrows—some abnormal condition of things within has set you astray as to your relations to things without.'

'Then you think,' cried the poor man, almost joyfully, 'that I am not necessarily diseased in brain?'

'Necessarily? No. The body of a man is a mere bundle of organs for condensing external facts, as says a writer with whom I hope by-and-bye to make you acquainted. The man has a hearing organ, a seeing organ, and so on. In each organ there is a receiving nervous surface; from this surface, leading into the man, is a communicating nervous cord; while, at the end of this cord, is a nervous centre, which takes up the impression conveyed and makes it part of the individual's experience.'

'And mischief may be present anywhere and in any of these parts?'

'Exactly. But to lay the finger of science on the particular part is often impossible. The surface, the cord, or the centre may be to blame, and we thus pass, at a bound, from the merest physical investigation into a psychological speculation of the most intricate and uncertain nature.'

Major Molineux cast a wistful glance at Val Helmont and the rest.

'But is it not possible for science to reason with something like certainty in such matters? The universe is governed by fixed laws. Fixed laws rule the bodily and mental health of man. I have twenty times calculated the chances of the periodical return of my malady. An astronomer can as accurately calculate the return of a passing world. Anatomy has laid open to us all the secrets of the human machine. Is there none, then, who can penetrate into this poor body and pluck forth the heart of its mystery?'

He spoke with eagerness, but without passion; and as I saw him there, and recalled his awful doom, I felt my heart throb with a pity which swallowed up, once and for ever, all other feelings.

'Dear Major Molineux, dear friend,' I said, 'science cannot do what you ask. See, here,' and I drew down a chart of the nervous system, which was affixed in its box to the wall. "Here are the nerves which emanate from the brain, and which are under the control of the will. Here are the ganglionic nerves, which are not under the control of the will. See how all the great vital organs depend upon these last for the performance of their functions. And these ganglionic organs tell us nothing. The heart beats, the lungs breathe, the stomach digests, but we take no note of their motions. It is only when these organs are *diseased* that we become conscious of their existence. A reflex action now begins. Sense on soul and soul on sense, discussing, arguing, disputing. The body is slowly informed of the capacities of the mind: the mind gradually takes upon itself the functions of the body. See here, here, here—these myriads of glands, each working under the influence of the nerves distributed to them. Each filament, each follicle participates in the general disorder, and a chain of morbid association between mental and corporeal organs binds mind to body—a chain the woven links of which are intertwisted beyond human skill to loose. You ask me to show you the heart of your mystery; as well ask me to show you Thought made visible."

'And yet these men,' said the Major, glancing at his shelves, 'more than half believed that among the many forces of great nature was one—supreme, eternal—which, in its varying shape, was health, air, gold, love, jealousy and death.'

'Others besides your mystics,' said I, 'have recognised such a force, but they have given it a name. So far as man is concerned, there are in him two distinct manifestations of this force—the Will and the Intellect. Will is instinctive and unwearied; Intellect is reflective and fatigable. But the Intellect is as a bridle to the Will, and sometimes it happens that Will takes the bit in its teeth and runs away. Then takes place something like that of which you complain, and the mere instinctive and animal part of the man assumes sole control of his personality. Is this Madness? If the deliberative faculties cannot regain the mastery over the executive faculties—yes.'

'No,' said Major Molineux; 'if such a force exists, Madness and Sanity are but terms. We are all parts of one great whole, and discord is impossible. Nay, that which seems discord may be harmony, and my awful sufferings a necessary part of the universal joy. Yet why should I bear this burden? I am not a wicked man. Heaven is my witness that I have lived uprightly according to my lights. Why am I singled out from all my fellow-men to be the subject of so fearful an outrage? If my body has sinned, let it be punished; but why make sport of my intellect, and leave God-like reason at the mercy of the basest part of man?'

He walked up and down as he spoke, and I watched him with increased interest. He had evidently thrown off the mask, and was speaking in his real character. The genial *militaire*, the entertaining host, the learned mathematician, the well-read physiologist—these were mere characters assumed by him as garments of disguise. The real man was before me—no longer calm, courteous, and self-restrained, but fevered with suffering, and wild with undefined anxiety. This man interested in the speculations of Holland or Van Holst, the discoveries of Laplace, and the philosophy of Newton! The wide world held for him but one subject—the maddening speculation on his own madness.

'We have talked long enough this evening,' said I, 'and Rochford will be here to bid us goodbye directly. Calm yourself, and receive him with your wonted ease.'

He grasped my hand convulsively, and after a few moments' silence, resumed, in a less high-strung tone, 'I will be calm, Doctor. I always try to be so. But is it not terrible, this fight between a strong Will and a flagging Intellect? And each mysteriously helps the other, for I feel that if for an instant I relax my determination to be sane, at that instant I shall become a raging madman. Did we live in olden times one would say that an angel and a devil were fighting for my soul.'

He fell back on the sofa with a faint laugh, and, at the same moment, Rochford entered hurriedly. 'Major,' he said, 'forgive me for disturbing your chat, but Beatrice has given signs of consciousness.'

The young girl's name recalled us both to present surroundings.

'Go to her at once, Fayre,' said Major Molineux; 'I am tired, and shall seek rest. Remember, the house is as your own, Rochford, and do not scruple to use it.'

'When did it happen?' I asked, as we ascended the stairs.

'About ten minutes since. Her mother was watching her, when suddenly the child opened her eyes and said, "Agnes!"'

'The name of Miss Tremayne. I confess you somewhat surprise me. I should have expected that any remark she might have made would have been in reference to the accident. I wonder if she regained consciousness earlier, and unknown to you?'

'I was asleep,' said Mrs. Rochford, 'nearly all last night, and I certainly fancied when I awoke that Beatrice had slightly changed her position, but there was no other sign of increased vitality, and I dismissed the matter from my mind.'

I raised Miss Rochford on her pillows, and took her hand. The fingers closed on mine, and a faint smile passed over her lips.

'You are right,' I said; 'she is conscious. The greatest care is now required. No noise, no conversation; above all, no sudden excitement. This is the most critical period in a case like hers.'

I remained for some time in the apartment, and persuaded Rochford to stop the night. We passed an agreeable *tête-à-tête*, and on the next day had the satisfaction to find that the invalid was growing steadily convalescent. In the afternoon Major Molineux made his appearance. He was in unusually good spirits, and told me that he had felt better than he had done for many a day.

'Whether it is your medicine or your society, doctor, which has so benefited me, I don't know, but I feel a new man.'

We expressed our congratulation, and the Major surprised us both by stating that he had determined to visit the village of Green Ponds, where he had an estate.

'Do you know,' said he, 'that I have been going through my banker's book and looking up some land valuations, and I find that I am worth more than ninety thousand pounds.'

'And what do you intend to do with it?' asked Rochford, lighting his cigar. 'Some fortunate relative in England, I suppose.'

'By no means,' said Major Molineux. 'I have left it to your daughter.'

There could be, of course, no further discussion after so startling a statement, and I hastened to change the subject by suggesting that a sojourn of two or three days at Green Ponds would assist the cure which had been so happily begun.

'You have lived too long here,' I said. 'This house is gloomy, and you know every tree and shrub by heart. There is nothing like change of scene. Each object brings with it new associations, and opens up new trains of thought. Take my advice.'

'I will,' said Major Molineux, cheerily. 'I feel benefited already by the mere thoughts of the journey. May I see Miss Beatrice before I go?'

Rochford looked at me for a reply. I had rather that she had not been disturbed, but, after the magnificent avowal of the legacy, it would seem churlish to have refused.

'You may, but for a moment only,' I said. 'You will forgive me, but it is important that her newly-recovered intelligence should be allowed healthy sleep after its enforced fainting fit.'

Together we mounted to the room. Beatrice was breathing regularly, and her eyes were closed in peaceful slumber.

'Poor girl,' said Major Molineux. 'She was a great favourite with my little Agnes,' and, leaning over the bed, he touched the forehead of the sleeper with his lips.

An astonishing, and, to me, unaccountable, change took place in the features and conduct of the invalid. Her face flushed crimson red, she opened her eyes, and, raising herself to a sitting posture, stared wildly about her. At sight of Major Molineux, she fell back as though life had suddenly left her.

'Some ugly dream, perhaps, has disturbed her,' said I, 'and the touch of your lips brought about the imagined catastrophe. She will soon recover.'

In effect, so soon as Rochford and our host had withdrawn from the room, Beatrice revived; tears rolled from beneath her eyelids and she feebly sought for my hand, holding it fast in hers, as though clinging to some saving stay.

'I was wrong to have admitted him,' I said to Mrs. Rochford. 'I should have remembered that your daughter had always a dislike to him.' Low as were the tones in which I spoke, Beatrice must have heard and understood them, for she increased the pressure of her slender fingers on mine. 'He visits Green Ponds to-day,' I continued, 'and, at my persuasion, will stay a day or two there; so that he is not likely to alarm us again, however foolish we may be.' As I concluded my sentence, Beatrice released my hand with a sigh of relief.

That sigh betokened much that was unpleasant to my self-love. From the moment when I had seen her life in danger I had confessed to myself that I had loved her. It is true that I was almost old enough to be her father, but love is a passion which takes no thought of years, and my affection had sensibly increased with my prolonged attendance on her. I had saved her life, and it would seem as if that life belonged to me, and I might hope, in the future, to bend it to my will. The glance of her eyes, the smile on her lip, the pressure of her hand, seemed, I thought, to indicate that she, in her inmost heart, owned a feeling for me warmer than friendship. But the instant relaxation of the muscles at the mention of the Major's absence showed me that she had besought my attention merely to shield her against some threatened danger. Her unreasoning dislike to Major Molineux had returned at the sight of him, and she wanted me near her only because she imagined that I would prevent a repetition of his visit.

Nevertheless, I did not despair of winning her, and, taking my hat, went in search of Rochford. He knew my position and my prospects. The island in which he lived, lovely though its climate and scenery might be, was not a place where he would be likely to meet with a better match than myself for his daughter, despite the difference in our ages. Captain Rochford was not rich. He had often told me that his income never amounted to more than £700 a year, and—I suddenly stopped. I had forgotten the statement made by Major Molineux concerning the disposition of his fortune. Beatrice Rochford, with £90,000 dowry, might choose, even in London, among men of rank and estate. It was impossible, moreover, that I should, after hearing the promise concerning the legacy, go to the father of the heiress and ask for her hand. I should appear a mercenary adventurer, whose unblushing conduct was dictated by the meanest motives.

The position was embarrassing. Now that I clearly perceived that Beatrice Rochford was beyond my reach, my love for her grew more intense. I could put away the thought of her so long as I knew that she was near me, and that there was, at least, a possibility of my being able to win her for closer companionship. But now I realised that I must think of her no more. I began to suffer the pangs of sudden remorseful jealousy. 'Why had I not spoken earlier? Why had I not, at least, allowed Rochford to have guessed at my feelings?' And this misfortune had come upon me by the act of the man upon whose behalf I had assumed a responsibility that darkened my waking hours, and bid fair to cause me profound mental disturbance. What could have induced Major Molineux to become generous so abruptly? Angry with myself and circumstances, I resolved to put an end to this state of suspense. I would return at once to India, and, in the meantime, would see Beatrice as little as possible.

'Rochford,' I said, after dinner, 'I have received letters from Calcutta which I have too long neglected. I must return forthwith.'

'You are sudden in your determination,' said Rochford, with a slightly wounded air.

'I should have mentioned it before, but the precarious condition of Miss Rochford forbade my inflicting on you any inconvenience. She has now recovered consciousness, and, with careful nursing, needs small medical attendance.'

'Well,' said Rochford, 'we shall be all sorry to lose you—Beatrice, especially, I know—but a man of talent cannot be expected to spend his days in an out-of-the-way nook like this.'

It was on the tip of my tongue to say that I should ask nothing better than such a fate under certain conditions; but I thought of the £90,000, and was silent.

The next day I went to Hobart to make preparations for departure, and found that it would be impossible for me to leave for at least three weeks. I resolved, however, that I would not spend that time in the society of the Rochfords, but make one of a fishing party to the south-west coast of the island.

I was prevented from going by the following circumstance, which I simply record here without any speculation as to how it came about or what induced it.

On Thursday evening, the second day after I had left Castle Stuart, I was playing a rubber of whist in the card-room of the Club, when I felt someone touch me on the left shoulder. I turned round, and saw no one. Somewhat puzzled, I commenced to deal, when I heard a sharp sound, as if produced by the swish of a descending whip, and the cards were—so it seemed—struck from my hands. I raised my eyes, and, over my partner's head, I saw the face of Beatrice Rochford, floating as though in air. The lips were almost blue, and the wildly-sweeping hair framed a face of waxen pallor. The eyes—those wonderful eyes into which I had so often gazed— were alone alive, and they were fixed on me with an expression of imploring agony. Muttering some incoherent excuse, I hurried from the table, ordered out my horse, and galloped down the road to New Norfolk.

I had no doubt whatever then, and I have none now—I have already said that I do not intend to speculate upon the peculiarity of the case— that I was summoned to witness a catastrophe of some kind. I was not prepared for that which awaited me at Castle Stuart. The house was lit in the whole of the upper front, and there were lights moving about the lower rooms. Rochford himself took my horse.

'I had some instinct that you would come. Go upstairs.'

I went straight to Beatrice's room, and found her dead.

But death, in its mercy, usually leaves, for the last look of the sorrowing survivors, composed features and restful eyelids. Miss Rochford's body was rigid. Her hands were clenched and her eyes wide open, while that once lovely face was deformed with an expression of such supernatural horror that I could not glance at it again.

'How did this happen?' said I, to the mumbling and shivering Pennithorne, who had been set by Rochford on guard at the door, with strict orders not to let the bereaved mother see the fearful sight within.

'Why didn't you take her away?' she said, mopping and mowing in her usual fashion. 'I told you what would happen. She has seen him.'

My blood ran cold.

'Has the Major returned?'

'He returned last night, and kept his room all day as usual. We left Miss Rochford for a few minutes, and when we came back she was like you saw her, and *this* was on the table.'

She gave me an unopened letter, addressed to myself, in Major Molineux's handwriting. Without waiting to inspect its contents, I crossed the corridor and made my way direct to the Major's bedroom. He was lying on his face on the floor—dead, and standing on the table was an empty two-ounce phial, and an empty wine-glass.

Hastily I tore open the letter. It was written in a firm, bold hand, and evidently intended to be read by other eyes than mine. It was, in fact, Major Molineux's last effort to keep from the world's knowledge the fact that his mental life had in it anything to conceal.

Castle Stuart,
24th Nov., 1835.

MY DEAR DOCTOR FAYRE,—My mind is so unhinged by long suffering, that I have at length determined on committing suicide. I have left the whole of my property, save some small legacies, to Miss Beatrice Rochford. Turner and Thompson have the will, and I have written to them to come to Castle Stuart so soon as my letter is received. Keep my keys in your possession until their arrival, and then deliver to them my effects. They will settle all my accounts. I wish you health and happiness.

I am, yours truly,
J. MOLINEUX.

Chapter VIII

An inquest was held the following day and I stated as much of the foregoing history as I thought desirable.

It was clear that, if a verdict of *felo-de-se* was returned, the will would be set aside and the immense fortune forfeited to the Crown.

I repeated in brief the account of the late Major's malady, saying that he was subject to a delusion of a nature which I could not reveal, which seized him on every Thursday, and that during that time I did not consider him responsible for his actions. The whole city was aware of his peculiar conduct in secluding himself on that day, and the jury returned, by direction, a verdict of 'temporary insanity.'

Twenty-seven hours after death an examination was held by the doctor of the regiment, a resident surgeon, and myself, the result of which I carefully preserved.

The emaciation was considerable. The deceased having fallen on his face, there were marks of contusion on his left temple. The body exhaled an odour of prussic acid. The eye did not present any particular appearance. The stomach was remarkably capacious, and the contents were set aside for analysis. In some parts of the mucous membrane of this organ, especially near the upper and inferior orifices, there were marks of recent inflammation, particularly in stellated patches, where slight marks of extravasation were visible. In several portions of the small intestines the external hue was dark, almost approaching to livid, and the mucous membrane of these portions was vividly or darkly red, but without extravasation or perceptible injection of the vessels. The large intestines exhibited no marks of disease of any kind, and the liver, spleen, mesentery, kidneys, and abdominal viscera were all perfectly sound.

Before a knife was laid on the body I expressed a wish that the ganglionic centres might be carefully examined, as I conceived that perhaps some irritation of the nerves of organic life played an important part in the phenomena exhibited by the patient. The solar plexus was therefore minutely investigated, but nothing abnormal was perceptible.

In the thorax there was great and varied disease. The lungs were studded with tubercles, especially the superior lobes, and extensive adhesions existed between the pleuræ-costales and the pleuræ-pulmonales. None of the tubercles had broken down so as to discharge their contents through the bronchial tubes.

The heart was not larger than usual, but the pericardium was universally adherent. The organ itself presented one of the finest specimens of 'simple hypertrophy' which I have ever seen. The parietes of the left ventricle were an inch and a quarter in thickness, and the cavity was with difficulty discovered. It could not have contained four drachms of blood, if so much, scarcely a third of that which a healthy left ventricle would be capable of throwing off at each contraction. There was nothing abnormal in the arteries, and the blood in every part of the body was perfectly fluid.

The brain was large and remarkably firm, the vessels rather congested, but there was no visible trace of disease in the head. The skull was of unusual thickness and density.

And now comes the most remarkable part of the pathology. Upon the pneumo-gastric, or *vagus* nerve of the left side, just before the re-current is given off, there was affixed a hard, jagged body, the size of a kidney bean, composed of calcareous matter, and, probably, a diseased bronchial gland, converted into this substance. The union of the nerve and the ragged mass was so intimate that no dissection, without cutting the nerve or the calcareous matter itself, could separate them. The foreign body had, in fact, penetrated, or at least invaded, the nerve, which was thickened at this part. Lower down, and involving the cardiac, pulmonic and œsophageal plexuses in a labyrinth of perplexity, were several diseased bronchial glands, rendering the dissection a tedious and difficult operation.

When we consider that the *vagus* nerve rises in the medulla oblongata, and is distributed chiefly to the great organs not under our control, and that it communicates with almost all the ganglionic nerves, we can form some idea of the disturbance produced in the system by a jagged calcareous mass implanted, as it were, in one of the most important nerves of the great vital viscera. It will be noticed that the majority of the organs to which the pneumo-gastric nerve distributes its functions were found changed in structure or disordered in function. The state of the heart probably accounted for the great emaciation, combined with the incessant craving for animal food, while the fact that it could not circulate more than one-third the usual quantity of blood through the lungs, must have produced deficient sanguification in the pulmonary apparatus whatever was the amount of digestion. Diseases of the heart are very apt to affect the brain, and my colleagues and myself agreed that dissection showed that the mental functions were disturbed by physical changes, and that the monomania in this instance, as probably in many others, was dependent on corporeal rather than moral causes.

I followed to the grave the remains of the lovely girl I had once thought to make my wife, and a few weeks afterwards quitted Hobart Town, and I have never revisited it.

The mystery of Major Molineux has now been told—at least as much as can be told without violating a confidence which I even now hold sacred. There are many points in this strange and dreadful history which I cannot attempt to explain. The periodicity of the attack is one of these; the exact relation which the injury to the nervous system bore to the peculiarly horrible form which the delusion assumed is another. The *Par vagum* are the agents of communication between the mind and matter of a man, between his soul and his body, and their derangement would affect both spirit and flesh. How, I cannot say. Nor dare I speculate on the dread question why Providence permitted a poor wretch to endure tortures incomparable even among the torments of the heathen's fabled hell, and that without a particle of moral guilt.

'Tasma' (Jessie Couvreur)

Monsieur Caloche

1890

CHAPTER I

A MORE un-English, uncolonial appearance had never brightened the
prosaic interior of Bogg & Company's big warehouse in Flinders Lane.
Monsieur Caloche, waiting in the outer office, under fire of a row of
curious eyes, was a wondrous study of 'Frenchiness' to the clerks. His
vivacious dark eyes, shining out of his sallow face, scarred and seamed by
the marks of small-pox, met their inquisitive gaze with an expression that
seemed to plead for leniency. The diabolical disease that had scratched the
freshness from his face had apparently twisted some of the youthfulness
out of it as well; otherwise it was only a young soul that could have been
made so diffident by the consciousness that its habitation was disfigured.
Some pains had been taken to obviate the effects of the disfigurement and
to bring into prominence the smooth flesh that had been spared. It was
not chance that had left exposed a round white throat, guiltless of the
masculine Adam's apple, or that had brushed the fine soft hair, ruddily dark
in hue like the eyes, away from a vein-streaked temple. A youth of
unmanly susceptibilities, perhaps—but inviting sympathy rather than
scorn—sitting patiently through the dreary silent three-quarters of an
hour, with his back to the wall which separated him from the great head
of the firm of Bogg & Co.

The softer-hearted of the clerks commiserated him. They would have liked to show their goodwill, after their own fashion, by inviting him to have a 'drink,' but—the possibility of shouting for a young Frenchman, waiting for an interview with their chief! Any one knowing Bogg, of Bogg & Co., must have divined the outrageous absurdity of the notion. It was safer to suppose that the foreigner would have refused the politeness. He did not look as though whisky and water were as familiar to him as a tumbler of *eau sucrée*. The clerks had heard that it was customary in France to drink absinthe. Possibly the slender youth in his loose-fitting French paletôt reaching to his knees, and sitting easily upon shoulders that would have graced a shawl, had drunk deeply of this fatal spirit. It invested him with something mysterious in the estimation of the juniors, peering for traces of dissipation in his foreign face. But they could find nothing to betray it in the soft eyes, undimmed by the enemy's hand, or the smooth lips set closely over the even row of small French teeth. Monsieur Caloche lacked the happy French confidence which has so often turned a joke at the foot of the guillotine. His lips twitched every time the door of the private office creaked. It was a ground-glass door to the left of him, and as he sat, with his turned-up hat in his hand, patiently waiting, the clerks could see a sort of suppression overspreading his disfigured cheeks whenever the noise was repeated. It appeared that he was diffident about the interview. His credentials were already in the hands of the head of the firm, but no summons had come. His letter of recommendation, sent in fully half an hour back, stated that he was capable of undertaking foreign correspondence; that he was favourably known to the house of business in Paris whose principal had given him his letter of presentation; that he had some slight knowledge of the English language; that he had already given promise of distinguishing himself as an *homme de lettres*. This final clause of the letter was responsible for the length of time Monsieur Caloche was kept waiting. *Homme de lettres!* It was a stigma that Bogg, of Bogg & Co., could not overlook. As a practical man, a self-made man, a man who had opened up new blocks of country and imported pure stock into Victoria—what could be expected of him in the way of holding out a helping hand to a scribbler—a pauper who had spent his days in making rhymes in his foreign jargon? Bogg would have put your needy professionals into irons. He forgave no authors, artists, or actors who were not successful. *Homme de lettres!* Coupled with his poverty it was more unpardonable a title than jail-bird. There was nothing to prove that the latter title would not have fitted Monsieur Caloche as well. He was probably a ruffianly Communist. The French Government could not get hold of all the rebels, and here was one in the outer office of Bogg & Co. coolly waiting for a situation.

Not so coolly, perhaps, as Bogg, in his aggrieved state of mind, was ready to conclude. For the day was a hot-wind day, and Bogg himself, in white waistcoat and dust-coat, sitting in the cool depths of his revolving-chair in front of the desk in his private office, was hardly aware of the driving dust and smarting grit emptied by shovelfuls upon the unhappy people without. He perspired, it is true, in deference to the state of his big thermometer, which even here stood above 85° in the corner, but having come straight from Brighton in his private brougham, he could wipe his moist bald head without besmearing his silk handkerchief with street grime. And it was something to be sitting here, in a lofty office, smelling of yellow soap and beeswax, when outside a north wind was tormenting the world with its puffs of hot air and twirling relays of baked rubbish and dirt. It was something to be surrounded by polished mahogany, cool to the touch, and cold iron safes, and maps that conveyed in their rippling lines of snowy undulations far-away suggestions of chill heights and mountain breezes. It was something to have iced water in the decanter at hand, and a little fountain opposite, gurgling a running reminder of babbling brooks dribbling through ferntree valleys and wattle-studded flats. Contrasting the shaded coolness of the private office with the heat and turmoil without, there was no cause to complain.

Yet Bogg clearly had a grievance, written in the sour lines of his mouth, never too amiably expanded at the best of times, and his small, contracted eyes, full of shrewd suspicion-darting light. He read the letter sent in by Monsieur Caloche with the plentiful assistance of the tip of his broad forefinger, after a way peculiar to his early days, before he had acquired riches, or knighthood, or rotundity.

For Bogg, now Sir Matthew Bogg, of Bogg & Company, was a self-made man, in the sense that money makes the man, and that he had made the money before it could by any possibility make him. Made it by dropping it into his till in those good old times when all Victorian storekeepers were so many Midases, who saw their spirits and flour turn into gold under their handling; made it by pocketing something like three thousand per cent. upon every penny invested in divers blocks of scrubby soil hereafter to be covered by those grand and gloomy bluestone buildings which make of Melbourne a city of mourning; made it by reaching out after it, and holding fast to it, whenever it was within spirit-call or finger-clutch, from his early grog-shanty days, when he detected it in the dry lips of every grimy digger on the flat, to his latter station-holding days, when he sniffed it in the drought which brought his neighbours low. Add to which he was lucky—by virtue of a certain inherent faculty he possessed in common with the Vanderbilts, the Stewarts, the Rothschilds of mankind—and far-seeing. He could forestall the news in the *Mark Lane Express*. He was almost clairvoyant in the matter of rises in wool. His luck, his foresight, were only on a par with his industry, and the end of all his slaving and sagacity was to give him at sixty years of age a liver, a paunch, an income bordering on a hundred thousand pounds, and the title of Sir Matthew Bogg.

It was known that Sir Matthew had worked his way to the colonies, acting indiscriminately as pig-sticker and deck-swabber on board the *Sarah Jane*. In his liverless, paunchless, and titleless days he had tossed for coppers with the flat-footed sailors on the forecastle. Now he was bank director, railway director, and a number of other things that formed a graceful flourish after Sir Matthew, but that would have sounded less euphonious in the wake of plain 'Bogg.' Yet 'plain Bogg' Nature had turned him out, and 'plain Bogg' he would always remain while in the earthly possession of his round, overheated face and long, irregular teeth. His hair had abandoned its lawful territory on the top of his head, and planted itself in a vagrant fashion, in small tufts in his ears and nostrils. His eyebrows had run riot over his eyes, but his eyes asserted themselves through all. They were eyes that, without being stronger or larger or bolder than any average pair of eyes to be met with in walking down the street, had such a knack of 'taking your measure' that no one could look at them without discomfiture. In the darkened atmosphere of the Flinders Lane office, Sir Matthew knew how to turn these colourless unwinking orbs to account. To the maliciously inclined among the clerks in the outer office there was nothing more amusing than the crestfallen appearance of the applicants, as they came out by the ground-glass door, compared with the jauntiness of their entrance. Young men who wanted colonial experience, overseers who applied for managerships on his stations, youths fresh from school who had a turn for the bush, had all had specimens of Sir Matthew's mode of dealing with his underlings. But his favourite plan, his special hobby, was to 'drop on to them unawares.'

There is nothing in the world that gives such a zest to life as the possession of a hobby, and the power of indulging it. We may be pretty certain that the active old lady's white horse at Banbury Cross was nothing more than a hobby-horse, as soon as we find out in the sequel that she 'had rings on her fingers and bells on her toes,' and that 'she shall have music wherever she goes.' It is the only horse an old lady could be perpetually engaged in riding without coming to grief—the only horse that ever makes us travel through life to the sound of music wherever we go.

From the days when Bogg had the merest shred of humanity to bully, in the shape of a waif from the Chinese camp, the minutes slipped by with a symphony they had never possessed before. As fulness of time brought him increase of riches and power, he yearned to extend the terror of his sway. It was long before he tasted the full sweetness of making strong men tremble in their boots. Now, at nearly sixty years of age, he knew all the delights of seeing victims, sturdier and poorer than himself, drop their eyelids before his gaze. He was aware that the men in the yard cleared out of his path as he walked through it; that his managers up-country addressed him in tones of husky conciliation; that every eye met his with an air of deprecation, as much as to apologise for the fact of existing in his presence; and in his innermost heart he believed that in the way of mental sensation there could be nothing left to desire. But how convey the impression of rainbow-tints to eyes that have never opened upon aught save universal blackness? Sir Matthew had never seen an eye brighten, a small foot dance, at his approach. A glance of impotent defiance was the only equivalent he knew for a gleam of humid affection. He was accustomed to encounter a shifting gaze. The lowest form of self-interest was the tie which bound his people to him. He paid them as butts, in addition to paying them as servants. Where would have been his daily appetiser in the middle of the day if there had been no yard, full of regulations impossible to obey; no warehouse to echo his harsh words of fault-finding; no servile men, and slouching fast-expanding boys, to scuttle behind the big cases, or come forth as if they were being dragged by hooks, to stand with sheepish expression before him? And when he had talked himself hoarse in town, where would have been the zest of wandering over his stations, of surveying his fat bullocks and woolly merinos, if there had been no accommodating managers to listen reverentially to his loudly-given orders, and take with dejected, apologetic air his continued rating? The savour of life would have departed,—not with the bodily comfort and the consequence that riches bring, but with the power they confer of asserting yourself before your fellow-men after any fashion you please. Bogg's fashion was to bully them, and he bullied them accordingly.

But, you see, Monsieur Caloche is still waiting; in the position, as the junior clerks are well aware, of the confiding calf awaiting butchery in a frolicsome mood outside the butcher's shop. Not that I would imply that Monsieur Caloche frolicked, even metaphorically speaking. He sat patiently on with a sort of sad abstracted air; unconsciously pleating and unpleating the brim of his soft Paris hat, with long lissome fingers that might have broidered the finest silk on other than male hands. The flush of colour, the slight trembling of lips, whenever there was a noise from within, were the only signs that betrayed how acutely he was listening for a summons. Despite the indentations that had marred for ever the smoothness of the face, and pitted the forehead and cheeks as if white gravel had been shot into them, the colour that came and went so suddenly was pink as rose-coloured lake. It stained even the smooth white neck and chin, upon which the faintest traces of down were not yet visible to the scrutinising eyes of the juniors.

Outside, the north wind ran riot along the pavement, upsetting all orderly arrangements for the day with dreadful noise and fussiness, battering trimly-dressed people into red-eyed wretches heaped up with dust; wrenching umbrellas from their handles, and blinding their possessors trying to run after them; filling open mouths with grit, making havoc with people's hats and tempers, and proving itself as great a blusterer in its character of a peppery emigrant as in its original *rôle* of the chilly Boreas of antiquity.

Monsieur Caloche had carefully wiped away from his white wristband the dust that it had driven into his sleeve, and now the dust on his boots— palpably large for the mere slips of feet they enclosed—seemed to give him uneasiness; but it would seem that he lacked the hardihood to stoop and flick it away. When, finally, he extended surreptitiously a timid hand, it might have been observed of his uncovered wrist that it was singularly frail and slender. This delicacy of formation was noticeable in every exterior point. His small white ear, setting close to his head, might have been wrapped up over and over again in one of the fleshy lobes that stretched away from Sir Matthew's skull. Decidedly, the two men were of a different order of species. One was a heavy mastiff of lupine tendencies—the other a delicate Italian grey-hound, silky, timorous, quivering with sensibility.

And there had been time for the greyhound to shiver long with expectancy before the mastiff prepared to swallow him up.

It was a quarter to twelve by the gloomy-faced clock in the outer office, a quarter to twelve by all the clerks' watches, adjusted every morning to the patriarch clock with unquestioning faith, when Monsieur Caloche had diffidently seated himself on the chair in the vicinity of the ground-glass door. It was half-past twelve by the gloomy-faced clock, half-past twelve by all the little watches that toadied to it, when Sir Matthew's bell rang. It was a bell that must have inherited the spirit of a fire-ball or a doctor's night-bell. It had never been shaken by Sir Matthew's fingers without causing a fluttering in the outer office. No one knew what hair-suspended sword might be about to fall on his head before the messenger returned. Monsieur Caloche heard it ring, sharply and clamorously, and raised his head. The white-faced messenger, returning from his answer to the summons, and speaking with the suspension of breath that usually afflicted him after an interview with Sir Matthew, announced that "Mister Caloosh" was wanted, and diving into the gloomy recess in the outer office, relapsed into his normal occupation of breathing on his penknife and rubbing it on his sleeve.

Monsieur Caloche meanwhile stood erect, more like the startled greyhound than ever. To the watchful eyes of the clerks, staring their full at his retreating figure, he seemed to glide rather than step through the doorway. The ground-glass door, attached by a spring from the inside, shut swiftly upon him, as if it were catching him in a trap, and so hid him in full from their curious scrutiny. For the rest, they could only surmise. The lamb had given itself up to the butcher's knife. The diminutive greyhound was in the mastiff's grip.

Would the knife descend on the instant? Would the mastiff fall at once upon the trembling foreigner, advancing with sleek uncovered head, and hat held in front by two quivering hands? Sir Matthew's usual glare of reception was more ardent than of custom as Monsieur Caloche approached. If every 'foreign adventurer' supposed he might come and loaf upon Bogg, of Bogg & Company, because he was backed up by a letter from a respectable firm, Sir Matthew would soon let him find out he was mistaken! His glare intensified as the adventurous stripling glided with softest football to the very table where he was sitting, and stood exactly opposite to him. None so adventurous, however, but that his lips were white and his bloodless face a pitiful set-off to the cruelly prominent marks that disfigured it. There was a terror in Monsieur Caloche's expression apart from the awe inspired by Sir Matthew's glare which might have disarmed a butcher or even a mastiff. His large, soft eyes seemed to ache with repressed tears. They pleaded for him in a language more convincing than words, 'I am friendless—I am a stranger—I am—' but no matter! They cried out for sympathy and protection, mutely and unconsciously.

But to Sir Matthew's perceptions visible terror had only one interpretation. It remained for him to 'find out' Monsieur Caloche. He would 'drop on to him unawares' one of these days. He patted his hobby on the back, seeing a gratification for it in prospective, and entering shortly upon his customary stock of searching questions, incited his victim to reply cheerfully and promptly by looking him up and down with a frown of suspicion.

'What brought you 'ere?'

'Please?' said Monsieur Caloche, anxiously.

He had studied a vocabulary opening with 'Good-day, sir. What can I have the pleasure of doing for you this morning?' The rejoinder to which did not seem to fit in with Sir Matthew's special form of inquiry.

'What brought you 'ere, I say?' reiterated Sir Matthew, in a roar, as if deafness were the only impediment on the part of foreigners in general to a clear comprehension of our language.

'De sheep, Monsieur! La Reine Dorée,' replied Monsieur Caloche, in low-toned, guttural, musical French.

'That ain't it,' said Sir Matthew, scornfully. 'What did you come 'ere for? What are you fit for? What can you do?'

Monsieur Caloche raised his plaintive eyes. His sad desolation was welling out of their inmost depths. He had surmounted the first emotion that had driven the blood to his heart at the outset, and the returning colour, softening the seams and scars in his cheeks, gave him a boyish bloom. It deepened as he answered with humility, 'I will do what Monsieur will! I will do my possible!'

'I'll soon see how you shape,' said Sir Matthew, irritated with himself for the apparent difficulty of thoroughly bullying the defenceless stranger. 'I don't want any of your parley-vooing in my office—do you hear! I'll find you work—jolly quick, I can tell you! Can you mind sheep? Can you drive bullocks, eh? Can you put up a post and rail? You ain't worth your salt if you can't use your 'ands!'

He cast such a glance of withering contempt on the tapering white fingers with olive-shaped nails in front of him that Monsieur Caloche instinctively sheltered them in his hat. 'Go and get your traps together! I'll find you a billet, never fear!'

'Mais, Monsieur'—

'Go and get your traps together, I say! You can come 'ere again in an hour. I'll find you a job up-country!' His peremptory gesture made any protest on the part of Monsieur Caloche utterly unavailing. There was nothing for him to do but to bow and to back in a bewildered way from the room. If the more sharp-eared of the clerks had not been in opportune contiguity to the ground-glass door during Sir Matthew's closing sentences, Monsieur Caloche would have gone away with the predominant impression that 'Sir Bang' was an *enragé*, who disapproved of salt with mutton and beef, and was clamorous in his demands for 'traps,' which Monsieur Caloche, with a gleam of enlightenment in the midst of his heart-sickness and perplexity, was proud to remember meant 'an instrument for ensnaring animals.' It was with a doubt he was too polite to express that he accepted the explanation tendered him by the clerks, and learned that if he 'would strike while the iron is hot' he must come back in an hour's time with his portmanteau packed up. He was a lucky fellow, the juniors told him, to jump into a billet without any bother; they wished to the Lord they were in *his* shoes, and could be drafted off to the Bush at a moment's notice.

Perhaps it seemed to Monsieur Caloche that these congratulations were based on the Satanic philosophy of 'making evil his good.' But they brought with them a flavour of the human sympathy for which he was hungering. He bowed to the clerks all round before leaving, after the manner of a court-page in an opera. The hardiest of the juniors ran to the door after he was gone. Monsieur Caloche was trying to make head against the wind. The warm blast was bespattering his injured face. It seemed to revel in the pastime of filling it with grit. One small hand was spread in front of the eyes—the other was resolutely holding together the front of his long, light paletôt, which the rude wind had sportively thrown open. The junior was cheated of his fun. Somehow the sight did not strike him as being quite so funny as it ought to have been.

CHAPTER II

The station hands, in their own language, 'gave Frenchy best.' No difference of nationality could account for some of his eccentricities. As an instance, with the setting in of the darkness he regularly disappeared. It was supposed that he camped up a tree with the birds. The wit of the wool-shed surmised that 'Froggy' slept with his relatives, and it would be found that he had 'croaked' with them one of these odd times. Again, there were shearers ready to swear that he had 'blubbered' on finding some sportive ticks on his neck. He was given odd jobs of wool-sorting to do, and was found to have a mania for washing the grease off his hands whenever there was an instant's respite. Another peculiarity was his aversion to blood. By some strange coincidence, he could never be found whenever there was any slaughtering on hand. The most plausible reason was always advanced for necessitating his presence in some far-distant part of the run. Equally he could never be induced to learn how to box—a favourite Sunday morning and summer evening pastime among the men. It seemed almost to hurt him when damage was done to one of the assembled noses. He would have been put down as a 'cur' if it had not been for his pluck in the saddle, and for his gentle winning ways. His pluck, indeed, seemed all concentrated in his horsemanship. Employed as a boundary-rider, there was nothing he would not mount, and the station hands remarked, as a thing 'that beat them once for all,' that the 'surliest devils' on the place hardly ever played up with him. He employed no arts. His bridle-hand was by no means strong. Yet it remained a matter of fact that the least amenable of horses generally carried him as if they liked to bear his weight. No one being sufficiently learned to advance the hypothesis of magnetism, it was concluded that he carried a charm.

This power of touch extended to human beings. It was almost worth while spraining a joint or chopping at a finger to be bandaged by Monsieur Caloche's deft fingers. His horror of blood never stood in his way when there was a wound to be doctored. His supple hands, browned and strengthened by his outdoor work, had a tenderness and a delicacy in their way of going to work that made the sufferer feel soothed and half-healed by their contact. It was the same with his manipulation of things. There was a refinement in his disposition of the rough surroundings that made them look different after he had been among them.

And not understood, jeered at, petted, pitied alternately—with no confidant of more sympathetic comprehension than the horse he bestrode—was Monsieur Caloche absolutely miserable? Granting that it were so, there was no one to find it out. His brown eyes had such an habitually wistful expression, he might have been born with it. Very trifles brought a fleeting light into them—a reminiscence, perhaps that, while it crowned him with 'sorrow's crown of sorrow,' was yet a reflection of some past joy. He took refuge in his ignorance of the language directly he was questioned as to his bygone life. An embarrassed little shrug, half apologetic, but powerfully conclusive, was the only answer the most curious examiner could elicit.

It was perceived that he had a strong objection to looking in the glass, and invariably lowered his eyes on passing the cracked and uncompromising fragment of mirror supported on two nails against the planking that walled the rough, attached kitchen. So decided was this aversion that it was only when Bill, the black-smith, asked him chaffingly for a lock of his hair that he perceived with confusion how wantonly his silken curls were rioting round his neck and temples. He cut them off on the spot, displaying the transparent skin beneath. Contrasted with the clear tan that had overspread his scarred cheeks and forehead, it was white as freshly-drawn milk.

He was set down on the whole as given to moping; but, taking him all round, the general sentiment was favourable to him. Possibly it was with some pitiful prompting of the sort that the working manager sent him out of the way one still morning, when Sir Matthew's buggy, creaking under the unwelcome preponderance of Sir Matthew himself, was discerned on its slow approach to the homestead. A most peaceful morning for the initiation of Sir Matthew's blustering presence! The sparse gum-leaves hung as motionless on their branches as if they were waiting to be photographed. Their shadows on the yellowing grass seemed painted into the soil. The sky was as tranquil as the plain below. The smoke from the homestead reared itself aloft in a long, thinly-drawn column of grey. A morning of heat and repose, when even the sun-light does not frolic and all nature toasts itself, quietly content. The dogs lay blinking at full length, their tails beating the earth with lazy, measured thump. The sheep seemed rooted to the patches of shade, apathetic as though no one wore flannel vests or ate mutton-chops. Only the mingled voices of wild birds and multitudinous insects were upraised in a blended monotony of subdued sounds. Not a morning to be devoted to toil! Rather, perchance, to a glimmering perception of a golden age, when sensation meant bliss more than pain, and to be was to enjoy.

But to the head of the firm of Bogg & Company, taking note of scattered thistles and straggling wire fencing, warmth and sunshine signified only dry weather. Dry weather clearly implied a fault somewhere, for which somebody must be called to account. Sir Matthew had the memory of a strategist. Underlying all considerations of shorthorns and merinos was the recollection of a timid foreign lad to be suspected for his shy, bewildered air—to be suspected again for his slim white hands—to be doubly suspected and utterly condemned for his graceful bearing, his appealing eyes, that even now Sir Matthew could see with their soft lashes drooping over them as he fronted them in his darkened office in Flinders Lane. A scapegoat for dry weather, for obtrusive thistles, for straggling fencing! A waif of foreign scum to be found out! Bogg had promised himself that he would 'drop on to him unawares.' Physically, Bogg was carried over the ground by a fast trotter; spiritually, he was borne along on his hobby, ambling towards its promised gratification with airy speed.

The working manager, being probably of Bacon's way of thinking, that 'dissimulation is but a faint kind of policy,' did not, in his own words, entirely 'knuckle down' to Sir Matthew. His name was Blunt—he was proud to say it—and he would show you he could make his name good if you 'crossed' him. Yet Blunt could bear a good deal of 'crossing' when it came to the point. Within certain limits, he concluded that the side on which his bread was buttered was worth keeping uppermost, at the cost of some hard words from his employer.

And he kept it carefully uppermost on this especial morning, when the quietude of the balmy atmosphere was broken by Sir Matthew's growls. The head of the firm, capturing his manager at the door of the homestead, had required him to mount into the double-seated buggy with him. Blunt reckoned that these tours of inspection in the companionship of Bogg were more conducive to taking off flesh than a week's hard training. He listened with docility, nevertheless, to plaints and rating—was it not a fact that his yearly salaries had already made a nest-egg of large proportions?—and might have listened to the end, if an evil chance had not filled him with a sudden foreboding. For, pricking his way over the plain, after the manner of Spencer's knight, Monsieur Caloche, on a fleet, newly broken-in two-year-old, was riding towards them. Blunt could feel that Sir Matthew's eyes were sending out sparks of wrath. For the first time in his life he hazarded an uncalled-for opinion.

'He's a good working chap, that, sir!'—indicating by a jerk of the head that the lad now galloping across the turf was the subject of his remark.

'Ah!' said Sir Matthew.

It was all he said, but it was more than enough.

Blunt fidgeted uneasily. What power possessed the boy to make him show off his riding at this juncture? If he could have stopped him, or turned him back, or waved him off!—but his will was impotent.

Monsieur Caloche, well back in the saddle, his brown eyes shining, his disfigured face flushed and glowing, with wide felt-hat drawn closely over his smooth small head, with slender knees close pressed to the horse's flanks, came riding on, jumping small logs, bending with flexible joints under straggling branches, never pausing in his reckless course, until on a sudden he found himself almost in front of the buggy, and, reining up, was

confronted in full by the savage gleam of Sir Matthew's eyes. It was with
the old scared expression that he pulled off his wideawake and bared his
head, black and silky as a young retriever's. Sir Matthew knew how to
respond to the boy's greeting. He stood up in the buggy and shook his fist
at him; his voice, hoarse from the work he had given it that morning,
coming out with rasping intensity.

'What the devil do you mean by riding my 'orses' tails off, eh?'

Monsieur Caloche, in his confusion, straining to catch the full
meaning of the question, looked fearfully round at the hind-quarters of
the two-year-old, as if some hitherto unknown phenomenon peculiar to
Australian horses might in fact have suddenly left them tailless.

But the tail was doing such good service against the flies at the
moment of his observations, that, reassured, he turned his wistful gaze
upon Sir Matthew.

'Monsieur,' he began apologetically, 'permit that I explain it to you. I
did ga-lopp.'

'You can ga-lopp to hell!' said Sir Matthew with furious mimicry. 'I'll
teach you to ruin my 'orses' legs!'

Blunt saw him lift his whip and strike Monsieur Caloche on the chest.
The boy turned so unnaturally white that the manager looked to see him
reel in his saddle. But he only swayed forward and slipped to the ground
on his feet. Sir Matthew, sitting down again in the buggy with an
uncomfortable sensation of some undue excess it might have been as well
as to recall, saw this white face for the flash of an instant's space, saw its
desperation, its shame, its trembling lips; then he was aware that the two-
year-old stood riderless in front of him, and away in the distance the figure
of a lad was speeding through the timber, one hand held against his chest,
his hat gone and he unheeding, palpably sobbing and crying in his
loneliness and defencelessness as he stumbled blindly on.

Run-away boys, I fear, call forth very little solicitude in any heart but a
mother's. A cat may be nine-lived, but a boy's life is centuple. He seems
only to think it worth keeping after the best part of it is gone. Boys run
away from schools, from offices, from stations, without exciting more than
an ominous prognostication that they will go to the bad. According to Sir
Matthew's inference, Monsieur Caloche had 'gone to the bad' long ago—
ergo, it was well to be rid of him. This being so, what utterly inconsistent
crank had laid hold of the head of the great firm of Bogg & Company, and
tortured him through a lengthy afternoon and everlasting night, with the

vision of two despairing eyes and a scarred white face? Even his hobby cried out against him complainingly. It was not for this that it had borne him prancing along. Not to confront him night and day with eyes so distressful that he could see nothing else. Would it be always so? Would they shine mournfully out of the dim recesses of his gloomy office in Flinders Lane, as they shone here in the wild bush on all sides of him?— so relentlessly sad that it would have been a relief to see them change into the vindictive eyes of the Furies who gave chase to Orestes. There was clearly only one remedy against such a fate, and that was to change the nature of the expression which haunted him by calling up another in its place. But how and when!

Sir Matthew prowled around the homestead the second morning after Monsieur Caloche's flight, in a manner unaccountable to himself. That he should return 'possessed' to his elaborate warehouse, where he would be alone all day—and his house of magnificent desolation, where he would be alone all night, was fast becoming a matter of impossibility. What sums out of all proportion would he not have forfeited to have seen the white-faced foreign lad, and to be able to pay him out for the discomfort he was causing him—instead of being bothered by the sight of his 'cursed belongings' at every turn! He could not go into the stable without seeing some of his gimcracks; when he went blustering into the kitchen it was to stumble over a pair of miniature boots, and a short curl of hair, in silken rings, fell off the ledge at his very feet. There was only one thing to be done! Consulting with Blunt, clumsily enough, for nothing short of desperation would have induced Sir Matthew to approach the topic of Monsieur Caloche, he learned that nothing had been seen or heard of the lad since the moment of his running away.

'And 'twasn't in the direction of the township, neither,' added Blunt, gravely. 'I doubt the sun'll have made him stupid, and he'll have camped down some place on the run.'

Blunt's insinuation anent the sun was sheer artifice, for Blunt, in his private heart, did not endorse his own suggestion in the least degree. It was his belief that the lad had struck a shepherd's hut, and was keeping (with a show of common-sense he had not credited him with) out of the way of his savage employer. But it was worth while making use of the artifice to see Sir Matthew's ill-concealed uneasiness.

Hardly the same Sir Matthew, in any sense, as the bullying growler who had driven by his side not two days ago. For *this* morning the double-seated buggy was the scene of neither plaints nor abuse. Quietly over the bush track—where last Monsieur Caloche, with hand to his breast, had run sobbing along—the two men drove, their wheels passing over a wideawake hat, lying neglected and dusty in the road. For more than an hour and a half they followed the track, the dusty soil that had been witness to the boy's flight still indicating at intervals traces of a small footprint. The oppressive calm of the atmosphere seemed to have left even the ridges of dust undisturbed. Blunt reflected that it must have been 'rough on a fellow' to run all that way in the burning sun. It perplexed him, moreover, to remember that the shepherd's hut would be now far in their rear. Perhaps it was with a newly-born sense of uneasiness on his own account that he flicked his whip and made the trotter 'go,' for no comment could be expected from Sir Matthew, sitting in complete silence by his side.

To Blunt's discerning eyes the last of the footprints seemed to occur right in the middle of the track. On either side was the plain. Ostensibly, Sir Matthew had come that way to look at the sheep. There was, accordingly, every reason for turning to the right and driving towards a belt of timber some hundred yards away, and there were apparently more forcible reasons still for making for a particular tree—a straggling tree, with some pretensions to a meagre shade, the sight of which called forth an ejaculation, not entirely coherent, from Blunt.

Sir Matthew saw the cause of Blunt's ejaculation—a recumbent figure that had probably reached 'the quiet haven of us all'—it lay so still. But whether quiet or no, it would seem that to disturb its peace was a matter of life or death to Sir Matthew Bogg. Yet surely here was satiety of the fullest for his hobby! Had he not 'dropped on to the "foreign adventurer"' unawares? So unawares, in fact, that Monsieur Caloche never heeded his presence, or the presence of his working manager, but lay with a glaze on his half-closed eyes in stiff unconcern at their feet.

The clerks and juniors in the outer office of the great firm of Bogg & Co. would have been at some loss to recognise their chief in the livid man who knelt by the dead lad's side. He wanted to feel his heart, it appeared, but his trembling fingers failed him. Blunt comprehended the gesture. Whatever of tenderness Monsieur Caloche had expended in his short lifetime was repaid by the gentleness with which the working manager passed his hand under the boy's rigid neck. It was with a shake of the head that seemed to Sir Matthew like the fiat of his doom that Blunt unbuttoned Monsieur Caloche's vest and discovered the fair, white throat beneath. Unbuttoning still—with tremulous fingers, and a strange apprehension creeping chillily over him—the manager saw the open vest fall loosely asunder, and then——

Yes; then it was proven that Sir Matthew's hobby had gone its extremest length. Though it could hardly have been rapture at its great triumph that filled his eyes with such a strange expression of horror as he stood looking fearfully down on the corpse at his feet. For he had, in point of fact, 'dropped on to it unawares;' but it was no longer Monsieur Caloche he had 'dropped on to,' but a girl with breast of marble, bared in its cold whiteness to the open daylight, and to his ardent gaze. Bared, without any protest from the half-closed eyes, unconcerned behind the filmy veil which glazed them. A virgin breast, spotless in hue, save for a narrow purple streak, marking it in a dark line from the collar-bone downwards. Sir Matthew knew, and the working manager knew, and the child they called Monsieur Caloche had known, by whose hand the mark had been imprinted. It seemed to Sir Matthew that a similar mark, red hot like a brand, must now burn on his own forehead for ever. For what if the hungry Australian sun, and emotion, and exhaustion had been the actual cause of the girl's death? he acknowledged, in the bitterness of his heart, that the 'cause of the cause' was his own bloodstained hand.

It must have been poor satisfaction to his hobby, after this, to note that Blunt had found a tiny pocketbook on the person of the corpse, filled with minute foreign handwriting. Of which nothing could be made! For, with one exception, it was filled with French quotations, all of the same tenor— all pointing to the one conclusion—and clearly proving (if it has not been proved already) that a woman who loses her beauty loses her all. The English quotation will be known to some readers of Shakespeare, 'So beauty blemished once for ever's lost!' Affixed to it was the faintly-traced signature of Henriette Caloche.

So here was a sort of insight into the mystery. The 'foreign adventurer' might be exonerated after all. No baser designs need be laid at the door of dead 'Monsieur Caloche' than the design of hiding the loss which had deprived her of all glory in her sex. If, indeed, the loss were a *real* one! For beauty is more than skin-deep, although Monsieur Caloche had not known it. It is of the bone, and the fibre, and the nerves that thrill through the brain. It is of the form and the texture too, as any one would have allowed who scrutinised the body prone in the dust. Even the cruel scars seemed merciful now, and relaxed their hold on the chiselled features, as though 'eloquent, just, and mightie Death' would suffer no hand but his own to dally with his possession.

It is only in Christmas stories, I am afraid, where, in deference to so rollicking a season, everything is bound to come right in the end, that people's natures are revolutionised in a night, and from narrow-minded villains they become open-hearted seraphs of charity. Still, it is on record of the first Henry that from the time of the sinking of the *White Ship* 'he never smiled again.' I cannot say that Sir Matthew was never known to smile, in his old sour way, or that he never growled or scolded, in his old bullying fashion, after the discovery of Monsieur Caloche's body. But he was none the less a changed man. The outside world might rightly conjecture that henceforth a slender, mournful-eyed shadow would walk by his side through life. But what can the outside world know of the refinement of mental anguish that may be endured by a mind awakened too late? In Sir Matthew's case—relatively as well as positively. For constant contemplation of a woman's pleading eyes and a dead statuesque form might give rise to imaginings that it would be maddening to dwell upon. What a wealth of caresses those stiff little hands had had it in their power to bestow! What a power of lighting up the solemnest office, and—be sure—the greatest, dreariest house, was latent in those dejected eyes!

Brooding is proverbially bad for the liver. Sir Matthew died of the liver complaint, and his will was cited as an instance of the eccentricity of a wealthy Australian, who, never having been in France, left the bulk of his money to the purpose of constructing and maintaining a magnificent wing to a smallpox hospital in the south of France. It was stipulated that it should be called the 'Henriette' wing, and is, I believe, greatly admired by visitors from all parts of the world.

Ernest Favenc

A Haunt of the Jinkarras (A Fearsome Story of Central Australia)

1890

IN May, 1889, the dead body of a man was found on one of the tributaries of the Finke River, in the extreme North of South Australia. The body, by all appearances, had been lying there some months and was accidentally discovered by explorers making a flying survey with camels. Amongst the few effects was a Lett's Diary containing the following narration, which although in many places almost illegible and much weather-stained, has been since, with some trouble, deciphered and transcribed by the surveyor in charge of the party, and forwarded to THE BULLETIN for publication.

TRANSCRIBED FROM THE DEAD MAN'S DIARY.
March 10, 1888.—Started out this morning with Jackson, the only survivor of a party of three who lost their horses on a dry stage when looking for country; he was found and cared for by the blacks, and finally made his way into the line where I picked him up when out with a repairing–party. Since then I got him a job on the station, and in return he has told me about the ruby-field of which we are now in search; and

thanks to the late thunder-storms we have as yet met with no obstacles to our progress. I have great faith in him, but he being a man without any education and naturally taciturn, is not very lively company, and I find myself thrown on to the resource of a diary for amusement.

March 17.—Seven days since we left Charlotte Waters, and we are now approaching the country familiar to Jackson during his sojourn with the natives two years ago. He is confident that we shall gain the gorge in the McDonnell Ranges to-morrow, early.

March 18.—Amongst the ranges, plenty of water, and Jackson has recognised several peaks in the near neighbourhood of the gorge, where he saw the rubies.

March 19.—Camped in Ruby Gorge, as I have named this pass, for we have come straight to the place and found the rubies without any hindrance at all. I have about twenty magnificent stones and hundreds of small ones; one of the stones in particular is almost living fire, and must be of great value. Jackson has no idea of the value of the find, except that it may be worth a few pounds, with which he will be quite satisfied. As there is good feed and water, and we have plenty of rations, we will camp here for a day or two and spell the horses before returning.

March 20.—Been examining some caves in the ranges. One of them seems to penetrate a great distance—will go to-morrow with Jackson and take candles and examine it.

March 25.—Had a terrible experience the last four days. Why on earth did I not go back at once with the rubies? Now I may never get back. Jackson and I started to explore this cave early in the morning. We found nothing extraordinary about it for some time. As usual, there were numbers of bats, and here and there there were marks of fire on the rocks, as though the natives had camped there at times. After some searching about, Jackson discovered a passage which we followed down a steep incline for a long distance. As we got on we encountered a strong draught of air and had to be very careful of our candles. Suddenly the passage opened out and we found ourselves in a low chamber in which we could not stand upright. I looked hastily around, and saw a dark figure like a large monkey suddenly spring from a rock and disappear with what sounded like a splash. 'What on earth was that?' I said to Jackson. 'A jinkarra,' he replied, in his slow, stolid way. 'I heard about them from the blacks; they live underground.' 'What are they?' I asked. 'I couldn't make out,' he replied; 'the blacks talked about jinkarras, and made signs that they were underground, so I suppose that was one.'

We went over to the place where I had seen the figure and, as the air was now comparatively still and fresh, our candles burnt well and we could see plainly. The splash was no illusion, for an underground stream of some size ran through the chamber, and on looking closer, in the sand on the floor of the cavern, were tracks like a human foot.

We sat down and had something to eat. The water was beautifully fresh and icily cold, and I tried to obtain from Jackson all he knew about the jinkarras. It was very little beyond what he had already told me. The natives spoke of them as something, animals or men, he could not make out which, living in the ranges underground. They used to frighten the children by crying out 'jinkarra!' to them at night.

The stream that flowed through the cavern was very sluggish and apparently not deep, as I could see the white sand at a distance under the rays of the candle; it disappeared under a rocky arch about two feet above its surface. Strange to say, when near this arch I could smell a peculiar pungent smell like something burning, and this odour appeared to come through the arch. I drew Jackson's attention to it and proposed wading down the channel of the stream if not too deep, but he suggested going back to camp first and getting more rations, which, being very reasonable, I agreed to.

It took us too long to get back to camp to think of starting that day, but next morning we got away early and were soon beside the subterranean stream. The water was bitterly cold but not very deep, and we had provided ourselves with stout saplings as poles and had our revolvers and some rations strapped on our shoulders. It was an awful wade through the chill water, our heads nearly touching the slimy top of the arch, our candles throwing a faint, flickering gleam on the surface of the stream; fortunately the bottom was splendid—hard, smooth sand—and after wading for about twenty minutes we suddenly emerged into another cavern, but its extent we could not discern at first for our attention was taken up with other matters.

The air was laden with pungent smoke, the place illuminated with a score of smouldering fires, and tenanted by a crowd of the most hideous beings I ever saw. They espied us in an instant, and flew wildly about, jabbering frantically, until we were nearly deafened. Recovering ourselves we waded out of the water, and tried to approach some of these creatures, but they hid away in the darker corners, and we couldn't lay hands on any of them. As well as we could make out in the murky light they were human beings, but savages of the most degraded type, far below the ordinary Australian blackfellow. They had long arms, shaggy heads of hair, small twinkling eyes, and were very low of stature. They kept up a confused jabber, half whistling, half chattering, and were utterly without clothes, paint, or any ornaments. I approached one of their fires, and found it to consist of a kind of peat or turf; some small bones of vermin were lying around, and a rude club or tool. While gazing at these things I suddenly heard a piercing shriek, and, looking up, found that Jackson, by a sudden spring, had succeeded in capturing one of these creatures, who was struggling and uttering terrible yells. I went to his assistance, and together we succeeded in holding him still while we examined him by the light of our candles. The others, meanwhile, dropped their clamour and watched us curiously.

Never did I see such a repulsive wretch as our prisoner. Apparently he was a young man about two or three and twenty, only five feet high at the outside, lean, with thin legs and long arms. He was trembling all over, and the perspiration dripped from him. He had scarcely any forehead, and a shaggy mass of hair crowned his head, and grew a long way down his spine. His eyes were small, red and bloodshot; I have often experienced the strong odour emitted by the ordinary blackfellow when heated or excited, but never did I smell anything so offensive as the rank smell emanating from this creature. Suddenly Jackson exclaimed: 'Look! look! he's got a tail!' I looked and nearly relaxed my grasp of the brute in surprise. There was no doubt about it, this strange being had about three inches of a monkey-like tail.

'Let's catch another,' I said to Jackson after the first emotion of surprise had passed. We looked around after putting our candles upright in the sand. 'There's one in that corner,' muttered Jackson to me, and as soon as I spotted the one he meant we released our prisoner and made a simultaneous rush at the cowering form. We were successful, and when we dragged our captive to the light we found it to be a woman. Our curiosity was soon satisfied—the tail was the badge of the whole tribe, and we let our second captive go.

My first impulse was to go and rinse my hands in the stream, for the contact had been repulsive to me. Jackson did the same, saying as he did so—'Those fellows I lived with were bad enough, but I never smelt anything like these brutes.' I pondered what I should do. I had a great desire to take one of these singular beings back with me, and I thought with pride of the reputation I should gain as their discoverer. Then I reflected that I could always find them again, and it would be better to come back with a larger party after safely disposing of the rubies and securing the ground.

'There's no way out of this place,' I said to Jackson.

'Think not?' he replied.

'No,' I said, 'or these things would have cleared out; they must know every nook and cranny.'

'Umph!' he said, as though satisfied; 'shall we go back now?'

I was on the point of saying yes, and had I done so all would have been well; but, unfortunately, some motive of infernal curiosity prompted me to say—'No! let us have a look round first.' Lighting another candle each, so that we had plenty of light, we wandered round the cave, which was of considerable extent, the unclean inhabitants flitting before us with beast-like cries. Presently we had made a half-circuit of the cave and were approaching the stream, for we could hear a rushing sound as though it plunged over a fall. This noise grew louder, and now I noticed that all the natives had disappeared, and it struck me that they had retreated through the passage we had penetrated, which was now unguarded. Suddenly Jackson, who was ahead, exclaimed that there was a large opening. As he spoke he turned to enter it; I called out to him to be careful but my voice was lost in a cry of alarm as he slipped, stumbled, and with a shriek of horror disappeared from my view. So sudden was the shock, and so awful my surroundings, that I sank down utterly unnerved comprehending but one thing: that I was alone in this gruesome cavern inhabited by strange, unnatural creations.

After a while I pulled myself together and began to look around. Holding my candle aloft I crawled on my stomach to where my companion had disappeared. My hand touched a slippery decline; peering cautiously down I saw that the rocks sloped abruptly downwards and were covered with slime as though under water at times. One step on the treacherous surface and a man's doom was sealed—headlong into the unknown abyss below he was bound to go, and this had been the fate of the unhappy Jackson. As I lay trembling on the edge of this fatal chasm listening for the faintest sound from below, it struck me that the noise of the rushing water was both louder and nearer. I lay and listened. There was no doubt about it—the waters were rising. With a thrill of deadly horror it flashed across me that if the stream rose it would prevent my return as I could not thread the subterranean passage under water. Rising hastily I hurried back to the upper end of the cavern following the edge of the water. A glance assured me I was a prisoner; the water was up to the top of the arch, and the stream much broader than when we entered. The rations and candles we had left carelessly on the sand had disappeared, covered by the rising water. I was alone, with nothing but about a candle and a half between me and darkness and death.

I blew out the candle, threw myself on the sand and thought. I brought all my courage to bear not to let the prospect daunt me. First, the natives had evidently retreated before the water rose too high, their fires were all out and a dead silence reigned. I had the cavern to myself; this was better than their horrid company. Next, the rising was periodical, and evidently was the cause of the slimy, slippery rock which had robbed me of my only companion. I remembered instances in the interior where lagoons rose and fell at certain times without any visible cause. Then came the thought, for how long would the overflow continue. I had fresh air and plenty of water, I could live days; probably the flood only lasted twelve or twenty-four hours. But an awful fear seized on me. Could I maintain my reason in this worse than Egyptian darkness—a darkness so thick, definite and overpowering that I cannot describe it, truly a darkness that could be felt? I had heard of men who could not stand twenty-four hours in a dark cell, but had clamoured to be taken out. Supposing my reason deserted me, and during some delirious interlude the stream fell and rose again.

These thoughts were too agonising. I rose and paced a step or two on the sand. I made a resolution during that short walk. I had matches— fortunately, with a bushman's instinct, I had put a box in my pouch when we started to investigate the cavern. I had a candle and a half, and I had, thank Heaven! my watch. I would calculate four hours as nearly as possible, and every four hours I would light my candle and enjoy the luxury of a little light. I stuck to this, and by doing so left that devilish pit with reason. It was sixty hours before the stream fell, and what I suffered during that time no tongue could tell, no brain imagine.

That awful darkness was at times peopled by forms that, for hideous horror, no nightmare could surpass. Invisible, but still palpably present, they surrounded and sought to drive me down the chasm wherein my companion had fallen. The loathsome inhabitants of that cavern came back in fancy and gibbered and whistled around me. I could smell them, feel their sickening touch. If I slept I awoke from, perhaps, a pleasant dream to the stern fact that I was alone in darkness in the depth of the earth. When first I found that the water was receding was perhaps the hardest time of all, for my anxiety to leave the chamber, tenanted by such phantoms, was overpowering. But I resisted. I held to my will until I knew I could safely venture, and then waded slowly and determinedly up the stream; up the sloping passage, through the outer cave, and emerged into the light of day—the blessed glorious light, with a wild shout of joy.

I must have fainted; when I came to myself I was still at the mouth of the cave, but now it was night, the bright, starlit, lonely, silent night of the Australian desert. I felt no hunger nor fear of the future; one delicious sense of rest and relief thrilled my whole being. I lay there watching the dearly-loved Austral constellations in simple, peaceful ecstasy. And then I slept, slept till the sun aroused me, and I arose and took my way to our deserted camp. A few crows arose and cawed defiantly at me, and the leather straps bore the marks of a dingo's teeth, otherwise the camp was untouched. I lit a fire, cooked a meal, ate and rested once more. The reaction had set in after the intense strain I had endured, and I felt myself incapable of thinking or purposing anything. This state lasted for four and twenty hours—then I awoke to the fact that I had to find the horses, and make my way home alone—for, alas, as I bitterly thought, I was now, through my curiosity, alone, and, worst of all, the cause of my companion's death. Had I come away when he proposed, he would be alive, and I should have escaped the awful experience I have endured.

I have written this down while it is fresh in my memory; to-morrow I start to look for the horses. If I reach the telegraph-line safely I will come back and follow up the discovery of this unknown race, the connecting and long-sought-for link; if not, somebody else may find this and follow up the clue. I have plotted out the course from Charlotte Waters here by dead-reckoning.

March 26.—No sign of the horses. They have evidently made back. I will make up a light pack and follow them. If I do not overtake them I may be able to get on to the line on foot.

END OF THE DIARY.

NOTE.—The surveyor, who is well-known in South Australia, adds the following postscript:—

The unfortunate man was identified as an operator on the overland line. He had been in the service a long time, and was very much liked. The facts about picking up Jackson when out with a repairing party have also been verified. The dead man had obtained six months' leave of absence, and it was supposed he had gone down to Adelaide. The tradition of the jinkarras is common among the natives of the Macdonnell Range. I have often heard it. No rubies or anything of value were found on the body. I, of course, made an attempt to get out, but was turned back by the terrible drought then raging. As it is now broken, I am off, and by the time this reaches you shall perhaps be on the spot.

Ernest Favenc

Doomed

1899

JIM Turner sat in the verandah of his modest homestead reading a letter. The mailman had just left the bag, and amongst the miscellaneous contents was a letter from an old friend, one Dick Beveridge, and in the contents was an item of information which made him feel rather uncomfortable.

'You perhaps have not heard that Charley Moore is dead, and how he died. His horse fell on him and crippled him. He lay there for four and twenty hours before he was found, and then he had been only dead for about one hour. The ants were swarming over him. Fancy what he must have suffered! So now that he is gone, you and I are the last of the five.'

Five of them. Yes, he remembered it well—five of them, eager, young, and hopeful, who came into the untrodden district just sixteen years ago. They found good country, and each took up a run. Now there was only Beveridge and himself alive, and the other three had all died violent deaths. How distinctly he recalled the occurrence, which had given rise to the looming fate that seemed to be overhanging them.

They were camped one afternoon on the bank of the river; the same river he could now see from the verandah, bordered by luxuriant-foliaged tea-trees, with flocks of white cockatoos screaming and frolicking amongst the bushes, varied by flights of the Blue Mountain parrots crowding and chattering round the white flowers.

'Hullo!' said Moore, 'there are some niggers coming.' Across the wide stretch of sand on the opposite bank some wandering blacks from the back country had just put in an experience. Tired, thirsty, and burdened with their children and their camp furniture, they trooped down the bank to the water, and drank at the grateful pool in the river bed.

'What a start it would give them to drop a bullet in amongst them,' said Daveney; 'I'm blessed if I don't do it.'

'Take care you don't hit one; there are a lot of gins and children amongst them,' said Moore.

Daveney took up his carbine and fired. There was a start of dismay amongst the natives, and they bolted up the bank. One stopped behind a black patch prostrate on the sand.

'By heavens, you've hit one, you clumsy fool,' said Beveridge, and the whole party went across the sand to the water. Not only one, but two, had been hit. The Martini bullet had gone clean through a gin's body and killed the baby she had been nursing. The gin was still alive. She looked at the white faces still gazing down at her, and commenced to talk. What she said of course none of them could understand, but that it was a wild tirade of vengeance against the murderers of her child and herself they could pretty well understand. Death cut her speech short, and almost at the same time there was a wild yell from the bank above, and a shower of spears fell amongst the run-hunters. Only one man was hit badly, and that was Daveney, the man who fired the fatal shot. The blacks had retreated after throwing their spears, and the whites helped their wounded comrade across to camp. Pursuit was impossible; the evening was well on, and by the time the horses could be got together the blacks would be beyond reach.

Then Turner's memory recalled Daveney's death in raging delirium, when the tropic sun had inflamed his wound, and fever had set in.

'Keep that gin away, can't you? Why do you let her stop there talking, talking, talking? What is she saying? You will all die, die violent deaths. Ha! Ha! Ha! Funny a myall blackgin can talk such good English, but that's what she says, "You will die violent deaths!" Keep her away, you fellows, can't you? There's no sense in letting her stand talking there!' He died, and was buried in a lovely valley, where never a white man has been near since. Then Strathdon was drowned in the wreck of the Gothenburg, and now Moore had met a horrible fate. Turner got up with a shudder. Who would go next, he or Beveridge? He had no wish to die just then. He had but lately married, and in a few years the station would be clear of all back debt. He took up the letter, and read it through. At the end Beveridge said, 'I am coming your way, and will see you in a few days.' Turner banished all memories of the past, and went in and ate a hearty dinner and his fair young wife congratulated him on his good appetite.

Beveridge came in due time. Like Turner, he had seemingly banished dull care, and had chosen to ignore the doom that strangely enough seemed hanging over him. Nay, he even declined to talk of it with his host, and resolutely declared it was 'all bosh.'

It was a sultry, thunderous evening, and Turner and his wife, with their precious first baby, had driven their guest out to a point of interest in the neighborhood, and were returning, when the thunderstorm suddenly burst over their heads. Turner kept his horses going, but the rain overtook them some five miles from the homestead, and pelted them in their faces. Then came a flash, and darkness, as though the electric fluid had struck their eyeballs blind. With the flash came a roar, as though the world was splitting in twain, and then the horses, which had bolted off the road, went headlong into a wire fence, instead of pulling up at the sliprails.

'It's as dark as pitch,' said Turner, getting on his legs unhurt. 'Where are you all?' There was no answer, and he commenced groping about, and came on the struggling horses. 'Whoa! Beveridge, man, where are you? It can't be night, but it's all dark. Didn't you see that cursed old gin standing in the road and startling the horses? Beveridge!'

One of the men fortunately came along and found Turner, stricken blind, crouching against a tree. One of the horses was dead, with a broken neck; the other was much cut about with the wire. The baby was uninjured, and Mrs. Turner was unconscious; while Beveridge's head had been smashed in by the hoof of one of the struggling horses; he was dead. Mrs. Turner recovered, but her unfortunate husband never did, and to the day when a merciful death took him away from the blind earth, whose beauty he would see no more, he asserted that the last thing he saw was the form of a blackgin, with a child in her arms, standing in front of the sliprails and blocking the horses.

Rosa Campbell Praed

The Bunyip

1891

EVERY one who has lived in Australia has heard of the Bunyip[1]. It is the one respectable flesh-curdling horror of which Australia can boast. The old world has her tales of ghoul and vampire, of Lorelei, spook, and pixie, but Australia has nothing but her Bunyip. There never were any fauns in the eucalyptus forests, nor any naiads in the running creeks. No mythological hero left behind him stories of wonder and enchantment. No white man's hand has carved records of a poetic past on the grey volcanic-looking boulders that overshadow some lonely gullies which I know. There are no sepulchres hewn in the mountain rampart surrounding a certain dried-up lake—probably the crater of an extinct volcano—familiar to my childhood, and which in truth suggests possibilities of a forgotten city of Kör. Nature and civilisation have been very niggard here in all that makes romance.

No Australian traveller ever saw the Bunyip with his own eyes; and though there are many stockman's yarns and black's *patters* which have to do with this wonderful monster, they have all the hazy uncertainty which usually envelops information of the legendary kind. Some night, perhaps, when you are sitting over a camp fire brewing quart-pot tea and smoking store tobacco, with the spectral white gums rising like an army of ghosts around you, and the horses' hobbles clanking cheerfully in the distance, you will ask one of the overlanding hands to tell you what he knows about the Bunyip. The bushman will warm to his subject as readily as an

Irishman to his banshee. He will indignantly repel your insinuation that the Bunyip may be after all as mythical as Alice's Jabberwock; and he will forthwith proceed to relate how a friend of his had a mate, who knew another chap, who had once in his life had a narrow escape from the Bunyip, and had actually beheld it—and in a certain lagoon not a hundred miles from where you are squatting. He himself has never set eyes upon the Bunyip, nor has his mate, but there is not the smallest doubt that the other chap has seen it. When facts come to be boiled down, however, 'the other chap's' statements will seem curiously vague and contradictory; and if the details are to be accepted as they stand, a remarkable contribution to natural history must be the result.

The Bunyip is the Australian sea-serpent, only it differs from that much-disputed fact or fiction in that it does not inhabit the ocean, but makes its home in lagoons and still deep water-holes. For rivers and running creeks it appears to have an aversion. No black fellow will object to bathe in a river because of the Bunyip, but he will shake his woolly head mysteriously over many an innocent-looking water-hole, and decline to dive for water-lily roots or some such delicacy dear to the aboriginal stomach, on the plea that 'Debil-debil sit down there.'

Debil-debil and Bunyip are synonymous terms with the black fellow while he is on the bank of a lagoon, though 'Debil-debil' in the abstract represents a much more indefinite source of danger, and has a far wider scope of action than most mythological deities. 'Debil-debil' is a convenient way of accounting, not only for plague, sickness, and disaster, but also for peace, plenty, and good fortune. According to the religious code of the Australian aboriginal, Ormuzd and Ahriman do not work at opposite poles, but combine and concentrate themselves under one symbol. The supremacy of Debil-debil is uncontested, and he deals out promiscuously benefits and calamities from the same hand. A medicine-man professing to be in confidential communication with Debil-debil may kill or cure a black fellow according to his pleasure. The natives have a superstition, in common with many primitive nations, that if an enemy possesses himself of a lock of hair from the head of one to whom he wishes ill, and buries it in the ground beneath a gum tree, the despoiled person will sicken and die as the hair rots away. In that case Debil-debil must be 'pialla-ed' (entreated) by the sick person to unbury the hair and cast it in the fire, when the charm will be dissolved. The medicine-man, therefore, has but to assure his patient that Debil-debil has refused or acceded to his request, and death or speedy recovery will be the consequence.

The blacks have an impish drollery and love of mischief, and they delight in imposing on the credulity of their white auditors. Thus the stories of their superstitions must not be accepted too literally. But it is certain that when they show a distinct reticence in regard to any reputed article of faith, it may safely be looked upon as genuine. The blacks never will volunteer information about the Bunyip; it has always to be dragged out of them. When a black fellow disappears, it is generally understood that the Bunyip has got hold of him, and the particular water-hole in which the monster is supposed to live becomes more than ever an object of terror, and a place to be avoided. The water-hole may have been hitherto uncondemned by tradition, and the blacks may choose to disport themselves in it; but if one of them, seized with cramp or enmeshed in weeds, sinks to rise no more, the terrible cry of 'Bunyip' goes forth, and those waters are henceforth shunned.

The Bunyip is said to be an amphibious animal, and is variously described: sometimes as a gigantic snake; sometimes as a species of rhinoceros, with a smooth pulpy skin and a head like that of a calf; sometimes as a huge pig, its body yellow, crossed with black stripes. But it is also said to be something more than animal, and among its supernatural attributes is the cold, awesome, uncanny feeling which creeps over a company at night when the Bunyip becomes the subject of conversation; and a certain magnetic atmosphere supposed to envelop the creature, and to spread a deadly influence for some space around, rendering even its vicinity dangerous, is particularly dwelt upon. According to legend, it attracts its prey by means of this mysterious emanation, and when sufficiently near, will draw man or beast down to the water and suck the body under, and without sound or struggle the victim disappears, to be seen no more. It is silent and stealthy, and only very rarely, they say, and always at night, has been seen to rise partially from the black water which it loves, and utter a strange moaning cry like that of a child or a woman in pain. There is a theory that water is a powerful conductor for the kind of electricity it gives out, and that a pool with dry abrupt banks and no outlying morass is tolerably safe to drink from or to camp by; but a lagoon lying amid swamp has always an evil reputation, and in some districts it is very difficult to persuade a black fellow to venture into such a place.

One of the most famous haunts of the Bunyip, round which all sorts of stories gathered, though I never could really authenticate one of them, is a lagoon that we all knew well, and which used to furnish my brothers with many a brace of wild-fowl for our bush larder.

This lagoon is about four miles long, in some parts very deep, in others nothing but marsh, with swamp-oaks and ti-trees and ghostly white-barked she-oaks growing thickly in the shallow water. The wild-duck is so numerous in places that a gun fired makes the air black, and it is impossible to hear oneself speak, so deafening are the shrill cries of the birds which brood over the swamp.

We were none of us very much afraid of the Bunyip, though I confess to many an anxious shudder, and to having stopped and switched a stick behind me in order to make sure that all was right, when I found myself at dusk walking by the banks of the lagoon. A curious fascination, which was assuredly not the magnetic attraction of the Bunyip, used to draw me there; the place was so wild and eerie and solitary, and appealed so strongly to my imagination. I liked nothing better than to go with my brother on moonlight nights when he went down there with his gun over his shoulder to get a shot at wild-duck; the creepy feeling which would come over us as we trod along by the black water with dark slimy logs slanting into it, and reeds and moist twigs and fat marsh plants giving way under our footsteps, was quite a luxurious terror. There were such strange noises, the faint shivering sound made by the spiky leaves of the swamp-oak, the flapping of the she-oaks' scaly bark, the queer gurgling 'grrur-urr-r' of an opossum up a gum tree, the swishing of the ducks' wings when they rose suddenly in the distance, the melancholy call of the curlews,—all these, breaking the silence and loneliness of the night, were indescribably uncanny and fascinating; but I am bound to say that during these expeditions we never saw a sign of the Bunyip.

We were travelling once up country,—my brother Jo and I,—and had arranged to camp out one night, there being no station or house of accommodation on the stage at which we could put up. The dray, loaded with stores and furniture for the new home to which we were bound, had been started some days previously, and we had agreed to meet the drivers at a certain small lagoon, known as the One-eyed Water-hole, and camp there under the dray tarpaulin. We were riding, my brother driving a pair of pack-horses with our swags, and we were unable to carry any convenience for spending a night in the bush.

It was the month of November, and the heat was overpowering. The red gum oozed from the iron-bark trees and fell in great drops like blood. The deafening noise of the forest was in strange contrast to the night silence and loneliness of the lagoon I have described. All the sounds were harsh and grating—the whirring of grasshoppers and locusts, the chattering of parrots and laughing-jackasses, the cawing of cockatoos and scuttling of iguanas through the coarse dry blady grass. It was a relief to the heat and monotony, when, as the sun set, we left the timbered ridges and came down upon a plain, across which a faint breeze blew, and where we could see, at the foot of a distant ridge, the One-eyed Water-hole and our dray beside it, loaded high, and covered with a huge tarpaulin that hung all round it like a tent.

The men were busy making a fire and watering the bullocks. They had got down their blankets and the rations and tin billys and quart pots from the dray, and Mick, who had been hut-keeper to a party of shearers, was mixing Johnny-cakes on a piece of newly-cut bark, ready for baking when the logs had burnt down into ashes and embers. Some of the others had cut tufts from the grass trees on the ridge, and strewn them on the earth under the dray for us to lie upon. Very soon we were all comfortably camped, and as night closed in and the stars shone out, the scene became more and more picturesque. Our fire had been lighted a few yards away from the lagoon, which, deep and black where the banks were high, widened out at the lower end into a swamp of she-oaks, their white lanky stems standing out against the darker background of ridge, densely covered with jungle-like scrub.

We had eaten our meal of beef and hot Johnny-cakes all together by the dray, and there was something striking about the appearance of the men, in their bright Crimean shirts and rough moleskin trousers and broad-brimmed cabbage-tree hats, as they lounged in easy attitudes, smoking their pipes and drinking quart-pot tea, while they waxed communicative under the influence of a nip of grog, which had been served out to them apiece.

They were telling shearing stories—how Paddy Mack and Long Charlie had had a bet as to which could shear a sheep the fastest; how Father Flaherty, the priest from the township, who has come over to see the shearing in full swing, timed them by his watch; how at the word 'off' the shears slashed down through the wool, and how the quickest man sheared his sheep in less than a minute, and the other a second and a half later. Then Mick had to tell of a man who used to shear his hundred and twenty sheep in the day, and on his way from the wool-shed to the hut jump over a four-foot-six post and rail fence, which after having been bent double all day was a feat he might be proud of.

Then somehow—perhaps it was the wildness and loneliness of the place, or the wind across the plain, or the sighing of the she-oaks, or the weird 'poomp' of the bullock bells—the talk got on to eerie things, and from the authentic story of Fisher's Ghost it was an easy transition to the Bunyip and all its supernatural horrors. Most of the men had some Bunyip tale to relate; and as we talked a sort of chill seemed to creep over us, and one could almost fancy that the horrible monster was casting its magnetic spell upon us from the dark swamp close by. After a bit, when it was discovered that the billys were empty, and that we wanted more water to make some fresh tea, no one seemed inclined to go down to the lagoon to fetch it, and Mick, taking a firestick to light his pipe, said slowly,—

'Begorra, Charlie, we must look out here for the Bunyip. You ask old Darby Magrath if he'd like to camp down by the swamp of the One-eyed Water-hole all night by himself. I remember Darby telling me that when he was riding across this plain one night after shearing, his horse stopped of a sudden and trembled all over under him—just like a bullock in the killing yard when you drop the spear into his neck. Darby says he felt cold all through his bones; and then a queer sort of noise came up from the water,—a kind of sound like a baby moaning,—and he just clapped spurs into his old yarraman (horse), and never pulled up out of a gallop till he had got over the range and was at the "Coffin Lid" public, five miles on. The horse was all dripping with sweat, and poor old Darby as white as a corpse.'

'Well, I don't know much about the thing myself—never had no Bunyip experiences myself; but unless Gemmel Dick is *the* most almighty liar'—began Long Charlie, taking out his pipe in preparation for a blood-curdling yarn and then stopping suddenly, for at that moment there came a curious sound from the lagoon, or the swamp, or the plains to our left, we could not tell whence—a wild, thrilling sound, which at first seemed scarcely human, but which, when repeated after the interval of a moment or two, struck my heart as if it were the cry of some dying animal, or of a child in dire distress and agony.

We all started and looked anxiously at each other, waiting until it came again, and not quite liking to confess out tremors, when one of the men exclaimed nervously,—

'Say, what's that?'

'Wallabi bogged,' pronounced Long Charlie oracularly, and was beginning once more,—

'Well, as I was telling you, if Gemmel Dick ain't *the* most'—

But that strange, horrible cry from the lagoon—yes, it must come from the swamp end of the lagoon—broke the night silence again, and stopped

Long Charlie a second time. It was more prolonged, more certain, than it had been before. Beginning low, a sort of hoarse muffled groan, it swelled into a louder, shriller note, which we at once imagined might be the strained broken coo-ëë of a child in pain or terror.

Every one of us rose.

'By Jove! I'll tell you what I believe it is,' said my brother Jo excitedly. 'That's some free-selector's kid lost in the bush. Come along, you fellows. Don't be funky of the Bunyip.'

He darted down towards the swamp, which lay some little distance from our camp, the dark heads of the she-oaks rising above a thick veil of white mist, that shrouded completely the less lofty and more straggling branches of the ti-trees. The rest of us followed him closely. It must be said that we were not deterred at that moment by any thought of the Bunyip and its supernatural atmosphere. Long Charlie, the most practical of the party, waited to detach a rough lantern which hung from one of the staples of the dray, and caught us up as we reached the borders of the swamp. The sound had ceased now. Coo-ëëing loudly, we peered through the cold clinging mist among the brown twisted branches of the ti-trees, which shook their scented bottle-brush blossoms in our faces. Under our feet, the ground, which had been trodden into deep odd-shaped ruts by the cattle coming down to drink, gave way at every step. We could hear the soft 'k—sssh' of the displaced water, and we shivered as the slimy ooze mounted over our insteps and trickled down through our boots, while the pulpy rushes sprang back as we forced ourselves through, and struck our hands with clammy touch.

It was a dreary, uncanny place, and even through our coo-ëës the night that had seemed so silent on the plain was here full of ghostly noises, stifled hissings, and unexpected gurglings and rustlings, and husky croaks, and stealthy glidings and swishings.

'Look out for snakes,' said Long Charlie, flourishing his lantern. 'And don't all of us be coo-ëëing all the time, or when the little chap sings out we shan't be able to hear him.'

We stopped coo-ëëing, and presently the wail sounded again, fainter and more despairing, we fancied, and urging us to greater energy. Though we tried to move in the direction of the voice, it was impossible to determine whence it came, so misleading and fitful and will-o'-the-wisp-like was the sound. Now it seemed to come from our right, now from our left, now from the very depths of the lagoon, and now from the scrub on the ridge beyond.

I don't know how we got through the deeper part of the swamp without getting bogged; but we did at last, and reached the scrub that straggled down to the water's edge. Here was dense, and in places impenetrable foliage; rough boulders were lying pell-mell at the foot of the ridge, and creepers hung in withes from the trees, with great thorns that tore our hands and our clothes. We did not know which way to turn, for the cry had ceased, and the dead silence of the scrub was like that of the grave. We waited for a minute or two, but it did not come again.

'I believe it was the Bunyip after all,' said Mick, with a shudder. 'And look here, I shall head the lagoon, I ain't going to cross that swamp again. It's all nonsense about the little 'un, not a child nor a grown man or beast could have forced theirselves down here.'

Long Charlie flashed his lantern along the wall of green, and, stumbling over stones and logs, we walked as well as we could, skirting the scrub and making for the head of the lagoon. We paused every now and then, straining our ears for the voice that had led us hither, and once it sounded faint but thrillingly plaintive, and guided us on.

At last there came a break in the jungle, a narrow track piercing the heart of the scrub, and then a wider break, and a warning cry from Long Charlie in advance,—

'Hello! Look out! It's a gully—pretty deep. You might break a leg before you knew it. Keep along up the track.'

We kept along up the track, waiting to let Long Charlie go first with his lantern. Suddenly the moon, which had risen while we were in the swamp, sent a shaft of light down through the opening, and showed us, a little way ahead, where the track widened out and then stopped altogether, a tiny plateau, in the centre of which stood a great white bottle tree, its trunk perfectly bare, bulging out in the centre like a garment swelled by the wind, and looking in its fantastic shape like a sentinel spectre.

It gave one a strange creepy feeling to see this huge white thing rising up so solemnly in the midst of the gloom and the solitude. There was something else white on the grass—something almost the same shape as the bottle tree lying across at its foot. The moon was dim for a moment or two. Nobody spoke, we pressed up the ridge side, then a hoarse smothered ejaculation burst from Long Charlie's lips, and as he spoke the moon shone forth again, and he shifted his lantern so that its gleam fell athwart the white prostrate form and upon a snake, brown and shiny and scaly and horrible, which uncoiled itself, and with a swift, wavy motion disappeared into the depths of the scrub.

It seemed to us, we said afterwards, as though we could hear each other's hearts beating. The men were too horrified to utter a sound. At last Long Charlie said, in a deep, awe-stricken voice,—

'By God! that beats me.'

And then Mick, moving a little nearer, cried, with a sob in his brawny throat,—

'It's Nancy—little Nancy—Sam Duffy's girl from the "Coffin Lid," and it was only the other day she came out and served me with a nobbler.'

Paddy Mack was sobbing too, they all seemed to know and love the child.

'She wur so fond of looking for chuckie-chuckies in the scrub, and quantongs and things. And she might have knowed, poor little Nancy! that if she wanted quantongs, I'd have got 'em for her; and didn't I string her a necklace only last shearing! But she was always a child for roaming,— she wasn't afraid of snakes, nor blacks, nor nothing,—she said she liked to hear the bell-bird call, and that it seemed to be always calling *her*. I've heerd her say that—poor little Nancy !—always smiling when she carried a chap out a nobbler. And now the bell-bird has rung her home.'

Long Charlie only said again, 'That beats me.'

They couldn't account for it; the child had been dead some hours, they said. They couldn't believe it was that snake which had bitten her, and they declared that the cry we heard must have been the Bunyip, or little Nancy's ghost.

[1] While looking through files of the *Sydney Morning Herald* for 1848, I came across the following paragraph, under date August 1st of that year. It was headed 'The Bunyip again.' 'A Mr. R. Williams, of Port Fairy, a correspondent of the *Portland Gazette*, reports the discovery of a real Bunyip in the Eumeralia. Mr. W. says: 'A stockman in the employ of Mr. Baxter was fishing in the Eumeralia, when he was suddenly startled by what he at first imagined to be a huge black fellow swimming in the river, but which I think must be the Bunyip. I went with the stockman the next day, and was fortunate enough to get a good view of him. He was of a brownish colour, with a head something the shape of a kangaroo, an enormous mouth, apparently furnished with a formidable set of teeth, long neck, covered with a shaggy mane which reached halfway down his back; his hind quarters were under water, so that we could not get a full view of him, but if one may judge by what was seen, his weight must be fully equal to that of a very large bullock. On trying to get a closer examination, he took alarm and immediately disappeared; and although a strict watch has since been kept, he has never again been seen, but it is hoped that the exertions now being made by Mr. Baxter to catch him will be crowned with success.'—ED.

Francis Adams

The Hut by the Tanks

1892

I never knew but one man who thought he had seen a ghost. Of ghost stories at second-hand, third-hand, and so on up to the twentieth-hand, we most of us know plenty. This man I spent six months with. We were on the same station, working together, sleeping in the same room. He was a simple, kindly soul, eminently honest and truthful. I cannot remember him ever telling an apocryphal yarn. This ghost story of his was only produced by accident. One winter night, when we were both in bed and the lights out, the subject of the supernatural came up and I pretty freely expressed my scepticism. A peculiar silence on the part of friend Holmes (Jonnie Holmes was his name, and I had got in the way of calling him Jonnie as often as Holmes) led me to suspect dissent. Of course I began to investigate. Strictly speaking, Jonnie was the first 'Australian native' I ever knew. I had been in the bush before and was at home in the life, but I can't think of any other genuine sample of young Australia whom I had been much thrown with before Jonnie. He had been born and bred in the bush, and, except one short and hopelessly bewildering and bewildered visit to Brisbane, had never been out of it. He was one of the numerous offspring of a small selector, and looked forward to one day being a small selector himself. Meantime he and I were boundary riders on a sheep station. He had had the normal education of a lad who had luckily lived within reach of a State school and had parents sensible enough to keep him pretty regularly at his 'scholarship.' (The old English peasant word sounded so curiously to me, I remember, in his Australian mouth.) The besotting and fuddling effects of the appalling solitude of the life of the lonely bushman had so far fallen lightly on him. He had intelligence, and took an interest in all he did, keeping a sort of stock and station journal, which was the record of his advance in all sorts and conditions of knowledge. We all have the element of superstition in us somewhere. It is not for nothing that for countless unknown ages our speechless but reflective ancestors grew into articulation and shuddering dread of the terrible caprices of unknown forces. Jonnie Holmes had a larger share of this superstition than I, that was all. I felt this as I began questioning him. I have had 'bush fright' more than once, and know all about it.

'You don't mean to say, Jonnie,' I said, 'that you believe in ghosts?'

He hesitated a moment, and then got ready to own up.

'Well,' he said, 'Acheson, I must say I do.'

I laughed. It was the wont of Holmes' front hair to stand erect, and this habit neither oil, nor water, nor brush could perceptibly modify. I had a vision of Holmes seeing a ghost when he was a 'kid,' and that hair taking a lift ever after.

'What are you laughing at?' he asked.

I explained.

He took the matter seriously, I perceived at once. I lay, still hilarious but only inwardly so, waiting till he enunciated solemnly:

'No, Acheson, I don't think it was seeing the ghost made my wool so terribly uppish. I remember it used to be that way before. But—p'raps it made it worse!'

His solemn tone was altogether too much for me. I began to shout, laughing helplessly. This was a bad move, as, like all bushmen, Jonnie was frightfully thin-skinned in the matter of ridicule. It took much persuading to get him to renew the subject, and I had to be very explanatory and serious. At last, however, I succeeded, and the questioning went on.

'What sort of ghosts do you believe in?' I asked. 'Apparitions, spectres, lights, rappings, or what?'

'I believe,' he replied deliberately, 'in two sorts of ghosts. There's the bush ghost, and there's the ghost of murderers and murdered people. I've never seen the bush ghost, not myself; at least, I'm not sure. But I know those who have, and I believe in it.'

'What *is* the bush ghost?' I asked.

'Well,' he said, 'no one seems to know what it *is*. It's a rum sort of thing,' he added dubitatively.

Suppressing the almost overwhelming temptation to be flippant and say that it might also be a *whisky* sort of thing, I inquired: 'Well, but it must have a shape of some sort. What's it like? Is it the bunyip?'

'The bunship,' he said dogmatically, 'is bunkum. It's not a fool of a thing like that. It's real. It means great misfortune or death, almost always death. If you see it, you generally die before the year's out. I knew three fellows who died that way, and the other fellow broke his back at a fence and is a living corpse at this hour.'

'And what did they say they *saw?*'

'None of 'um were quite certain about it. They all said it was black, and like a ball, and that it rolled along in front to the left of them, and all the while you saw it you kept running cold shivers from behind your ears down your backbone. One of 'um—that was Ned Lane (he died of the fever in Brisbane four years ago)—said he thought it might be the ghost of an animal, and he was pretty sure it had eyes and feet and a tail, but all rolled-round and confused-like. The others thought it was more like a glass globe half full of black liquor that kept whirling about and seemed to be flying round the outside of the globe somehow. It kept going and coming. They were all riding at the time, and after a bit the horses got frightened and sweated all over into a lather as if they'd been stuffing themselves on soft food for months.'

'*After a bit?* Not at once?'

'No, not at once. They all noticed that. At first none of 'um could make the thing out. It looked quite thin and unsubstantial-like. Ned said he took it for a shadow, and wasn't afraid for a bit, till he knew what it was.'

'Was it at night they all saw it?'

'No; Ned saw it about two o'clock. He died a month after—wiped clean out after two days' seedy, and they tell me he was worse than dead before the life was out of him. Morris saw it about the after-glow; Walker on a moonlight night. Walker was riding through the scrub. He died six or seven months after—got scratched by a nail and blood-poisoning did for him. Morris died three or four months after, I was told. A deaf-adder bit him. He was droving horses up North. He put his elbow on it just by the camp fire. He was dead like lightning.'

It was evident that Jonnie felt he was merely stating cause and effect.

'And did you think you saw it once yourself?' I asked.

'Well,' he said, 'I don't think it *could* have been, for it's sixteen months past, and I'm all right. And the horse got frightened first, and, though I saw a round, dark thing rolling ahead of me, to the left, it didn't move, but just kept on there. I couldn't get the horse past anyway. I had to ride right back and round.'

'Didn't you go and look at it yourself?'

'No. But you be sure I kept a pretty sharp look out for it as I went along. It was dusk, and I was going into a little place under the Range, Helidon-way, to see a friend of mine who's an orange orchard there. I was coming down the road over the Range from Toowoomba.'

I could get no further particulars about the bush ghost. Jonnie had given me his whole information and belief on the subject. I returned to the second sort of ghost.

'Then it wasn't the bush ghost," I said, which made your ... which you saw for certain? Did you ever see any other sort of ghost for certain, Jonnie?'

'Yes,' he said slowly, 'I did, Acheson.'

'What was it like?'

There was a long pause.

'It was like,' he said in a low voice, 'it was like a man and woman, just the same as living, only they were shadowy a bit, and I think you might have almost looked through them.'

'And you—saw—them?'

'I saw them.'

'How long ago?'

'Just on two years.'

'Will you tell me about it?'

Jonnie seemed to consider. It was evident that he did not relish going through his experience again. Even in the kindly and matter-of-fact daytime I do not think it would have pleased him. How much less, then, at the present hour? It was pitch dark. The wind surged and pressed outside, every now and then booming down the chimney and out through the large, whitewashed, empty fireplace, gently fanning our faces with the breath of the outer darkness. The only sound of life was the mournful stridulation of the curlews in the adjoining swamp. Directly opposite his eyes was the room's one window looking out directly into the black, cloud-thick and wind-swept sky. I realised all this for the first time in this long pause. We had been sitting with the two sons of the boss, chatting pleasantly over the great red ember fire of a more than half consumed log of box, in the cosy little workshop and den they had—still called 'the school-room' in memory of educative efforts in the past. The conversational atmosphere of the den had been transferred to our bedroom as we undressed by the dim candle light, continuing the conversation, but with the added candour that springs from the absence of some of the original talkers. Now for the first time a something of uneasiness, eeriness—funk, if you like—subtle, indefinable, but unmistakeable, got hold of me. Let me be candid. At such an hour, in such a place, I should not have been altogether put out if this solemn believer in a *bonâ fide* ghost, seen by his own eyes and recognised as 'shadowy a bit,' and quite uncomfortably transparent, had kept his story for some other occasion. But it was not to be. The demoniac instinct of retailing a horrible experience and thus making somebody participate therein (that well-known personage, the Ancient Mariner, had a finer but less genuine explanation of his gruesome inflictions on the Wedding Guest, who rose the morrow morn a sadder but a wiser man)—this demoniac instinct had got hold of Jonnie, and I felt it. Presently, in a slow, hushed voice, he began.

'It was about two years ago,' he said, 'a little earlier than this—in June. I've been here just a year. The boss engaged me in Brisbane. I went down from Toowoomba with Fenwich and a mob of horses, and I never thought I should get to Brisbane alive, or, any way, get back again. That was after I thought I saw the bush ghost by Helidon. Well, before that, I was on a cattle station fifty or sixty miles off the line, to the north, Hilburn way. The boss himself was alright. He was the son of an old army captain who came here in the convict time. He took no notice of things much, and left it all to the overseer. That overseer, Davis, was just a terror, and no one could stop with him. I put up with him for two years, for he knew a lot about cattle. And, though there's no money in cattle, and hasn't been for years, and isn't likely to be, a man ought to know all about it. Well, at last I got out of him all he knew, and then his ways came unbearable to me, and I made up my mind to go. It may seem a curious thing, but it's a fact.'

'I didn't know the land more than twenty or thirty miles round, and especially the other twenty miles or so 'twixt there and the line! I came down from the north-west, and Davis wasn't the man to let you get your nose up off the grindstone and look round a bit if he could help it. The country's all plain about there; some parts with no trees on at all, other parts pretty bushy, and if you don't know it, it's sing'ler how easy you can get lost there. There's always that everlasting circle of trees down on the horizon' (Jonnie always said 'horizon' with the *i* short), 'and, if you've no landmarks, why, I don't care how good a bushman you are, you can pretty quick get lost.'

131

He paused. He was still talking in that deliberate dreamy way. I suppose a bird, hopping round and round and down and down to a staring snake or a cat, would, if it could talk, talk something in this style about very ordinary matters.

'Well,' he said, 'I set off to ride Charcoal into Hamilton—that's a bit over sixty miles—and the way seemed as clear as could be. Hamilton's a station on the line, and I was going into Too'mba from it. I set off early in the morning. It was cold and clear, with a slight north-west breeze blowing. You know it's dreadful cold on the plains at night.' (This was information to me, who had been boundary riding on them for three or four months! But I don't think Jonnie was altogether aware of my existence just then.) 'I don't think they can have it colder anywhere else in the earth. The wind goes right through you and out behind. Nothing'll stop it. A coat doesn't seem to make any difference. Men have freezed to death out on the plains at nights. What you've got to do is to light a fire and get behind a lorg and make the best of it. Well, towards sunset the wind moved round a bit more west, and presently I began to feel it getting at me. By dark it would be freezing. And, to tell you the truth, I was beginning to feel more and more sure that I'd lost myself. Things got to look bluer and bluer every minit, and, by George, when I made up my mind to it that I was clean bushed, I tell you I had a bit of a creep in my back hair, and began thinking of the cosy room at home with Jack Hawthorne and Tom Birkett, and felt like as if I was going back that way presently as a sort of ghost.'

He paused again. The wind rose, pressing upon the window panes, rolling into the room from the fire-place that glimmered like a faint, tall, white, threatening figure in the middle of the opposite wall.

'I knew now,' he said, 'that I was in for a regular night of it in the open, with the wind blowing harder and harder and colder and colder, but I couldn't make up my mind to stop, but kept riding irresolute on. I think Charcoal knew I was bushed long before I did myself, and just made up his mind to go for water, having smelt it this way. Anyhow, just at this moment, passing into a belt of trees, I heard a whirr, and up went nine or ten whistling ducks out of a fine little tank just ahead. I was a bit startled. It came upon me when I was troubled. In an ordinary way, you know, noises in the bush don't startle you. You know what they are. If you get startled by a noise, it's because you don't know what it is, or because you're unprepared or thinking or troubled. I've got startled by a magpie whopping onto my hat as I was riding along under a tree by her nest.'

Another pause.

'I recognised in a moment that it wasn't a waterhole. There was work at one side of it—a bit of an embankment. I could tell that by the shape of it, but it was too dark to see any more. Charcoal went right on to the water, while I sat loose in the saddle, looking at it. I was just making out that there was two tanks here leading into one another, with a bit of an island or a promontory in the middle, when he turned a bit to the right, and I looked right up the second tank. That instant I saw a line of straight on it, and the next I gave a bit of an expression of rapture, as you may say, for there was a window, right enough, in a hut or a house of some sort on the top of the far bank. I was that glad and impatient that I couldn't scarcely wait to let Charcoal have his fill, but turned him off to the right and, with a dig in the ribs, rode along at a quick trot, with my eyes on the window. I've good sight and can see better than most people, but I tell you I was a bit surprised to make out that hut so well when it was so far off, and the night almost down. The light that came out of the window was astonishingly bright; it lit up all the window, and poured right out. Perhaps that was it. "Why," thinks I to myself presently, "they've got a bit of an illumination on in there to-night. P'raps they've company."'

He paused. A curlew stridulated close to the window, and then, turning on the wind, must have whirled away down it, for the next moment its cry came faintly from the distance.

'Do you hear?' he said, almost in a whisper. 'That's the very curlew p'r'aps that got up and went wheeling round me as the lights went out.'

'Lights went out?' I asked. 'What do you mean?'

'Why,' he said, 'as I was riding on, with my eyes on that window (I counted the panes—there were four of 'um, with a cross-bar down the middle), it went right out black.'

'The land on the promontory got between you and it.'

'That was what I thought, and I held straight on round the tank, that curlew crying to right and left of me all the time, till I came up to a fence and made out the hut not fifteen yards off, as dark as could be.'

'The window was on the other side.'

'That fence was a short one and didn't go up to the hut. I reckoned it must be a vegetable garden, closed in to keep out sheep or cattle. As I came up to the door, the curlew following me, something small and white slanted off along the front—a cat, as I thought. But when I drew up, *the door was half open and all as black as pitch!*'

He paused.

'I wasn't altogether frightened, but I'd got a bit of a scare and a puzzle, and I sat there staring at the place. There was a rail ran round it to right and left, I found, and p'raps there was once a gate in front of the door. I drew back Charcoal a bit, and we went round the hut, the curlew with us. It was fairly big—two rooms as I reckoned—and a bit of an outhouse. On the one side was a window, the side to the left of the door. I caught the glaze of the glass. Just then I saw the white thing again on the ground and called to it several times, "Puss, puss, puss." Then it mewed back, and a wild, half-starved sort of mew it was. I sat and considered. You know, I've seen mirage dozens of times, and once a mirage that looked just like two trenches half full of water took me in. P'raps, I thought, that window was a bit of a *night* mirage, so to speak. For I never had the least idea that anyone was inside the hut. I reckoned it was deserted. I can't tell you why.'

He paused again.

'Well,' he said, 'the long and the short of it was that I jumped down, tied up Charcoal to the rail, got ready to hit at anything, went in through the door, and brought a vesta round the back of my moleskins and up into the air in a moment. I had my fingers round it, and the wind was on the opposite wall, and the match burned up. I looked about. It was just an ordinary slab hut. There was a big empty fireplace at the right end. A little door at the left end, half open, led into another room. The fireplace had a few half-burned lorgs in it, blurred with rain. The floor was beaten earth. There wasn't a sign of furniture, or anything except a shut-down—a table-slab—up against the wall under the little window by the door. All the glass was broken out of the window, and a few bits were on the ground. I lit another vesta and went into the second room. There I got a surprise. It was quite small, scarcely big enough to turn in, but there was a stretcher in it— a frame with sacking sewn across it, and above the head of it were some shelves. The four window-panes were all unbroken. As I was looking again at the sacking, I got a bit of a scare. At the end of it, just to the right, was a great black stain. I tell you I had to look on the ground underneath to see if there was anything there, and all the while I was afraid somebody was going to come at me from behind. I tell you, when the vesta burned my fingers, and I dropped it with a start onto the earth, I got up and began staring round me, trickling with sweat all over.'

'Well?' I said.

'Well,' he said, 'there was nothing. I went out there, leaving it flaring and waving in the draught on the earth, and set off round to the out-house. What I wanted was wood. I intended camping there for the night.

I wasn't going to freeze out in the open for the sake of that stretcher, and a deserted hut. "What's a deserted hut?" thinks I. "There's piles of 'um all over Queensland, and there's dozens of reasons why they're given up." I got into the out-house, and set a vesta burning. If I couldn't find wood there, I would pull down the fences round the house; but in one corner I lit on quite a little pile. It was piercing cold all this time, but I scarcely noticed it, I was that taken up with my thoughts. Just as I was coming to the out-house door, with my arms full of wood, I saw the cat on the top of some timber by the wall, and called to her again. This time she seemed to take more heed, and followed along behind, mewing all the way, and entered the hut after me. I threw down the wood on the floor, and after a little trouble got a flame going. All the while I was doing this, I can't tell you why, but I thought someone was looking at me round the corner of the door by the stretcher. Once or twice I turned my head and stared, but there was no one. Then I got up and went and closed it, and it was a great relief.'

Jonnie paused and emitted a slight but protracted sigh.

'I went back into the shed,' he continued, 'several times, and brought in enough wood and lorgs—(there was a pile of regular cut lorgs, just the size of that across the fire-place in there)—enough to keep a blazing fire all night. The cat followed me to and fro, mewing all the time, and I tried to get her to come to me, but she wouldn't. When I got into the house, she'd stand at the door, arching her back and mewing, but she wouldn't come in any further, and the moment I got to the door to go out, she cleared off ahead of me. But I had a good look at her. She was a most curious cat. She was a sort of glazy white, quite *shaggy*, you might say, with the biggest blazing eyes I ever saw on any beast in my life. She was very thin and bony, though she'd a regular pot-belly. I suppose she was a tame cat that had gone on the wild. Their bellies get pot like that. You see, one day they gorge and then maybe for a week they starve. It's either a feast or a famine with them, as they say.'

He paused.

'I felt awful queer. I never felt quite like that ever before or since. I couldn't make up my mind to let Charcoal loose: no, nor even to hobble him, though I knew the poor brute wanted a feed and there was grand grass about. To tell you the truth, I'd been glad to have had him in the hut with me. There was something in that next room I wouldn't have looked at for worlds. I knew it. I knew that, if I saw it, I'd never forget it, and I didn't want to see it. Once or twice I felt like going into the outhouse and lighting a fire outside, but the door faced west, and there was no show. I might wake up frozen, or fizzling in the blazing shed. I put on my great coat again (I'd pulled it off when I began to make the fire), and took the horse-cloth from under Charcoal's saddle. I wanted it to squat on. But I did up the girths again. I couldn't make up my mind to unsaddle him. I tied him by the bridle, so that he could get at some grass by the rails, and went over on chance to the garden fence and broke in. There I found lots of green stuff, carrots, lettuces, potatoes, all running wild and seeding, and brought him back a feed. And all the while that cat keep skirting round me, and followed me into the garden; and, just as I got to the door, hang me, if that curlew didn't come bansheeing up about me again. I said to myself: 'Now either that cat's going to come in for the night or stop out for the night.' So I went in and sat down on the horse-cloth to the left of the fire, and the cat crept into the doorway. But it was just no good. For she wouldn't come in further, and edged off when I got up. At that I just shut the door to, and shoved in the rusty bolt, and sat down again.'

A pause.

'Well, I was cold and tired, and I began bit by bit to feel that that thing in the next room was going to keep quiet—'

'What thing?' I asked.

'That horrible thing I didn't want to see. How should *I* know what it was? Why, I didn't *want* to know! Well, I sat and sat, and I suppose I was just dozing off when I heard a dreadful scramble and a crying, and jumped up onto my feet and pretty well out of my skin at the same time. It was at the window. It was the cat. She must have clambered upon the rails outside and jumped at the window. She was struggling to get through one of the squares where a pane had been, but her pot belly stopped her. I can't say why, but I just began to laugh like mad. I kept on laughing and laughing and laughing, till she dragged herself through and fell clumsily down onto the floor. And that set me off laughing again, and the curious thing is, that she got up and came straight to me, and arched her back against my legging. I stroked her, and sat down on the horse-cloth, still laughing (it was quite foolish), and she arching her back and staring up in my eyes in the most strange, wild, eager way I ever saw in an animal.'

A pause again.

'Well,' he said, 'this went on for some time, till I began to feel a bit confident-like, and left off stroking her, and she cuddled up against me, and I went right off to sleep. When I woke ...'

A longer pause.

'Yes,' I said, 'when you woke?'

'I didn't wake. Some one woke me. Some one laughing. I just opened my eyes and looked right at the door. It was open. I knew it was open. It was open wide enough to see the bottom of the stretcher. I saw the bottom of the stretcher.'

He could not get on.

'Well?' I said.

'There was a sheet on it—a sheet and two feet. Naked. Fat and small. The toes crinkled. With earth on them. There was a bright light. And some one was laughing—laughing like mad.'

Once more he could not get on.

'Well?' I said; and again, 'Well?'

'I got up. I had to get up. I went over to the other wall. By the window. I stood. I looked in. I knew it all at once. There were candles in bottles on the shelves. Three of 'um. There was a candle in a candlestick on the chair at the foot of the bed. She was lying stretched out on the bed, her arms by her side. She was almost naked, dirty, smeared with earth. There was earth in her eyes, on her lips, in her hair. Her eyes were hollows and her teeth were snarling. You could see 'um all. The cat was standing on her chest. It was arched up, staring into her eyes. Its tail was right stiff out, with a bend at the top—ridiculous. It almost made me laugh. He'd dug her up. I knew it. Right on her breast was a great black mark—black, thick, clotted. That's where he stabbed her as she lay asleep, and there he was kneeling beside her, holding her hand and laughing like mad. Then he howled like a wild beast—like a starving dingo does when it's alone in the dark night in the scrub. Then he cried and sobbed, and then he laughed like mad, and I began to laugh too. He said she'd deserved it. He said he'd do it again. Then he called her: "Maggy, Maggy, Maggy, Maggy, Maggy, Maggy!" And then he took to laughing again. Then, all at once, like a flash, the lights went out. It was gone. I knew it was gone. I put my hand up to my head and wiped off the sweat. The fire had burned low. I threw on some wood, and it blazed up. I could see into the room. It was all dark. I made up my mind I'd go and shut the door. It was close on morn. I got to the door and was closing it when something stopped it. I cried out. I couldn't have stood any more. I should have gone mad. I looked down. It was the cat, lying on the floor. I pulled the door to, and the cat with it. I took her up, and went with her to the fire. She was limp and warm, but dead.'

'*Dead?*'

'Quite dead.'

'I sat with her on my knees till the dawn came out pale and then ruddy and then yellow on the wall opposite the window over my head. Then I took her up and the horse-cloth and went out. The wind was on the lull. All round was a lovely wooded country, beautifully grassed, and the first sunlight glinting on the waterpools right out across the plain. A little shepherd's-companion was frisking about Charcoal's head, teasing him. I took and buried the cat and rode away. That's all.'

'And you never heard anything more about... You never asked about the hut and who lived there?'

'No. But I can tell you exactly where it is if you like, for I struck the line about ten miles further on and came straight into Hamilton.'

I lay silent for a bit.

'Do you hear that curlew outside?' he asked. "P'raps it's the very curlew. There's no knowing.'

Henry Lawson

The Bush Undertaker (or A Christmas in the Far West)

1892

'Five Bob!' The old man shaded his eyes and peered through the dazzling glow of that broiling Christmas Day. He stood just within the door of a slab-and-bark hut situated upon the bank of a barren creek; sheep-yards lay to the right, and a low line of bare brown ridges formed a suitable background to the scene.

'Five Bob!' shouted he again; and a dusty-looking sheep-dog rose wearily from the shade by the side of the hut and looked inquiringly at his master, as the latter pointed towards some sheep which were strangling away from the main flock.

'Fetch 'em back,' he said confidently. The dog went off obediently, and his master returned to the interior of the hut.

'We'll yard 'em early,' he said to himself; 'the super won't know. We'll yard 'em early, and have the afternoon to ourselves.'

'We'll get dinner,' he added, glancing at some pots on the fire. 'I cud do a bit of doughboy, an' that theer boggabria'll eat like marrer, along of the salt junk.' He rose and slightly moved one of the black buckets from the blaze. 'I likes to keep it jist on the bile,' he said in explanation to himself. 'I don't like it to bile too hard. It makes it tough,—I likes to keep it jist a-simmerin'.'

Here his meditations were interrupted by the entrance of the dog.

'All right, Five Bob,' said the hermit; 'dinner'll be ready dreckly. Jist keep yer eye on the sheep till I calls yer; keep 'em well rounded up, 'n' we'll yard 'em arterwards and have a holiday.'

This speech was accompanied by a gesture evidently intelligible to the dog, who retired as though he understood English,—and the cooking proceeded.

'I'll take a pick 'n' shovel with me and dig up that old black fellow,' mused the shepherd, evidently following up an old train of thought; 'I reckon it'll nearly do now. I'll give it a minet's more bilin' 'n' put in the spuds.'

The last sentence referred to the cooking, the first to a supposed black fellow's grave about which he was curious.

'The sheep is a-settling down to camp,' said the soliloquiser, glancing through the door. 'So me an' Five Bob'll be able to get our dinner in peace. I wish I had enough fat to make the pan siss, I'd treat meself to a leather-jacket; but it took three weeks' skimmin' to get enough for them doughboys.'

In due time the dinner was dished up; and the solitaire seated himself on a block, with the lid of a gin-case across his knees for a table. Five Bob squatted opposite with the liveliest interest and appreciation depicted on his intelligent countenance.

Dinner proceeded very quietly, except when the carver paused to ask the dog how some tasty morsel went with him; and Five Bob's tail declared that it went very well indeed.

'Here y'are, try this,' cried the old man, tossing the dog a large piece of 'doughboy;' a click of Five Bob's jaws and the dough was gone.

The old shepherd then 'washed up' the tinware in the water in which the 'duff' had boiled, and afterwards, with the assistance of the dog, yarded the sheep.

This accomplished, he took a pick and shovel and an old bag from under his bunk, and started out over the range, followed, of course, by his faithful friend and confidant. After tramping some three miles a 'spur,' running out from the main ridge, was reached. At the extreme end of this, under some gum-trees, was a little mound of earth barely defined in the grass. This was the supposed black fellow's grave, about which the old man had some doubts.

He set to work to dig it up, and, sure enough, in about half an hour, he bottomed on 'payable dirt,' or, rather, a skeleton.

As soon as he had raked up all the bones, he amused himself by putting them together on the grass and speculating as to whether they belonged to black or white or male or female. Failing, however, to arrive at any satisfactory conclusion, he dusted the bones with great care, put them in the bag, and started for home.

He took a short cut this time, over the ridge and down a gully which was full of dead ring-barked trees and long white grass. He had nearly reached its mouth when a great greasy black 'gohanna' (iguana) suddenly clambered up a sapling from under his feet and looked fightable.

'Dang the jumpt-up thing!' cried the old man. 'It did give me a start!'

At the foot of this tree he then espied an object which he at first took to be the blackened carcase of a sheep, but on closer examination discovered to be the body of a man, which lay on its stomach with its face resting on its hands, dried to a mummy by the intense heat of the western summer.

'Me luck's in for the day!' said the bushman, scratching the back of his head while he took stock of the remains. He then picked up a stick and tapped the body on the shoulder: the flesh sounded like leather, and he turned the body over on its side; it fell flat on its back like a board, and the shrivelled eyes seemed to peer up at him from under the blackened wrists.

He stepped back involuntarily, but, recovering himself, he leaned on his stick and took in all the ghastly details.

There was nothing in the blackened features to tell aught of name or race, but the dress proclaimed the remains to be those of a European. Suddenly the old man caught sight of a black bottle in the grass close beside the corpse. This set him thinking. Presently his gathering suspicions settled into convictions, and exclaiming 'Brummy!' he knelt down and examined the soles of the dead man's Blucher boots, and then, rising with an air of conviction, said impressively, 'Yes, it's Brummy!—busted up at last! I told yer so, Brummy; I allers told yer as how it 'ud be—an' here y'are. Yer allers was a fool, Brummy. Yer cud earn mor'n any man in the colony, but yer'd slush it all away in drink. I allers sed as how it 'ud end, an' now yer kin see fur y'self.'

'I 'spect yer was a comin' ter me ter get fixt up 'n' set straight, same as yer allers uster come; then yer was agoin' to sweer off, same as yer allers uster sweer off; 'n' here y'ar', 'n' now I expect I'll have ter fix yer up for the last time an' make yer decent, for t'won't do ter leave yer a-laying here like the fool yer allers was.'

He picked up the corked bottle and examined it. To his great surprise it was more than half full of rum.

'Well, this gets me,' exclaimed the old man; 'me luck's in for this Christmas, sure. Yer must 'a' got the jams pretty early in yer spree, or yer wouldn't be making for me with near a bottleful left. Howsomenever, here's t'yeh health, Brummy.'

The old man looked round until his eyes fell upon some sheets of bark which lay close by, and he now took two pieces of bark, one about four and the other six feet long, and each about two feet wide, and brought them over to the body. He laid the longest strip by the side of the corpse, which he proceeded to lift on to it.

'Come on, Brummy,' he said, in a softer tone than usual. 'Come on, Brummy, 'n' don't be layin' there in that state any longer. Yer ain't as bad as yer might be, considerin' that it must be three months since yer slipped yer wind. I'spect it was the rum as preserved yer. It was the death of yer when yer was alive, 'n' now yer dead 'n' no good to nobody (which yer never warn't), it preserved yer in good condition.'

He then placed the other sheet of bark on top, with the hollow side downwards,—thus sandwiching the defunct between the two pieces— removed the saddle strap which he wore in the place of braces, buckled it round one end of the elongated sandwich, while he puzzled himself to think of something to tie up the other end.

'I can't afford any more strips off my shirt,' he said, critically examining the skirts of the old blue overshirt he wore. 'I might git a strip or two more off, but it's short enough already. Let's see; when did I buy that shirt? Oh, I remember, it was jist two days arter Five Bob was pupped. I bought the cabbage-tree hat a week before. I can't afford a new shirt jist yet;— howsomenever, seeing it's Brummy, I'll jist borrow a couple more strips. I kin sew 'em on agen when I git home.'

So saying, he tore another strip off his shirt, and fastened up the other end of the improvised mummy-case. The corpse now looked as though it was in splints for a broken back.

'I'll have ter leave the tools here,' reflected the old man. 'I can't carry everythink. I'll shove 'em in a log till termorrer. Come on, Brummy, we'll git home.'

He up-ended Brummy, and, placing his shoulder against the middle of the lower sheet of bark, lifted the corpse to a horizontal position, then, taking the bag of bones in his hand, started for home.

'I ain't spending such a dull Christmas arter all,' he reflected as he plodded on; but had not walked above a hundred yards when he suddenly saw a black 'gohanna' sidling off into the grass by the side of the path.

'That's another of them dang things!' he exclaimed. 'That's two I seen this morning.'

'Yer don't smell any too sweet, Brummy,' he continued presently, addressing the corpse. 'It must have jist been about the middle of shearing when yer pegged out. I wonder who got yer last cheque. Shoo ! there's another black gohanna—there must be a flock on 'em.'

He rested Brummy on the ground while he had another pull at the bottle, and, before starting again, packed the bag of bones on his shoulder under Brummy, but soon stopped again.

'The thunderin' jumpt-up bones won't keep straight,' he said. 'Ole on, Brummy, 'n' I'll fix 'em;' and he leaned the dead man against a tree while he settled the bones on his shoulder, and took another pull at the bottle.

About a mile further on he heard a rustling in the grass to the right, and, looking round, saw another black 'gohanna' gliding off sideways with its long snaky neck turned to watch him.

This puzzled the old man considerably, and the strangest part of it was that Five Bob would not touch the reptile, even when ordered to 'sick 'em,' but slunk off with his tail between his legs.

'Theer's sothin' uncanny about them theer gohannas,' said the old man at last. 'I seen swarms of grasshoppers 'n' big mobs of kangeroos, but dang me if ever I seen a flock of black gohannas before!'

On reaching the hut the old man dumped the corpse over his shoulder against the wall, wrong end up, and stood scratching his head while he endeavoured to collect his muddled thoughts; but he had not placed Brummy at the correct angle to the wall, and consequently that individual fell forward and struck him a violent blow on the shoulder with the iron toes of his Blucher boots.

The shock sobered him. He sprang a good yard and instinctively hitched up his moleskins in preparation for flight, till a backward glance revealed to him the true cause of this attack from the rear. Then he lifted the body, stood it on its feet against the chimney, and ruminated as to where he should lodge his mate for the night, not noticing that the shorter sheet of bark had slipped down on the boots and left the face exposed.

'I 'spect I'll have ter put yer into the chimney-trough for the night, Brummy,' said he, turning round to confront the corpse. 'Yer can't expect me to take you into the hut, though I did it when yer was in a worse state than—Lord!'

The shepherd was not prepared for the awful scrutiny (if so it might be named) that gleamed on him from those empty sockets; his nerves received a severe shock, and it was some time before he recovered himself sufficiently to speak.

'Now look here, Brummy,' said he, shaking his finger severely at the delinquent, 'I don't want to be hard on yer; I'd do as much for yer 'n' more than any other man, 'n' well yer knows it; but if yer starts playin' any of yer jumpt-up larks on me, and a-scarin' of me after a-humpin' of yer home, by the holy frost ('n' that's sweerin' to it) I'll kick yer to jim-rags.'

This admonition delivered, he hoisted Brummy into the chimney-trough, and with a last glance towards the sheep-yards, he retired to his bunk to enjoy a well-earned nap.

He had more than a nap, however, for when he woke it was dark, and the bushman's instinct told him that it must be nearly nine o'clock.

He lit the fat lamp and poured the remainder of the rum into a pannikin; but just as he was about to lift the draught to his lips he heard a peculiar rustling sound on the roof, and he put the pot down on the table with a slam that made some of the contents jump out.

The dog crept close to his master and whimpered, and the old shepherd, used, as one living alone in the bush must necessarily be, to all that is weird and dismal, felt for once, at least, the icy breath of fear at his heart.

He then loaded his old single-barrel shot-gun hastily, and went out to investigate. He walked round the hut several times and examined the roof on all sides, but saw nothing; the corpse appeared to be in the same position.

At last, persuading himself that the noise was caused by 'possums or the wind, the old man returned to his hut, boiled the billy, and after composing his nerves somewhat with a light supper and a meditative smoke, retired for the night. He was aroused several times before midnight by the same peculiar rustling sound above his head, and though he rose and examined the roof on each occasion by the light of the moon, which had risen, discovered nothing.

At last he determined to sit up and watch until daybreak, and for this purpose took up a position on a log a little distance from the hut, with his gun laid across his knees in readiness.

About an hour later he saw a black object coming over the ridgepole, and fired. It fell, and he ran round to the opposite side of the hut, where there was an immense black 'gohanna' in violent convulsions on the ground.

Then the old man saw it all. 'The thunderin' jumpt-up thing!' he exclaimed; 'it's that same danged first gohanna a-follered of me home, 'n' has been havin' his Christmas dinner of Brummy, and a-hauntin' of me into the bargain.'

As there was no one by whom he could send a message to the station, and the old man dared not leave the sheep and go himself, he determined to bury Brummy the next afternoon, reflecting that the authorities could disinter the corpse for inquest if they pleased.

So he brought the sheep home early, and made arrangements for the burial by measuring the outer casing of Brummy both ways, and digging a hole according to those dimensions.

'Come on, Brummy, it's time yer turned in,' said he, lifting the body down. He carried it to the grave and lowered it down in one corner, end first, like a post. He then arranged the bark so as to cover the face, and by means of a line dropped the body to a horizontal position, threw in an armful of gum leaves, and then very reluctantly took the shovel and dropped in a few shovelfuls of earth; then he paused.

'Arter all,' he said, leaning on his spade and wiping his brow—'arter all it war Brummy!'

This reflection seemed to engender a flood of memories, in which the old man became absorbed. He leaned heavily upon his spade and thought.

'Brummy,' he said at last, 'it's all over now; nothin' matters now; nothin' didn't ever matter, nor don't. You uster say as how it 'ud be all right termorrer (pause); termorrer's come, Brummy—come fur you—it ain't come fur me yet, but it's comin'.'

He threw in some more earth. 'Yer don't remember, Brummy, 'n' mebbe yer don't want to remember—I don't want to remember—but—but—well, yer see that's w'ere yer got the pull on me.' His mind was evidently wandering.

He shovelled in some more earth and paused again.

The dog rose with ears erect and looked anxiously first at his master and then down into the grave.

'Theer oughter be somethin' sed,' muttered the old man; ''tain't right to put 'im under like a dog. There oughter be some sort of sarmin'.' He sighed heavily in the silence that followed this remark, and, proceeding with his work, filled the grave to the brim this time, and fashioned the mound carefully with his spade. Once or twice he muttered the words, 'I am the rassaraction.' He was evidently trying to remember the something that 'oughter be sed,' and stood by the side of the grave. He removed his hat, placed it carefully on the grass, held his open hands out from his sides and a little to the front, drew a long deep breath, and said with a solemnity that greatly disturbed Five Bob, 'Hashes ter hashes, dus ter dus, Brummy.' Then he sat down and covered his face with his hands.

And the sun sank again on the grand Australian bush—the nurse and tutor of eccentric minds, the home of the weird, and much that is different from things in other lands.

'Price Warung' (William Astley)

The Pegging-Out of Overseer Franke

1892

I — THE PRELIMINARIES

I.

PHILIP Franke was his name, and his grade was Overseer of the Outer Domain Gang. Originally a drummer-boy in the 73rd Regiment, he, by much musical beating of the tattoo and reveille, and by a fine enthusiasm in the use of the cat when a comrade was lashed to the halberds in Barrack Square, had achieved promotion in the regiment. He had won the sergeant's stripes, and with them the commendation of his superiors, and the hearty, undisguised hatred of every one—'Government labour,' soldier, or lower class 'free'—over whom at any time he exercised authority. A pleasant fellow to look at, save that he was rather undersized, he had a round chubbiness of feature which was suggestive of Primeval Innocence and Uncorrupted Virtue. No man could look more un-Systematic or more cherubic; and when Mr. Lewin, the distinguished botanist and artist, was searching for models for the group of angels he was painting for the lady of his Excellency Governor Macquarie—Mrs. Macquarie favoured Mr. Lewin with many commissions—it is not surprising to learn, firstly, that Lieutenant-Colonel O'Connell promised to send him some one from the Barracks who he thought would serve Mr. Lewin's purpose; and, secondly, that Sergeant Philip Franke was, in consequence, depicted by the artist as reposing on a remarkably neat arrangement of snowy *cumuli.*

The incident is mentioned here as demonstrating the regard in which his officers held Franke, and also as indicating the foundation for the widespread convict belief that Franke would never get any nearer heaven than those pictured clouds would carry him.

Truth to say, the qualities which were most generally manifested by Philip Franke were not such as to commend him to the loving appreciation of the 'Government labour,' or of the rank-and-file. And when on the 19th day of March, 1814, it was known that Sergeant Franke had received his Excellency's special permission to remain behind when his regiment was relieved by the 46th under Colonel Molle, there was a wild break-out of hilarity in Barrack Square, and a corresponding depression of spirits among the out-labour passports. For in the same breath that it was made known that Franke had received Governor Macquarie's permission, it was announced that he retired on pension to the Overseership of the O. D. Gang.

His Excellency the Major-General's farewell proclamation to the 73rd was read out by the Brigade-Major at morning parade. When the paragraph—

> In adverting to their Services in this Colony, although unhappily Events have occurred which must always occasion the deepest Regret, as well to the Corps as to the Major-General, it must be recollected that the Odium attending those ACTS OF DEPRAVITY ought in Justice only to extend to the Perpetrators of them,

was reached, a murmur rolled through the ranks—'Acts o' depravutty! Th' spyin o' Sargeant Franke, th' measley sot!' The files on parade had memories that at that particular moment were not to be appeased by rounded periods of glowing eulogy. His Excellency went on to express his opinion that—

> This Station has not afforded the usual Field for Military Glory, but, in as far as the industrious Exertions of those Non-commissioned Officers and Privates who could be spared from Military Duty have

been concerned, this Colony is much indebted for many useful Improvements, which, but for the soldiers of the 73rd Regiment, must have remained only in the Contemplation of those anxious for its Civilization for a Length of Time.

He might go even beyond that magnificent tribute—he might go to the length of averring that—

The Comforts enjoyed by the Colonists in Consequence of the zealous and laborious Exertions of the Soldiers of the 73rd Regiment will long be remembered with their grateful Recollections.

But even balm of that sort could not heal the wound Macquarie had inflicted when he had given Corporal Franke an extra stripe for playing the sneak and turning barrack-room and parade-ground into sub-divisions of hell.

Healing for that wound came only when it was known later the same day that Sergeant Franke was to stop behind, having obtained fifty acres of land and an overseership.

'But O Lord, boys, what'll life be worth now for them convicts as he's over?'

This was the barrack-room sentiment. And it was not thought merely and kept in the thinker's own mind, but spoken openly without reserve as a soldier should speak. And it was applauded bravely when spoken.

For with the sergeant would pass away the chief spy of the regiment, and the lesser spies feared the rank-and-file more than they were regarded by the officers. None of the lesser spies were gifted like Phil Franke with sweet manners and a cherub's face, and consequently none could get the ear of the Colonel and the Major-General. With every disposition to emulate Franke's career as a reporter to the High Powers to barrack and guard-room discontent, two or three non-coms. and several privates had been unfortunately deprived by Nature of the qualities necessary for success. Which circumstance, if looked at in the proper light, will appear a matter for regret, inasmuch as in the barrack-room of the 73rd rebellion was always in an incipient stage, and the expenditure on a few military executions would have conduced greatly to the prosperity of the country.[1] At any time in our colonial history up to 1825 it would have been an easy thing for our Prætorian Guards to have wrested the control of the colony from the Constituted Powers, and more than one such plot had been in

course of incubation within the quarters of the 73rd. That the eggs were
addled was largely due to our hero, Franke.

II.

Overseer Franke was installed in office the day after the 73rd had marched
down to the Cove and embarked for Calcutta. The Outer Domain Gang,
as was the case with all low-class labour (as distinguished from the
mechanics), were quartered on the west side of the town in the sheds that
surrounded the Old Country Gaol. From their squalid living-place to the
scene of their daily work was a good three-mile walk, and that distance
suggested to the fertile brain of the Overseer an idea. It occurred to him
the very day he assumed command, but he was too astute to play the new
broom all at once, so he deferred promulgating it in the ears of the
Authorities till he had been some weeks in office.

Then he enunciated it to the Superintendent of Convicts, and the
Superintendent of Convicts passed it on approvingly to the Chief Engineer,
and the Chief Engineer quietly appropriated it as his own, and strongly
recommended it to Governor Macquarie, who was graciously pleased, in his
capacity of Head of the State and Deputy-Providence, to adopt it.

Now, the idea, when we come to state it in cold-blooded print at this
time of day, does not challenge admiration either by its daring audacity or
sublime originality. The defect, however, is not in the idea, but in us. To
appreciate an historic fact, you must weigh and estimate it in the light of
the day on which it happened. And the day when Overseer Franke
generated, and the Chief Engineer appropriated, and the Governor acted
upon the Idea, was the Day of Small Economies. The genius of Old
Sydney in Macquarie's early years of administration was the genius of
lavish expenditure, but in his later epoch, the fine old ruler worshipped at
the throne of another God. Things were so skimped that even the
hangmen were compelled to be economical in the matter of hemp. They
wished to hang twenty Condemned one day in '21 in Lower George
Street, and the Sheriff could not succeed in getting together more rope
than would suffice to 'top off' nineteen. It would have detained the crowd
and the Sheriff another hour from breakfast to have hanged No. 20 with
the rope which had already despatched No. 1, and so, as the high
functionary dare not anticipate his next quarter's advance by purchasing
rope on credit, he put back No. 20 for a week.

It is from the circumstance, then, that the spirit of economy was abroad
that Mr. Franke's idea derives its importance.

Instead of marching his gang from quarters to the site of their work every morning, and marching them back every night, he proposed that he should camp out with them the week through, bringing them in for muster—and divine service—from Saturday to Monday.

This was his plan. In the light of the Administration, it was Splendid, Capital! For it promised to save the Government, time, sinew, boots, money. If, in the process of economy, it also lost a soul or two, well, that consideration could not be permitted access to the Authorities' judgment for one second's audience.

Mr. F. A. Hely, Principal Superintendent of Convicts, once remarked to Father Ullathorne, Vicar-General of Roman Catholics: 'Absurd, my dear sir! You ask us to consider souls. That's your business! The Administration has to consider *cash*!'

And Mr. Hely was right. He generally was. When, for instance, he sent seventy-three assigned servants—exactly fifty more than he was entitled to—to his estate of 5120 acres, an estate for which he had paid £16 13s. 4d., there can't be the least doubt he was right. Consequently, being never in error, his opinion as to the folly of giving heed to souls when cash was concerned, must be respected.

III.

Nevertheless, that heedlessness was the weak spot in Franke's plan, as the sequel proved. It precipitated his pegging-out.

When Franke took charge of the gang there was about five years' clearing work to do on the hilly land which ran from Windmill Ridge to the South Head Road. All the area now known as Darlinghurst was then wooded, sparsely in places, but for the most part the timber was thick. The task of clearing and burning-off with such appliances as were at command of the outer gang was heavy, and the allowance of five years' time was by no means excessive for the undertaking. The Chief Engineer, however, was able to report, two years after the new Overseer had originated his idea, that the marked-out work would be completed by the gang a good twelve months under the allotted period. For this satisfactory achievement the C.E. not unnaturally took the most considerable proportion of credit, but still he did not withhold some tribute of appreciation from Franke. The Overseer, indeed, should have had all, as it was by his plan that the gang had got through so much work.

The only people dissatisfied were the gangers. The average number of men in the gang was twenty, and the official power which directly controlled them was made up by the Overseer, three soldiers, and a scourger. Notwithstanding this ample manifestation of care by the Authorities, the gang grew discontented, and had to be soothed back at sundry times into contentment and resignation by two hangings, about a dozen of imprisonments, and several score of floggings.

But even gentle remedies of that kind were not potent to keep always within bounds the turbulence of felon-spirits that feel themselves injured by three things which we shall enumerate in the order of their importance as they stood in the estimation of the genial Overseer's *protégés*.

Firstly, the gangers objected to the deprivation of their daily walk, or rather shuffle—men with single or double irons on could not walk—to and from the town barracks. They would not have minded so much had the time, ordinarily consumed by the out-gangs in passing from the barracks to the working-places and back again, been allowed them for rest. But that was not so; they had to work those two or three hours. Thus their hours of labour were literally from sunrise to sunset, though other gangs worked, say, three hours less.

Secondly, the camping-out system practically gave control of their ration and clothes allowances to Overseer Franke. And Overseer Franke, as became an intelligent officer of the System, was not slothful in the business of deriving a very substantial addition to his recognized emoluments from those same allowances.

And, thirdly, they lost the sweet solace of companionship with minds that ran in other grooves of duty, which they would have enjoyed had they been barracked nightly. 'There is no apparent motive for the prisoner's murder of the deceased!' remarked C. J. Forbes, at a later day, in the preface to his summing-up on a capital charge. 'Beg your Honour's parding!' interrupted the prisoner, with a courteous desire to set the judge—all things considered, the noblest man who ever sat on a N.S.W. Supreme Court Bench—right, 'my motive's plain 'nuff. I wanted a change! I got so wery tired of gang-work—there was no wariety in it at all!' Well, that was just the matter with Franke's gangers. The nightly chat in barracks would have been a safety-valve for their natures, and conveyed some refreshment to their minds; but in camp their speech was dammed-up, and their lips, if they did move audibly after 'lights out!' were in danger of being sealed with a leaden seal. 'Fire into the tents, sentry, if yer hear as the men's a-talkin' together. They may be concoctin' mutiny!' Thus the seven men who, on the average, were the occupants of each tent (eight by eight its floor area) were dumb perforce.

There is no tyranny like that of the petty tyrant, and there is no torture like that suffered by his victims. The very littleness of the source of authority adds another and acuter pang to the pain. Had the thousand and one miserable restrictions imposed by ex-Sergeant Franke been directly ordered by a nominal gentleman, or by an officer of commissioned rank, they would have been borne the easier. Only a man with vermin-soul could have designed and put into force some of the methods adopted by Mr. Franke for the subjugation of his men, and being what he was, he was not restrained by any regard for the common humanity which the convict shared with himself, such as even a Foveaux or a Rossell affected (if he did not feel) at times. Intoxicate a creature of his low stamp with the absolutism of power, and you would develop a wretch that even Pluto, who, so far as is known of him, has one or two gentlemanly instincts, would surely be loth to employ. Foveaux, after hanging a man in the presence of his wife and child, patted the latter on its back kindly and told it to 'Never mind! mammy'll get you a new daddy soon, p'r'aps!' Franke would not have done that—he would have shown the little one its father dangling at the rope's-end, and would have smiled as he did it.

For Franke was the most ingeniously devilish of the low-caste sons of the System that we have come across. To what degree of excellence he would have attained had the Outer Domain Gang not interrupted his official career it is impossible to say.

That thing they did: in the third year of his Overseership they shortened his official career—at least so far as the System was concerned, for there is no saying what use could be found for him otherwise—by terminating his life.

Now that was unkind of the gang, it will be admitted. The amount of work done by it under Phil Franke's intelligent direction was so much larger, as we have said, than could have been expected, that the Chief Engineer had marked out for Franke in his mind's eye a wider and still more remunerative field of labour. And of these new emoluments and this deserved promotion, Franke's gangers robbed him.

IV.

There had come a new man to the gang. Occasionally, though rarely, it happened that a ganger would remain deaf to the wiles of the System, and would refuse to extend his seven years to fourteen, or his fourteen to 'life.' The men of Old Sydney held out countless inducements to Government men to extend their term of 'Gov'ment labour' indefinitely, or till it reached the foot of the gallows, but now and then it would occur that a transport resisted the temptation in the shape of scourgings and starvings to remain on the muster-rolls, and became free.

Such an event had just happened. One Saturday evening when the gang went into the town for Sunday Chapel and muster, one of the gangers dropped out an expiree, and Mr. Overseer Franke was consequently able to present no more than eighteen at the muster.

'Overseer Franke, how is it your gang is only eighteen?' demanded the Barrack-master; 'your strength's twenty.'

'Yes, sir, but your Honour has forgotten that one man got his certificate yesternight____'

'That's nineteen!'

'And one is waitin' trial, your Honour, for assaultin' me.'

'Ah, that's the score, but you're still one short, then! There, go to No. 2 yard and pick out a likely fellow.'

'Yes, sir!'

And in a second, he had passed into the inner quadrangle of the Muster-yard—some of the stone wall is still standing—where one hundred and forty newly-landed transports were huddled, pending inspection.

Up and down the ranks of sickly wretches—they had been seven months on the voyage, and short of water and lime-juice for the last month—he passed, closely scrutinizing the cargo. It was a regulation that the Governor, or, if that was not convenient, the Colonial Secretary, should allot each new-comer to the work for which he was best suited. The regulation had been obeyed in the case of the *Coromandel* cargo. On the previous morning (Saturday) his Excellency had inspected the 'indent,' and had selected every man who said he was, or seemed to be, a mechanic. Then he had ordered the rest to 'gang-labour,' and thus left them to the tender mercies of the Overseer. There are more ways than one of carrying out a regulation.

'A crawling, scurvy lot!' commented Overseer Franke to the yard constable. 'I want a strong, wiry 'un, an' there don't seem to be one in the batch.'

'Try this cove wots over here,' suggested the constable, and pointed as he spoke to where a man, under the medium height, but otherwise well proportioned, stood, the centre of a ragged group. 'This chap ain't much muscle to look at, but he's blooded—he's got sperrit, I should say, an' 'udn't prove a shiser. You try him, Mr. Franke, sir. Here, you feller, stand out!'

The 'fellow' stood. The grime of confinement did not blur altogether the fine lines of his face, and the delicate nostrils of the long nose, the sweep of the eyelashes, and the chiselling of the mouth, indicated blood and gentle nurture, while the straightforward, lucid eyes spoke equally clearly of a disposition of integrity. It was a mystery how such a man came to be included in the ring of degraded scum, possibly only to be explained by a sudden lapse into a criminal deed, or, as an alternative (of which there are many instances in convict archives), that he was bearing the brunt of some rich or great man's crime.

'Your name, feller?'

'Edgar Allison Mann,' was the reply, respectful in tone.

'Edgar *Man*!' exclaimed the Overseer, aghast at the fancied affront to his dignity. '*Man*! Do you know as you're talking to a Hoverseer?'

'Mann, sir, I said—M-a-n-n! Edgar Allison are my Christian names.'

'Ah, that's it, is it! Now, jest look here, young feller, we ain't a-goin' to put up with your inserlence.'

'I meant no insolence! You misunderstood me, sir!'

'Misunderstood yer, did I! Now, wot's that but inserlence, I'd like to know? Ain't it inserlence, constable?'

'It must be, Mr. Franke, sir, if you say so; you have 'ad more experience than me, sir.'

'By my lights, my flash cove, I'll have to take your flashness out of yer. A-tellin' me that I misunderstood yer! Wot'll yer say next, I wonder!'

'That—you—are—a—blackguard—who—has—been—invested—with—a—little—brief—authority—over—your—betters!'

The yard-constable held his breath; Overseer Franke let his tongue loll out in amazement; did he hear aright, or had his senses deceived him? Did the audacious transport really mean to call him all that? The only sound to be heard in that yard for some seconds was the half-suppressed chuckle from a transport who was out on his second voyage: 'Lord, ain't the swell a-crackin' a whid in prime twig!'[2]

'Wot's that yer say?' Franke, when he had got over the shock, said. 'Wot's that?'

Word for word, pausing between each as he had done before, the transport repeated his former speech.

The whole yard looked for a burst of anger, and an immediate presentment of the offender before the Barrack-master with a request for condign punishment. A genius like Franke, however, was above doing what common constables and newly-landed transports expected from him. He knew a trick worth two of immediate punishment.

'Yer'll do, my man! I likes a feller with pluck for my gang, for it gives me som'at to do to break him in! March to the outer yard there—yer are a-going to jine No. 3 Outer, d'ye hear that?'

When Mr. Franke marched back on Monday morning to the heights beyond Windmill Ridge, there went with him Edgar Allison Mann, No. 14–736, as the twentieth man of his gang.

V.

Mann adjusted himself with philosophic fortitude to the terrible conditions under which he was placed. Reticent as to his past, he strove by whispered word and the example of a manly bearing where the whole routine was carefully designed to stamp out even the physical type of manliness, to encourage his wretched fellow-gangers to look to the future, to bear up under the infinite degradations of the present by forcing their minds to anticipate a brighter and happier time. His influence at the end of three months was extraordinary. Even the Overseer could not but notice it, and should have rejoiced at it, as in the quietude of the gang they worked better. But their superior discipline provoked Franke, for it was none of his doing—caused, instead, by a spirit which he regarded as rebellious, and by methods he considered insubordinate, and Mann's conquest over the rude hearts of his fellow-gangers was the more galling as it was a proof that he, the Overseer, had failed to break Mann's spirit in the first week of the young transport's inclusion in the gang.

He had taken offence at the way Mann saluted him, and understanding clearly that nothing was more harassing to a convict of 'superior position' than the necessity he was hourly under of 'capping' to the penal officers, he put him through a course of instruction. He had permitted the soldier-guard to supervise the labour of the gang one forenoon while he devoted himself to 'a-larnin' the gen'elman how to s'lute.'

For three mortal hours he kept Mann marching to and fro on a path six yards long in front of the tents. He sat on a stool in the opening of a tent, midway between the points at which the convict had to turn upon his heel, and every time of passing, he ordered the prisoner to salute.

'One, two, three, four—s'lute. Hand to your peak; higher, feller!' Mann would obey and proceed. Returning, it would be—

'One, two, three, four—s'lute. Left hand to left leg, right brought smartly up, an' held there till yer pass the orf'cer as yer payin' honour to—d'ye hear that, pris'ner, *a-payin' honour to!*'—he would laugh gaily here, as though to accentuate the stabbing insult; then 'One, two, three, four.' And so to the end of the walk.

After that exercise of three hours' duration, Mr. Franke turned to the transport, and said, with a heavenly smile lighting up his cherub's visage—

'And now, Mann, d'yer think yer'll know another day 'ow to salute properly?'

'I think so, sir!' responded Mann, with as sweet a smile. 'I think so! I'll not forget this lesson.' And in the self-abasement which dare not groan aloud, he resolved he would not.

He dare not groan at that or countless other insults, because groaning would have provoked the application of the lash to his back. And Mann dare not, for his soul's sake, do that. Like the poor sinner at Macquarie Harbour, who told Surgeon Barnes that once he was flogged he did not care a brass farden what became of him—he'd as soon go to hell as not—for his thoughts were hell after the lash had bitten him (Charles Buller, to whom the Australias owe so much, wept as he heard Barnes' narrative)—Mann knew he was done for once the cat stung him. He would no longer be a man—a human being; he would be an animal that cringed before such a creature as Phil Franke, or he would be a desperate, blood-craving beast. No, he *dare not* be flogged. Always he held himself up with that hope that he would always keep to the weather-side of the Overseer's mad passion.

But there was no knowing what a day would bring forth in Old Sydney times, when the monarch of the hour was a cherub of the Franke variety. Mann *was* flogged—forty stripes save one. 'That's Scriptooral, pris'ner,' grinned the Cherub—forty was Overseer's limit—'an' I'll take care the scourger don't give yer more. Peel!'

'Peel,' he, Mann, perforce did; and as he stripped for the punishment, he swore to his Maker that, before the next Saturday, the Cherub should have a chance of seeing what the earth looked like from another sphere.

The cause of the punishment was Mann's championship of another ganger.

The weekly ration of O. D. Gang consisted of four pounds of salt pork one week, and seven pounds of fresh beef the next, the flour-food being, week in and week out, ten pounds of wheat and six pounds of maize, ground by the prisoners themselves, in *their own time*, mixed with cold water.

But Overseer Franke, having been appointed, by reason of being in 'detached camp,' a storekeeper, was entitled to make issues from store to himself, as Overseer. And he would not have attained to the eminence he possessed as an official if he had not contrived to turn this arrangement to account.

As Storekeeper, he was entitled to buy, at the rate fixed by the Governor, meat, wheat, and maize, giving an order on the Deputy-Commissary-General for the payment.

As Storekeeper, he would issue to the Overseer (himself) the scheduled allowance of rations, taking his own receipt for the quantity of produce.

And as Overseer, he would issue to his men what he pleased. And he pleased to issue very little. He, as a fact, robbed them of nearly half.

One Monday an elderly transport, a coarse, languid, brutish 'First-fleeter,' working in the hot sun, fell ill. He was thrust into the shade of the gums till knock-off time, and then carried to the tent, one of the tent-party being Mann.

In the still watches of a moonlit night, the sick man became delirious for want of nourishment or from the sunstroke. Mann rose and, as noiselessly as possible, so as not to disturb the other poor fellows whom slumber mocked, asked him, 'Could he do anything for him?' But the First-fleeter, in his delirium, made no coherent answer.

Mann went to the fly-opening, and called: 'Sentry!'

The one sentinel on night duty—twelve hours at a stretch—challenged him and ordered him to stand.

'Prisoner's dying!' Mann never would permit himself to fall into the use of the corrupt form 'pris'ner,' though nearly everybody, from the Governor, Judges, and parsons, down to the children in the streets, made the word a dissyllable. 'Prisoner's dying!'

The challenge had awoke the Overseer. He came to the mouth of his tent: 'What's that?'

'Pris'ner sick in No. 1,' reported the sentry.

'Who's that talking?'

'I—Mann—No. 20.'

'Back to your bed, Mann! Wot d'yer mean, my fine swell, disturbin' the gang at this hour?'

'The man—Cummings—is dying!'

'Wot's that to yer if he is! The rule o' camp is no talkin' arter "lights out." Back—'

'You are a murdering villain if you let this poor devil die!'

'Fire, sentry! Fire!' And by virtue of the authority which reposed in the bosom of the Overseer, the sentry obeyed. He fired point-blank—Mann had thrown himself down on his side of the tent—and First-fleeter Cummings' delirium merged into and ended with one deep, low groan.

In the flapping of a swallow's wing the young convict was out in the moonlight.

'Shoot me, you murderous scoundrel! Shoot me, if you dare, and all the soldiers in the colony will not save you from the dogs. Shoot me as you've shot that prisoner after starving him—he was ill because you robbed him of his rations. You've as much right to shoot me as that other, for you've robbed me, all of us, of our rations.'

A minute of silence. Then the Cherub spoke to some purpose.

'No, no, my fine feller—we don't waste powder an' shot on gentles. That's the death they like. It's the cat as yer don't like, an' it's the cat as yer a-goin' to have. Scourger!'

At two o'clock in the morning, on the height of Woolloomooloo, with the soft sea-breezes chanting plaintively through sassafrass and eucalyptus, Mann got his thirty-nine! Thirty-nine was scriptural.

VI.

From that morning Mann changed bodily, mentally, morally. From that morning he lived only for revenge; he would not even wait to see what justice would come forth at the Sunday muster.

When the gang went out to day-labour, the camp was in charge of the soldier who had gone on duty at daybreak. This day the soldier, instead of taking his usual sleep, was obliged to continue his sentinelship, for he had to watch over the writhing body of Convict Mann and the stiff one of Convict Cummings.

What passed between Mann and the sentry can be inferred by the circumstance that the soldier threw in his fate with the gang when they made their bolt, as they did three nights later—on the Thursday.

On the Thursday night they bolted, under Mann's leadership, and seized a schooner which lay out in the main stream. Overseer Franke, of course, raised a remonstrance as to their going, but they treated it as unpolitely as they did his complaint that they were hurting him, when they pegged him out—*alive*—with tent-pegs and lines—on an ant-hill in the heavily-timbered gorge between two hills.

Alive—with food just *outside* of his reach—and a bullet-hole through his right hand, into which aperture the ants were directed by the ingenuity of one Mann, who made a sweet track of the Overseer's ration sugar from a hole in the hill to the hole in the hand.

About eight or nine years afterwards, Mr. Absalom West was clearing some ground in Bark 'Um Glen—now refined into Barcom—when he came upon a skeleton—pegged out.

II — The Completion of the Deed

I.

Overseer Franke, of the Outer Domain Gang, working on the heights of Woolloomooloo, and engaged in clearing (by means of convicts' agony) the wooded ranges of hills and network of gullies, so as to make room for the perfume-breathing plants of civilization, had been rudely interrupted in his slumbers. One of the gang, Convict Cummings, being half-starved, sun-smitten, and overworked, had become delirious in the mid-hours of the night, and another transport—Mann—had set the Regulations at defiance by imploring the sentry's aid for the sick wretch, his tent-mate. Thereupon, Mr. Overseer Franke had awoke from his beauty-sleep and had ordered the sentry to still Mann's rebellious tongue with a bullet. The sentry fired in Mann's direction, but the bullet had found its destined billet in Convict Cummings' body—and Convict Cummings had ceased from troubling. Unfortunately, the wicked Mann, having evaded the shot, did not rest. He upbraided Overseer Franke for having murdered Cummings. He became positively insulting—and was flogged.

At two o'clock in the morning, at a spot somewhere, we take it, about where Liverpool Street of Modern Sydney dips into Womerah Avenue, Darlinghurst, Convict Edgar Allison Mann received thirty-nine lashes.

And Mann was 'gently born;' and when the back of a gently-born transport had once been stained with the infamous stigma of the lash-point, only two things, if he were not to become utterly bestial, remained for him to do: to kill his tyrant, and—to die.

And Convict Mann, being at heart a really fine fellow—being, moreover, a firm believer in Shandy's doctrine that a man's name influenced his character; being, in a word, manly, lost not a minute in coming to the resolve to do both things.

'Peel!' had ordered Overseer Franke.

Mann had obeyed, making a remark as he did so:

'Flog me, and by God who looks from the heaven above, you're a dead man, Mr. Franke!' And then correcting himself, as though before he were subjected to the degrading ordeal he would assert his manhood, he repeated the words, but dropped the title.

'You're a dead man, *Franke!*'

'Scourger—thirty-nine!' laughed Franke. He might have made the penalty forty lashes—beyond forty an overseer could not go—but he read his Bible, did Franke—also the Regulations. 'Thirty-nine' was scriptural. And it was one on the safe side of the Regulation allowance.

All through the next day when the only living occupants of the camp were the sentry (the one who had shot Cummings) and himself—Cummings was, of course, also there, but though he was a present horror and outrage, he was in the past tense—Convict Mann nourished himself upon the lees of his cup of shame. And the draught turned to the acid of revenge in his mouth. By the time the gang returned to work after the nooning repast, he had forgotten, however, for a brief space, his physical pangs in the pleasure of anticipation.

He had formed a scheme by which to obtain the freedom of the gang and his revenge upon Overseer Franke.

The one recreation permitted to the gangers was a rare plunge into the waters of the inlet since known as Rushcutter's Bay, which was granted to them whenever they visited the Bay for the purpose of renewing the stock of rushes which composed their beds. The sedge at that time not only covered densely the low-lying areas between the arms of the Bay, but ran out in the inlet itself, and to gain a clear plunge the convicts were obliged to advance some hundreds of yards from the proper beach-line. More than one poor devil, having got so far, thought he would go farther, and had sought to dive and swim beyond the military guards' range. If the soldiers missed, however, there were other and still more vigilant guards (the sharks), and these never, so the Authorities believed, missed their man.

On the last occasion, six weeks before, on which Overseer Franke had thought it desirable to refresh his 'labour' with a bath and with new bedding, Mann, with another ganger, going out a little farther than the others, found that a derelict ship's boat had been tide-borne into the Bay, and had nosed a short way into the spiky sea-growths. Their hearts had laboured mightily at the discovery, for the fates would be cruel indeed if, with such a tool to their hands, they could not win freedom somehow. They had kept the knowledge of the boat to themselves. They had driven the craft with all their might farther into the sedge, and then had diverted the attention of their fellow-gangers from the vicinity by raising the cry of 'A shark! a shark!' and by retreating hurriedly from the spot. And all the time that had intervened, the knowledge of the boat hidden in the rushes had soothed the ache of the hearts and hands of the two men. The boat was oarless, that was one disadvantage, but they did not always think of the deficiency. They dwelt upon what they had, not upon that which they had not.

This day—a Tuesday—which Convict Mann spent in camp, brooding over his shame and his revenge, he thought less, perhaps, of the boat than he had on other days—till the afternoon. Then, the recollection flashed upon him, and, all gashed and pain-stricken as he was, he strove to act upon it. He called the sentry.

'Sentry! Can I speak to you?'

The solider paused in his wearisome walk by the tent-month.

'Yes, Mann.'

'Will you do me a favour?'

'Ef it ben't agen Reg'lashuns.'

There was a moment's silence. Then—

'It's against the letter of the Regulations, but not against their spirit.'

'I don't know wot yer mean.'

'Well, the Regulation is that flogged prisoners should be turned out to work as soon as possible after the flogging, isn't it?'

'Yes.'

'Then I wish to get better soon—to get about the quicker. And a dip in the bay'll heal—the—back—quickly. The salt is good for it!'

'No-a! I'll not let yez go. Yez 'ud drounded yesself!'

'Sentry, what do they call me in the gang?'

'Gen'elman Ned.'

'Yes, Gentleman Ned! And though I'm lying here flogged'—then, for a second, restraint to which he was subjecting himself gave way, and he shivered and sobbed—the wrung agony of a strong man's sob!—in the impotency of his wrath. 'Though I'm here under punishment, I hope—I hope—I'm still a gentleman in that I won't lie. I'll come back, sentry, if you'll allow me to go!'

'Yez u'd not get there ef I let yez go. Yez too sick.'

'By Heaven, I would, sentry. My *will* will carry me, and back, if I had no other power.'

The solider—a pock-marked, skimpy-eyebrowed-and-haired fellow, with the irresoluteness expressed in his features of the creature who always been subject to rule—grew dubious.

'Ef it be th' salt as yez wants, th' Overseer 'ud 'a issued some 'a yez spoken for it. I might give yez some now.'

'The Overseer would place you under arrest for stealing the salt, if you did.

No; I would not ask you to do that, but the salt of the sea-bath would cure me quickly. On the word of a man who never *lied*, sentry, I'll come back.'

The sentry hesitated. If Mann did not keep his word, or became too ill to return before the Overseer and the gangers came back to camp at six o'clock, then he would be ruined. Mann read his thought.

'On my word of honour, sentry, I will be back before five o'clock. It is now about two. Weak as I am, I can do the distance in the time.'

'Strike your breast, an' swear be God that yez 'ud not ruin me.'

The crude, childish oath was taken. Mann struggled to his feet, swinging involuntarily round on his heel from weakness as he did so, and then invoking what strength he could, set out. Under some scrubby gums, offending the day with the rigidity of its contorted nakedness, lay the murdered thing. Feeble as he and blood-exhausted, Mann spent a little of his poor force in breaking off the feathery crest of a young wattle; and threw it on the corpse. There had been no opportunity to bury Cummings before the gang went to labour in the morning, and the interment would have to be performed by the men in their own time at night.

The sound of the breaking sapling directed the sentinel's notice to Mann. He ran up. 'Yez mustn't do that, Mann; Overseer left no orders,' he said, as he pulled the branch off the dead man.

At no era in its history did the System inculcate respect for the convict dead. The convict alive was carrion; dead, was carrion still.

II.

Mann dragged himself to the waterside through the scrub and timber. It was awful work—heroic in the endurance of suffering of the acutest kind. But he was whipped onwards by the shadow of the cat. Again and again he fell; and once when he fell he burst out in a wild spasm of anger, and swore by the heaven that smiled upon him and upon the System that he would not move from the spot. He grew delirious for a few minutes and fancied that Franke was chasing him with the sentries. 'Come on! Come on, ye devils!' he shouted, but they did not come, for they were not there. And then the rustle of the breeze in the wattles and the gums, while it cooled his brain for the moment, and momentarily banished the fever of madness, played, too, its tricks with his fancy. The interlacing shadows caused by the movement of the branches seemed to him a horrid play of floggers' whips. The air was full of 'cat-tails'—they whistled, they were falling upon him, they would lacerate him yet again! In his dread he rose and turned to flee, and in the turning dashed his head against the jagged end of a limb that had been ruptured by a southerly squall. The wood ripped into his cheek, but the gashing of the flesh was his salvation. The inflamed blood was eased through the wound, and he became rational again.

He cursed his fate that he had become clearer in head, though his weakness of body had increased with the outflow of blood. And he cried against the God that would not let him die in a blessed unconsciousness of dying. But again his mood changed. He remembered his promise to the sentry and addressed Heaven once more. This time it was in prayer. He bent his head, and craved strength to keep his word. 'Let it not be said that Gentleman Ned had proved false to the trust placed in him by the miserable wretch of a soldier-guard!' A poor prayer, indeed, and if wholly sane he would have spurned the paltry vanity that prompted it. Perhaps, however, all unknowing to himself the Power whom he approached had Himself framed the pleading. The only evidence the lower-class creature, free or convict, had in those days of the existence of a Power that was true and righteous and just, was a brother-man's word. A broken vow, a violated promise—and away went the betrayed one's faith in God, truth, honour, justice, everything.

Stumbling, staggering, now leaning against a tree for rest, now pressing his lips against the exuding gum on eucalyptus boles, he went on to the rushes, crying aloud sometimes for help and sometimes hoarsely whispering to himself in pity of his own plight—moving while two voices echoed in his ears: 'The boat! The sentry!' If he could only find the boat safe! If he could only return to the sentry in time to prevent the man being punished for the breach of good discipline caused by his permitting him to leave camp! Onward to the boat, back to the tents! Once—he gave up and moved in his return path! And then, the thought of the boat spurred him forward again.

III.
At last, he reached the Bay. Then his strength came back to him impetuously. He crashed through the reed-beds out to the circle of blue water, and plunged into the shallows. The brine stung him, pricked him— it punctured him in a thousand pores, but it renewed his vigour, and supposing there had been human eye to see, he had been cheered for the boldness with which he parted the waves as he swam towards the point in the sedgy arc where the boat had been driven in by himself and the other convict. With the boat was freedom, perhaps happiness, for the gang; and

though the rush-edges cut his back and thighs, he was reckless of the smarts in the exhilaration of the conquest over himself, his weakness, Franke, the System—a victory symbolized by that swim through the cool, foam-flecked billows. He laughed in his sense of triumph as he recognized where his brother-ganger, in forcing his way out again from the dense growths, had broken off short the dagger-points of a cluster of reeds. He laughed again when the outer line of sedges closed behind his own path, as, treading water, he drove himself into the springy mass, and saw the plants which he and his mate had bent and bruised as they had pushed the boat before them. It was a note of mighty exultation that laugh—which changed in its last accents to the dry cackle of a parching mouth.

The boat was gone!

Had freedom, and wealth, and home, and woman's love, and the prattle of one's child, and all other things that make life glorious, been offered to Convict Mann the next hour as a condition of his telling, he could not have related how he reached the camp again. But at five o'clock, just when the clod's brain of the guard was dimly pondering the question as to whether it was not time for Gen'elman Ned to be showing up, he flung himself gaspingly on his rush-bed. He could have told to an interrogator nothing but the one thing—that the recollection of the sentry waiting for the fulfillment of his vow had alone kept him from there and then throwing away the life so ridiculed of fate. To march through an Inferno to reach the boat—and then to find it gone! God!

Now, the sentry could not know of this disappointment, of course. All that the stupid fellow saw was that Mann had returned, and, diverging a yard from his 'go,' he strove to make himself as pleasant as it was right for Authority to condescend to when the person to be patronized was only a transport.

'Yez a-got back then, Mann? 'Ope as yez 'ad a raal noice swim, now!'

'Oh, blast you, blast you! Go away!' the tortured wretch exclaimed, and turning his head upon the rushes, recked nothing of the anger of the insulted soldier. Which, nevertheless, was not to be despised, for was he not the representative of the military power, and the civil power, and every other power on that hill-side, pending Overseer Franke's return.

IV.

At five minutes past six that personage came back to camp, closing with his two soldiers the procession of ironed labourers. He was affable, and, as the sentry saluted, asked him how the 'gen'elman' had passed the day.

' 'E war inserlent to me, y'r Honour—blarsted me!' reported the soldier.

'Mann!'

In his tent, the transport heard the command, and dragged himself to his feet to obey it.

'Mann!'

Haggard with his shame and with the horrible recoil from his hope that had acted as a new blister upon his hurts, Mann went out, and saluting, faced his tyrant.

'Yer've bin inserlent, Mann?'

The transport looked towards the sentry. And the sentry then remembered that, after all, it was Gentleman Ned who had cursed him— and Gentleman Ned had kept his word—and once upon a time Gentleman Ned had doubtless enjoyed the right to swear at common people like himself; and so—

'Mister Franke, I don't wish to press th' charge!'

'Oh, very well! Then we'll let yer orf this time lightly. An' so yer'll jest dig that stiff 'un's grave for punishment! I won't flog yer agen—yet!'

Mann's first impulse was to refuse—the next to strike Franke, and he had actually stepped a pace nearer to the latter when another and wiser thought occurred to him. He would dig the grave, for by so doing he would obtain a shovel which would serve the fell purpose he had in his mind. The hand he had raised to strike Franke he carried to his forehead in salute. Franke noticed the transition and laughed.

'That's right, Mann! Yer a-gettin' broken in, I see! There's nothin' like the cat for gentles arter all—it breaks the spirit so purtily.'

At 6.30—the gang had returned from labour at six o'clock—the evening muster was held. 'Tea'—twelve ounces of maize meal (reduced by the Overseer's peculation to ten) mixed with cold water—was rationed out, and then two men were told off to dig Cummings' grave.

'No. 20' (Mann).

'No. 7.' This was a feeble old fellow, one of the 'passengers' by the fatal 'second fleet'—'built in eclipse and rigged with curses dark'—whose constitution had never regained vigour after the terrible privations of a voyage that had been one long feast for the sharks which followed the vessels' wake.

'Nos. 20 an' 7—no, we don't give no precedunse to gentles in this 'ere neighb'rood. Nos. 7 and 20'll dig th' late Mister Cummins's' grave—an' make a tidy job of it—an' sink four foot!'

Mann and his co-sexton limped towards the scrub where the dead body lay. The Overseer followed them to mark out the grave. He ordered Mann to take from the heap of tools thrown down by the labourers a pick, and No. 7, a shovel. 'Ye're the younger man, No. 14-736'—when Franke was unusually genial he would address the convicts by their register numbers, and not merely by those of the gang-roll (and when Mr. Franke was genial the scourger was busy and happy)—'Ye're the younger man, an' jest yer take the pick, an' begin 'ere. Oh, it's the pick—an' the cat—as is good fer yer gentles. Oh'—the jeer changed dreadfully—'oh, help! Mutiny—'

The crashing of the pick closed the sentence. Well was it for Overseer Franke that the torture of the forenoon had drawn the strength from Mann's limbs and the oil from his sinews. The smooth handle of the tool slipped round in the transport's hands as he lifted it, and the pick struck the official's head with the side instead of the point. It was well, we say, for Franke; for the blow did not kill but only stunned him. Perhaps, though, it was ill that he survived.

The Overseer's cry had roused the guard. The few minutes that they could call their own of the whole twenty-four hours were those immediately following the muster for 'tea,' and before the night guard was set. It had been always a thought of Franke's that at that time of the day the convict mind was less disposed to study the whys and wherefores of a 'bolt' than at any other period, because the gangers would then be suffering from the lassitude of the day's severe labour, and the inertia which comes from stomachs filled—such filling!—after long fast. Consequently, he had never objected to a brief relaxation of military discipline. For a few minutes their muskets would be laid down by the three sentinels—their pipes would be lit—and they could feel themselves a trifle freer than the transports they guarded.

Now, by this circumstance—this illustration of his own magnanimity—was Overseer Franke undone. Had he permitted no relaxation of sentry-duty then, his cry would no sooner have reached the guards' ears than it would have elicited the speedy aid of a bullet—and it is quite unlikely that Convict Mann would have been missed a second time that day. As it was, though the three soldiers heard the sharp appeal for aid, they were some yards away from their muskets, and before they could reach the weapons, several of the convicts had rushed between them and the guard-tent. In the passing of the eye-gleam in which they saw Mann's deed, some of the wretches apprehended the consequences of the act, and, and, on the instant, became—men. Sottish they were one moment with the debased cravings of the creature that exists only to work, and be fed, and to sleep sleep that gives no rest; but they were men the next, under the influence of that blow for mastery. It wooed their manhood back to them.

And the guard were powerless to help the Overseer.

V.

Mann, having struck Franke to the earth, threw the pick down and strode towards the startled but pleased transports. One or two of the more adventurous of them, in that rebound towards mental independence, abandoned all caution, and cheered him. 'Well done, Gen'elman!' 'Well done, Mr. Mann!'

'I don't think I've killed him, coves,' said Mann, hardened into a vulgar familiarity of speech by the very deed which had strengthened the others' respect for him, 'he'll come to, presently. But I'll kill him then.'

A soldier—one of the two that had formed the gang-guard—at this, thought to withdraw himself quietly from the group. Instantly the action was noticed, and a ganger stopped him. 'No,' said the fellow, 'you don't get to the town. We've got a chance to bolt now, and we'd be—fools not to use it. What d'ye say, pals?'

Then Mann knew his task was easy—even without the boat. Unless he could tell them of the boat, he had not thought to win the assent of every member of the gang to an attempt to escape. Now, he understood that they had responded to his rebellious act as tinder to the spark.

'Yes,' he exclaimed, 'hold the lobsters.'

'You won't murder me, Mann?' entreated the soldier.

'No—but we will bind you till we have made our run.'

''Ear, ear,' was gasped by some of the transports.

'We'll tie 'em up!' And, in a second, two tents were on the ground, and the lines were being cut for the pinion-cords for the military guard, who, once assured of their lives, made but slight resistance.

The whole camp of transports was now seized with semi-madness. They were a long way from being out of the wood, for, as yet, none (not even Mann himself) had the least idea of how they were to effect their escape. Inland, or over sea? None knew. All they cared to understand for the moment was that their oppressor, who was to them the only Visible Authority, lay senseless—destitute of life apparently as he was of power.

In their wild burst of licence some rushed on the store-tent, others sat down to 'oval' their own or their comrades' irons. Nearly all whistled or sang. The soldiers—two tied to tree-trunks, the third supine on the grass—were amazed at the antics; Overseer Franke did not remonstrate; and was it fancy altogether that suggested there was a grin on Cummings' face?

Mann, as befitted the leadership which he had assumed without dispute, was the first to recover himself. His back was torturing him. The pain reminded him of his vow.

'Coves—mates!' he cried. 'Silence! we have business to do!'

Instantly they stopped their clamour. Two or three, however, went on 'ovalling,' and the ring of the hammer as they forced the anklet-bands out of their true shape so that the feet could be withdrawn, disturbed, with a singular sharpness, the suddenly-created silence. Disturbed also Mr. Overseer Franke. He came to himself.

The gang heard the rustle as he turned on the gum-leaves where he had fallen; they heard him moan and his cry for a drink; they heard—and for answer looked at Mann.

And Mann made due reply.

He walked up to the prostrate official and asked him did he know him—him, Mann. He put the question courteously—oh, so courteously—'May I have the pleasure of this valse?' was the style of it. And Franke nodded a 'yes,' and prayed for a drink.

'Cummings craved for a drink—and you gave him a bullet!' said Mann.

Did Franke respond to that retort? Not that Mann knew, for with that insight with which the gang, inspired by sudden liberty, had been endowed, the transports who had handled the sentries' muskets seized the weapons once more and rushed simultaneously to tender to Overseer Franke the cooling draught he had proffered Convict Cummings.

'Don't kill him, boys!' said Mann; 'only wound him!' Then—

'Stay!' he continued. And motioning for help he erected the still half-dazed Overseer against a tree, and called for more cord. They bound him to the bole, but at Mann's order left the wretch's right hand free.

Free—for a second it was. Then Mann himself took it (as limp and nerveless as Cummings' own) and stretched it outwards by a piece of line, the other end of which was fastened to another tree. The cord was tautened, and thus the hand of the Overseer was between two trees.

Mann went to the camp fire-place and, lifting a charred bit of fuel, returned with it and inscribed a circle, and, within the circle, 'a bull's-eye,' on the palm of the suspended hand.

'There!' he exclaimed, as he threw away the charcoal. 'There's a target. Fire away!'

The second shot riddled the hand, and the third smashed the wrist.

Then the leader stopped the musketry practice.

'That's enough for the present,' he said. 'We may want these bullets for living men. And this one is as good as dead!'

VI.

Thereupon Mr. Franke—whose portrait may be seen in Government House, Sydney—realized vividly his fate; and banishing all weakness—even a tyrant may be strong when pleading for his life—cried out for mercy.

'Yes!' replied Mann, 'the mercy you showed Cummings and myself and all of us!'

'Wot d'yer fight fer Cummin's fer?' moaned the Overseer. 'He peached on yer!'

'Yes?' Mann could not restrain the note of curiosity in his voice.

'Yes, 'e did. 'E tol' me 'bout yer findin' the boat. An' I gave 'im two figs of chaw-stuff fur a-tellin' me!'

Mann turned, as though he would have spit upon the dead body. But his better self was not yet dead. He thought that, after all, the System had made Cummings a traitor—and to a meanly-endowed creature such as he was, two figs of tobacco in the hand were worth a dozen boats in the sedge.

'Where is the boat?' he demanded.

Between the groans and the tears his wounds were wringing from him, Overseer Franke tried to effect a bargain.

'Will yer give me my life if I tells yer, 'an 'ow yer can get orf?'

The gang waited breathlessly for the reply of their leader. When it came, after a moment's deliberation, it was 'Yes!'

'On yer word as a gen'elman?' bartered the infamy.

A lump rose in Mann's throat. Still, he confirmed his previous answer. 'Yes!'

And the gang breathed freely. And so did Overseer Franke.

Then the Overseer told Mann and the others how he and Cummings and a soldier had gone to the Bay, upon Cummings' betrayal of the boat, after dark one night, and had removed the boat to another part of the inlet. And Cummings had kept that new secret, because he was to have a fig weekly till the boat was sold. For, needless to say, being a representative Government official, though the boat was properly Government's, Mr. Franke intended selling it for his own profit.

'And how will we get off?' questioned Mann.

'Ter-day's Tuesday. Ter-morrer the coaly-town (Newcastle) schooner's due, an' the night arter she comes in, skipper an' crew go 'shore. There ain't a soul on board. Thursday night—yer can go—an' I'll not report yer till Friday.'

' 'Ear, 'ear!' applauded the gang. But Mann remained silent.

'Yer won't break yer promise, *Mister* Mann?' pleaded the prisoner.

How the gang enjoyed the 'Mister!' But Mann's face clouded the deeper.

'What promise?' he exclaimed, at last.

'Yer promise to give me my life.'

'I made you no such promise!'

The gang shrank into stupid silence.

'Oh, yer a gen'elman—an' break yer word!' The misery of that expostulation from the Overseer!

'Blast you—yes! You cut the gentleman out of me with the cat. You die!'

And in the late-fallen dusk there mingled, curiously, the rapturous applause of the transports, and the alternate prayers and imprecations of the doomed officer.

VII.

That was on the Tuesday evening. On the Wednesday the gang had a merry day. They found the boat in the morning, and stored her with provisions from the store-tent. And in the afternoon, they pegged-out Overseer Franke. On an ant-hill, on a wooded gully-rise, they fastened him down with tent-lines. His right hand was stretched out with tightened cord again—this time to a special peg. A track of sugar was made from the orifice of the ant-bed to the hole in the hand, in case the industrious little creatures should not otherwise perceive so appetizing a banquet as that shattered fragment of official humanity.

Before they pegged him out they flogged Overseer Franke.

After they pegged him out, they placed some victuals and water—just outside of his reach. It was Mann who suggested that last refinement. In fact, it was the gentleman whom the cat had robbed of his gentle-hood that devised the means for keeping the latter-day Tantalus busy while he lived. And it was not Mann's fault that he did not make Franke immortal.

The soldiers threw in their lot with the convicts. Such a thing happened as a matter of course, when there was no superior officer of the System to say nay.

And on the Thursday they seized the schooner, and, after a successful trip, reached a South Sea island.

Sydney heard of them later—when the missionary, William Ellis, complained to the British authorities that they were playing havoc with his mission-field.

But Mann was not with them then. Mann, in fact, never left Port Jackson. He committed suicide just as the vessel was stealing out of the Heads in the midnight darkness of Thursday night. His last words were: 'I've done all I can for you, coves! Good-bye!' And then he pulled the trigger.

He was privileged to receive an oration over his grave in the sea.

'Damn him! W'y didn't he drown hisself? That shot might be 'erd at South 'Ead Signal Stashun.'

Absalom West found Franke's skeleton in 1824.

1 Colonel Arthur, in transmitting a return of expenditure to the Secretary of State for the Colonies, remarked 'that every item of the expenditure would be found conducive of the prosperity of the colony.' The statement included £20 3s. 4d., executioners' expenses.
2 'Cracking a whid in prime twig.'—Making a speech in a stylish or masterly manner.

Hume Nisbet

The Haunted Station

1894

IT looked as if a curse rested upon it, even under that glorious southern morn which transformed all that it touched into old oak and silver-bronze.

I use the term silver-bronze, because I can think of no other combination to express that peculiar bronzy tarnish, like silver that has lain covered for a time, which the moonlight in the tropics gives to the near objects upon which it falls—tarnished silver surfaces and deep sepia-tinted shadows.

I felt the weird influence of that curse even as I crawled into the gully that led to it; a shiver ran over me as one feels when they say some stranger is passing over your future grave; a chill gripped at my vitals as I glanced about me apprehensively, expectant of something ghoulish and unnatural to come upon me from the sepulchral gloom and mystery of the overhanging boulders under which I was dragging my wearied limbs. A deathly silence brooded within this rut-like and treeless gully that formed the only passage from the arid desert over which I had struggled, famishing and desperate; where it led to I neither knew nor cared, so that it did not end in a *cul-de-sac*.

At last I came to what I least expected to see in that part, a house of two storeys, with the double gables facing me, as it stood on a mound in front of a water-hole, the mellow full moon behind the shingly roof, and glittering whitely as it repeated itself in the still water against the inky blackness of the reflections cast by the denser masses of the house and vegetation about it.

It seemed to be a wooden erection, such as squatters first raise for their homesteads after they have decided to stay; the intermediate kind of station, which takes the place of the temporary shanty while the proprietor's bank account is rapidly swelling, and his children are being educated in the city boarding schools to know their own social importance. By and bye, when he is out of the mortgagee's hands, he may discard this comfortable house, as he has done his shanty, and go in for stateliness and stone-work, but to the tramp or the bushranger, the present house is the most welcome sight, for it promises to the one shelter, and to the other a prospect of loot.

There was a verandah round the basement that stood clear above the earth on piles, with a broad ladder stair leading down to the garden walk which terminated at the edge of the pool or water-hole; under the iron roofing of the verandah I could make out the vague indications of French doors that led to the reception rooms, etc., while above them were bedroom windows, all dark with the exception of one of the upper windows, the second one from the end gable, through which a pale greenish light streamed faintly.

Behind the house, or rather from the centre of it, as I afterwards found out, projected a gigantic and lifeless gum tree, which spread its fantastic limbs and branches wildly over the roof, and behind that again a mass of chaotic and planted greenery, all softened and generalized in the thin silvery mist which emanated from the pool and hovered over the ground.

At the first glance it appeared to be the abode of a romantic owner, who had fixed upon a picturesque site, and afterwards devoted himself to making it comfortable as well as beautiful. He had planted creepers and trained them over the walls, passion-fruit and vines clung closely to the posts and trellis work and broke the square outlines of windows and angles, a wild tangle of shrubs and flowers covered the mound in front and trailed into the water without much order, so that it looked like the abode of an imaginative poet rather than the station of a practical, money-grubbing squatter.

As I quitted the desolate and rock-bound gully and entered upon this romantic domain, I could not help admiring the artful manner in which the owner had left Nature alone where he could do so; the gum trees which he had found there were still left as they must have been for ages, great trees shooting up hundreds of feet into the air, some of them gaunt and bald with time, others with their leafage still in a flourishing condition, while the more youthful trees were springing out of the fertile soil in all directions, giving the approach the appearance of an English park, particularly with the heavy night-dew that glistened over them.

But the chill was still upon me that had gripped me at the entrance of the gully, and the same lifeless silence brooded over the house, garden, pool and forest which had awed me amongst the boulders, so that as I paused at the edge of the water and regarded the house, I again shuddered as if spectres were round me, and murmured to myself, 'Yes, it looks like a place upon which has fallen a curse.'

Two years before this night, I had been tried and condemned to death for murder, the murder of the one I loved best on earth, but, through the energy of the press and the intercession of a number of influential friends, my sentence had been *mercifully* commuted to transportation for life in Western Australia.

The victim, whom I was proved by circumstantial evidence to have murdered, was my young wife, to whom I had been married only six months before; ours was a love match, and until I saw her lying stark before me, those six months had been an uninterrupted honeymoon, without a cloud to cross it, a brief term of heaven, which accentuated the after misery.

I was a medical practitioner in a small country village which I need not name, as my supposed crime rang through England. My practice was new but growing, so that, although not too well off, we were fairly comfortable as to position, and, as my wife was modest in her desires, we were more than contented with our lot.

I suppose the evidence was strong enough to place my guilt beyond a doubt to those who could not read my heart and the heart of the woman I loved more than life. She had not been very well of late, yet, as it was nothing serious, I attended her myself; then the end came with appalling suddenness, a post-mortem examination proved that she had been poisoned, and that the drug had been taken from my surgery, by whom or for what reason is still a mystery to me, for I do not think that I had an enemy in the world, nor do I think my poor darling had one either.

At the time of my sentence, I had only one wish, and that was to join the victim of this mysterious crime, so that I saw the judge put on the fatal black cap with a feeling of pleasure, but when afterwards I heard it was to be transportation instead, then I flung myself down in my cell and hurled imprecations on those officious friends who had given me slavery and misery instead of release. Where was the mercy in letting me have life, since all had been taken from it which made it worth holding?—the woman who had lain in my arms while together we built up glowing pictures of an impossible future, my good name lost, my place amongst men destroyed; henceforward I would be only recognised by a number, my companions the vilest, my days dragged out in chains, until the degradation of my lot encrusted over that previous memory of tenderness and fidelity, and I grew to be like the other numbered felons, a mindless and emotionless animal.

Fortunately, at this point of my sufferings, oblivion came in the form of delirium, so that the weeks passed in a dream, during which my lost wife lived once more with me as we had been in the past, and by the time the ship's doctor pronounced me recovered, we were within a few days of our dreary destination. Then my wife went from me to her own place, and I woke up to find that I had made some friends amongst my fellow-convicts, who had taken care of me during my insanity.

We landed at Fremantle, and began our life, road-making; that is, each morning we were driven out of the prison like cattle, chained together in groups, and kept in the open until sundown, when we were once more driven back to sleep.

For fourteen months this dull monotony of eating, working and sleeping went on without variation, and then the chance came that I had been hungering for all along; not that liberty was likely to do me much good, only that the hope of accomplishing it kept me alive.

Three of us made a run for it one afternoon, just before the gun sounded for our recall, while the rest of the gang, being in our confidence, covered our escape until we had got beyond gun-shot distance. We had managed to file through the chain which linked us together, and we ran towards the bush with the broken pieces in our hands as weapons of defence.

My two comrades were desperate criminals, who, like myself, had been sentenced for life, and, as they confessed themselves, were ready to commit any atrocity rather than be caught and taken back.

That night and the next day we walked in a straight line about forty miles through the bush, and then, being hungry and tired, and considering ourselves fairly safe, we lay down to sleep without any thought of keeping watch.

But we had reckoned too confidently upon our escape, for about daybreak the next morning we were roused up by the sound of galloping horses, and, springing to our feet and climbing a gum tree, we saw a dozen of mounted police, led by two black trackers, coming straight in our direction. Under the circumstances there were but two things left for us to do, either to wait until they came and caught us, or run for it until we were beaten or shot down.

One of my companions decided to wait and be taken back, in spite of his bravado the night before; an empty stomach demoralizes most men; the other one made up his mind, as I did, to run as long as we could. We started in different directions, leaving our mate sitting under the gum tree, he promising to keep them off our track as long as possible.

The fact of him being there when the police arrived gave us a good start. I put all my speed out, and dashed along until I had covered, I daresay, about a couple of miles, when all at once the scrub came to an end, and before me I saw an open space, with another stretch of bush about half a mile distant, and no shelter between me and it.

As I stood for a few minutes to recover my breath, I heard two or three shots fired to the right, the direction my companion had taken, and on looking that way I saw that he also had gained the open, and was followed by one of the trackers and a couple of the police. He was still running, but I could see that he was wounded from the way he went.

Another shot was sent after him, that went straight to its mark, for all at once he threw up his arms and fell prone upon his face, then, hearing the sounds of pursuit in my direction, I waited no longer, but bounded full into the morning sunlight, hoping, as I ran, that I might be as lucky as he had been, and get a bullet between my shoulders and so end my troubles.

I knew that they had seen me, and were after me almost as soon as I had left the cover, for I could hear them shouting for me to stop, as well as the clatter of their horses' hoofs on the hard soil, but still I kept to my course, waiting upon the shots to sound which would terminate my wretched existence, my back-nerves quivering in anticipation and my teeth meeting in my under-lip.

One!

Two!!

Two reports sounded in my ears; a second after the bullets had whistled past my head; and then, before the third and fourth reports came, something like hot iron touched me above my left elbow, while the other bullet whirred past me with a singing wail, cooling my cheek with the wind it raised, and then I saw it ricochet in front of me on the hill side, for I was going up a slight rise at the time.

I had no pain in my arm, although I knew that my humerus was splintered by that third last shot, but I put on a final spurt in order to tempt them to fire again.

What were they doing? I glanced over my shoulder as I rushed, and saw that they were spreading out, fan-like, and riding like fury, while they hurriedly reloaded. Once more they were taking aim at me, and then I looked again in front.

Before me yawned a gulf, the depth of which I could not estimate, yet in width it was over a hundred feet. My pursuers had seen this impediment also, for they were reining up their horses, while they shouted to me, more frantically than ever, to stop.

Why should I stop? flashed the thought across my mind as I neared the edge. Since their bullets had denied me the death I courted, why should I pause at the death spread out for me so opportunely?

As the question flashed through me, I answered it by making the leap, and as I went down I could hear the reports of the rifles above me.

Down into shadow from the sun-glare I dropped, the outer branches of a tree breaking with me as I fell through them. Another obstacle caught me a little lower, and gave way under my weight, and then with an awful wrench, that nearly stunned me, I felt myself hanging by the remnant of the chain which was still rivetted to my waist-band, about ten feet from the surface, and with a hundred and fifty feet of a drop below me before I could reach the bottom. The chain had somehow got entangled in a fork of the last tree through which I had broken.

Although that sudden wrench was excruciating, the exigency of my position compelled me to collect my faculties without loss of time. Perhaps my months of serfdom and intercourse with felons had blunted my sensibility, and rendered me more callous to danger and bodily pain than I had been in my former and happier days, or the excitement of that terrible chase was still surging within me, for without more than a second's pause, and an almost indifferent glance downwards to those distant boulders, I made a wild clutch with my unwounded arm at the branch which had caught me, and with an effort drew myself up to it, so that the next instant I was astride it, or rather crouching, where my loose chain had caught. Then, once more secure, I looked upwards to where I expected my hunters to appear.

When I think upon it now, it was a marvel how I ever got to be placed where I was, for I was under the shelving ledge from which I had leapt, that is, it spread over me like a roof, therefore I must conclude that the first tier of branches must have bent inwards, and so landed me on to the second tree at a slant. At least, this is the only way in which I can account for my position.

The tree on which I sat grew from a crevice on the side of the precipice, and from the top could not be seen by those above, neither could I see them, although they looked down after me, but I could hear them plainly enough and what they said.

'That fellow has gone right enough, Jack, although I don't see his remains below; shall we try to get down and make sure?' I heard one say, while another replied:

'What's the good of wasting time, he's as dead as the other chap, after that drop, and they will both be picked clean enough, so let us get back to Fremantle with the living one, and report the other two as wiped out; we have a long enough journey before us, sergeant.'

'Yes, I suppose so,' answered the sergeant. 'Well, boys, we may say that there are two promising bushrangers the less for this colony to support, so right about, home's the word.'

I heard their horses wheel round and go off at a canter after this final speech, and then I was left alone on my airy perch, to plan out how best I was to get down with my broken arm, for it was impossible to get up, and also what I was likely to do with my liberty in that desolate region.

Desperate men are not very particular about the risks they run, and I ran not a few before I finally reached the bottom of that gulch, risky drops from one ledge to another, frantic clutchings at branches and tree roots; sufficient that I did reach the level ground at last more nearly dead than alive, so that I was fain to lie under the shadow of a boulder for hours without making an effort to rise and continue my journey.

Then, as night was approaching, I dragged myself along until I came to some water, where, after drinking and bracing up my broken arm with a few gum-trunk shards, and binding them round with some native grasses, while I made my supper of the young leaves of the eucalyptus bushes, I went on.

On, on, on for weeks, until I had lost all count of time, I wandered, carrying my broken fetters with me, and my broken arm gradually mending of its own accord. Sometimes I killed a snake or an iguana during the day with the branch I used for a stick, or a 'possum or wild cat at night, which I devoured raw. Often I existed for days on grass roots or the leaves of the gum-tree, for anything was good enough to fill up the gap.

My convict garb was in tatters and my feet bootless by this time, and my hair and beard hung over my shoulders and chest, while often I went for days in a semi-conscious state, for the fierce sun seemed to wither up my blood and set fire to my brain.

Where I was going I could not tell, and still, with all the privation and misery, the love of life was once again stronger in me than it had been since I had lost my place amongst civilised men, for I was at liberty and alone to indulge in fancy.

And yet it did not seem altogether fancy that my lost wife was with me on that journey. At first she came only when I lay down to sleep, but after a time she walked with me hand in hand during the day as well as in my dreams.

Dora was her name, and soon I forgot that she had been dead, for she was living and beautiful as ever as we went along together, day after day, speaking to each other like lovers as we used to speak, and she did not seem to mind my ragged, degraded costume, or my dirty, tangled beard, but caressed me with the same tenderness as of yore.

Through the bush, down lonely gullies, over bitter deserts and salt marshes, we passed as happy and affectionate as fond lovers could be who are newly married, and whom the world cannot part, my broken chain rattling as I staggered onwards while she smiled as if pleased with the music, because it was the chain which I was wearing for her dear sake.

Let me think for a moment—was she with me through that last desert before I came to that gloomy gully? I cannot be quite sure of that, but this I do know: that she was not with me after the chill shadows of the boulders drew me into them, and I was quite alone when I stood by the water-hole looking upon that strange and silent house.

It was singular that the house should be here at all in this far-off and as yet unnamed portion of Western Australia, for I naturally supposed that I had walked hundreds of miles since leaving the convict settlement, and as I had encountered no one, not even a single tribe of wandering blacks, it seemed impossible to believe that I was not the first white man who had penetrated so far, and yet there it loomed before me, substantial-looking in its masses, with painted weather-boards, shingles, iron-sheeting, carved posts and trellis-work, French windows, and the signs of cultivation about it, although bearing the traces of late neglect.

Was it inhabited? I next asked myself as I looked steadily at that dimly-illumined window; seemingly it was, for as I mentally asked the question, a darkness blotted out the light for a few moments and then moved slowly aside, while the faint pallor once more shone out; it appeared to be from the distance a window with a pale green blind drawn down, behind which a lamp turned low was burning, possibly for some invalid who was restlessly walking about, while the rest of the household slept.

Would it be well to rouse them up at this hour of the night? I next queried as I paused, watching the chimney tops from which no wreath of smoke came, for although it did not seem late, judging from the height of the moon, yet it was only natural to suppose that in this isolated place the people would retire early. Perhaps it would be better to wait where I was till morning and see what they were like before I ventured to ask hospitality from them, in my ragged yet unmistakably convict dress. I would rather go on as I was than run the risk of being dragged back to prison.

How chilly the night vapours were which rose from this large pool, for it was more like the moat from some ancient ruin than an ordinary Australian water-hole. How ominous the shadows that gathered over this dwelling, and which even the great and lustrous moon, now clear of the gable end, seemed unable to dissipate, and what a dismal effect that dimly-burning lamp behind the pale green blind gave to it.

I turned my eyes from the window to the pond from which the ghostly vapours were steaming upwards in such strange shapes; then crossed the reflections like grey shadows and floated over the white glitter which the moon cast down, like spectres following each other in a stately procession, curling upwards interlaced while the gaunt trees behind them altered their shapes and looked demoniac in their fantastic outlines, shadows passing along and sending back doleful sighs, which I tried with all my might to think was the night breeze but without succeeding.

Hush! was that a laugh that wafted from the house, a low, but blood-curdling cachinnation such as an exultant devil might utter who had witnessed his fell mischief accomplished, followed by the wail of a woman, intermixed with the cry of a child!

Ah! what a fool I was to forget the cry of the Australian king-fisher; of course that was it, of course, of course, but—

The shapes are thickening over that mirror-like pool, and as I look I see a woman with a chalk-white face and eyes distended in horror, with a child in her hands—a little girl—and beside them the form of a man whose face changes into two different men, one the face of death, and the other like that of a demon with glaring eyeballs, while he points from the woman and child to the sleeping pool.

What is the devil-spectre pointing at, as he laughs once more while the woman and child shrink with affright?

The face that he himself wore a moment ago, the face of the dead man whom I can see floating amongst that silver lustre.

I must have fainted at the weird visions of the night before, or else I may have fallen asleep and dreamt them, for when I opened my eyes again, the morning sun was pouring over the landscape and all appeared changed.

The pool was still there but it looked like a natural Australian water-hole which had been deepened and lengthened, and artificially arranged by a tasteful proprietor to beautify his estate; water-lilies grew round the edges and spread themselves in graceful patches about; it was only in the centre portion, where the moonlight had glinted and the other reflections cast themselves, that the water was clear of weeds, and there it still lay inky and dangerous-like in its depth.

Over the building itself clustered a perfect jungle of vegetable parasites, Star-of-Bethlehem, maiden-blush roses, and Gloire-de-Dijon, passion-flowers and convolvulus, intermingling with a large grape-laden vine going to waste, and hanging about in half-wild, neglected festoons; a woman's hand had planted these tendrils, as well as the garden in front, for I could see that flowers predominated.

As for the house itself, it still stood silent and deserted-looking, the weather-boards had shrunk a good deal with the heat of many suns beating upon them, while the paint, once tasteful in its dried tints, was bleached into dry powder; the trellis-work also on the verandah had in many places been torn away by the weight of the clinging vines, and between the window-frames and the windows yawned wide fissures where they had shrunk from each other.

I looked round at the landscape, but could see no trace of sheep, cattle, nor humanity; it spread out a sun-lit solitude where Nature, for a little while trained to order, had once more asserted her independent lavishness.

A little of my former awe came upon me as I stood for a few moments hesitating to advance, but at the sight of those luscious-looking bunches of grapes, which seemed to promise some fare more substantial inside, the dormant cravings for food which I had so long subdued came upon me with tenfold force, and, without more than a slight tremor of superstitious dread, I hurriedly crushed my way through the tangle of vegetation, and made for the verandah and open door of the hall.

Delicious grapes they were, as I found when, after tearing off a huge bunch, and eating them greedily, I entered the silent hall and began my exploration.

The dust and fine sand of many 'brick-fielders,' i.e., sand storms, lay thickly on every object inside, so that as I walked I left my footprints behind me as plainly as if I had been walking over snow. In the hall I found a handsome stand and carved table with chairs, a hat and riding-whip lay on the table, while on the rack I saw two or three coats and hats hanging, with sticks and umbrellas beneath, all white with dust.

The dining-room door stood ajar, and as I entered I could see that it also had been undisturbed for months, if not for years. It had been handsomely furnished, with artistic hangings and stuffed leather chairs and couches, while on the elaborately carved cheffonier was a plentiful supply of spirit and wine decanters, with cut glasses standing ready for use. On the table stood a bottle of Three-star brandy, half-emptied, and by its side a water-filter and glass as they had been left by the last user.

I smelt the bottle, and found that the contents were mellow and good, and when, after dusting the top, I put it to my mouth, I discovered that the bouquet was delicious; then, invigorated by that sip, I continued my voyage of discovery.

The cheffonier was not locked, and inside I discovered rows of sealed bottles, which satisfied me that I was not likely to run short of refreshments in the liquid form at any rate, so, content with this pleasant prospect, I ventured into the other apartments.

The drawing-room was like the room I had left, a picture of comfort and elegance, when once the accumulation of dust and sand had been removed.

The library or study came next, which I found in perfect order, although I left the details for more leisurely examination.

I next penetrated the kitchen, which I saw was comfortable, roomy and well-provided, although in more disorder than the other rooms; pans stood rusting in the fire-place, dishes lay dirty and in an accumulated pile on the table, as if the servants had left in a hurry and the owners had been forced to make what shifts they could during their absence.

Yet there was no lack of such provisions as an up-country station would be sure to lay in; the pantry I found stored like a provision shop, with flitches of bacon, hams sewn in canvas, tinned meats and soups of all kinds, with barrels and bags and boxes of flour, sugar, tea and other sundries, enough to keep me going for years if I was lucky enough to be in possession.

I next went upstairs to the bedrooms, up a thickly-carpeted staircase, with the white linen overcloth still upon it. In the first room I found the bed with the bed-clothes tumbled about as if the sleeper had lately left it; the master of the house I supposed, as I examined the wardrobe and found it well stocked with male apparel. At last I could cast aside my degrading rags, and fit myself out like a free man, after I had visited the workshop and filed my fetters from me.

Another door attracted me on the opposite side of the lobby, and this I opened with some considerable trepidation because it led into the room which I had seen lighted up the night before.

It seemed untenanted, as I looked in cautiously, and like the other bed-room was in a tumble of confusion, a woman's room, for the dresses and underclothing were lying about, a bed-room which had been occupied by a woman and a child, for a crib stood in one corner, and on a chair lay the frock and other articles belonging to a little girl of about five or six years of age.

I looked at the window, it had venetian blinds upon it, and they were drawn up, so that my surmise had been wrong about the pale green blind, but on the end side of the room was another window with the blinds also drawn up, and thus satisfied I walked in boldly; what I had thought to be a light, had only been the moonlight streaming from the one window to the other, while the momentary blackening of the light had been caused, doubtless, by the branches of the trees outside, moved forward by the night breeze. Yes, that must have been the cause, so that I had nothing to fear, the house was deserted, and my own property, for the time at least.

There was a strange and musty odour in this bed-room, which blended with the perfume that the owner had used, and made me for a moment almost giddy, so the first thing I did was to open both windows and let in the morning air, after which I looked over to the unmade bed, and then I staggered back with a cry of horror.

There amongst the tumble of bed-clothes lay the skeletons of what had been two human beings, clad in embroidered night-dresses. One glance was enough to convince me, with my medical knowledge, that the gleaming bones were those of a woman and a child, the original wearers of those dresses which lay scattered about.

What awful tragedy had taken place in this richly furnished but accursed house? Recovering myself, I examined the remains more particularly, but could find no clue, they were lying reposefully enough, with arms interlacing as if they had died or been done to death in their sleep, while those tiny anatomists, the ants, had found their way in, and cleaned the bones completely, as they very soon do in this country.

With a sick sensation at my heart, I continued my investigations throughout the other portions of the station. In the servants' quarters I learnt the cause of the unwashed dishes; three skeletons lay on the floor in different positions as they had fallen, while their shattered skulls proved the cause of their end, even if the empty revolver that I picked up from the floor had not been evidence enough. Some one must have entered their rooms and woke them rudely from their sleep in the night time, for they lay also in their blood-stained night-dresses, and beside them, on the boards, were dried-up markings which were unmistakable.

The rest of the house was as it had been left by the murderer or murderers. Three domestics, with their mistress and child, had been slaughtered, and then the guilty wretches had fled without disturbing anything else.

It was once again night, and I was still in the house which my first impulse had been to leave with all haste after the gruesome discoveries that I had made.

But several potent reasons restrained me from yielding to that impulse. I had been wandering for months, and living like a wild beast, while here I had everything to my hand which I needed to recruit my exhausted system. My curiosity was roused, so that I wanted to penetrate the strange mystery if I could, by hunting after and reading all the letters and papers that I might be able to find, and to do this required leisure; thirdly, as a medical practitioner who had passed through the anatomical schools, the presence of five skeletons did not have much effect upon me, and lastly, before sun-down the weather had broken, and one of those fierce storms of rain, wind, thunder and lightning had come on, which utterly prevented any one who had the chance of a roof to shelter him from turning out to the dangers of the night.

These were some of my reasons for staying where I was, at least the reasons that I explained to myself, but there was another and a more subtle motive which I could not logically explain, and which yet influenced me more than any of the others. *I could not leave the house, now that I had taken possession of it*, or rather, if I may say it, now that *the house had taken possession of me.*

I had lifted the bucket from the kitchen, and found my way to the draw-well in the back-garden, with the uncomfortable feeling that some unseen force was compelling me to stay here. I discovered a large file and freed myself from my fetters, and then, throwing my rags from me with disgust, I clad myself in one of the suits that I found in the wardrobe upstairs, then I set to work dusting and sweeping out the dining-room, after which I lit a fire, retrimmed the lamps, and cooked a substantial meal for myself, then the storm coming on decided me, so that I spent the remainder of the afternoon making the place comfortable, and when darkness did come, I had drawn the blinds down and secured the shutters, and with a lighted lamp, a bottle of good wine, and a box of first-class cigars which I also found in the cheffonier, with a few volumes that I had taken from the book shelves at random, and an album of photographs that I picked up from the drawing-room table, I felt a different man from what I had been the night previous, particularly with that glowing log fire in the grate.

I left the half-emptied bottle of brandy where I had found it, on the table, with the used glass and water filter untouched, as I did also the chair that had been beside them. I had a repugnance to those articles which I could not overcome; the murderer had used them last, possibly as a reviver after his crimes, for by this time I had reasoned out that one hand only had been at the work, and that man's the owner of the suit which I was then wearing and which fitted me so exactly, otherwise why should the house have been left in the condition that it was?

As I sat at the end of the table and smoked the cigar, I rebuilt the whole tragedy, although as yet the motive was not so clear, and as I thought the matter out, I turned over the leaves of the album and looked at the photographs.

Before me, on the walls, hung three oil portraits, enlargements they were, and as works of art vile things, yet doubtless they were faithful enough likenesses. In the album, I found three cabinet portraits from which the paintings had been enlarged.

They were the portraits of a woman of about twenty-six, a girl of five years, and a man of about thirty-two.

The woman was good-looking, with fresh colour, blue eyes and golden-brown hair. The girl—evidently her daughter—for the likeness was marked between the two, had one of those seraphic expressions which some delicate children have who are marked out for early death, that places them above the plane of grosser humanity. She looked, as she hung between the two portraits, with her glory of golden hair, like the guardian angel of the woman who was smiling so contentedly and consciously from her gilded frame.

The man was pallid-faced and dark, clean-shaven, all except the small black moustache, with lips which, except the artist had grossly exaggerated the colour, were excessively and disagreeably vivid. His eyes were deep set, and glowing as if with the glitter of a fever.

'These would be the likenesses of the woman and child whose skeletons lay unburied upstairs, and that pallid-faced, feverish-eyed ghoul, the fiend who had murdered them, his wife and child,' I murmured to myself as I watched the last portrait with morbid interest.

'Right and wrong, Doctor, as you medical men mostly are,' answered a deep voice from the other end of the table.

I started with amazement, and looked from the painting to the vacant chair beside the brandy bottle, which was now occupied by what appeared to be the original of the picture I had been looking at, face, hair, vivid scarlet lips were identical, and the same deep-set fiery eyes, which were fixed upon me intently and mockingly.

How had he entered without my observing him? By the window? No, for that I had firmly closed and secured myself, and as I glanced at it I saw that it still remained the same. By the door? Perhaps so, although he must have closed it again after he had entered without my hearing him, as he might easily have done during one of the claps of thunder which were now almost incessant, as were the vivid flashes of wild fire or lightning that darted about, while the rain lashed against the shutters outside.

He was dripping wet, as I could see, so that he must have come from that deluge, bareheaded and dripping, with his hair and moustache draggling over his glistening, ashy cheeks and bluish chin, as if he had been submerged in water, while weeds and slime hung about his saturated garments; a gruesome sight for a man who fancied himself alone to see start up all of a sudden, and no wonder that it paralyzed me and prevented me from finding the words I wanted at the moment. Had he lain hidden somewhere watching me take possession of his premises, and being, as solitary men sometimes are, fond of dramatic effect, slipped in while my back was turned from the door to give me a surprise? If so he had succeeded, for I never before felt so craven-spirited or horror-stricken, my flesh was creeping and my hair bristling, while my blood grew to ice within me. The very lamp seemed to turn dim, and the fire smouldered down on the hearth, while the air was chill as a charnel vault, as I sat with shivering limbs and chattering teeth before this evil visitor.

Outside, the warring elements raged and fought, shaking the wooden walls, while the forked flames darted between us, lighting up his face with a ghastly effect. He must have seen my horror, for he once more laughed that low, malicious chuckle that I had heard the night before, as he again spoke.

'Make yourself at home, Doctor, and try some of this cognac instead of that washy stuff you are drinking. I am only sorry that I cannot join you in it, but I cannot *just yet.*'

I found words at last and asked him questions, which seemed impertinent in the extreme, considering where I was.

'Who are you? Where do you come from? What do you want?'

Again that hateful chuckle, as he fixed his burning eyes upon me with a regard which fascinated me in spite of myself.

'Who am I, do you ask? Well, before you took possession of this place I was its owner. Where do I come from? From out of there last.'

He pointed backwards towards the window, which burst open as he uttered the words, while through the driving rain a flash of lightning seemed to dart from his outstretched finger and disappear into the centre of the lake, then after that hurried glimpse, the shutters clashed together again and we were as before.

'What do I want? You, for lack of a better.'

'What do you want with me?' I gasped.

'To make you myself.'

'I do not understand you, what are you?'

'At present nothing, yet with your help, I shall be a man once more, while you shall be free and rich, for you shall have more gold than you ever could dream of.'

'What can I do for you?'

'Listen to my story and you will see. Ten years ago I was a successful gold finder, the trusting husband of that woman, and the fond father of that girl. I had likewise a friend whom I trusted, and took to live with me as a partner. We lived here together, my friend, myself, my wife and my daughter, for I was romantic and had raised this house to be close to the mine which I had discovered, and which I will show you if you consent to my terms.'

'One night my friend murdered me and pitched my body into that water-hole, where the bones still lie. He did this because he coveted my wife and my share of the money.'

I was calm now, but watchful, for it appeared that I had to deal with a madman.

'In my lifetime I had been a trusting and guileless simpleton, but no sooner was my spirit set free than vengeance transformed its nature. I hovered about the place where all my affections had been centred, watching him beguile the woman who had been mine until he won her. She waited three years for me to return, and then she believed his story that I had been killed by the natives, and married him. They travelled to where you came from, to be married, and I followed them closely, for that was the chance I waited upon. The union of those two once accomplished, he was in my power for ever, for this had established the link that was needed for me to take forcible possession of him.'

'And where was his spirit meantime?' I asked, to humour the maniac.

'In my grasp also, a spirit rendered impotent by murder and ingratitude; a spirit which I could do with as I pleased, so long as the wish I had was evil. I took possession of his body, the mirage of which you see now, and from that moment until the hour that our daughter rescued her from his clutches, he made the life of my former wife a hell on earth. I prompted his murder-embrued spirit to madness, leaving him only long enough to himself after I had braced him up to do the deed of vengeance.'

'How did the daughter save the mother?'

'By dying with her, and by her own purity tearing the freed spirit from my clutches. I did not intend the animal to do all that he did, for I wanted the mother only, but once the murder lust was on him, I found that he was beyond my influence. He slew the two by poison, as he had done me, then, frenzied, he murdered the servants, and finally exterminated himself by flinging himself into the pool. That was why I said that I came last from out of there, where both my own remains and his lie together.'

'Yes, and what is my share in this business?'

'To look on me passively for a few moments, as you are at present doing, that is all I require.'

I did not believe his story about his being only a mirage or spectre, for he appeared at this moment corporal enough to do me a considerable amount of bodily harm, and therefore to humour him, until I could plan a way to overpower him, I fixed my eyes upon his steadfastly, as he desired.

Was I falling asleep, or being mesmerized by this homicidal lunatic? As he glared at me with those fiery orbs and an evil contortion curling the blood-red lips, while the forked lightning played around him, I became helpless. He was creeping slowly towards me as a cat might steal upon a mouse, and I was unable to move, or take my eyes from his eyes which seemed to be charming my life-blood from me, when suddenly I heard the distant sound of music, through a lull of the tempest, the rippling of a piano from the drawing-room with the mingling of a child's silvery voice as it sang its evening hymn, and at the sound his eyes shifted while he fell back a step or two, with an agonized spasm crossing his ghastly and dripping wet face.

Then the hurricane broke loose once more, with a resistless fury, while the door and window burst open, and the shutters were dashed into the room.

I leapt to my feet in a paroxysm of horror, and sprang towards the open door with that demon, or maniac, behind me.

Merciful heavens! the drawing-room was brilliantly lighted up, and there, seated at the open piano, was the woman whose bones I had seen bleaching upstairs, with the seraphic-faced child singing her hymn.

Out to the tempest I rushed madly, and heedless of where I went, so that I escaped from that accursed and haunted house, on, past the water-hole and into the glade, where I turned my head back instinctively, as I heard a wilder roar of thunder and the crash as if a tree had been struck.

What a flash that was which lighted up the scene and showed me the house collapsing as an erection of cards. It went down like an avalanche before that zig-zag flame, which seemed to lick round it for a moment, and then disappear into the earth.

Next instant I was thrown off my feet by the earthquake that shook the ground under me, while, as I still looked on where the house had been, I saw that the ruin had caught fire, and was blazing up in spite of the torrents that still poured down, and as it burned, I saw the mound sink slowly out of sight, while the reddened smoke eddied about in the same strange shapes which the vapours had assumed the night before, scarlet ghosts of the demon and his victims.

Two months after this, I woke up to find myself in a Queensland back-country station. They had found me wandering in a delirious condition over one of their distant runs six weeks before my return to consciousness, and as they could not believe that a pedestrian, without provisions, could get over that unknown stretch of country from Fremantle, they paid no attention to my ravings about being an escaped convict, particularly as the rags I had on could never have been prison made. Learning, however, that I had medical knowledge, by the simple method of putting it to the test, my good rescuers set me up in my old profession, where I still remain — a Queensland back-country doctor.

Guy Boothby

With Three Phantoms

1897

So I prophesied as I was commanded. And as I prophesied there was a noise, and behold a shaking, and the bones came together bone to his bone ... but there was no breath in them.

—EZEKIEL xxxvii.

I DATE the whole business from one muggy, horrible night, such as can only be produced by Port Darwin in her Season of Torment.

Remember, I am writing of years ago, when sarongs were permitted in the open streets, and more top-hamper than a singlet was deemed an impossibility. To-day everything is changed—solar topees, white umbrellas, and cotton ducks have overrun the settlement, and Comfort, as usual, has disappeared behind the smirking grin of Conventionality. Being observant, you will see in this the steady increase of a female population.

The entire township was in commotion. The mail-steamer was in harbour, and as that was an event which only happened once in seventy days, we donned festive attire, and resumed, for the time being, the manners and appearance of a civilised community.

The arrival of the mail-boat was of more importance than would at first appear, not only on account of the news it brought, but because the Government Resident invariably asked her commander to dinner, and an invitation to meet him was invariably the occasion of intrigue and diplomacy.

Besides a recognised status, a Residency dinner meant a good meal, the sight of new faces, unadulterated liquors, and not unfrequently female society. True, the latter was not always of the most cultured kind; but in those days we had not learned to be either critical or fastidious.

On this occasion it was a bachelor dinner, and a distinct success. The Chinese cook excelled himself, the wines were above suspicion, and the company irreproachable.

The great gun was a newly arrived explorer, who next day was to leave for the interior in the hope of discovering traces of the long-lost Leichardt expedition.

Now, beings who, of their own desire, sentence themselves to starvation, hardship, and almost certain death, in attempts to discover a thing which can be of no possible use to them when they have obtained it, can scarcely fail to be interesting companions, and this particular specimen was even more so than usual. We saw the night out together, with the boom of the Barrier surf in our ears, and, over some of the Resident's own particular brand of port, wished his trip a speedy and successful issue.

Next morning he disappeared, the mail-boat went on to China, and we returned to the unending monotony of our daily life.

The weeks and months rolled by, another mail-boat arrived, and before the traveller could have reached the Catherine River, we had almost forgotten that such a man existed.

Three years later I left the Territory and set off with pack-horses to seek a fortune in Northern Queensland, and, because I couldn't help myself—the only reason which induces any man to go there—drifted as far south-west as Boulia.

In those days the present settlement was as yet undreamt of. Now it calls itself a township, boasts a turf club, a shifting population of, perhaps, a hundred souls, and is altogether grand and metropolitan. Nevertheless, the heat, the sand, and the utter desolation must be there as of yore, and will continue for the delectation and delight of hopeless man as long as the earth remains to hold them.

The Sub-inspector of Police in charge of the district came of pedigreed stock, and rejoiced in the name of Vesey. He was a well-conditioned youth, of glib speech and easy manners, visibly impressed with the belief that to tail-twist niggers was his special mission upon earth.

Perhaps it was just as well that he believed in his work, for his life was rough in the extreme, and his quarters partook more of the nature of a dog-kennel than a civilised abode. However, he was perfectly happy, and never grumbled save when compelled by the good behaviour of the natives to remain inactive for any length of time.

I reached the barracks one evening at sundown, and introduced myself. In the words of the song, 'Though he had not much to offer, all he had he gave;' and because I had nothing whatsoever to do, and wanted a home, I accepted his invitation and billeted myself upon him for nearly three months.

The barracks were composed of his own quarters (a hut of three rooms), the sergeant's tent, and a couple of native gunyahs, while for his staff he had a white sergeant and six black troopers, who at his command would have stormed the gates of hell itself.

His district comprised a tract of country about twice the size of England, and when the natives in any quarter made themselves more than usually objectionable, he would descend upon them tooth and nail, until there remained not a man among them to tell the story. Humanitarians would have called his work murder, but lonely men, compelled to dwell in the Far West, derived a feeling of security from the bare sound of his name. In his own phraseology 'he was the hand of Providence engaged upon the extermination of the aboriginal in the interests of a higher civilisation.'

It was from this interesting specimen that I learnt the fate of the explorer mentioned earlier.

The bodies of the man and his party had been found on the rim of that hopelessly impassable desert which lies between Hooker's Creek and Sturt's furthest exploration west. Judging from their report, the rescue party had barely time to complete the burials before they were compelled, by want of water, to hurriedly retrace their steps. But to return to my story.

It had been intensely hot all day, and the thermometer, with a consistency which would have been commendable in any other cause, had for ten long hours stood at 118° in the shade. Not a sound broke the suffocating stillness of the night, and even the moon, rising blood-red above the horizon, seemed to jar upon the overstrung nerves.

Propping ourselves in the veranda, we sat and smoked, thinking our own thoughts. Our conversational energy had evaporated earlier in the evening, so there was nothing for it but to listen to the buzzing of the mosquitoes and the occasional moan of a night bird across the still lagoon.

Suddenly from the distance of the plain came a noise of ridden horses.

They crossed the creek and turned towards the camp. Then the moon showed us three travellers, and Vesey said in explanation—

'Dougherty and one of the boys; don't know the other chap. But whoever he is he seems to be precious shaky in the saddle.'

When the party pulled up, it took some time to get the third man from his horse, but with the assistance of two or three lounging troopers it was eventually accomplished, and they started towards us.

Stopping at the edge of the veranda, the sergeant saluted. The rag-bag groaned.

'What have you there, sergeant?'

'Well, that's more than I can say, sir! He's a man, but what sort of a man, I'm blessed if I can tell you. We found him on Pituri Creek unconscious, so I strapped him on the pack-saddle and brought him in!'

'Lift him up and let's have a look at him.'

I brought the lamp from the room and held it aloft, while the sergeant and a boy straightened the bundle out.

He was certainly a man, and might once have been a white man, but of what age or nationality it was impossible even to conjecture. He was neither more nor less than a living skeleton. A long, knotted beard straggled on his breast, and his great sunken eyes seemed devoid of even the faintest spark of life.

Of clothes he wore none, if you except an indescribable garment of skins, which only served to lend an additionally wild effect to his general weirdness. He was too weak to stand alone, and when addressed vouchsafed no reply.

'Rum fish, ain't he?' said Vesey, after a careful examination. 'Lost, I should say, and been living with the niggers. Take him away, sergeant, get those rags off him and put what's left to bed! We'll wait till he's got a few cargoes of grub aboard, and then see what he's made of.'

But it was more than a week before the stranger could leave his bunk.

Then came Christmas Eve—a sweltering mockery of the day, with the thermometer at 120° in the coolest spot. From sunrise to sunset we broiled in the veranda, cursing our luck for being in such a place, and only turning out to welcome three congenial spirits who had ridden in from neighbouring stations to help us keep the feast.

Out of respect to the day we spent the evening inside the house, and the consequences were uproarious to a horrible degree. One of the new arrivals had brought a banjo, another was an accomplished songster, and prolonged applause followed each combined attempt.

The room itself was simply an Inferno; the lamps smoked and the fumes of half a dozen different tobaccos blended with the complex horrors of the night. In all stages of undress we beat time with our glasses on the table, related anecdotes which nobody heard, proposed toasts which nobody heeded, and enjoyed ourselves generally as only desolate men can, when they foregather in the World's Waste Places.

Then Yerburgh re-tuned his banjo, and, with a brief introduction, burst into—

'Way down upon de Swanee Ribber,
Far, far away,
Dere's wha my heart is turning ebber,
Dere's wha de ole folks—

The music stopped abruptly. Mylrea, who was seated opposite the door, suddenly seized a glass, and was in the act of hurling it when Vesey caught his arm.

'Steady with the family china, old man. What's up? Great Scott!'

We all turned instantly, to find gazing at us from the doorway the loathsome Wanderer of the Bush. His appearance was enough to frighten any man.

We thought that Vesey held the right to speak.

'What the devil brings you out of bed at this time of night?' he inquired.

The apparition pulled itself together, and the blank look faded from its eyes just as breath draws off a sabre blade. We waited for the reply.

Very slowly, and as if desirous of securing our united sympathies, it said—

'I—am—an—Englishman!'

'Why doesn't he say 'was'?' whispered Mylrea.

But the stranger only clung to the door-post, and hunted for words with which to express himself.

'Well, I don't see that it matters much who or what you are,' said Vesey, rising and pushing a chair towards him; 'it's Christmas Eve, so come in and sit down. Here's liquor, which might be better and couldn't very well be worse; take a pull and see if it'll bring your memory back. That's the way! Now try and spin your yarn, for I suppose you've one to tell!'

The man clawed his long hair back with a hand that was own cousin to a monkey's paw, and a brighter look came into his eyes. It didn't require much observation to see that the spirit was bringing both his memory and his mother-tongue back to him.

'What day do you say this is?'

'Christmas Eve.'

'Christmas Eve! Oh, God! And of what year?' He asked the question nervously, as if he dreaded the answer he would receive.

We told him, and when he had grasped the fact he sank his head upon his hands. After a while he spoke again, and his voice had a note in it pitiful to hear.

'If that's so, I've been in hell four years, and now—I'm an old man—an old man.' He paused a moment. 'Have any of you ever heard of a man, Alexander McKinnon—an explorer?'

'Hope he's no friend of yours,' said Vesey; 'the poor devil perished with all his party in the desert over three years ago!'

'No—no—he didn't die.'

We all took a hand in the question.

'What do you mean?'

'Only that —*I am Alexander McKinnon!*'

'What! You Alexander McKinnon, who left Port Darwin for the Catherine River four years ago?'

'The same.'

'Why, man!' cried Vesey, 'the rescue party's report says that they found your dead body in the desert, recognised it, and buried you.'

'I know nothing of that. Nevertheless, I *am* Alexander McKinnon.'

After this we hung upon the wanderer's words, like men listening to the voice of one returned from the dead.

The heat was awful, the lamp flared, and the reek of perspiring humanity filled the room. I remember noticing a tarantula crawling up the back of Vesey's chair, but was too interested to acquaint him of the fact. We had no attention for such minor matters then.

'Why should I tell you my story? You wouldn't believe it. You are men who live in real houses and eat your fill daily. But yet—it must be true—fatally true!'

He covered his face with his hands and was silent. The cheap nickel-plated clock on the mantelpiece ticked undisturbed for five full minutes. We hadn't the heart to hurry him.

When he recovered his composure he said:—

'As you know, I left Port Darwin on the 24th of September, four years ago, with a party of three men and six pack-horses, to seek for traces of

Leichardt's Expedition.'

'Our first camp was in the jungle, eighteen miles from the town, and from that point we struck in a direct line for the Catherine River, reaching it on the 10th of October. After camping a week there we made final arrangements, and then steered through open forest and high grass, over stony ridges and enormous gorges to the Victoria, which we struck on the 30th of October, and left again, our party all well, on the 4th of November.'

'So far we had journeyed without adventure, and, what was strange, although the country thereabouts was explored by Wyckham, of the *Beagle,* early in the forties, and again by Gregory some time in the fifties, without discovering any traces of previous expeditions.'

'On the 4th of December we found the head of Sturt's Creek, and followed it down until the 16th, when it disappeared in the sands of the Great Desert. With food and water very scarce we retraced our steps to Hooker's Creek, and here met with our first great misfortune, losing two pack-horses, and, what was worse, all the stores they carried, while crossing a deep water-hole.'

'In view of the position, we held a consultation as to whether it would be better to follow our tracks back along the Victoria, or do what no man had ever done before—that is to say, cross the unexplored country which lies between lat. 18.11 and long. 132, and which I now know to be the most hopeless stretch of awful desert on the face of this godless continent.'

'Eventually we decided to attempt the latter, and accordingly set off, steering a north-of-east course for three days, when we reached a large water-hole, where we camped a day to rest.'

'Leaving this water, we passed on to a stretch of sandy table-land thickly covered with trees of a type somewhat resembling the Morton Bay fig. That night we were compelled to camp without water, and in the morning pushed on till midday, when we left the table-land and descended to a tryodia-covered plain, where once more we had a dry camp.'

'About ten o'clock on the day following we entered the desert pure and simple, an endless sandy plan, where no sign of water, animal life, or any vegetation whatsoever was discernible, save the interminable and eye-wearying spinifex.'

'The heat was terrible, and by this time our personal water supply was reduced to six pints. Before nightfall a riding horse and two pack-horses knocked up and had to be abandoned. These things had a most depressing effect upon us all, so much so that during the night my second in command must have gone suddenly mad, for he wandered away, and next morning was found dead, with a bullet in his brain, about a mile from the camp. We buried him in the wilderness, and so ended our Christmas Eve four years ago.'

'Three days later only two of us were left, with less than a pint of water, to push ever on and on towards the rising sun.'

'Picture it for yourselves! Picture the hopelessness of our position! To go backwards or forwards almost certain death!'

The poor wretch stopped and gazed from one to the other, throwing his hands out before him with a sort of gesture of despair.

'Now commences the part of my story you will not believe, though I swear it is, if possible, truer than anything I have told you yet. If you want proof my presence here should satisfy you, and surely better evidence you could not have.'

'On the fourth night, weary and more than sick at heart, we were camped in what seemed to be the eternal centre of that endless plain. We were in piteous plight, our stores were well-nigh done, and we had drunk our last drop of water twelve hours before. A low wind moaned across the spinifex, and then the moon rose to show us the naked horrors of the desert by night.'

'Suddenly my companion sprang to his feet and pointed to some dim shadows moving in the far distance.'

'Black or white men, their presence would mean our salvation. We tried to coo'ee, but our parched throats emitted no sound; we could only wave our hands and beckon wildly to them in the moonlight.'

'To our unspeakable joy they turned towards us, and then we saw they were horsemen, and three in number. But save the sigh of the wind across the spinifex, no sound came with them.'

'Nearer and nearer they approached till we could almost discern their faces, and still they made no noise. When they were within a dozen paces they halted. And then—my God! I can feel the horror of it now—*I could see the moon shining through each horse and rider!*'

'Without speaking or appearing to see us, they fixed their camp within a stone's throw, hobbled and belled their phantom steeds, and turned them loose. Not a detail did these three dead men omit from the ordinary camp routine; and so all through that hot miserable night they watched and waited with us.'

'In the dim light of dawn they saddled up, and once more started on their way.'

'We followed their example, and henceforward day by day journeyed in their wake.'

'How I lost my companion and my horse, how I lived through the remainder of that awful desert, I do not know. My mind for that period is a partial blank, and I remember nothing save three shadowy horsemen, who glided continually before me.'

'They never spoke, they neither ate nor drank, but through scorching day and starry night, over sand and over rock, they were my constant and never-failing companions.'

'At length, after what seems now to have been an eternity, we came to the borders of a dense black scrub, which stretched away to north and south as far as the eye could reach. Here they left me, and I laid down to die. I recollect no more.'

'Where or how I have spent the last three years I cannot tell you, but that three dead men took me from the West and set me in the East, I am myself a living witness. And—and—your pardon—but I am—an old man now—virtue is gone—out of me. I can go no further, mates. The sun is down. It—is—time—to—camp!'

His voice had been gradually getting lower and lower, and on the last words he slipped from his chair and fell unconscious to the floor.

Between us we carried him to his bunk, and took it in turn to sit with him throughout the night.

The sun of Christmas morning rose before his sightless eyes, and when, its long day's work accomplished, it disappeared in a flood of crimson splendour behind the creek timber, the lingering shadows touched a new-made grave—the Wanderer's last camp and resting-place.

'Coo-ee' (William Sylvester Walker)

The Evil of Yelcomorn Creek

1899

There are more things in heaven and earth, Horatio,
Than are dreamt of in your philosophy.

— WILLIAM SHAKESPEARE

'I'M right glad to see you, sir,' said old Baines. 'I'm out of tobacco, and I don't think I ever felt the time go so slow.

'Generally got something to do so, sir, always making or scheming something, but I can't get on without my "bacca."

'Seems to put a "considering cap" on a fellow's head.

'But the sun's gone, our Australian twilight don't last long, like the twilight in the old country.

'The "more's the pity," say I.

'There's more poetry in the gloaming, the real old English gloaming, with its changing light and shade, some folks would say, but even here it's right pleasant and cool after the long hot day.

'Ay, and it's pleasant to sit and think, your duty done, and the sheep looked to, and yarded for the night, just the time when the crickets and tree frogs are chirping, and the cool breeze comes murmuring up, whilst the evening star twinkles brightly, as if making believe it was night.

'And there's lots of strange sounds of birds and beasts all around you. One takes to it wonderfully after a bit. I don't think I'd swop it for the

English twilight, after all, unless I'd made my "pile," and I'm a'most too old for that now, sir.

'Now I'll take your horses up there in the "hop" ridge nigh to the tank, and fill the water-trough for them. There's plenty of grass there, sir. I never let the sheep go within coo-ee of that ridge, and "Bally" and "Jessie" wouldn't even let them look that way if they saw 'em. Why, that's my garden, sir, and it grows more for me than most people thinks.'

Old Baines was the queerest old customer on the river, and I never felt more comfortable than when my duty as ration-carrier certified my sojourn for the night at his hut.

Full of anecdote on the spur of the moment, he was nevertheless a little whimsical, and his dancing dolls and niggers—his 'merry people' as he called them—were the talk of the district.

From a feeling of loneliness, I suppose, in his 'back block' shepherd's hut, he made these puppets from some light cork-like scrub wood, and on whistling a jig tune and pulling some invisible strings, they would all set to dancing like fun.

Queer as the old fellow was—and there were not wanting some who said he was 'touched'—he liked his comforts, and was particularly fond of reading, so I generally contrived to bring him as much literary matter as possible.

'Have a drop of beer, sir? Likely enough you're thirsty after your long ride,' queried this enigma when he returned.

And the draught was delicious, made as it was from one of his recipes, from the wild hop-bush—not from the vine.

'What's that book you've got for me, sir?

'Never too Late to Mend. Just what my poor dad used to say to me when I was a whelp after a good "lambastin." Charles Reade? Ah, he's an author, he is.

'I've wanted to come across that very book. There's a lot of convict history in it, I think. Ah, well, it'll keep. Have you seen my "Columbine" and "Harlequin," sir?'

And from a box filled with all sorts of carvings he produced the two representatives of pantomime loosely jointed in some peculiarly clever way.

After a capital supper, cooked by the old fellow, and enjoyed by us both, he occupied himself with his books and his pipe, dipping into the former rather than reading them.

'That's a queer scene on the diggings, sir,' he said at length, 'where Robinson the ex-thief (as Judge Lynch) making his speech in defence of the prisoner, says to the excited crowd: "When I was in California,"—my word, mustn't he have been startled when he heard that whisper in his ear: "I guess I was thyar!"—and him a thief, too! My word, those digger fellows seem to get everywhere.

'I've seen a lot of them in my time. I've been on Lambing Flat in the old days, ay, and on Bendigo and Ballarat too, but the worst time I ever had was in Queensland prospecting for opals.

'You've heard tell, I dare say, sir, that the Queensland opal is the true 'noble' opal, the same as the Hungarian. It's rather rough knocking about on the mulga ridges in the blazing sun, but I've seen the opals as big as bantams' eggs, and bigger, with all the colours of the rainbow in them. If you get a piece only as big as a pin's head in the hard brown matrix, it'll blaze out like fire when the sun catches it.

'And the real "fire opals," you'll see them now in plenty in most of the best jewellers' shops in Sydney, on little trays one above the other, worked by mechanism to revolve slowly so as to show off the stones.

'But I reckon I was the first discoverer of both the blue opal deposit and perhaps a later one of the opal itself.

'Well, about six years ago, before I came to this district, I had been shepherding on the Nardoo in Queensland.

'I had the finest flock of wethers on the station, and open country. One of the plains might have been an old lake once, from the look of it, and that was the end of my tether.

'I'd get to about the middle of it if I made an early start, and let my sheep go their "own way." They was fond of that plain. From the middle of it back home would take me till sundown.

'Wild dogs? Well, there was a sight of them, but my little bitch, "Fly," she never let one come near the place, and my brave old "Rover," he was a match for the biggest of them, and they were more like wolves up there than dingoes.

'Well, one day I says to myself: My beat hedges on to some queer country, I'll see if I can do a bit of exploring.

'The station waggon wasn't due for a week, so I took four days' "tucker" and started.

'The first night I got to the end of the big plain, up to a range that had been tantalising me every day, for being a born "fossicker," I wanted to see what was in it, but the sheep had always been like hobbles to me, and I couldn't leave them.

'A nice camp it was that night. The scent of the sandal-wood bushes was sweet, and it was nice and cool near the ridge.

'I had the sheep camped on a rise near the end of a small water hole, and, thinks I, there's summat in those ranges far or near.

'They trend to the south as far as the eye can reach, and to-morrow we shall see what we shall see.

'Well, next morning we got through a fine gully on to one of the queerest plains you ever see.

'There were three conical hills on it—one right in the centre of the plain, the others one on each side of it; and they looked so striking that I steered my sheep to the nearest, and went "fossicking."

'I had seen something on the sides of them glitter in the sun. It was native talc, plenty of it; where it had been laid bare on the sides by the rain; and I found some stuff like layers of blue enamel on some stones, and lots of things for all the world like stone jars, or more properly speaking, like halved cocoanuts, but some were longer. I thought the natives must have had a pottery there one time or another, but I soon reasoned it out as only a natural formation of hardened sandstone, balled, and worked into layers by water action, probably by rolling before it. They had broken across in drying.

'Then I filled a bag with specimens of all kinds, and turned back for my first camp, reaching my own yard next day.

'Now, the blue stuff like china I found on the stones was the first blue opal deposit found in Queensland, and it's my first and last try for those precious stones that I am going to tell you about.

'Ah, and that same blue deposit cost my mate's life too, being the direct cause of our setting out to hunt for the stones.

'I found out all that about the deposit from a scientific chap, who came along with two horses and stopped a night at my hut. Says he:—

"Somewhere about the district where you got that blue deposit, Baines, you will find the opal itself.

"It mightn't be just where you found the stones, because they have come on flood water long ago. When you strike a hill or a big reef of that hard chocolate-coloured stone you peg in for opals, break up the rock and look for the opal in the stone itself."

'I minded those words, sir, and gave him some specimens to take down to Sydney, where he was bound for.

'Not long after he was gone, a young "jackeroo," who used to come out with rations, brought me a letter from Mr Clark the overseer, with word in it that my sheep, 2000 fine fat wethers, were to be on the roads for the Adelaide market in a week.

'There were 8000 sheep going altogether, and the gentleman who was to take charge of them, Mr Miles, was waiting at the home-station until they were delivered over to him.

'The overseer complimented me on my sheep, saying that they were the best on the run, and that he could always depend upon me, etc. etc. He wanted to know if I would go down with them, as they would be all mixed together at night, "boxed" for camping, or split into two mobs of about 4000 each. I should have to shepherd about the same number I had.

'I liked being "on the roads." There is nothing much to do, except to let your sheep feed leisurely forward, and this year it would be still easier, as it had been a fine season, and there would be plenty of grass.

'Adelaide was 1000 miles away; so there was a six months' job—wages extra, of course, and a cook to cook your grub. Nothing to do but head your sheep in the right direction, and let 'em feed quiet.

'Well, I didn't know which way to look at it at first.

'I'd saved over a hundred pounds, and it was safe in the bank. The trip would put another forty into my pocket.

'But I'd got those opals in my head, and though I knew Mr Clark would be disappointed, I meant to beg him to put another man into my place.

'I'd got attached to them sheep too, sir. I'd seen them grow from two-tooth to prime wethers, seen 'em shorn as the seasons came round, and all that, and I knew my marked sheep as well as I knew "Fly" and "Rover."'

'You see, sir, if one of those marked sheep (I had eighteen altogether scattered through the flock) went a-missing, I might calculate to have lost 100 to 150. You'd hardly tell that number out of 2000 without counting the whole flock, and their bellies all full too!

'The marked sheep were nearly all black or brown ones, but one fellow had only a black patch on his rump including the tail; as round as a target, you could see him anywhere, unless he was facing you, and I called him "the Bull" partly for bull's-eye, and partly for being a bit of an Irishman and trying to be black, when he was supposed to be white.

'When the "jackeroo" went away, I sent no word, only "that I would think it over."'

'I lit my pipe, and sat me down on the old log outside my hut door that had served me as a seat for twelve months in that place and was wore pretty smooth. Then I thought the matter over as I puffed the bacca.

'Here was I, then.

'The sheep and myself belonged to each other, so to speak. Say, I goes. Well, there's one hundred and forty odd pounds for me in Adelaide, new clothes, new boots, new fixin's, and hotel dinners, with the barmaids wheedlin' money out of you at every turn.

'Perhaps I gets drunk, and runs through that money in a fortnight; well, that ain't much. I done the same thing pretty often.

'I'm safe to get back with Mr Clark if I go back with the waggon-driver. Mr Clark wants me to go. There's no one can look after sheep on the roads like me. I'd like to see those fellows top the market, says I out loud, and I'm blest if the "Bull" didn't turn right round (he was near the gate), and look me straight in the face, as much as if to say, "Don't leave us, old man. We can't forget you, you know. You're too ugly."

'Well, I argued it that way. Then I says:—

'Now, Baines, you know you're a thundering fool in a big town, and you can't keep your money, but up here in the bush, there's few fellows can pull along as well as you do.

'You're in good health, probably you've got a good time to live if you take care of yourself.

'Why don't you make a big "pile," and give up shepherding? *Those opals, sonny!* Now, what do you think of it?

'Well, there you were. I was in a quandary, "between the horns of a dilemma," as the scientific chap would have called it. I never see a dilemma. If there had been any at Yandilla, our head-stockman would have had 'em in the yard, and branded 'em quick.

'Well, I brought out my old silver watch, and puts it on the stump beside me, and I says: There's fourteen bronze-wing pigeons gone down to water past the old copper-leaved gum tree at the end of the water-hole.

'If there's five more pass before you get once round the "second" dial, old ticker, I'll give up the sheep and go prospecting. There was six: so it was opals.

'Mr Clarke laughed when I told him after I had taken my sheep into the head-station, and says; "There's a strong 'Eepai' tribe out there somewhere. Take care you don't get 'boomallied' or speared by the 'warrigal' blacks, Baines."

'I told him I was sorry to leave the sheep, but he knew as well as I did that I shouldn't have a farthing of my money left if I went to Adelaide.

'I got a first-class rig-out from the Yandilla store—so some of my money benefitted the station anyway—picks, shovels, three horses, and a rare lot of "tucker." Who was my mate? Only a black fellow, but a rare good one. He did not belong to that part of the country, but had been brought down from the Roper River in the far north, and it was a favour of Mr Clark to let me have him, for he was Bobbie, Mr Clark's own boy, but he wanted a spell hunting, so the overseer let him go.

'Well, the sheep started, and I sold my dogs. It was a lovely summer, and after three days' travelling, Bobbie and me was in as pretty a bit of country as you ever see, but it ran out against awful ranges and thick scrub. Mortal man couldn't get over them ranges, let alone a pack horse, and the range on the other side of it was the Boree range, the one I wanted to go to. The Boree range was a "oner" also, and none of the Boree fellows wanted to climb that; but I wanted to get to the bottom of it on the Yandilla side. Now, the geography of this part of the country is so peculiar, that I took a bit of a map of it.

'Here you see is Yandilla to the north. *That's* the Tarcoo River. Right; two days down that, Bobbie and me camps *there*. It was a big water-hole.

'Next day we left the river, and steers due east. We come to the range, and the range beyond it I knew was in a direct line with my old camp, back up the Tarcoo River beyond Yandilla. You see it *here,* sir, on the paper. *I'm after the chocolate-coloured matrix of the opal!*

'You remember the sheer range I told you of, sir, which the Boree fellows didn't care to climb. That's *all* chocolate-coloured stone, and there's enough opals in it, sir, to make your hair stand on end.

'But you won't care to carry any away when you get there!

'Why? I'll tell you why, sir.

'Bobbie and me strikes this country *there*, the bottom all rough scrub and boulders, the sides inaccessible. It's forty miles from the main river, at the head of a creek called the "Yelcomorn."

'In our days up there in Queensland, the main river, wherever it was, was the road, the highway of civilisation.

'No fear of any traveller being forty miles back from it, unless he was exploring, or prospecting like me, especially when he knows the dividing range between the Tarcoo and the Boree is called the "Never Never" Mountains. Ah, the sort of country the "Barrier" was before they found the silver there, pretty well unknown, except to a few stockmen, and a shepherd or two. Sheer precipices on one side, and alarming steep, and uninteresting on the other.

'And the scrub—that's enough to settle any one. The Boree sweeps the base of the big range on the other side of these "Never Never" Mountains, and the traveller, when he's left that long, brown, wearisome, ungovernable pile of hills far behind him, is truly thankful.

'But inside, down them steep cliffs, ah! it is lovely!

'The creek we had followed up—the Yelcomorn—I knew something about, only five miles up though, no further, and it was the knowledge of a certain outcrop of chocolate-coloured stone that brought me there.

'It took us a day and a half hard dragging with the pack-horse and the others to get to the extreme end of the creek, and where we ought to have gone on through a deep, straight up and down ravine where the creek branched, we were brought up all standing by a wall of rock which seemed to have been built by giants.

'You couldn't get horses or anything else *up* the hills around us. They were like the sides of houses, and the wall of rock was just a whole hilltop slid into the hollow.

'Well, I thought we were beat, and should have to go back and try some other route. Bobbie climbs up some fifteen feet on the ledge of one of the great rocks which were strewn about like paving stones. There was hundreds more on top. Presently he beckons me. I joined him. Would you believe it? there was a tunnel about four feet high, by the same breadth. In we goes!

'It was dug between the boulders, in the rubble which lay between the great blocks, zig-zag, black as pitch. After about one hundred yards, I wanted to go back. Thinks I: We may be in a python's lair, and it won't be at all pleasant if his majesty is at home.

'But we lights matches, and on we goes, winding round and on again, in and out. At length we sees a glimmer of light.

'"By the Lord! we're *through*!" shouts I, mad with delight. "Come from nowhere to Paradise, one hundred yards or more in a straight line. Treble that, if you count the turns and twists." As I stood on the ledge of the last rock inward and saw what I saw, "Bobbie," I says, "I've seen some queer sights in my time, but this and that together (meaning the hole) beats all I ever *did* see."

'"Mine think it," says Bobbie coolly. "Where 'yarramen?'" (horses).

'You might have knocked me down with a blow, and I wouldn't have opened my lips. Horses indeed! Our horses were the other side of an obstruction to anything larger than a man, impregnable, unalterable, unfathomable. And the millions of tons of convulsed nature had turned the real source of the old half-dried creek on the other side into the New

Yelcomorn, where we were, running through a valley like the garden of Eden.

'As far as I could estimate from where I was, there was a seven-mile block, that is, seven miles square of virgin country; the finest I had ever clapped my eyes on, and the timber was the finest I had ever dreamed of.

'There was enough "bloodwood," and "beefwood" on the ridges to have shingled a township, and the kangaroos and emus, shell parrots and cockatoos, white, and black! oh my, it was a fairy spot.

'But I have a queer name for it, sir. I call it the "Ghost's Glen"!

'There was no entrance to it in or out (unless you had a balloon) but by the tunnel. And that tunnel had been made by black fellows before I was born! whichever way I looked at it. And another thing, none of them had used it for half a century or more. There was no tracks, no half-burnt firesticks—nothing.

'"Bobbie," says I, "we'll camp in this here Paradise to-night, and do a bit of exploring on the morrow" (I could see the big Boree range, the one I wanted, sticking up high above the far trees). "You think it, we get pick and shovel along a hole."

'"Mine think it," said he, "fetch 'im 'billy,' blanket, 'picketul'" (pistol)

'"Well, my boy, we'll go back, and hobble the horses; we'll have to take 'em back half a mile to water, clear of the scrub." And we did it, and crawled back through the tunnel again, as the sun was shedding a golden light upon the "gidyahs" and "yapunyahs" of this unknown (to us) and marvellous region.

'It was too late to "prospect" that day, and "Bobbie's" tomahawk soon went to work upon the white gum trees by the creek, where we were rigging up a "gunyah" to camp in, made with sheets of bark so obtained, at the side of those lovely sedge rimmed sheets of water.

'As the first ringing stroke of the flashing blade fell upon the nearest tree, "Coo-oo-ee," very faint and far away, came to my ears, and there was a trembling cadence in the cry—a sort of quivering despair that wrung my heart, and almost made it stop beating. It seemed to float nearer and nearer till it mingled with the whispering of the leaves in the tree tops. Ah, the despair of that cry, the misery of it! It was a death cry if ever there was one yet!

'"That's not black fellows," thinks I; "they're *demons*. We're in a land of spirits!"

'Bobbie went chopping on, he hadn't heard 'em. I cocked my revolver and strolled across one end of the water-hole.

'Kangaroo grass and wild oats grew over your head.

'The bright green of the sedge-rimmed banks of the long sheet of water contrasted vividly with the wonderful blue of it, and every white-waisted gum tree shot its shadow straight down until it looked as if there was a whole army of ghosts watching that pool.

'Overhead, on the long, streaming branches, the Nankeen cranes, parrots, cormorants and wood-duck, sat as quiet as if they had never seen a human being before in their lives.

'I passed on quick. Oh, Lord, what's this? A native grave! And another! Great heavens, here's a skull and thighbones dragged up out of the ground. Under the "mulgas" more graves, hundreds of 'em.

'Spears, "heilamans" (shields of hard wood), stone tomahawks and boomerangs lying all about, strewing the ground, mildewed and rotting with many seasons of exposure.

'I fancied I traced an old stain of blood on one iron-wood "heilaman."

'On I went, the same thing meeting my eyes everywhere.

'More graves, more loose bones and skulls. Very old marks of the stone tomahawks could be seen on the trees. (The blacks had all steel tomahawks in *my* time), and the fallen poles of ancient "gunyahs" (bark or grass huts), were here and there.

'I stooped to pick up a boomerang. Ah, that dreadful cry, "Coo-oo-ee," moaning and writhing away through the air.

'I crossed over to where the "yapunyahs" stood in dusky groves, and beneath them also were the same mournful relics. Did my foot brush a grave:— "Coo-oo-ee."

'Did I sweep aside a bough to gaze into the shady vistas:—"Coo-oo-ee" in the same low, mysterious and frightful manner. I got back to camp. Bobbie's tomahawk was sticking in a tree, and he was lying at the foot of it, *dead*!

'His limbs were all drawn up, and his fingers crooked, as if he had died in agony or fright.

'He'd gone; his soul had gone out of his body to them "Coo-oo-ees."

'It was pretty bad to scare one, but worse was to come.

'When I had covered Bobbie with a rug, after moving him to the head of the water-hole, where it was all sand and easier dug, I kept watch in that dreadful place alone.

'"Coo-oo-ee."

'Ah, the weeping of it. Ah, the sorrow of it. Shivering away, away, away.

'The moon rose, sir, on a queer sight, and looked down upon that ghostly water-hole with its white sentinels. At the head of it lay dead Bobbie with his mate senseless beside him: whilst flitting in the 'corrobborree' dance close by amongst the tall "yapunyahs" went the skeleton-painted wraiths, tall and weird, of those warriors who fought and fell in the dim long ago, between the two dividing ranges. "No man's land," I call it.

'As the battalions of twenty, spear in hand, "heilaman" on left shoulder, foot to foot, shoulder to shoulder, trooped forth, their eyes blazing with the light of battle, they'd stop and bow their heads by Bobbie and cast phantom ashes of the sacred "wambiloa" upon him.

'And I reckon that made him a ghost like themselves.

'How did I know if I was senseless? I saw them do it, sir, and my nerve held good until I fired a revolver slap through a fellow who was standing about six yards off, with a spear up, to throw at me. He was a king, I think, for I never saw such a feather mat as he had on him. It was like bronze-gold.

'When I saw him still there, just the same after the shots, I fainted, or anyhow became senseless.

'At daylight I came to myself and buried poor "Bobbie," with my revolver close handy. Not that it was much use in that place, but it was company like.

'It was time too that poor "Bobbie" was buried. The flies told me that. I struck a blow with my pick on some chocolate-coloured rock, on which I could see blue deposit, and a lot of different sized opals; when that ghostly awful cry came pealing out again directly.

'"So," I says, "if it's meddling with things beyond my knowledge, I am, I'm off," and I got back with my traps through the tunnel, blocked up the other end, so that a mouse couldn't get through, got my horses and went clean out of the country.

'I never stopped till I got down here, 700 miles from the spirit-land.

'How do I know them opals are there, sir? Why, bless you, I saw them then, and I've seen 'em often since in my dreams, for I've been there many times a-hunting with poor Bobbie.'

Barbara Baynton

A Dreamer

1902

A SWIRL of wet leaves from the night-hidden trees decorating the little station, beat against the closed doors of the carriages. The porter hurried along holding his blear-eyed lantern to the different windows, and calling the name of the township in language peculiar to porters. There was only one ticket to collect.

Passengers from far up-country towns have importance from their rarity. He turned his lantern full on this one, as he took her ticket. She looked at him too, and listened to the sound of his voice, as he spoke to the guard. Once she had known every hand at the station. The porter knew everyone in the district. This traveller was a stranger to him.

If her letter had been received, someone would have been waiting with a buggy. She passed through the station. She saw nothing but an ownerless dog, huddled, wet and shivering, in a corner. More for sound she turned to look up the straggling street of the township. Among the sheoaks, bordering the river she knew so well, the wind made ghostly music, unheeded by the sleeping town. There was no other sound, and she turned to the dog with a feeling of kinship. But perhaps the porter had a message! She went back to the platform. He was locking the office door, but paused as though expecting her to speak.

'Wet night!' he said at length, breaking the silence.

Her question resolved itself into a request for the time, though this she already knew. She hastily left him.

She drew her cloak tightly round her. The wind made her umbrella useless for shelter. Wind and rain and darkness lay before her on the walk of three bush miles to her mother's home. Still it was the home of her girlhood, and she knew every inch of the way.

As she passed along the sleeping street, she saw no sign of life till near the end. A light burned in a small shop, and the sound of swift tapping came to her. They work late to-night, she thought, and, remembering their gruesome task, hesitated, half-minded to ask these night workers, for whom they laboured. Was it someone she had known? The long dark walk—she could not—and hastened to lose the sound.

The zigzag course of the railway brought the train again near to her, and this wayfarer stood and watched it tunnelling in the teeth of the wind. Whoof! whoof! its steaming breath hissed at her. She saw the rain spitting viciously at its red mouth. Its speed, as it passed, made her realise the tedious difficulties of her journey, and she quickened her pace. There was the silent tenseness, that precedes a storm. From the branch of a tree overhead she heard a watchful mother-bird's warning call, and the twitter of the disturbed nestlings. The tender care of this bird-mother awoke memories of her childhood. What mattered the lonely darkness, when it led to mother. Her forebodings fled, and she faced the old track unheedingly, and ever and ever she smiled, as she foretasted their meeting.

'Daughter!'

'Mother!'

She could feel loving arms around her, and a mother's sacred kisses. She thrilled, and in her impatience ran, but the wind was angry and took her breath. Then the child near her heart stirred for the first time. The instincts of motherhood awakened in her. Her elated body quivered, she fell on her knees, lifted her hands, and turned her face to God. A vivid flash of lightning flamed above her head. It dulled her rapture. The lightning was very near.

She went on, then paused. Was she on the right track. Back, near the bird's nest, were two roads. One led to home, the other was the old bullock-dray road, that the railway had almost usurped. When she should have been careful in her choice, she had been absorbed. It was a long way back to the cross roads, and she dug in her mind for landmarks. Foremost she re-called the 'Bendy Tree,' then the 'Sisters,' whose entwined arms talked, when the wind was from the south. The apple trees on the creek— split flat, where the cows and calves were always to be found. The wrong track, being nearer the river, had clumps of sheoaks and groups of pines in places. An angled line of lightning illumined everything, but the violence of the thunder distracted her.

She stood in uncertainty, near-sighted, with all the horror of the un-known, that this infirmity could bring. Irresolute, she waited for another flash. It served to convince her, she was wrong. Through the bush she turned.

The sky seemed to crack with the lightning; the thunder's suddenness shook her. Among some tall pines she stood awed, while the storm raged.

Then again that indefinite fear struck at her. Restlessly she pushed on till she stumbled, and, with hands out-stretched, met some object that moved beneath them as she fell. The lightning showed a group of terrified cattle. Tripping and falling, she ran, she knew not where, but keeping her eyes turned towards the cattle. Aimlessly she pushed on, and unconsciously retraced her steps.

She struck the track she was on when her first doubt came. If this were the right way, the wheel ruts would show. She groped, but the rain had levelled them. There was nothing to guide her. Suddenly she remembered that the little clump of pines, where the cattle were, lay between the two roads. She had gathered mistletoe berries there in the old days.

She believed, she hoped, she prayed, that she was right. If so, a little further on, she would come to the 'Bendy Tree.' There long ago a runaway horse had crushed its drunken rider against the bent, distorted trunk. She could recall how in her young years that tree had ever after had a weird fascination for her.

She saw its crooked body in the lightning's glare. She was on the right track, yet dreaded to go on. Her childhood's fear came back. In a transient flash she thought she saw a horseman galloping furiously towards her. She placed both her hands protectingly over her heart, and waited. In the dark interval, above the shriek of the wind, she thought she heard a cry, then crash came the thunder, drowning her call of warning. In the next flash she saw nothing but the tree. 'Oh, God, protect me!' she prayed, and diverging, with a shrinking heart passed on.

The road dipped to the creek. Louder and louder came the roar of its flooded waters. Even little Dog-trap Gully was proudly foaming itself hoarse. It emptied below where she must cross. But there were others, that swelled it above.

The noise of the rushing creek was borne to her by the wind, still fierce, though the rain had lessened. Perhaps there would be someone to meet her at the bank! Last time she had come, the night had been fine, and though she had been met at the station by a neighbour's son, mother had come to the creek with a lantern and waited for her. She looked eagerly, but there was no light.

The creek was a banker, but the track led to a plank, which, lashed to the willows on either bank, was usually above flood-level. A churning sound showed that the water was over the plank, and she must wade along it. She turned to the sullen sky. There was no gleam of light save in her resolute, white face.

Her mouth grew tender, as she thought of the husband she loved, and of their child. Must she dare! She thought of the grey-haired mother, who was waiting on the other side. This dwarfed every tie that had parted them. There was atonement in these difficulties and dangers.

Again her face turned heavenward! 'Bless, pardon, protect and guide, strengthen and comfort!' Her mother's prayer.

Steadying herself by the long willow branches, ankle deep she began. With every step the water deepened.

Malignantly the wind fought her, driving her back, or snapping the brittle stems from her skinned hands. The water was knee-deep now, and every step more hazardous.

She held with her teeth to a thin limb, while she unfastened her hat and gave it to the greedy wind. From the cloak, a greater danger, she could not in her haste free herself; her numbed fingers had lost their cunning.

Soon the water would be deeper, and the support from the branches less secure. Even if they did reach across, she could not hope for much support from their wind-driven, fragile ends.

Still she would not go back. Though the roar of that rushing water was making her giddy, though the deafening wind fought her for every inch, she would not turn back.

Long ago she should have come to her old mother, and her heart gave a bound of savage rapture in thus giving the sweat of her body for the sin of her soul.

Midway the current strengthened. Perhaps if she, deprived of the willows, were swept down, her clothes would keep her afloat. She took firm hold and drew a deep breath to call her child-cry, 'Mother!'

The water was deeper and swifter, and from the sparsity of the branches she knew she was nearing the middle. The wind unopposed by the willows was more powerful. Strain as she would, she could reach only the tips of the opposite trees, not hold them.

Despair shook her. With one hand she gripped those, that had served her so far, and cautiously drew as many as she could grasp with the other.

The wind savagely snapped them, and they lashed her unprotected face. Round and round her bare neck they coiled their stripped fingers. Her mother had planted these willows, and she herself had watched them grow. How could they be so hostile to her!

The creek deepened with every moment she waited. But more dreadful than the giddying water was the distracting noise of the mighty wind, nurtured by the hollows.

The frail twigs of the opposite tree snapped again and again in her hands. She must release her hold of those behind her. If she could make two steps independently, the thicker branches would then be her stay.

'Will you?' yelled the wind. A sudden gust caught her, and, hurling her backwards, swept her down the stream with her cloak for a sail.

She battled instinctively, and her first thought was of the letter-kiss, she had left for the husband she loved. Was it to be his last?

She clutched a floating branch, and was swept down with it. Vainly she fought for either bank. She opened her lips to call. The wind made a funnel of her mouth and throat, and a wave of muddy water choked her cry. She struggled desperately, but after a few mouthfuls she ceased. The weird cry from the 'Bendy Tree' pierced and conquered the deep throated wind. Then a sweet dream voice whispered 'Little woman!'

Soft, strong arms carried her on. Weakness aroused the melting idea that all had been a mistake, and she had been fighting with friends. The wind even crooned a lullaby. Above the angry waters her face rose untroubled.

A giant tree's fallen body said, 'Thus far!' and in vain the athletic furious water rushed and strove to throw her over the barrier. Driven back, it tried to take her with it. But a jagged arm of the tree snagged her cloak and held her.

Bruised and half conscious she was left to her deliverer, and the back-broken water crept tamed under its old foe. The hammer of hope awoke her heart. Along the friendly back of the tree she crawled, and among its bared roots rested. But it was only to get her breath, for this was mother's side.

She breasted the rise. Then every horror was of the past and forgotten, for there in the hollow was home.

And there was the light shining its welcome to her.

She quickened her pace, but did not run—motherhood is instinct in woman. The rain had come again, and the wind buffeted her. To breathe was a battle, yet she went on swiftly, for at the sight of the light her nameless fear had left her.

She would tell mother how she had heard her call in the night, and mother would smile her grave smile and stroke her wet hair, call her 'Little woman! My little woman!' and tell her she had been dreaming, just dreaming. Ah, but mother herself was a dreamer!

The gate was swollen with rain and difficult to open. It had been opened by mother last time. But plainly her letter had not reached home. Perhaps the bad weather had delayed the mail boy.

There was the light. She was not daunted when the bark of the old dog brought no one to the door. It might not be heard inside, for there was such a torrent of water falling somewhere close. Mechanically her mind located it. The tank near the house, fed by the spouts, was running over, cutting channels through the flower beds, and flooding the paths. Why had not mother diverted the spout to the other tank!

Something indefinite held her. Her mind went back to the many times long ago when she had kept alive the light while mother fixed the spout to save the water that the dry summer months made precious. It was not like mother, for such carelessness meant carrying from the creek.

Suddenly she grew cold and her heart trembled. After she had seen mother, she would come out and fix it, but just now she could not wait.

She tapped gently, and called 'Mother!'

While she waited she tried to make friends with the dog. Her heart smote her, in that there had been so long an interval since she saw her old home, that the dog had forgotten her voice.

Her teeth chattered as she again tapped softly. The sudden light dazzled her when a stranger opened the door for her. Steadying herself by the wall, with wild eyes she looked around. Another strange woman stood by the fire, and a child slept on the couch. The child's mother raised it, and the other led the now panting creature to the child's bed. Not a word was spoken, and the movements of these women were like those who fear to awaken a sleeper.

Something warm was held to her lips, for through it all she was conscious of everything, even that the numbing horror in her eyes met answering awe in theirs.

In the light the dog knew her and gave her welcome. But she had none for him now.

When she rose one of the women lighted a candle. She noticed how, if the blazing wood cracked, the women started nervously, how the disturbed child pointed to her bruised face, and whispered softly to its mother, how she who lighted the candle did not strike the match but held it to the fire, and how the light bearer led the way so noiselessly.

She reached her mother's room. Aloft the woman held the candle and turned away her head.

The daughter parted the curtains, and the light fell on the face of the sleeper who would dream no dreams that night.

Mary Gaunt

The Lost White Woman

1916

THE brig was a wreck. Now and again through the foaming breakers they could see the dark mass of her stern, but the white water covered it and it was gone; a spar or two came washing ashore and some of the deck hamper, but it was utterly impossible that any living thing could be aboard the *Britannia*. On the beach stood the little band of survivors, three men and a woman. It was a November day, the storm had passed, overhead was a cloudless blue sky, and the bright sun was rapidly drying their damp clothes and putting a little warmth into their frozen limbs. The woman, hardly more than a girl she was, drew her red cloak round her and shivered drearily. She felt sick and ill and terrified, and she wished with all her heart that the sea had not been so merciful.

'Heart up, my pretty,' said the old man beside her, putting a kindly hand on her shoulder.

'Where are we?' she asked.

The old man looked towards the mate who was carefully nursing a broken arm.

'Ninety Mile Beach, I think,' said he, sinking down on the sand, 'the Gippsland coast.'

And in 1839 they knew less about Gippsland than we do about Central Africa. Behind them was dense tea-tree scrub, its dark green tops vivid and bright in the sunshine, and before them the long yellow stretch of sand that went right away to the horizon, and the treacherous sea sparkling and dancing in the sunlight.

'We can walk back to the settlement,' suggested the old sailor.

But the mate shook his head.

'Scrub's too dense, so I've heard, and there's Corner Inlet and Western Port to be negotiated if we go round the coast. No, bo'sun, Twofold Bay's our only hope,' and he looked pitifully at the woman.

'Then we'd better start at once,' said the bo'sun, and he put one arm round her, lifted her to her feet, and turned his sturdy old face to the east. The other two quietly followed him.

They had no food, they had no water, they had absolutely nothing but what they stood up in, and for all they knew, the thick scrub on their left hand might be swarming with blood-thirsty savages.

At noon they came to some rocks jutting out into the sea. They searched and found shell-fish, and their overpowering thirst they quenched at a rill of water that came out of the scrub. The woman was done, and so was the mate. They had just as soon lie down and die there as crawl a step farther, and since the others would not leave them, they all lay down and rested in the shade of the tea-tree. They slept, too, and they kept no watch. There might be lurking savages, but their plight could hardly be worse. Death possibly would not be so cruel as that weary tramp along the coast to Twofold Bay.

And at evening death came. Just as the sun was setting and the swift darkness coming down on the land, there were strange rustlings in the scrub about them, so soft and gentle it might have been the wind among the leaves, only there was no wind.

Ellen Hammond heard it first. She pushed her thick hair back from her ears and sat up and listened, then her eyes fell on a dark hand beside a tea-tree stem; she stifled a cry, and in a moment the scrub was alive with leaping, dancing figures. There came a flight of spears; the old man beside her died with a moan, and the other two scrambled to their feet. But their eyes were heavy with sleep; they had only their fists to defend themselves with, and those black figures, with skeletons marked on them in white, outnumbered them ten to one.

The unhappy woman crouching there saw them butchered before her eyes, and crouched still lower. It was useless her trying to escape, and she covered her face with her long, fair hair, gave a yearning, tender thought to the husband and home she had been going to in Sydney, and bent her head to meet her fate. Oh that it might come quickly! That it might come quickly! The white men had died so quietly, with scarce a groan, and now there was in her ears only the uncouth yabbering of savage tongues. How horrible, how weird, how unearthly it all seemed! But still death did not come.

And then a new terror seized her; she thought no more of husband and home, she only realised she was alone and unprotected among those horrible savages, and she envied with all her heart the quiet men beside her. The suspense was more than she could bear, and she sprang to her feet with a terrified cry, and started down for the beach. If she could but reach the sea, the kindly sea, then would all her troubles be over.

But she had not gone half-a-dozen steps before strong hands were laid upon her, she was turned round sharply, and found herself facing a stalwart savage with a bearded face smeared with grease and a piece of bone stuck in his hair. He uttered a sort of grunt of astonishment and admiration. Probably in all his days he had not seen anything so fair as this English girl, with the sunny hair about her shoulders and her blue eyes wide with horror and terror. He appeared to be a sort of chief amongst them, for he pushed off the others who came crowding round, and put his hand on her shoulder. It made her shudder, but she dared not shake it off. At least he kept the other savages away, and she closed her eyes to shut out the sight of them stripping the dead men who had been her friends all this long, weary day.

At last the hand on her shoulder began to urge her forward, and the whole band went in single file through the scrub. It was dark now, and the savages were evidently afraid. They huddled close together, and moved in silence. The tea-tree was high above their heads; sometimes it met and shut out the dark sky, but generally she could see a star looking down on her, reminding her of her courting days, when she and Tom had looked at the stars together, and it comforted her somehow, though she could hardly have told how. By and by they passed the belt of tea-tree, the scrub and undergrowth were different now, and immense trees towered overhead; then the ground cleared a little, there were little points of leaping flame in the darkness, shrill coo-eyes, the guttural sound of many voices shouting in an uncouth, barbarous tongue, and the pattering of bare feet, and she knew they had reached the blacks' camp.

She was so weary now nothing seemed to matter. She would have dropped to the ground but for the strong hand on her shoulder. A stick in a small fire, a blackfellow's fire, leaped into sudden light, and she saw she was standing beside a hollow tree, and that the interior seemed to be carpeted with soft rotten wood and dead leaves, and with a touch and a kindly look at her captor—necessity had made her diplomatic—she slipped inside and dropped down there, and with the shouts of the people still in her ears she fell into a sleep that was almost a stupor.

'I tell you what, my man,' said Captain Dana of the Native Police, not unkindly, 'you'd very much better let us go alone. See here, you're nothing much of a bushman, and you won't be any mortal good to us. You go back to the settlement like a good fellow, and I'll send Bullet here along to put you on the right track. If there's a white woman there——'

'If—if——" stammered Hammond, whose dark hair was already streaked with grey, and whose young face had many lines in it. "When that stockman from Western Port way saw no less than two trees with E. H. marked on them. I—I——'

'And you know,' said Dana soothingly, 'the average stockman will see anything that's worth a glass of rum.'

'And that leaf he picked up out of Dr Jamieson's big bible. He swears there was something written on it in charcoal when first he saw it, but it got rubbed off in his trousers' pocket.'

'It might have been there before the blacks raided Jamieson's station,' mused Dana, 'and—well—it's but a slender clue, specially as we can't read it. Look here, do you know, Hammond—I mean—do you understand— what I mean is, if there's a woman with the blacks we're bound to find her, and we'll bring her in any way. My dear fellow, you haven't realised what the life of a woman among them is like, what she'd be after two or three months, let alone two or three years!'

The unhappy man groaned, and the policeman thought he was going to see reason.

'We'll hand her over to the first white woman we come across, and then you shall see her when she's properly clothed and——'

'I'm going on with you,' said the man sullenly.

'On your head be it then,' and Dana rolled his blanket round him, put his head on his saddle and his feet to the fire, and stared up at the stars, musing on the impracticability of white men and black troopers. Occasionally he looked round and saw his men dimly in the darkness out of range of the firelight, and the white man, full in the blaze, with his head buried in his hands.

'I don't suppose,' said he to himself, 'there is any danger, but if some wandering scallawag of a warrigal does throw a spear that ends it, I don't suppose the poor devil'll mind very much.'

It was weary work trailing through the dense forests. It was late autumn, too, and the rain—it rained every day; the ground was a quagmire—soft, loose ground on which the foot of a white man had never trod; the huge trees, the trailing creepers, the fern, and the tea-tree loomed up dimly through the mist and the rain, and the four black troopers were as miserable as only blackfellows can be. Only the stern command of their leader kept them going forward. Whenever they came to a sheltered spot they were anxious to 'quamby' there, and whenever they got the chance they gorged themselves so with food that there was serious danger of the supplies running short. As for the other white man, he grew more like a ghost every day. Even if he found the woman he loved, would it not be better for him and her that she should be dead? How were they ever to blot out those cruel years? And what must she have suffered! What must she be suffering still! Oh God! Oh God! No wonder he spent sleepless nights and watched the dawn come creeping slowly, grey and dreary, through the dripping bush.

They found traces of the aborigines more than once. More than once Bullet, a big black trooper, came back saying that 'Plenty blackfellow yanem from scrub,' but never did they get a sight of them, though they found their deserted fires over and over again.

'One day more and we must turn back,' said Dana at last. 'No, Mr Hammond, it's no good protesting. I assure you we haven't two days' flour left, and if I didn't go the troopers would go without me. There's not much chivalry among these sons of darkness. Back to Jamieson's station we must go. If he can lend us some rations, well, we'll come back for another two days, and that's all I can promise you.'

And that day Bullet found a tree and pointed it out to Dana. It was marked, as if with some rude instrument unskilled fingers had tried to cut thereon the letters E. H. And it was freshly done. Dana looked at it gravely, and the man beside him trembled like a leaf. The sun was bright in a cloudless sky to-day, and his face was ghastly.

'Well,' said the leader kindly.

Hammond moistened his dry lips.

'It is—it must be—'

'I think so too.'

The day was bright and fairly warm, and the troopers went gaily ahead. The blacks had passed that way, and they were following quickly. A broken twig, a little trampled grass, to the eyes of the white men there was nothing, but Bullet went ahead briskly and they followed in silence.

Hammond was sick with weariness and suspense. He could hardly sit his horse.

'I see nothing,' he said anxiously. 'Can they possibly be following anything?'

'It's as plain as the high road,' said Captain Dana. 'It won't be long now. We shall come upon them before night, and then at least we shall learn something.'

By and by Bullet stopped short and came back to his leader.

'Plenty blackfellow this time sit down alonga waterhole.'

'Then,' said Dana, dismounting, 'we'll leave the horses here and creep in on them. Here, Johnny Warrington, you sit down alonga yarramen.'

Johnny Warrington didn't exactly seem to like being left alone in the gathering darkness with the horses, but there was no gainsaying Captain Dana's orders. He would have liked to have left Hammond, too, but one glance at the man's strained, anxious face stopped him.

It was getting dark now, the outlines of the tree trunks were hazy with the evening mists. Captain Dana followed close behind Bullet, and behind him came Hammond. He knew that the other two troopers were on either side, but the gathering gloom hid them from him. He could see nothing but the tall, slight figure of the leader of the black troopers.

So impressive had been the command for silence that he hardly dared breathe; the others slipped along like ghosts, only his own footsteps seemed to ring out above all other sounds. He was thankful for the wind that arose and rustled the leaves of the trees overhead, for the mocking laugh of a belated jackass, for the mournful hoot of the little white owl that flitted like a lost soul across their path.

Then the figure in front came to a halt, and, turning, caught his hand and pointed to three fiery eyes that looked out of a background of gloom.

'Blackfellows' fires,' said Dana, 'at the bottom of the gully. We'll get a little closer and make a rush when I say "Go."'

The minutes seemed to crawl, they were stretching themselves into hours, the very sound of his heart beating seemed to fill all the night; then there was the sharp snap of a breaking branch. He had trodden on it.

'You fool,' said Dana's voice angrily. 'Go; now go,' he shouted, and he ran forward.

Then followed a scene of wild confusion in the dying light. The troopers raced forward with a savage yell. The blacks in the camp returned it with a cry of unmistakable terror. There was a flight of spears, and then another as the troopers closed. And then came the sharp report of the white man's firearms.

Dana swore an angry oath.

'Who did that?' But there was no reply. The camp was vacant, and its late occupants were rapidly scuttling away into the scrub. Only there was a dark form lay close to one of the little fires. Hammond stood still bewildered, and Dana cried to his men to see that they weren't all speared from the scrub.

The opossum skin rug at the fire moved feebly, and a woman's voice with a sob in it cried:

'Are you white men?'

In a moment Hammond was at her side, and Dana had stirred the smouldering fire to a blaze. It was a white face that lay there among the folds of the rug, a very white face, the hair all round it like an aureole was flaxen, but alas, there was a dark stain on the fur and it was growing larger every minute.

'Nellie! Nellie! Nellie! My God! At last!'

She put up a feeble hand and touched his face. There were still the ragged remains of a sleeve on the thin arm.

'I'm glad, I'm glad, sweetheart. I have wanted you so much.'

The tears were blinding his eyes and raining down on the face that was growing so still.

'Man,' said Dana's pitying voice, 'she is dying.'

'No, no.'

She turned her face into his shoulder.

'Tom, Tom dear.'

Dana bared his head. In the bright firelight they were a target for every spear from out the blackness of the surrounding scrub. But he reckoned that a blackfellow when he was scared was scared badly, and would not stop to see if things might not be mended.

A moment or two passed, and Captain Dana touched his shoulder again.

'Dead,' said he. 'She is dead. God rest her soul.'

'Who shot her?' said Dana when he told the story to his particular friend in Melbourne a fortnight later; 'well, between ourselves, just between ourselves, you know, I think it was Hammond himself. There were two reports, and I've dismissed Racy Bob from the force for firing without orders; the beggar was pining to get back to his tribe and would have made himself scarce in a week if I hadn't, and I've made Hammond clearly understand that he didn't. He thinks I've eyes that see the bullets in the air, but if the bullet that came whistling past my arm didn't bury itself in the opossum skin rug I'm a Dutchman.'

'She was better dead,' said Captain Lonsdale quietly; 'much better dead. But you're right, we'll keep the story quiet.'

And so quiet did they keep it that many people to this day think that the white woman who was captured by the Gippsland blacks was never found.

William Hay

*An Australian
Rip Van Winkle*

1921

In some states of Australia—especially in the South—there are those
curious survivals to be seen as you thread the wild ranges in motor or
coach—the roads that lead nowhere. Many will recognize the
phenomenon indicated. There used to be scores of them threading the
hills and flats that rise immediately over Encounter Bay. And it is the same
to-day; as you flash along the fine valley causeways, you see winding up
into the uninhabited bushland on either side, these tracks of white sand,
just wide enough to take a vehicle, and choosing one, you can sometimes
trace it with the eye before you are away—ribboning for miles over the
silent piney ranges.

Of course those neat little roads leading so persistently where by all
human conjecture there is *nothing*, and never was anything, of permanent
consequence (appearing so startlingly in the boundless scrub like a path in
an enchanted shrubbery) have quite a steady romantic interest for youth,
and a certain family of children which this story concerned, who
sometimes took their pleasure on these high flats over the sea, would often
turn their cobby little horses into some specially inviting road to *nowhere*,
only to find it breaking off into lesser new ones, or threading unalteringly
into the unknown, beyond their courage or the daylight.

The charm of these roads may be painted in a paragraph. The soil of the uplands is almost entirely whitish sand, and as bush-fires are not infrequent, there is hardly any time for undergrowth to grow, so that the pretty little piney trees, and gums, and bushes, and wild flowers grow formally as if niggardly planted here and there by the hand of man. Starting up among these green formalities are the mysterious roads, nearly always pure white, in places quite hard and scattered with white crystals, in others sprinkled with transparent, reddish gravel like a private driveway, but generally speaking simply soft, white sand, into which your horse sinks to the ankles, and in whose heaviness he frets a great deal, perspiring much and shuddering off the pleasant-sounding flies.

In the minds of the children, these roads led to more than one remarkable place of the imagination, but perhaps the more pleasing and generally accepted were that of a strange little solitary church, a Grecian temple left by the soldiers of Alexander or the lonely tomb of a great explorer, all fearfully distant and found by guess and wonderful persistence, of the kind (but for the jew-lizards and large black iguanas) just expected to be found at the end of so homely an approach. The attractions of the find varied with the hour of the discussion. If not too late in the day, the church would be conspicuous for a grove of little green peaches; if towards twilight, there were sounds of a wonderful organ. In these harmless romances, the children had something more than an amused abettor in Jake, the stockman, whose duties after the cattle in the back-scrub led to occasional meetings and homeward rides in company. In appearance, Jake was very romantic, with a head and face something resembling the portraits of R. L. Stevenson, only that he was exceedingly fair, and slightly more melancholy. He often wore his hair quite long. When at work he always wore a white handkerchief knotted loosely round his neck. But in the evening, when he would come up to see the master, or chat with the maids, he donned a beautiful fresh suit, and a handkerchief of exquisite pink or blue silk.

Looking back, we suppose Jake was a man of quite forty. He was a beautiful rider, and carried a small stock-whip, a weapon which, like the finished swordsman of old, he would seldom use. He never varied in his dress or address. There was something soothing in his slow voice, but sometimes—very seldom—his remarks were not exactly coherent. Perhaps this was owing to his solitary life—the life of his choice. Every year—we think it was every year—he would take a month's holiday, sometimes riding off to the capital on his horse, sometimes by coach. What he did with himself on these occasions was not quite clear. On one of them he informed me he went to Tasmania to see the caves, but finding his bush dress and manners not suitable to some fine company in which he found himself, took careful pencil notes of the clothing of a member of the party, purchasing exactly similar articles as near as he could remember from neck-tie to hat, and restricting himself to one single ornamental cup of tea who had been used to swig from his capacious billy-can. He also, he said, stopped himself in a habit he had of running down everything he saw, as it seemed to worry the party. 'For the time,' he would half sadly reflect, 'he seemed to pass comparatively well as a sort of harmless companionable joker.'

Jake seemed but absently amused at childish attempts to find romance in 'nowhere' roads or anything else, yet he would exert himself sufficiently now and then to answer a civil question about a road; and one or two specially brought to his notice of the more respectable sort were even found to possess some sort of distinction. This one led to lime-stone. The one yonder that fell in lumps into the valley was 'fire-wood.' While one approached romance and danger so far as to lead to some disused 'wells,' which same were afterwards privately inspected, and found grim enough among their rushes in the grey sand, guarded by ancient railings. However, on one inspiring occasion Jake pulled them all up before a string of no less than seven mingling tracks, and pointing over these with his sunburnt hand spread out palm downwards, said 'Now, master and young misses, if you were to follow one of those roads, and knew which one to take, and knew how to keep in it and not be coaxed off among the others further on, and never grew weary of it, why, there you'd come on a peculiar thing—yes, the queerest end, right in there in the bush that you would fancy a road could come to.' Of course this was a wonderful remark for a person like Jake to make, but it was a long time before there was won from him any more about it. He would just look wonderfully superior like a sad poet and slap his hand suddenly down on his knee, making all the horses jump. All got a notion somehow (not that his face was any less calm) that it was rather serious. At last one of the children by an oblique and then a direct question discovered that this silent, quiet track led like a ghostly guide actually to a house, and that the house was empty. In the moment's awed outcry, three other facts were extracted, that it was none of your mud and whitewash places, but built of good bricks and stone, with chimneys and a staircase. So here was the strangest information, aye, deep in one of these very roads, so wild, so disused, so quiet, so suggestive of romantic ends, so eloquent with silent mystery, there was—if a person were persistent enough, were brave enough, were, alas, impossibly and Olympically skilful and crafty enough—there was to be found a building, alone and empty.

Before we go further, it is time to narrate an incident in Jake's history, of which these children were then only dimly aware.

For years without number it had been the habit of the maids to chaff Jake about a certain 'Biddy Laurence,' an eccentric character, who dwelt somewhere on the road to the capital, and dealt, as the fit took her, in garden produce, though possessed of private means. Dowered with great personal strength, and capable of being roused to an awful scathing eloquence, she lived alone, associating only with those with whom she met when driving to village or capital, and certain favoured males—of whom Jake was one—who, in accordance with some tie of understanding or good feeling, undertook on occasion her ploughing and some of the heavier work. Of this strange scolding *solitary* it was not known whence she came, or what had been her history, if I fear (as is the fate of such eccentrics) they generally heard her spoken of partially in jest. Face to face, however, from her mature powers of sarcasm, and the sharp, cynical, efficient expression of her eyes, she was treated with more respect. I remember seeing her (a tall, dark woman) and have never been able to forget the extraordinary power and beauty of her expression of tired scorn.

It was not quite clear in what light Jake and his sparse brotherhood of helpers should have really been looked upon in their relations with the woman—whether actually suitors for her hand, or men approved of by her difficult eye, or merely acquaintances in whom existed a sort of freemasonry of solitude—whichever it was, when we heard one day Biddy Laurence had died, there seemed some uncertainty whether Jake should be laughed at as one in a sort of mock-bereavement, or treated rather carefully as one who had really suffered a sort of loss. As a whole I think he was accepted generally as one who did not consider himself much the worse off, and this I perceive was the suggestion of his rather smirky demeanour on the subject, if as I distinctly remember he was known to be one of those named by the dead in the distribution of her belongings. A faint interest lay in the fact that these were left to the children of a relation whose whereabouts it had been left to Jake and two visionary shepherds— his co-executors—to discover. Jake was believed to be going to look into the matter on his next visit to the capital, but there the interest lapsed.

It was not long after this, that Jake was late one windy night in returning home, in fact he did not come home till the following morning, looking very ill and grey. He gave, however, no more than a trivial excuse connected with his work, and not long afterwards he was again absent all night, and at yet another time was two whole days away upon his duties, without returning. This was very unusual with him. Some one chaffed him on one of these occasions as having been 'visiting with Biddy Laurence's ghost,' and though he put them off with a laugh, he looked weary and nervous. However, he soon seemed to recover himself, though he more than once repeated his absences, and we heard him chaffed most unmercifully by a certain ancient maid-servant, for 'mooning like a lunatic about Biddy Laurence's place.' Perhaps they thought he was doing himself a harm. He took it always pretty well, though slowly requesting them to 'stop their nonsense.' Finally, the children gathered from various asides that silly Jake had got a scare about the belongings in the dead woman's house, and had been watching there to see if he could discover if any one was tampering with them … as if any one would have wanted the poor rough things!

Out of this, one day, came quite naturally to the children in private discussion the strange conclusion that the house along the secret road, of which Jake had told them, must be 'Biddy Laurence's place.' What a fancy! What a gruesome idea to think of Jake hanging about the strange place in the night!

But the story turned out stranger than this.

There occurred that terrible summer storm, still remembered for its savagery and persistence, and Jake did not come home, and was not found for twenty-one days and nights. Searchers, having heard he had been hanging about the cottage of Biddy Laurence, went there among other places. He was, however, not found at that cottage, which was padlocked on the outside (or his horse, though it had been stalled there in a shed) nor at any of the nearer houses, including those of the two lonely shepherds, his familiars, who had neither of them seen him for some while.

It might have been supposed he had taken French leave and ridden off to the capital, but that his little collie dog had come home covered with mud and matted with burrs. The animal was wild and savage with a sort of bewilderment and seemed to be trying to convey something to every one. With great difficulty it was caught and tied up in the stable in the possibility that it might lead them after the vanished bushman, but it severed the rope with its teeth and disappeared in the night.

Some one had gone off to the capital to see if Jake was there.

One evening one of the gardeners, who was milking a cow in the further paddock, heard a curious quick barking and growling, and glancing scrubward, he saw what at first looked like a horse calmly walking along and cropping the bushes with a dog 'yapping' queerly about it. But suddenly he concluded there was something amiss as something like a saddle hung under the horse's belly, and at once he perceived that the horse (bridled though matted with mud) was hung upon by an awful, tottering figure, who leant against it, clutching the reins and girths, sometimes in a sort of frightful weariness dropping his head on his hands, again slyly raising it and urging the wonderful beast forward a meander of a few cropping steps.

Jake fell when he saw the gardener running, and was picked up quite cracked in the head. He wore no hat, and his shirt and trousers were caked with mud, like the coat of the horse, and fearfully torn. His hair and beard were long and stained with earth like his face. He looked as if he had been dug up from a grave. The poor horse had been rolling and rolling till you couldn't tell his colour, till there was only a hanging remnant of the saddle ratcheted by the martingale; while his beautiful mane and tail, over which Jake had lavished so much care, were tangled up with mud and stones. The little dog, besides being extremely wild and important, had, so it was found, the remains of blood on his jaws. The children called it 'the return of Rip Van Winkle' because when Jake became more coherent he could not understand that he had been away more than a single night.

Before we relate Jake's story we must return to the children. As we shall be some time before returning to Jake, we may mention that his strange narration was at first very contradictory and hovered on the supernatural—in fact *there*, in spite of stern moments of self-correction, it has hovered ever since. There are wicked men, however, who think he was hiding with this tale a more ugly and ordinary one.

The children heard next day that Jake had been taken ill in the scrub, but they were not told how he had managed alone in his long absence. They knew of course of Jake's condition when first sighted, and two of them hurried off and examined grievsomely his tracks backward for a part of a mile. Though it had rained in the night, these were easily traceable where they now and then marred the surface of the scrub roads. Immediately after lunch, one of the children, privately retiring, rounded in and saddled his pony. He wished to see for himself what happened to Jake's tracks further back on the uplands. He intended to follow them swiftly back on the chance of their taking him to Jake's seven roads, one of which, so he said, led to the forgotten house. In short, it was his splendid thought that, given Jake's tracks led to the seven roads, and onward along one of them, surely he might take it that he knew whence his sick friend had come, surely here was the key to the puzzle and the discovery of that mysterious dwelling.

What a chance! Nor would there be any danger in following Jake's tracks to untold depths of lonely scrub, since he could find his way home again by them, enlarged by his own!

The boy got off unseen, and was soon out of sight of dwelling and sea in the higher scrub. Jake's tracks were scarred so deep every now and then upon the road or among the brush that they were followed back at a trot: though horse and swinging Jake seemed often of two minds, the former pushing instinctively for the track, the latter from all appearances making now and then an effort to pull him upon a piece of clear going. At first the road rose over patches of red gravel bright enough among the piney foliage, but presently he was led off into a white soft road, he and his pony sinking deeper between narrow shrubberies. Out of this he galloped by a strange way again into the open, and but for Jake's footsteps and a vista of the sea and its mountain was entirely upon unknown ground. At length, with a panting cry, he recognized some configuration of the trees and view which told him he was actually being led towards the place of Jake's puzzle of the seven roads. These in a few seconds opened out before him, while away into the raggedest, most unused of the seven the bushman's footsteps sauntered on beside his horse in uneven strange distortions.

Imagine the Investigator's feelings of excitement at approaching such a romantic mystery. Here were old Jake's tracks like a string leading him through this labyrinth of intersecting roads to an actual habitation, somewhere hidden among these miles and miles and miles of empty wilderness rising and falling in unbroken change before him. It was the possibility. There is such a difference between dreams and stories, and reality. It is not quite so pleasant. There is a difficulty in *doing* the thing. It is as if a person who had been making believe with you grew rather grave. A young fellow breathes hard! Along the white track, between the countless, stiff, wild shrubs, would Jake's solitary house indeed be found?

The boy pulled in an instant; and then drew off his horse, and urged it into the new road. At first it was hardly a road at all, and so much a discarded human way did it seem, and so many little bushes had grown up in the surface of it, and hemmed it close about, that it was only their bruising and the fantastic bruising of the sand by Jake that drew the explorer further. He went now at a trot, more often at a walk, and was able to observe a certain prettiness in the path. It was impossible to help reflecting how like a private driveway were some places, if only they had cleared the bushes growing in the fair red gravel. At one spot where the hard marble whiteness of the surface was powdered with little crystals, he breathlessly dismounted and pocketed one as large as 'an almond.' On either side grew the wild fuchsias, about a span high, the honey-scented bells, like the cottage-flower, only made of leather. And smaller than these, but spreading more, things covered with garnet and gold. In great numbers were the double great white everlastings on silver stalks. He disappeared entirely now into a grove of banksias with serrated leaves, and now he pushed through trailing grey bushes with soft mauve flowers. But generally speaking the forsaken way passed agedly through formal shrubs, most of them spiked and prickly, and each living, as it were, severely exclusive. There seemed something sacred in such an old road, and to ride upon it was like troubling something that was shyly dead.

Quite early Jake's footsteps had vanished from beside the horse's, so it was plain that for a time at least he was on its back. Of course there were moments when the boy was full of scepticism, not only that Jake's tracks were leading true, but that such a track would lead to anything of human solidity. How could it lead to anything more satisfying than some withered erection of its own too plentiful walls of greenery under which the sick Jake had sought to shelter himself! Then the road was now and again crossed by others, some in better use, across which Jake led with a persistence barely trustworthy, while at one point he himself waveringly forsook his own road, for one not a whit more respectable. It was difficult to retain faith with a little restive horse continually pointing out how little it had in our purpose, or any purpose at all leading that way. But to hasten our story, just sufficient will was retained to push with Jake down the long, long slope, and on over flat after flat till the gums and wattles thickened darkly about the road and down a little dip in front, half buried in sand and banksias, suddenly appeared the half of an old grey gate and chain.

As the boy pulled in, feeding his eyes on these foreign things, he heard a curious sound, like the wind in the trees but never ceasing. He felt if he should discover nothing else in the empty silent wild but a gate and chain, it would be rather peculiar. Slowly he resumed. Just a little on, a dog-leg fence poked out of the banksias, which had almost overgrown it, and two wires that had been once twisted across, were now sunken in the sand.

He pushed his way along the choked old road for a few dawdling paces, when there opened in through the front leaves, just below, a little flat that had once been cleared, and showed a few cow-eaten apple-trees. Over beyond was a rise like his own, under which a creek ran with a loud constant serene sound. Just on the north of the orchard, was a bare mound, on which, quite ghastily, stood a lean looking house, of two stories, fearfully plain and strong, two windows and a blind one above, two windows and a door below. *There it was*, Jake's house, but how plain from what had been imagined! At last the awed Investigator pushed down the tale of Jake's wonderful 'nowhere' road, and jigging out on the flat, saw lonely away against the scrub, eighty yards behind, a shed and barn of great logs, rudely roofed with straw held down by wires strangely suspending great stones.

Nothing could have been more motionless than the place was, or more lacking in animal life. Round the windows of the house, as he came nearer, he saw the wood had gone quite black for want of paint, while the door was just old, grey wood. If this was a little ugly, the brick-work of the house was nice and pleasant, while it was good to have the creek in there, calling all the while so loud and serene. Also the great apples on the tops of the trees were very homely, though when one was snatched and tested, it was found to be dreadfully sour. Afar—very far—in the scrub some jackasses were effusively laughing. When the mound was mounted and the house encircled at a polite distance, it was seen that two of the windows were mended with black sacking, and the old blinds, discoloured by the rain, were little more than coarse bits of stained rag. There was an enclosed plot before the front of the house, but nothing in it of human planting, not a shrub or a flower. This was just the same at the rear, where presently he arrived, not a poor bit of ivy or even a single ragged bush of geraniums. The owner had been one who had no love for flowers, or had somehow ceased to love them. What a sardonic woman! The boy wondered if this was what Jake meant when he said there was something peculiar about the house, or if there was something else. Jake's manner had not implied that there was anything awful, but only rather strange. There seemed nothing stranger than that. The back of the place was very bare. There were two lower windows, boarded up, and a door of old grey wood. There was a sphere-shaped tank half sunk in the ground. A small shed faced the door, in which were the wheel-marks of a cart, but nothing else. A path ran down to the river, passing on its way a dairy sunk in the slope, and down below, some remnants of tree-cabbages.

The child found courage in the persistent noise of the water, and

slowly sliding off his horse, tied it protesting to the shed. He thought he
would go round to the front, and see if he could perceive anything
through a pane of glass on one side of the door. Parting from his irreverent
pony with reluctant hand, he was passing slowly round the building, when
the back door drew him nearer. It hung uneven on its hinges, and there
was a gap at the bottom. Surely something might be seen through the gap.
When he had come close up, he found to his great surprise that the
padlock was undone and hung against the post. He was surprised because
he remembered when the other day Jake's searchers visited the house, that
the doors were fast.

He was awed. For the instant he thought of quickly remounting. But
it was wonderful how calming was the silence and that pretty creek. It
occurred gradually to him that Jake must have returned here after the
searchers had left, have entered the house, and then forgotten the door. He
had felt too ill perhaps to fasten it. If there were any one inside, it could
only be one of Jake's two friends, with one of whom he was acquainted.
Slowly his awe lessened. He could not hear the slightest sound. He took
courage and knocked with his whip. If one of Jake's friends came, he
would ask him if he might see inside.

There was no answer to his knock, which was so solitary it seemed to
echo into the trees. He waited with a proper decency, and knocked again.
If there was one thing he had no belief in it was the existence of ghosts of
dead people. The house was silent. He put his hand on the old door and
ventured to push it. Had he known what had happened, he would not
have done so. He saw inside some nice stone flags. He pushed the door
yet further, and then quite wide, so that the light crept in. This was the
room where the woman had lived. Jake knew this room well of course. It
smelt of incense, the smell of burned shea-oak. It was quite a decent sort
of place. Two black kitchen chairs with flowers along the tops; she had to
have flowers somewhere; a brown cupboard made of rough boarding; a
few plates in a rack, with pictures of the Rhine; a bare table under the
window; a low stove in which the ashes still lay. Before the latter a heavy
milking stool. The flag-stones were clean and grey. There was a bit of
sacking by the table for people's feet. All was quite clean except the ashes.
The stove itself was nice and black.

Against the wall there was a piebald stone, evidently for keeping the
door open, and the boy pulled this before it. He took another peep about
the room. Past the door there was another table, scarred with burning on
which lay a penny ink-bottle, a pen, and some paper with something

written upon it. Past the table, in the back wall, near the cupboard, there was a door, very rough, crossed with level beams. By this you would enter the interior of the house. To enter by this door you would have needed to mount a step. The boy began to wonder what sort of a strange look had the rest of the stern rooms. There was something strange about it, as Jake said. One peep through the door!

The door had no latch, but a bit of fretted rope hung down for a handle. He took a peep back at his pony. It was straining and snorting after a bit of grass, but the reins were strong. Advancing on tiptoe, he mounted the step and pulled at the rope. The door opened rather heavily but as easily as if it were oiled. Inside it took his breath away, it was such a change. There was a narrow old carpet along the passage, which was varnished at the sides. A narrow staircase led up above him, with polished banisters. Only a cobweb here and there. On the walls a faded wallpaper with hundreds of little black baskets of fruit, and two walnut-framed engravings, one with a great many figures of men—probably great men, for they wore frockcoats—and in the other, too, a great many figures, among which he thought he saw Wellington. There were two beautiful baskets made of 'everlastings' hanging from the dim ceiling, and there was a hat-stand, in which stood a fishing-rod; but he could hear no noise, only that of some flies moving to and fro.

It was not long before he thought he would go further. There was a door on either side of the front door (painted here a dusky yellow), that on the left being just open, as he could see through the banisters. The kitchen door fell behind him, pushing him in, and he advanced breathless up the carpet. The stairs, he now saw, were covered with an ivory patterned linoleum, and at the bottom, inside, hung a large cross of 'everlastings.' This reminded him that the woman was quite dead, and for a moment he fluttered in the hall like a frightened butterfly—dead as the road on which he had found his way to this lost place, along which, when Jake's footsteps were gone, he could never come again. He clung desperately to a chair of polished wood by the door that was ajar. To this presently, he reached, and gave a dreadful knock. There was nobody moving but the flies. He felt the door again and it moved like a live door from near the hinges. It allowed itself to be pushed, and he sprang up with an exclamation of amazement. The room was a pretty little sort of drawing-room, if hardly faded. A number of little chairs of dark carven wood, with cushions of a kind of green worsted covered the carpet. The light came dully through the thin blind, shining half-darkly on the faded flowers of the wall-paper, on which hung a number of interesting things, including a guitar, one string of which was broken and hung down over the dull gleam of a mirror. It was a surprisingly pretty place. There was a large engraving on the left wall which interested him greatly. It was that of a man in armour with a dark brooding face like a faithful dog, seated beside a woman who stood by a table with strange, wild, haunted eyes. What could it mean? When presently he entered the room, he several times caught the man watching what he did. It was surprisingly pretty. There was a gold clock on the mantelpiece opposite, and on either side two beautiful greyhounds carved in marble, almost as large as live dogs. On the left there was a cabinet piano, with a bit of satin on the front, and some songs on the top. Beyond the chimney, there was a faded-looking orange-coloured bookcase, with perhaps twenty books behind the glass in the top portion. But there was one little chair, as pretty a thing as any one ever saw, covered with satin of different colours, red, and washed-out blue, and parrot green and gold. It might have been made for a child. A cruel-looking Afghan sword, without a scabbard, hung on the wall past the curtains, so long it was difficult to believe it was really meant for use. In the corner too, beyond the window, there was a large fan of peacock's feathers, the brown ones below (which you see when he flaunts his tail) and the beautiful blue ones above. He remembered superstitious people saying that peacock's feathers were unlucky except at Christmas; the eyes were rather dark. Everything was spick and span, except the broken string of the guitar, which perhaps a mouse had gnawed. Through the crack of the door, in the corner, there was a green sofa, a Chinese mat, and a round table with books on mats of green wool, besides a Swiss cottage and something else carved out of wood. Above on the wall was a coloured picture of a pretty woman with hair hanging on her shoulders, lying back, fanning herself and staring smilingly out of the frame. It would have been as startling as if you had seen somebody, if she hadn't been so sleepy. When presently he stepped right into the room to see if he was accurate about the bit of wood-carving behind the door (it was as he thought a stock-whip handle such as Jake cut with his knife and beautifully done like a snake), when he was standing examining everything, he was afraid something jumped on the wall, but it was his face in the mirror, and this wouldn't have sent him away, nor the man watching him from beneath his helmet, only suddenly, on the mantelpiece, extraordinarily faintly, he was nearly sure he heard the clock going.

He was immediately in the hall again, where he listened himself to his senses, concluding there was no sound of ticking in the room at all, and after eyeing the stairs with exceeding longing, he pushed over the hall, turned the handle of the opposite door, and took just one quick polite look.

This was a pleasant dark sort of dining-room, with a great deal of grey earthenware on the tall sideboard opposite, and an engraving of Venice over the mantelpiece. This picture was an old dull friend of the child's; also a coloured picture of the Prince of Wales hunting, which he had seen in the Christmas numbers. Everything was very neat. There were some glass jugs shimmering on the tablecloth reminding a young fellow of lime-juice and well-water. There were some very nice brown chairs with benobbed horseshoe backs. By the fender was a yellow rocking-chair without any arms. There were some pictures over the sideboard. They seemed of dogs or of claves; and there was something in a glass case whose eyes gleamed. He was quite certain it was not the head of any one, but rather just a small wild animal or perhaps a little dead parrot. Over the table hung the usual basket of 'everlastings,' round which some silent files were swimming.

He would like to have examined everything, but thought he would not. Lingeringly closing the door, he moved to the stairs and looked up. They led straight to the back wall, and up the other side. Mounting three steps up, he eyed the stairs to the top, where they stopped before a grey-white door. Now he crept carefully up to the corner, and peeping round, perceived another door across in the left wall, like the one into the drawing-room. It was dark up here, but a glow came from somewhere. The glow he found, when he had stopped and craned just a little further up, came through the left hand door, which, like the one below, stood open a little, and from the top of which somebody had cut out a large V of wood, either for the light, or some peculiar reason. The boy presently cried out: 'Please, is there anybody here?' but he couldn't hear a sound in the house. He had mounted a little further. He would like to have seen what the bedrooms were like.

It was rather a courageous thing to ascend the stair into the dark. However, he would not need to open any door, since that one was open over the drawing-room, while the jagged cut in its top had given the house a look as of nobody caring so much for it, or what any one did with it. He crept up three steep little steps and took another survey. In the dark at the back of the stairs, there was a third door. It was shut, and between the banisters and it, there was a red wooden trunk with brass nails. At the top of the stairs, where he at last breathlessly climbed, he felt a nice carpet; and ignoring the door beside him, he moved, coughing twice, across the blind window to the door which was open. A large piece seemed to have been sawn out of the top. He could not see the piece anywhere.

With a fumbling knock, he pushed the door in a little. It was a wonderful peaceful dark room. There was a green bed against the back wall, with white frills and curtains. Over on its other side was a varnished mantelpiece, on which was a clock with a gable top and a picture in the front of a trotting horse and trap. The pendulum had stopped rocking. There were numberless blue flowers on the wall-paper, like those the children call 'snake-flowers,' which come out to warn you when the summer begins to blaze. In the surprise of it, it was quite possible to see some interesting and even beautiful things. On the mantelpiece there were two black wooden candlesticks, and two large yellow sea-shells. On one side hung a Japanese mat with pockets. On a round table by the window, there stood a work-box with mother-of-pearl in the lid, and opposite to it one of those writing-boxes which, when opened, offer the correspondent a little eminence of lavender plush from which to address her friend or her enemy. Besides these, upon the dim table, there was a basket of wax flowers of all kinds of colours which he wished rather to examine.

There was yet another 'basket' of yellow and white 'everlastings.' There were such a number of things he could never remember all. On the back wall there hung a dim text, which, however, he was just able to read. It said: 'Wherefore did'st thou doubt, O ye of little faith?' On the same wall besides this, there were two small engravings in orange frames, the nearer of a man lying dead or fast asleep with his hair hanging down. The other beyond the bed seemed to be a woman kneeling. He could not be certain with so little light. There was a dressing-table beyond the bed, and some small pieces of china. Beyond the door was a chest of drawers with china handles, and beyond the window a washing-stand, with marble-top, and a curious low square basin and jug which would have been nice to wash your hands in in boiling weather. In the plain brick grate, which was clean and black, there was that kind of bitter bush they put in fireplaces.

There was just one other thing about the room that was not neat, and that was a mat at the side of the bed which was dragged up in a great fold instead of lying flat on the carpet. Like the cut in the door near his head, it made him wonder if any one cared any more what was done. It occurred to him perhaps when they lifted the dead woman from the bed to take her away, they displaced the mat without knowing it. But more likely a 'possum' had climbed down the chimney and been playing about with his little hands like the little monkeys they are. It was troublesome among those many interesting things so dimly there ... The child drew slowly out of the memorable place, pulling the door after him. Crossing over the passage, he paused for a moment at the head of the stair beside the other door there. It would be nice, he thought, to take a look into this room before going. It would be like the other, only just so much more different to be peculiar. His hand felt for the handle, and he opened the door a fraction. It was not as he thought: it was lighter, and the flooring was uncarpeted. He hesitated and then pushed and stared his way in. It was a quite empty room, and had the pleasant, winey smell of a place where pears have been kept. There was nothing whatever in it, nor were the walls papered. It might have been a room in a ruined forsaken house. There was a hole in the blind through which considerable light entered, and there must have been a broken pane in the window glass, for into the place the sound of the river came, loud and remote, like the breathing of some serene bosom. And suddenly, all of a heap as the child stood in the bare room, he remembered that all the intimate, pretty things he had been seeing, were alone in a far away wild forest.

He stood beside the door, listening to the calm sound, and wondering about the woman. He speculated upon how she spent her Sunday evenings. It occurred to him to suppose she went to bed early and read in bed, a dangerous but pleasant habit. While thinking about her he thought of the man listening to his movements in the picture below, and this would have given him rather a grisly feeling, if it hadn't been for the sleepy woman on the wall opposite to it. He decided to go away now, while there was plenty of light for Jake's road. It would not do to be caught by twilight in such a place. The creek was nice. It would never let you think anything about it, but that it was always quite quiet. It never ceased to say it—even to the empty house.

He closed the door on the empty room, and climbed quietly in the shadow downstairs. Partly to avoid panic, and partly because he knew he would be sure to be asked by somebody or other if he was certain he was right in thinking it was *Wellington* in the engraving in the hall, he passed the open door at the bottom of the stairs and made certain it was the Duke with his cocked hat crooked as usual. In the sitting-room door as he turned back, he had a dark glimpse of the things on the wall, and the backs of chairs. He pulled himself away in a sort of panic of hurry (he was still afraid of the clock there), and passing another little door, arrived at that which led into the kitchen. This—painted russet—pulled him with a squeak into the stony room, and as he crept across the floor, he saw that there was a hole in the flags by the stove, where the solitary person had stood while she stirred at her cooking. The ghostly incense of her fires was still there ... He found his little horse staring skittishly at something over the river (as if the quiet had bothered it) but it was quite secure. It did not seem to have had any doubt that he would ever return through the open door. As usual it would not wait till he mounted, but was moving off round the lonely house while he was still clambering. He reined it up in the orchard, and wrested another great apple from the protecting branches. It was rather better than the first, but very awful. Such as it was it must be made to content him, however, on the way home. Ah, what a burden of news and deeds he carried! How incredible! He took a last scared look at the house before he galloped out of the open. Who would have thought there were so many beautiful things in the lonely and ruined place?

How Jake's life was saved is half-revealed in the following occurrence. If we are to believe Jake he was kept alive by the dead woman. We learn it is a fact of medical science, that a person in a certain state of health, and especially in cases of bereavement, may lie in a condition of swoon without food, water, or nourishment of any kind, for a space of time measured in weeks. He may return to his senses with system hardly impaired. His body may be tended by artificial nourishment, or even lie untended. Though this does not apply to Jake in that he had a different story to tell, yet remembering that he was not quite like other people, and that he may have been suffering from grief, we are helped by the point to a passable clearance of the mystery.

Before accounting for Jake's 'two days' absence (in all two weeks and three days), and his other absences, we throw in a picture of his shepherd companions, who with himself constituted the sole society made free of her house by Biddy Laurence. Of these, his two co-executors, one was a powerful gipsy sort of creature, who might be said to live in a state of perpetual sulk. He was tall, almost black of skin, and self-possessed; most masterful and efficient in everything he cared to put his hand to; and so excellently poised in his nature, so completely at ease with his own company, that to meet and address him in the scrub alone with his gun seemed a sort of intrusion on his dark good-natured privacy. The other was a Dane, nicknamed 'the Crusader,' from the air with which he approached any form of work, whether it was to clean a sty or a wine glass. He wore a red peaked beard and had an obstinate, grim expression in his small, light eyes.

To go direct from these to Jake's account of them, after the woman's death, they kept her house cleanly and decent between them, taking the singular pride of three singular men in the preservation of her pretty possessions and that each should be in the place and condition in which it was left. Each man possessed a key to the cottage, and while they met there on certain occasions to give the house a thorough overhaul, any one of them dropped in as he cared to and went through the rooms to see that all was as it should be. There were some worldly people who whispered that they met in the dead woman's hermitage to gamble, and that the natural result of such proceedings occurred. But Jake sufficiently quashed such accusers by refusing to entertain a word of evidence against the two men. His liking for the two had never allowed much beyond a sort of shrugging contempt for two more human freaks, but such as it was, it was unaltered by what happened to himself. They may have gambled and quarrelled, or they may have simply quarrelled as partners in a delicate transaction, but if they had, Jake had forgiven them extraordinarily easily. It was not easy to breed a crime out of the story, when the wounded man laughed the only reasonable plot away.

Nevertheless the web had a blackish look for one of the men as it was first spun from Jake; if against the man's denials and the victim's, there was no more to be said. It seems there had arisen a sort of troubled discussion—without a trace of heat in any of them—about a certain shifting and misplacing of sundry ornaments in the rooms, first noticed by Jake. These peculiar circumstances were rather pooh-poohed by the other two, led by the Dane, till the gipsy became half-persuaded there was something in it. At last the doubt began to grip all three, until to clear themselves in one another's eyes of the slightest suspicion of fooling with the rest, and to free themselves of the fear (less possible yet) that someone entered the locked cottage in their absence, a sort of agreement was one night come to to set a trap in the house of which they should all, of course, be cognisant.

This rather gruesome suggestion again originated with Jake and was taken up scientifically by the gipsy, who was of course an adept at such things. Several suggestions, promising bodily hurt to an intruder, were discussed, though they parted undecided yet which to adopt. It spoke for the reverent care with which the men kept the rooms that the disorder agreed upon by all as most troubling to them was of a nature hardly noticeable to an outsider. In the sitting-room a string had been found broken as by a presumptuous hand in the woman's guitar. Then the pictures, especially in hall and dining-room, were constantly found crooked on the walls, not (as Jake agreed) that they hadn't each of them a different notion of what was 'straight in a picture,' but these were at such a vicious angle, and often a different one on the same wall, as could hardly be dismissed as the work of earth-shock or shock of thunder. There was as well sometimes a strange smell in the rooms which it was difficult to account for, a sort of bitter, herby smell as might have come rather from an old well, or from down in a tomb, than a warmly furnished house. On top of this a pair of horse-clippers, whose peculiar design all had much admired, had disappeared from a shelf in the kitchen, and no one would countenance the thought of having borrowed them.

There were some of a few objects whose disturbance seemed peculiar, but what most troubled the minds of all three, and what they had all three privately replaced and privately found disturbed again, was the disorder of the carpet in the woman's bedroom (a place, according to Jake, held with a feeling almost of veneration by them) which was constantly found drawn up in large folds about the room. It is strange how persistent had been this rather grisly untidyness, yet having quite captured the (perhaps disordered) imagination of the three watchers, it was agreed that in this composed and sleepy room some experiment in the nature of a man-trap might be made.

Jake had been previously much disturbed at the loss of the clippers and had spent one or two nights watching the clearing, without any result but a strange heaviness of mind. Not long after the 'trap' suggestion, Jake was waylaid near the clearing by a great storm, and thought he would take shelter in the house. He turned into the orchard about twilight. The lightning was the fiercest he had ever seen, almost ripping open the low canopy, while there was an awful close noise of thunder as if they were moving heavy furniture in a narrow room. Two storms were approaching beside one another, forking and banging like struggling beasts and giving little respites of wicked silence, in which the quiet creek rippled by with a dove-like sound. Jake rode to the house and let himself in at the back door. He was in the kitchen waiting for the rain to come on or the thunder to cease, when he thought he heard something drop on a floor somewhere up in the house. He opened the inner door and listened, and though he did not hear it again, he tip-toed into the passage. The storm was flashing through the blinds and fissures, and cracking loosely overhead. Inside, the house seemed to cower. He looked into the sitting-room, and came out, and went up the stairs. The last thunder-roar had made the doors rattle, and awed even Jake, whose ears were still straining after that little sound. When nearly up he thought he heard a movement in the woman's bedroom. Somewhat disordered, he struck a match, and half-dazed with the alternate clamour and silence, advanced steadily as far as her room. (When asked if he noticed in the dark, the piece cut out of the door, he said he did not notice anything of the kind, though the gipsy, who acknowledged to cutting it, said he removed it before that time.) Jake then hurled open the door and at the moment he entered it, there was a ghastly crash of thunder, and a blue light came out of the chimney and advanced over the floor towards him. He received at the same instant a sort of sickening blow at the back of the neck and fell in a swoon beside the bed.

The gipsy afterwards explained that he had removed the piece of wood from the door and taken it away, with a view to constructing the trap as agreed. It looked rather black for this man, supposing him to have entered the locked house by some private way. If you assume him to have made a murderous attack upon Jake, he might have afterwards removed the piece of wood as a blind. Some said, crediting the gipsy with panic, that the man-trap was actually in its place, being removed afterwards, and that Jake was the first to suffer from his own punishment, like the Scotch Regent of singular memory. The gipsy, however, vehemently denied that the trap was in place. Jake's story, as we have said, amusedly laughed him out of suspicion.

When Jake came to a few hours after (it is supposed he lay insensible for *days*) he could not tell where he was. There he lay in the dark, conscious of a ghastly thirst. To assuage this became a motive for movement. He had waked on his side, with a fearful stiffness in his bones; and as he groaned over on his back, his elbow struck both the roof and the side of some tomb-like place. Had he not been convinced he had been insensible only a short time, he might have supposed himself beneath the ground, though if he was buried, he knew he was not buried deep, for he could hear the thunder still pounding. He was suddenly conscious of a gentle, infinitesimal light about him. His thirst roused him to straighten out a corroded arm, and touch the side of his prison. He clutched at something which tore in his hand. It was curtaining. In the half-swooning state in which his senses swayed, he concluded he was on the floor under the poor woman's bed.

How he got under the bed he did not know, but it is possible he was there while his rescuers were about the house, and so they would hardly have found him had they entered. The Dane himself had called at the cottage two days after Jake, found the door open, gone through the house, without seeing anything, and locked it behind him. Again, by order of the stipendiary, the Dane had called in at the clearing after the searchers had been, and unlocked the cottage door. But this was over a week after the accident happened. The Dane did not go again through the house, as he did not suspect Jake of lying hid in the place all that time.

This was all lost on Jake. According to him, he came to a sort of dazed consciousness a few hours after he fell and heard the thunder thudding. Somehow he rolled and wrestled his way out on the mat beside the bed. There was a bright moonlight behind the blind, and the objects of the room were dimly shrouded. For a while he essayed to focus a weak gaze on this and that, but when he was certain of the door, and had risen to his tottering legs beside it, a nausea of giddiness seized his brain, and he swayed hoarsely in a mad dance with floor and ceiling. So wild was the fantastic frolic of the furniture that it amused him and he laughed weakly as he took a third double-somersault with the friendly door. The wall beyond the bed swayed over below him, so that the white ceiling became the wall. The grey objects of the room dived and recovered themselves like awful birds. Impatient at last, he fell like a ninepin into the passage, and with only one steady thing in his consciousness, a dream of liquid on the dried paper of his throat, found his way over to the stair railing, and crawled in a whirligig of sagging darkness to the stairs. Down these, hold by hold, he felt his way, a swooning sailor on a swinging mast, and crouched at length at the bottom, panting loudly in the faded chaos of the hall and trying strangely to steady in his mind the half-remembered position of the kitchen door. As the goblin house rocked and reeled in mischievous phantasmagoria, there was a silent 'blast' of lightning, with a tremble and report of thunder, and it seemed to the poor fellow as if all the forces of Gehenna were gathering to confuse him and shut him away from his chance of succour. He was again swaying on his uncertain feet. His climb, however, had worse perplexed him, and he awoke in one side-room at least where the moonlight shone on some familiar furniture, and thought for one awful moment he was lost among the crazy medley of objects. So beside himself was he, that from one of the pictures in this room—an armoured man—he could not free his vision, and at last seemed to sway with the image in a mesmeric dance. Back and forth they reeled—

nay, he was almost lost—when the stupidity of his extremity goading him, he drove the gibbering obsession from his eyes, and slipped and tumbled along heaving walls, and drove his way by dancing banisters, till with a dive and a quaking laugh of triumph, he fell *crash* at the foot of a heavy door, pushed it with his elbow, and knew by the step on the other side that he had won his way to the dark kitchen.

The kitchen door was open slightly, and the moon shone on the floor. Jake remarked that strange herby smell in the room. It may be thought a simple thing for the swooning man to reach the door, but he was now in a bad way, and when he had dragged himself inside, seems to have sunk for a while into a dreamy stupor, in which the shaft of moonlight danced mockingly before his eyes like a whip-poor-will. So great was his yearning for the water that he several times thought himself risen and swaying towards the door, to find the stone flags yet against his hands. It must be noted that he had reasoned the cement tank useless to him, for if he could lower the bucket within, he could never raise it to his mouth; he must go downward to the river. Upon a sudden, in his almost swooning state (so he affirmed) he distinctly felt he was aided in an effort to gain his feet, and guided *outside the house*, where he quite swooned away.

This may be taken as the reader pleases. He awoke shortly after to find himself lying at the right side of the house on the mound above the orchard. He was conscious of a slight sound behind him. As he turned his head towards the back of the house, he quite clearly saw a figure in a bonnet and shawl blend with the moon-shadow by the shed. He was almost startled back into clear sense. When he stared upon it fixedly the shed was empty.

So fearful was his thirst, that he immediately rose and staggered down towards the river, which he could hear and indeed almost see in the uncertain yet bright night. The poor fellow got no further, however, than a large apple-tree at the bottom of the slope, 'neath which he fell, sinking again into oblivion.

He awoke in the long weeds under the tree, still (as he had it) in that night, which the moon still lit, but which was grown calm. He was conscious of waking twice, once with his throat a torture, yet unable to move, and again in perhaps a worse condition of want, yet just able to move his head. In this latter state he discovered not far from him in the grass an old white jug lying half on its side with its lip missing. It had the earth stained look of a vessel that has been cast aside for a long period. After some time staring at it, a hunger for the liquid it had once held, led him to drag himself over to it, in the hope of finding a drop or two of rain-water lying at the bottom. When he had pulled it from the sort of nest in which it lay, he found it heavy, and three-quarters full of a rather muddy liquid. Then and there it was trembling at his mouth, but when he would have finished it at a draught, he found it fiercely tart, burning his throat, yet so satisfying to his craving, that he put the old vessel down only half emptied. It may be that some apples had dropped from the tree into the jug and mingling with some rain-water fermented into an ardent spirit. Whatever it was, a drink of such power had never before passed his lips. The effect on him was extraordinary. He felt revived, and yet he felt mysteriously elated.

His body seemed to grow firmer, and the blood to dissolve in his aching limbs, but if anything he was become more light in the head. The landscape was clearer to his vision and quiet, but as the minutes passed and he lay there in the shade as wide-awake as the mean house out in the moon he began to imagine a curious thing. He thought that he could hear the footsteps of somebody passing to and fro above him. It was done very slowly as by one looking about him as he trod, and he might have given it up as his horse, which must have broken out of the shed, but that it kept to one spot. He rose up on his elbow and screwed his head about the tree but there was nothing on the slope but a few logs and a couple of young trees with dark shadows. When he again dropped his length, after a few minutes, he heard the slow, slow pacing. Jake could not get his mind off it, but he could not see the top of the slope for the apple-leaves. He gave it up and lay listening. Suddenly he smelt a strong odour of crushed hoarhound as the weed is called, followed by a *thump* in the grass behind him. When he had got round his slow, stiffened neck to its limit, he had, he was certain, another glimpse of that stooping human figure as it vanished up the orchard-side.

Soon after, as he lay there in the shade under the apple-tree, he heard the sound of voices up at the house. He insisted that he heard these voices because at first they were so ordinarily conversational that he mistook them for human ones, and tried to struggle himself up to call for help— but he began suddenly to doubt if they were human, for they began to sing the tune of a hymn, 'Though dark my path, and sad my lot,' yet never singing more than the first two lines, and repeating them again until they suddenly went. Jake had the muddled thought that perhaps these were spirits who had never been able to finish the spirit of the verse in their human existence. They had only just gone when loud and weirdly a bell rang down over the river, the sort of large homely bell they ring at picnics to tell the children it is time for tea. 'Te-rang, te-rang, te-rang.' But it too was gone in jerky inconsequence almost while it summoned so insistently. This was a strange experience for the poor bushman, but somehow (whether from the elation produced from the strong drink, or the still mazed condition of his mind) hardly at all terrifying. The noises ceased as the wind changes, and here he lay alone in the moonlit orchard, with the sad crickets and the creek simmering by always so beautifully unaltered.

He was dozing off, wondering at the nonsense of his brain, when—hark!—there was a sudden great crying-out behind the house, hardly beyond the raucous echo of something happening inside. Jake was almost struggled to his knees, with 'help' in his mind (so certain was he these were horrid doings), when it seemed lost in a fearful chaffering of shrieking birds. Sharp on this, exceedingly pretty, a small silver light sprang up by the water, and was answered by another in a black window in the house. Once again arose that funny, insistent, angry old bell, 'te-rang, te-rang, te-rong, te-rong,' dropping suddenly with an illogical clatter as if thrown on the ground. And a little after Jake was immeasurably astonished by the sound of two deep chords struck on the piano, followed by two impish trebles 'dotted,' as it were, with the point of the fore-finger. These were repeated again and again, till they were gone like a startling memory, and the calm river rippled alone in the solitary place.

But to hasten to the last of these dubious experiences—so far from all human aid and sympathy—little more occurred to surprise him, excepting that once, from half a doze, he heard a stock-whip 'cracked' close over the river: once, twice quickly, and then a while after away down the water, a loud, unbearable 'crack.' After that, for a long time on, the silence of the orchard was not broken in this strange way and he was left lying there in the normal night with his thoughts.

His mind was still excited and he could not sleep, but, as the effect of the drink, perhaps, began to wear off, his spirits became sad and disturbed. It was gathered from his guarded remarks that the poor woman was heavily on his mind—that her loss and the deprivation of her presence in the world, settled on him with dim grief. Doubtless he had reviewed his life without her before, and had found it at least bereft of something unreplaceable, and now, lying with powerless limbs, in a half-swooning state, he muddled her up with these half-real things with illicit longing, even would have followed after if he could that grey figure in the bonnet, in the hope of finding in it something resembling yet the woman who had

died. But with his doubtful head and tottering limbs, he was not able to
hunt the clearing after that figure, in which he only half believed (the
reader, doubtless, is convinced it was but one of the guilty men), or do
more than lie dreadly wondering if the dead woman were still among
these invisible beings about her haunted house. Here he was, quite
convinced he had received help from *something*, and while he had more
than the courage, if he could, to stare it in the face, was troubled at the
feeling that it might be connected with this strumming on the piano and
impish ringing of bells, that it might be transformed into some impish
ghost, among a set of impish spirits. It was worse to him, even than that
he could not pursue her, that having gone from the world that had known
her voice, she might not be happy away there. Jake felt that he had rather
the woman was locked in her grave, than that her particular look and
character should have changed, or lost in self-respect. This new dread
settled on him till he became bitter and inconsolable: filled him, poor
fellow, with an uneasiness that touched the vitals of his life.

At that time the thunder was still murmuring in the south, and a
hoarse noise of wind began to move sleepily in the trees. The river rustled
by before him, the very similitude of that line of the poet:

The poetry of the earth is never dead.

Its loud calm insistence reassured the bushman. Fear-stricken, he swayed up
upon his hands to look upon it—to listen to it rippling by. There it was
sweetly and somnolently washing the feet of its trees. It filled some of the
lonely emptiness of Jake's heart to see it. His eyes followed it up till they
looked once more on the house above. The tall narrow front of the building
was now in shadow. His eyes went hurriedly from window to window.
There was a vacant emptiness about them which seemed almost bottomless.
It seemed inconceivably desolate, ruined, and alone. The voice of the river
was all that was left of the woman in the moonlit solitude. He cried out
suddenly and fell on his side in the grass, his staring eyes caught on a log just
above him on the slope. Upon it there was a figure seated. It was stiff and
motionless. It wore no hat and its wild hair hung on its shoulders. Its chin
was in its hand, and calm as the river in the sound of which it had died, it
was looking down upon him with a scornful, half-smiling face.

Jake's troubles were not over with the morning. The reader remembers
how bemazed he was when found, and while absent at the clearing over

a fortnight, long held to it that he was away only the one night. It must also be remembered how some said the clearing had been the scene of just a common, hushed-up brawl. But many thought differently, and to the present day, when the thunder rolls heavily over the Bald Hills, the village wives will say, 'This reminds me of the fortnight Jake was lost,' or 'This is as bad as the night Jake Lewkner saw the ghost of Biddy Laurence.'

If Jake had seen the ghost of a good spirit that night, he was confronted by something like the image of an evil one in the morning. The sun waked him, shining right under the tree, but when he tried to rise he found himself, if clear in vision, so weak and feeble he was scarcely able to move his limbs. He turned at once to the broken jug, to which he was barely able to crawl, and felt a little better after his second drink. He was lying near the jug, head on arm, when he heard two loud sounds not far off, one of which led him to get up on his arms. The first was the unmistakable thumping of hoofs, and when he had looked this way and that, he saw somewhat to his pleasure, his horse moving near under the trees, and watching uneasily while it tore at the grass. It was in a fearful condition, its coat and mane matted with creek mud, and its saddle half torn away. He called it feebly by name, and it shot up its head, and stared in his direction. The other sound was a curious dragging and rustling just in front of the tree, and now that his head was higher, he saw swaying in the yellow grass, a great, black iguana, coming fair for him with its half-waddle, half-glide. He had never seen a larger specimen of these great lizards; it must have been eight feet from forking mouth to swaying tail. It perhaps had been approaching him in the morning dusk, for it was plainly making for him, and from its alert head and shooting fork, seemed already trying to fascinate him to rigidity or somehow to be triumphantly aware that he was unable now to crawl away from it. It dragged erect and stiffly through the rustling grass. He knew that it was capable of a flashing rush. The bushman, used as he was to these ugly things, felt he was at last in a corner with one. Perhaps it had in its mind to avenge its kind for the many he had shot. Swaying there on his arms, and staring the reptile in its ruthless eyes, he considered what sort of feeble defence he might make against it. Glancing to one side after some sort of weapon, he saw not far on his right a small branch which had been torn from the apple-tree. It was far too small, but better than his lethargic hands. Meanwhile the thing moved so near that he could see the sack-like pittings on its canvas skin. The horror was that it might flash upon him when it saw him move. He hoped the great thing would not get him with his hands on the ground.

Just as he made a half-swooning swing towards the weapon, the beast, as if it saw through him, altered its course a little to the left, and came dashing at him with high angry head. Jake shielded his face with unwieldy hands. At the same identical instant, there was a fierce cry from beyond the tree, and down the slope came the bushman's little dog, galloping straight for the arrested reptile. A rope hung round his neck, his fangs were bare, and his jaunty little tail was cocked over his back. Fair and straight for the great thing he ran,[1] growling shrilly, without a foot's change in his pace, while the iguana slowed towards him, forking like Satan. The dog looked a small ship to be thrown against so huge an enemy, but he seemed to know his business. As he came up, the great iguana flashed to one side, the dog jumping the other way. Then, with some unknown canine quickness, he was on the back of the flashing reptile, and had his teeth in its black neck, from which position he was whirled about, snarling awfully, and then shot off away over on his back, regaining his brave little legs and dodging round, and again getting in on the thing's back, in which something vital had been severed at the first onset, for it could no longer freely move. A third time the little animal sprang upon the creature, but this time he was not thrown off with the lashing of the other, but jumped aside and stood watchfully snarling and panting. The black skin of the reptile was terribly wounded, and it stared back at him writhing impotently, with a feeble flicker of its tongue. The little David had beaten his terrible Goliath. When the dog came warily at Jake's whisper, he still snarled, while his master somehow freed his neck of the vexing rope.

This strange rescue was near the end of Jake's adventure. He was immeasurably better for the presence of his dog and horse, and far from being incapacitated with the shock of his escape, seemed by the horrible occurrence, or that wonderful drink, to have been galvanized with a new strength. He almost immediately sat up against the tree, and began to fondly wonder if he would in a while be able to walk. Remarkably enough he experienced neither the cravings of hunger nor thirst, and had no longer any wish to reach the river where it lullabyed under the morning leaves, but he entertained a mounting hope that safety was now not beyond him. His horse had browsed nearer, and when he had been calling it awhile, it came up in the manner of these beasts and smelt his shoulder. He felt constrained to try his strength beside it and rising by the girth, the animal standing quiet, he secured and knotted the broken reins. He felt pretty well, his head steadily righting itself, and his legs promising better with use. Thus he stood collecting his strength, the beast eyeing him stealthily, and he lengthening the reins with the dog's rope. He thought that, mounting the horse, and sitting well back, with a hold on mane and girth, he might go a long way towards help ... To hasten our conclusion, he *did* by some means or other manage to get himself upon the horse, and slowly, very slowly, left the clearing. Some said he was a night upon the journey, and this is not impossible. For certain portions of the way he clung to the martingale on his chest and face, and even, for a short ecstatic period, lay, like Mazeppa, on his back. He appeared to have twice fallen insensible in the road. On both of these occasions he was roused by the importunity of his little dog and found the horse feeding beside him. After the first interruption, he mounted the animal by the aid of some timber. But on the second, when nearer home, he was unable to mount, and with many a fall, could but cling to and move with his browsing beast.

The finish of this matter of the 'nowhere roads' quite touches the poetical. It was connected with the boy explorer. If it hadn't been for his investigations, Jake would have been in a nice corner with the maids.

Just as Jake was getting well, a photograph reached the household of two children of a distant friend, whose name happened to be Laurence. The bushman became very interested in this photograph, and would examine it for long periods at a time, and even fancied that it had in the jumble of its background, a second picture of a cottage of two stories standing on a mound. In point of fact this was not only his fancy for every one could see the thing he pointed out to them—a quite common photographic phenomenon. When held in the hand it was merely the picture of two children seated on the grass of a lawn, in front of a small fountain and a glasshouse. But if looked at on a mantelpiece, or from an appreciable distance, the fountain and glasshouse had formed themselves into a narrow, tall house standing on a hillock. In many ways it was entirely unlike the house along the 'nowhere road,' yet there was a distinct resemblance. Jake was rather taken with this whim of the camera, and when soon after the children came to stay in the house, he seemed much interested in them, and, as if he really was inclined to connect them with the woman, Laurence, expressed a wish to show them some pretty things in the interior of the hermit's cottage ... Thus a party was made up of maids and children (though the maids, it must be told, were suspicious of exaggeration, and always sceptical of there being anything much worth the seeing in the woman's clearing) and one day, under Jake's guidance, two spring-drays of somewhat irreverent people jolted up into the scrub after cooking apples.

It is a point of the tale that when the boy returned from his first stolen visit, he was so frightened by the news that there had been foul play in the lonely place and one of Jake's friends was suspected of trying to do for him, that he kept secret the destination of that eventful ride, and in fear of a scolding, related his adventure, under secrecy, to two only of his play-fellows. They were as awed at their awful burden as they were for him, and if they let a hint drop in the kitchen it was only by way of expressing a belief in poor Jake and his cottage. Through various unexpected accidents and precautions, the truant had not yet confessed his escapade when enlisted for the apple-picnic, and, as they sat wedged in the carts among the apple-baskets, the three conspirators would nudge each other at some anticipatory hint of Jake's, or at the mere thought of approaching the place whose strange secret they shared.

After a pleasant journeying along the silent track (with an occasional groan as the wheels sank from the hard into the soft sand) they arrived, with cries of half-amused amazement, in the clearing. The house as they drove up was the object of some blunt criticism, and it even appeared to the child that it had a more ruinous, dilapidated look than when he first saw it, hardly a pane of glass, so it seemed, being whole in the windows. Jake eyed it rather speculatively, but he said nothing until they approached the front door, when he greeted with an exclamation of surprise, an official notice pasted upon it, threatening prosecution to trespassers. Somewhat less proudly he unlocked and threw open the door, disclosing the hall bare of carpet or furniture, the varnish scarred and colourless, the pictureless walls weather-faded and streaked with ribald drawings in red and white chalk, the only ornaments a cane chair with burst bottom, and the bare staircase. With an incredulous movement Jake turned to the door on his right, and threw it open, followed by some of the party. The room here was alike bare but for a few straws, the light streaming in through the blindless window on the blue-grey walls, the very mantelpiece having been torn away, leaving the bricks fallen outward across the littered flooring … Jake turned uncertainly back out of the room.

'Well, if this is your fine hall,' called one of the maids, half-mockingly, 'I don't think much of it. The staircase ain't so dusty.'

Jake attempted to reply. He began, as a man might draw palely on his imagination, to enlarge on the beauties that had been.

'Ah, goo arne! Ye're chaffing us, Jake!' (The girl was not certain there had been anything but card-playing in the place.)

Jake seemed incapable of defending himself.

At this point the Investigator stepped forward beside the helpless bushman, and stuttered out a rather excited story. He stated how he had ridden there, and seen the rooms as they once were; how it had been a 'perfectly beautiful place;' and how Jake was right in all he protested. He then, to prove his story, took them from room to room and showed them what had been here and here—here a picture, and here a beautiful chair, and here a guitar with a broken string, and here a piano with some tumbled music.

Well, everybody was *that amazed*! And Jake, followed about, taking his chaffing calmly, and listening while this or that was replaced on its legs on the varnished boards or hung for a moment on the empty nails. It gradually dawned on all that there must have been some rough play and Mr. L. the magistrate had taken the valuables out of harm's way. At length the party scattered noisily among the orchard trees, or gathered laughing down beside the loud-voiced creek, and at last returned, singing, in the apple-carts.

[1]   A fact.

Katharine Susannah Prichard

The Curse

1932

AZURE, magenta, tetratheca, mauve and turquoise: the hut, a wrecked ship in halcyon seas.

Sun steeped the valley among folding hills, dark with red gum and jarrah. No sign or sound of life, but the life of the trees, squirt of a bird's song, a bird's body through stirring leaves. Chatter of leaves. Clatter and clatter of leaves, husky, frail. Small green tongues, lisping and clicking together, twisting over and licking each other; whispering, gossiping, as we rode into the clearing.

'Come to see Alf!'
'Alf?'
'He's in gaol.'
'Ayeh!'
'Harness, a rifle and bridle.'

'That all?'
'All they found …'
'Under the floor of the hut.'
'Who?'
'The trooper …'
'Trooper and black tracker …'
'When they came for Alf.'

'In gaol ...'
'For a rifle, harness and bridle.'

Long slope of hill-side facing the hut, with scrub of saplings, tall, straight-stemmed, symmetrical fleece of leaves, young green and gold, tight-packed as wool on a sheep's back.

'Many's the time we've seen him ...'
'Come down this track?'
'On his brumby.'
'Rough-haired, chestnut ...'
'Weedy and starved looking.'
'Alf?'
'No, the brumby.'
'Both of them.'
'Hat tucked under the sides.'
'Hair over his ears.'
'And his kangaroo dogs ...'
'Two, black, snake-headed.'
'Tails curled in circles over their backs.'
'And the bitch ...'
'Tawny, fawn-coloured.'
'Eyes like Alf's ...'
'Light, empty eyes.'

Horses nudging, reins chinkle-chinkle over a post by the gate. Snuffing the blue, turned aside from it. Jim picked a flower. Blue and purple, the silky tissue swooning to his grip; a plushy leaf, harsh green. His hand, clutched fingers and jutty knuckles, crouched over it.

The blue cut itself into flowers about us; flowers holding themselves on stiff stalks, spires and pagodas of little umbrellas, folded and spread turquoise and azure, or fading mauve and magenta. Crowding upon us, reaching up to shin and calves, they thrust themselves against walls of the hut, lapping the doorstep; swirled under a fig tree and down through the orchard. Coarse, lush, growing stems of plants pressed so close, no weed, or bud, or blade could grow between them. Feeding, ravening on the earth, spread over ploughed land set to the mould of an old furrow, and under the fruit trees. The curse, sucking all the life blood from their soil, elixirs, manganese, phosphates, ammonia, and flaunting them in her seas—blue, sulphate of copper, and magenta, as the sari of a Tamil dancing girl.

Chatter and clatter of leaves; a vague, sly gibberish running through all the hills:

'The curse!'
'Patterson's curse?'
'A noxious weed ...'
'That's what it is, he says.'
'Salt and poisonous as the sea.'
'An enchanted sea.'
'Sea of dreams.'
'Dead sea.'
'Did for Alf all right.'
'Got him down?'
'Never tried to beat it!'
'No guts to let it.'
'What?'
'Beat him.'
'Alf?'
'No guts at all, he had.'
'Lost hope.'
'Starved.'
'Took to stealing.'
'Little things at first ...'
'Bridle and tommy-axe.'

'Drowned, was he?'
'Daft?'
'Not a bit ...'
'Touched, they said.'
'To let a place go, like this.'
'No.'
'Only done for.'
'Gutless.'
'Lazy.'
'Liked reading.'
' "Got any books?" he'd say.'
'Ride away with a bag full ...'

'Happy as Larry.'
'On his brumby.'
'With his kangaroo dogs.'
'Didn't like work.'
'Said so.'
'Liked reading.'
'And kangarooin'.'
'Bit of kangaroo tail soup ...'
'Goes all right.'
'Ever taste it?'

The hut, dead trees row by row to make walls, with sheet iron for roof, beaten by storms and sun to the gleam and white light of silver; empty, derelict. Rusty, the share of an old plough; a barrow of bush timber falling to pieces. Cart wheel under the fig-trees.

But prowling beside the door, she sprang at us, the fawn-coloured bitch. Fell back, snarling, too weak to stand, belly sagging, a white bag beneath her. Starved, she crouched waiting for Alf to return.

Laughter of leaves, inhuman, immortal. From time immemorial into eternity, leaves laughing; innumerable small green tongues clacking, their dry murmur falling away with the wind.

Dark in the forest, under the red gums and jarrah. The wood-carter's track, cicatrice of an old wound through the bush; but the leaves still chattering, lisping and muttering endlessly of Alf and the fawn-coloured bitch straining over her puppies down there in the sunshine. Gone from backsliding eyes the sun-steeped valley between folding hills, and hut, dim, ghostly, in calm seas, fading tetratheca and turquoise; birds flying across with jargon of wild cries.

Notes on the Authors

JOHN LANG (1816–64)

Lang was born in Parramatta, New South Wales, and educated in Sydney at Cape's School and Sydney College. He travelled to England in 1837 and studied law at Cambridge; he then returned to Sydney, where he was admitted to the Supreme Court as a barrister. In 1842 he left for India, where he practised at the Calcutta Bar and founded the influential newspaper *The Mofussilite.* Some of his novels were serialised in its pages. Lang later spent a few years in England in the 1850s where he contributed to Charles Dickens' *Household Words, All the Year Round, Fraser's Magazine* and various newspapers. Lang is best known in Australia for his novels *Lucy Cooper: an Australian Tale* (1846) and *The Forger's Wife* (1855) and his collection of short sketches and stories called *Botany Bay, or, True Tales of Early Australia* (1859). He died and was buried in Mussoorie in northern India.

MARY HELENA FORTUNE (C.1833–C.1910)

Fortune was born in Belfast, emigrating to Montreal, Canada, with her father. In 1851 she married Joseph Fortune. Her father later migrated to Australia to work on the goldfields, and she followed him there, with her first son, in 1855. She was briefly married again in Australia, to a mounted constable, Percy Brett. Fortune used the pseudonym 'Waif Wander' when she began to publish stories in the new, Melbourne-based *Australian Journal* in 1865. Early on, she co-wrote some detective fiction with James Skipp Borlase; her anonymously published 'Mystery and Murder' was later reprinted by Borlase in his collection *The Night Fossickers* (1867), under his own name. Fortune went on to contribute well over 400 short stories, as well as serialised novels and journalism, to the *Australian Journal* in a literary career spanning more than forty years. She is celebrated as one of the first female crime-fiction writers in the world; a collection of her detective fiction, *The Detective's Album: Tales of the Australian Police*, was published by Clarson, Massina and Co. in 1871. Even so, she died in obscurity; the exact place and date of her death are unknown.

MARCUS CLARKE (1846–81)

Clarke was born in Kensington, London, in privileged circumstances. Following his father's financial ruin and subsequent death in 1863, however, Clarke decided to emigrate to Australia, where he worked in a variety of occupations. In 1867 he became a staff writer for the *Argus*, where he wrote a regular, often humorous column, 'The Peripatetic Philosopher'. He was also heavily involved in colonial theatrical life, writing pantomimes and comedies as well as a libretto for a satirical, political operetta called *The Happy Land* (1880), which was subsequently banned. Burdened by debt, Clarke was forced into insolvency in 1874. His early writings were published in the *Australian Monthly Magazine*, *Colonial Monthly* (which he edited from 1868 to 1869), *The Australasian* and other newspapers and periodicals. His most famous work, the novel *His Natural Life*, was serialised in the *Australian Journal* from 1870 to 1872 and published by George Robertson in 1874. A different version, *For the Term of His Natural Life*, was published posthumously in 1884–85.

'TASMA' (JESSIE COUVREUR) (1848–97)

Couvreur was born in Highgate, London, coming to Tasmania with her family in the early 1850s. Her first marriage was a failure and she instituted divorce proceedings against her husband in 1883. With her second husband, a Belgian journalist and politician, she led a cosmopolitan life in Europe, later working as the Brussels correspondent of the *Times* newspaper. She began to publish stories in Australian periodicals in 1877 under the pseudonym 'Tasma'; the collection of stories *A Sydney Sovereign and Other Tales* was published in 1890, reprinting stories originally published in the *Australasian*. The best-known of her six novels, *Uncle Piper of Piper's Hill* (1889), was published to acclaim in both Australia and England.

Ernest Favenc (1845–1908)

Favenc was born in Surrey, England, and was educated in Berlin and Oxford. He came to Australia in 1864, working on north Queensland stations and, in 1877, leading an expedition to Darwin. His first book, *The History of Australian Exploration 1788-1888* (1888), became a major reference work. He published around 130 short stories in a number of colonial journals, including the *Bulletin*, which had printed an early collection, *The Last of Six: Tales of the Austral Tropics* (1893). Favenc is best known for his adventure and fantasy fiction, usually set in the Australian interior, the tropics or the Pacific.

Rosa Campbell Praed (1851–1935)

Praed was born at Bromelton in Queensland, where she grew up on her family's extensive country properties. She married Arthur Campbell Praed in 1872, living on a cattle station for several years—an experience described in a later novel, *The Romance of a Station* (1889)—before moving with him to England. She returned to Australia only once, in 1894–95. In the meantime she had become a celebrated London novelist. Her long literary career in fact saw her publish forty novels in fifty years, the first of which was *An Australian Heroine* (1880). A significant number of her novels had Australian themes and settings, including *Fugitive Anne* (1902) and *Lady Bridget in the Never-Never Land* (1915). Much of her later fiction reflected her growing theosophical interests. Separated from her husband in 1897, Praed lived with Nancy Harward, a psychic medium, until Harward's death in 1927. Her final years were beset with loneliness and illness; her three sons were dead and her daughter, Maud, who was born deaf, was in an asylum.

Francis Adams (1862–93)

Adams was born in Malta and educated mostly in England and later in France. He emigrated to Australia to improve his health in 1884, and soon became a committed republican, writing for the *Bulletin* as well as William Lane's left-wing paper *The Boomerang*. A collection of radical poetry, *Songs of the Army of the Night*, was published in 1888. But he also published across a range of popular genres; his first novel was a work of crime fiction, *Madeline Brown's Murderer*, published in Melbourne in 1887. Adams is also remembered for his social sketches and his journalism. Living in Margate, England, Adams became increasingly ill with tuberculosis and throat cancer. He shot himself with a pistol, with his wife close by.

HENRY LAWSON (1876–1922)

Lawson was born in Grenfell, New South Wales, growing up on his parents' selection often under difficult circumstances. His parents later separated, and in 1883 Lawson joined his mother, Louisa, in Sydney and became influenced by her commitment to the republican movement. His first poem, 'A Song of the Republic', was published in the *Bulletin* in October 1887. In 1892 the *Bulletin* commissioned Lawson to travel to Bourke; although the trip was a brief one, it heavily influenced his short stories, including 'The Bush Undertaker'. Louisa published his early collection, *Short Stories in Prose and Verse* (1894). Lawson's best-known work—*While the Billy Boils*—was published by Angus and Robertson in 1896 and was soon regarded as an Australian classic. He married Berthe Bredt the same year, and they travelled to New Zealand and England together, but on returning to Sydney in 1902 the couple separated. Lawson's later life was plagued by ongoing financial debt, alcoholism and mental illness.

'PRICE WARUNG' (WILLIAM ASTLEY) (1855–1911)

Astley was born in Liverpool, his family emigrating to Melbourne in 1859. He worked as a journalist, travelling around the south-east of Australia and finally settling in Sydney in 1891 with his wife, Louisa, after having worked for many years on a wide range of provincial newspapers. His reputation as a radical pro-Federation, pro-Labor journalist grew in the 1890s, which is when he also began to publish convict stories in the *Bulletin*—sustained and often heavily satirical critiques of the colonial administrative system. The *Bulletin* published some of these stories separately, as *Tales of the Convict System* (1892) and *Tales of the Early Days* (1892). Later, George Robertson published *Tales of the Old Regime* (1897) and *Half-Crown Bob and Tales of the Riverine* (1898), as well as the novel *Convict Hendy* (1898). His health and finances failing during the later 1890s, Astley became addicted to morphia and increasingly reclusive. He died in the Rookwood Benevolent Asylum.

HUME NISBET (1849–1923)

Nisbet was born in Stirling, Scotland, arriving at the age of sixteen in Melbourne, where he became involved in theatrical life. He returned to Britain to study art, and went on to teach and exhibit in Edinburgh. He became a prolific book illustrator, and was later commissioned by Cassell and Co. to visit Australia and New Guinea, contributing articles and sketches for *Cassell's Picturesque Australasia* (1887–89). Nisbet published seventeen novels, many of which are set in and around Australia and the Pacific. The first, *The Land of the Hibiscus Blossom: a Yarn of the Papuan Gulf*, was published in 1888 and then republished ten years later as part of Heinemann's Colonial Library of Popular Fiction. Nisbet's fiction in fact covered a range of popular genres, including romance, colonial adventure and crime. His autobiographical writings included *A Colonial Tramp: Travels and Adventures in Australia and New Guinea* (1891) and *Reminiscences of Early Australian Life* (1893).

Guy Boothby (1867–1905)

Boothby was born in Adelaide, but went to England with his mother for his early education. Returning to Adelaide at sixteen, he later became private secretary to the mayor and began to write for the theatre. After the failure of one his plays, *The Jonquille*, Boothby travelled with a friend through parts of Asia and tropical Australia, writing about his experiences in *On the Wallaby* (1894). He returned to England the same year and became a prolific and much-admired popular novelist, producing well over forty novels in just ten years. His *Dr Nikola* novels were international bestsellers, offering a sensational blend of thriller and orientalist fantasy.

'Coo-ee' (William Sylvester Walker) (1846–1926)

Walker was born in Heidelberg, Melbourne, a nephew of the popular novelist 'Rolf Boldrewood', who disapproved of Walker's literary writings. He worked on stations and as a miner, travelling to New Zealand and then to South Africa, before finally settling in Devon, England. Walker wrote under the pseudonym 'Coo-ee', publishing an early collection of stories, *When the Mopoke Calls*, with the English publisher John Long in 1898. He wrote seven novels, a number of which have Australian settings and themes.

Barbara Baynton (1857–1929)

Baynton was born at Scone, New South Wales, a seventh and possibly illegitimate child. She was educated at home, later working as a housekeeper and governess. She married Alex Frater in 1880, living in financial hardship in rural New South Wales. Divorcing Frater after discovering he was having an affair with her niece, she married Thomas Baynton, a retired Sydney doctor. Her wealthier circumstances enabled her to write. A collection of six short stories, *Bush Studies*, was published in 1902 by Duckworth in England, where she had travelled after failing to find an Australian publisher. After Thomas Baynton died in 1904 she led an affluent life in Australia and England, socialising with many well-known writers and celebrities. She married an English baron in 1921, but soon left him, returning to Australia in 1924. Baynton's only novel, *Human Toll*, was published as part of Duckworth's Colonial Library in 1907. *Bush Studies* earned great critical respect, and Duckworth republished the stories from the collection, together with two new ones, as *Cobbers* in 1917.

MARY GAUNT (1861–1942)

Gaunt was born at Chiltern, Victoria. In 1880 she became one of the first women to attend the University of Melbourne, leaving after only a year to pursue her writing. Some of her earliest short stories and articles appeared in *Cassell's Picturesque Australasia* in the late 1880s. Her first novel, *Bingley's Gap: A Tale of Old Colonial Days*, was published serially in the *Leader* in 1888. In 1894 she married Dr Hubert Lindsay Miller, and they settled in Warrnambool, Victoria. She continued to publish under her own name throughout the marriage and, after Miller's death in 1900, moved to England, supporting herself as a writer. Gaunt's growing success funded her extensive travel in Europe, Jamaica, Africa and China. Her adventures provided settings for her fiction, and she also wrote a number of autobiographical travel books, including *Alone in West Africa* (1912) and *A Woman in China* (1914). Several of her many novels are set in Australia, most significantly *Kirkham's Find* (1897) and *Deadman's* (1898), which were both published in Methuen's Colonial Library series.

WILLIAM HAY (1875–1945)

Hay was born in Adelaide, a distant relative of the famous Victorian literary writer Sir Edmund Gosse. Educated in Melbourne and at Cambridge, Hay returned to Adelaide in 1901, where he wrote his three best-known novels, each about Australian convict life: *Herridge of Reality Swamp* (1907), *Captain Quadring* (1912) and *The Escape of the Notorious Sir William Heans* (1919). Hay's writings were more or less ignored in Australia, however, and from 1925 he lived in seclusion with his wife and children near Victor Harbour in South Australia. His reputation in Australia was reassessed with the republishing of *The Escape of the Notorious Sir William Heans* in 1955 by Melbourne University Press. He had died ten years earlier, from an illness following overexertion while fighting a local bushfire.

Katharine Susannah Prichard (1883–1969)

Prichard was born in Fiji, later moving with her family to Melbourne, where she attended South Melbourne College. After working as a governess, she began a career as a journalist and travelled to London—with a letter of introduction from Alfred Deakin—to work for the Melbourne *Herald*. In 1915 she won the Hodder and Stoughton Novel Competition (Australasian Section) for her first novel, *The Pioneers*. Prichard married the Gallipoli veteran and VC recipient Hugo (Jim) Throssell, and they settled in the Perth suburb of Greenmount. She was a founding member of the Australian Communist Party, also campaigning against conscription and war and, much later on, for nuclear disarmament. Her best-known novels are *The Black Opal* (1921), *Working Bullocks* (1926), *Coonardoo* (1928) and *Intimate Strangers* (1937). She also wrote two autobiographical works, *Why I am a Communist* (1956) and *Child of the Hurricane* (1963).

Publication Sources

John Lang, 'The Ghost upon the Rail', from *Botany Bay, or, True Tales of Early Australia*, London: William Tegg, 1859.

Mary Fortune, 'Mystery and Murder', from the *Australian Journal*, 10 February 1866, pp. 376–8.

Marcus Clarke, 'The Mystery of Major Molineux', from *The Mystery of Major Molineux, and Human Repetends*, Melbourne: Cameron, Laing & Co., 1881.

'Tasma' (Jessie Couvreur), 'Monsieur Caloche', from *A Sydney Sovereign and Other Tales*, London: Trübner & Co., 1890.

Ernest Favenc, 'A Haunt of the Jinkarras', from the *Bulletin*, 5 April 1890, 8; and 'Doomed', from *The Australian Town and Country Journal*, 29 April 1899, p. 35.

Rosa Campbell Praed, 'The Bunyip', from Harriet Patchett Martin, *Cooee: Tales of Australian Life by Australian Ladies*, London: Griffith Farran Okeden & Welsh, 1891.

Francis Adams, 'The Hut by the Tanks', from *Australian Life*, London: Chapman & Hall, 1892; first published under the pseudonym 'Proteus' (with textual differences) as 'Jonnie Holmes—The Man Who Saw a Ghost' in *The Boomerang*, 19 May 1888, p. 9.

Henry Lawson, 'The Bush Undertaker', from *While the Billy Boils*, 1896; first published as 'A Christmas in the Far West; or, The Bush Undertaker' in the *Antipodean*, 1892, pp. 95–102.

'Price Warung' (William Astley), 'The Pegging-Out of Overseer Franke', from *Tales of the Early Days*, London: George Robertson, 1894; first published in the *Bulletin* as 'Overseer Franke's Pegging-Out,' 13 February 1892, pp. 21–3.

Hume Nisbet, 'The Haunted Station', from *The Haunted Station and Other Stories*, London: F.V. White & Co., 1894.

Guy Boothby, 'With Three Phantoms', from *Bushigrams*, London: Ward, Lock & Co., 1897.

'Coo-ee' (William Sylvester Walker), 'The Evil of Yelcomorn Creek', from *When the Mopoke Calls*, London: John Long, 1898; first published as 'The Mystery of Yelcomorn Creek' (with textual differences) in the *Centennial Magazine*, 8 March 1890, pp. 625–30.

Barbara Baynton, 'A Dreamer', from *Bush Studies*, London: Duckworth & Co., 1902.

Mary Gaunt, 'The Lost White Woman', from *The Ends of the Earth: Stories*, London: T. Werner Laurie, 1916.

William Hay, 'An Australian Rip Van Winkle', from *An Australian Rip Van Winkle and Other Pieces*, London: George Allen and Unwin, 1921.

Katharine Susannah Prichard, 'The Curse', from *Kiss on the Lips and Other Stories*, London: Jonathan Cape, 1932.
(Reprinted by Arrangement with the Licensor, The Estate of Katherine Susannah Pritchard c/- Curtis Brown (Aust) Pty. Ltd)

Acknowledgements

Publication of this work was assisted by a publication grant from The University of Melbourne and a subsidy from the university's School of Culture and Communication in the Faculty of Arts. We gratefully acknowledge these generous contributions.